# DARK METAMORPHOSIS

# DARK METAMORPHOSIS

JOHN COON

SAMAK PRESS

DARK METAMORPHOSIS



Samak Press
ISBN: 978-1-7324871-6-1



This novel is entirely a work of fiction. The names, characters and incidents portrayed in it are the work of the author's imagination. Any resemblance to actual persons or aliens, living or dead, events or localities is entirely coincidental.

Cover Design: 100 Covers
Interior Design: Formatted Books

# AUTHOR'S NOTE

Seeing so many readers from around the world embrace *Alien People* after I published it in September 2020 filled me with joy. I had so many more places to go and stories to tell with these characters. Now the door has flown open for me to take a deeper journey inside that universe.

*Dark Metamorphosis* chronicles another stop in the journey of Calandra and Xttra. This new chapter in their story places them in much a darker spot than ever before, challenging everything they embraced as truth. But what they experience also offers hope that dawn will soon arrive, and shadows will flee as light breaks forth to signal a new day. I felt extensive joy and had so much fun diving deeper into the universe I introduced in *Under a Fallen Sun* and expanded on in *Alien People*. I hope you all will enjoy the ride as well.

I am indebted, as always, to others who contributed to helping me to develop and polish the story you will soon read. Jeff Keyes, Joshua Coon, and Sandra Coon deserve special mention for offering valuable feedback on plot, characters, and setting while beta reading. I am also indebted to 100 Covers for creating an excellent eye-catching cover that fits thematically with my novel. And I appreciate Formatted Books for putting together a clean, appealing interior design for my latest novel. —JC

Nothing about this situation promised a path toward a happy resolution.

Xttra knew it once he laid eyes on the holoscreen. The unmarked vessel refused to respond to his repeated attempts to open a channel to communicate. Silence only confirmed what he suspected when the vessel first appeared on his scout ship's sensors.

This was indeed the saboteur whom Xttra and his crew were supposed to intercept.

"Plasma cannons are at full capacity."

Xttra snapped his head toward his weapons officer. Bo'un simultaneously glanced up from a holoscreen at his designated station on the bridge. Xttra answered him with a brisk nod.

"Good to hear." The master pilot turned back and faced the holoscreen above the helm console again. "Let's see if we can convince these people to stick around for a while longer."

Xttra scrutinized the holoscreen data and pinched his lips together into a frown. Fengar loomed on the horizon beyond Lathos. Impact scars pock-marked the silver-gray moon and dulled the natural luster of its icy crust. Colonies dotting that scarred surface harbored enough ports where this vessel could make a safe landing. From there, the saboteur had a clear path to exit their spacecraft, blend in with dissidents living inside a protected colony, and disappear forever.

Xttra refused to let this scenario unfold without a fight. Letting this traitor escape his grasp would only add another major blemish to his Stellar Guard service record. After the debacle on Earth, Xttra did not think his master pilot rank would survive another failed mission.

"We better head that vessel off before it lands on Fengar," Xttra said, glancing over at the navigator station again. "Give me an intercept course."

His navigator punched several buttons in a sequence. A moment later, a blue line charting a new flight path appeared on the helm holoscreen.

"Nice work, Talan," Xttra said, while keeping his eyes glued on the holoscreen. "Let's fly."

Their new flight path took his scout ship over the far side of Fengar. An enormous perpetual shadow blanketed the surface. That same side of the diminutive moon appeared forever tidal locked away from their sun's rays when Fengar journeyed across the Lathoan sky at night. Xttra guessed the unmarked vessel planned to use Fengar's dark half as a natural cloak masking its approach from visual sensors. A desperate rookie mistake from a pilot without enough experience or common sense to know better.

On cue, the unmarked vessel appeared dead ahead cloaked in shadow. The vessel's triangular nose pointed downward, and it rolled over on its left side as it approached the moon. This maneuver caused one rear triangular wing to protrude upward and the other to protrude downward.

"Looks like a Cassian dart." Bo'un echoed the perplexed feelings stirring inside Xttra. "How's that possible? I thought the Confederation discontinued the whole series."

Xttra shrugged.

"Still popular on the black market. Older models are harder to track on sensors, I suppose."

A flashing light lit up on the navigation station, accompanied by a short series of beeps.

"We're approaching orbital range," Talan said. He spun his chair around to face the helm. "What's your plan? What's hidden inside your armored sleeve?"

Xttra glanced over his shoulder and cracked a grin.

"I can't spoil the surprise. Where would be the fun in doing that?"

Talan scrunched up his pointed nose and green eyes and shook his head at Xttra's coy response. He turned his chair toward the medical officer's station.

"Is he always like this?"

Sarianna brushed back a short black bang and answered the navigator with a bemused expression.

"This is quite typical. Unfortunately."

Xttra laughed off her sarcastic remark. Sarianna knew what to expect. He always told new crew members this is what they signed up for when they joined his crew. Talan heard those same words on his first day.

As did Ohnro.

Xttra shot a quick glance at his new assistant pilot. Ohnro sat rigid in his seat, his eyes fixed in an unbroken stare on the other vessel looming in the distance. He let out a gruff sigh.

"Relax." Xttra shook his head. He refocused his attention on the unmarked Cassian dart ahead. "I'll let you know when it's time to worry."

Ohnro finally cocked his head toward the master pilot's chair and narrowed his gray eyes.

"I wonder what your last assistant pilot has to say about your bravado."

Bo'un and Sarianna both let out audible gasps. Xttra went from grin to hardened stare in a few seconds. He held up an index finger.

"You better shut your mouth before I shut it for you."

An uncomfortable silence permeated the bridge. Ohnro's remark reopened wounds Xttra spent the better part of a year trying to heal since he and Calandra returned from Earth. The sting of what they endured on that nightmarish expedition had not dulled with time.

Xttra still witnessed Lance making a grim death march to their aerorover if he allowed his mind to wander. A distinct image of the airborne vehicle exploding into a ball of flame, with his dying friend inside, haunted him with the tenacity of a vengeful spirit. Calandra also carried physical and emotional scars from their journey. Those scars weighed down her body and soul. No one—especially a novice assistant pilot—had a right to treat what they both endured with scorn.

He pressed his lips together for a moment and exhaled deeply. Xttra zigzagged the scout ship over Fengar's northern pole, hoping to conceal his approach from the other vessel.

His ploy did not work.

The unmarked vessel pulled out from starting descent maneuvers and leveled out. It executed a sharp turn and pointed toward the scout ship. Xttra's eyes widened, and he brushed a hand back through his light brown hair.

"The dart moved into an attack position." A surprised tone gripped his words. "Has that pilot lost their mind?"

"Desperate people end up doing desperate things," Bo'un replied.

Xttra nodded while continuing to stare straight ahead at the other vessel.

"I hope they're ready to learn a lesson. My scout ship can make a meal out of Cassian darts."

He pressed a small white button on the helm console. Two slots opened in the floor and cylindrical steering columns popped up through each opening. These stout metallic columns flanked each side of the pilot's chair. Xttra placed his hands into molded grooves on spheres topping each column and angled both spheres downward.

With shadow-like precision, the scout ship executed the same motion as the spheres. Tracking sensors on the holoscreen marked the vessel's position relative to Xttra's ship. Once red lines lined up with the back end of the vessel, he snapped his head toward Ohnro.

"Disable their weapons and secondary thrusters. Don't squeeze too much juice from our plasma cannons. We only want to cripple their vessel."

Ohnro nodded. A stoic frown graced his lips.

"I'll approach it like threading a needle."

The assistant pilot narrowed his eyes and squeezed a trigger stick below his console. Plasma bolts discharged from a pair of cannons embedded in the belly of the ship. A sudden flash followed.

Sparks burst forth from both secondary thrusters on the Cassian dart. Smoke mingled with flame billowed from brand new holes in each thruster.

Ohnro squeezed the trigger stick a second time. Two more plasma bolts slammed into the dart's short-range blasters. Protruding barrels from both weapons exploded in another cloud of smoke and flames on the underside of the vessel.

A wave of silent satisfaction swept over Xttra while watching the entire scene unfold.

"Perfect. This traitor is right where we want them."

Multiple rapid beeps greeted Xttra's ears. He flashed a smug grin at Ohnro.

"They want to talk now. Open a channel."

A hooded pilot materialized on the main holoscreen connected to an arca vox embedded within the helm console. They sat alone in the dart's cockpit. Dim lighting chased shadows across the pilot's face, obscuring their eyes and forehead from Xttra's vision.

Xttra leaned forward in his chair. His eyes locked into an unbroken hardened stare at the holoscreen.

"The Stellar Guard does not take technological sabotage lightly. We have nothing to discuss except the terms of your surrender."

The dart pilot visibly stiffened in their chair upon seeing Xttra and hearing his voice.

"Xttra?"

Silence permeated the bridge. Xttra's throat tightened, and his eyes widened. The pilot's voice sounded so familiar. Too familiar. He sensed all eyes on the bridge now focused on him and the main holoscreen.

"Whatever they told you, Xttra, is a lie." The dart pilot pierced a tense silence gathering on the bridge. "You need to listen to me."

"How does this person know you? Are you—"

Xttra turned, looked at Sarianna, and thrust a finger to his lips. The medical officer stopped mid-question. She tossed her hands up and sighed. Xttra refocused his attention on the hooded pilot and leaned forward again.

"Who are you? How do you know my name?"

At once, the dart pilot threw back their hood revealing their entire face to Xttra for the first time. His mouth fell open. Behind him, Bo'un gasped a second time.

"Kevin?"

A numbness gripped Xttra upon learning the pilot's identity. What drove Kevin to betray his trust in this manner? How could he turn against Ra'ahm and isolate himself from the only friends he had on Lathos?

The Earthian popped up as Xttra's first choice to replace Lance as his assistant pilot. Kevin sacrificed so much to help him and Calandra escape from the clutches of the Earth Defense Bureau and return home. Xttra should have known something was amiss when he turned down a chance to serve on his crew. A natural-born soldier like Kevin fit right at home in the Stellar Guard.

Xttra scolded himself internally for not seeing obvious warning signs.

"Who's Kevin?"

Ohnro's question drew an immediate sharp stare from Xttra. The assistant pilot frowned and answered with a defensive shrug.

"You're putting me in a difficult spot here." Xttra turned back and faced Kevin once again. "Give me one good reason I shouldn't turn you over to face a Stellar Guard tribunal."

Kevin rolled his eyes.

"I'll give you two reasons: I saved Calandra's life and your life back on Earth. And I didn't steal what old Delcor claims I stole."

Talan gasped and shook his finger at him.

"You should not refer to our chief sovereign in such flippant terms."

Kevin glared at the navigator. His image flickered on the holoscreen for a moment.

"Not my chief sovereign!" The Earthian's voice descended to a near growl. His eyes shifted to Xttra again. "Who's that jackass working for you?"

Xttra sighed.

"I disabled your secondary thrusters. You can't outrun my scout ship. But I can still help you if you'll let me."

"Really? How?

"Turn over the Caeco shield emitter prototype and we'll sort out the details.

Kevin let out a brief derisive laugh and shook his head. A slight tremor rippled through the holoscreen on his end while an alarm sounded behind him. He mashed down on a button near his steering controls.

The alarm ceased.

"You don't have a clue why they sent you after me. I guess I shouldn't be surprised."

"You stole top secret technology. Doesn't require a genius to solve that equation."

"No. I didn't." Kevin leaned forward as though preparing to whisper to Xttra in a crowded room. "I don't have any sort of prototype on me. But I did uncover intelligence threatening old Delcor's rule."

Xttra cocked an eyebrow at him.

"What intelligence?"

"The prime oracle lives."

"Of course, he does. In the heart of Luma."

Kevin shook his head.

"Not that one. The prime oracle named Valadius is alive and well."

Xttra bolted upright in his chair. His body stiffened from head to toe. A shudder raced through his spine.

"You lie." Bo'un's voice quavered as he spat out his accusation. "How dare you spread such seditious rumors, Earthian!"

"I'll never let you bring me back to the planet's surface alive, Xttra," Kevin replied, not even bothering to glance over at the weapons officer. "That tyrant Delcor wants me dead. You and Calandra are also stuck in his crosshairs. Soon, he'll go after you as well."

Xttra stared unblinking at the holoscreen. He could not find the right words to react to Kevin's revelation. If Valadius were truly alive, that changed everything he thought he knew about Ra'ahm. And the nature of the Order of Ahm itself.

"What makes you think you can escape?" Ohnro said. His hand hovered over the trigger stick like an agitated russakin, waiting for an order to strike.

"I'm not worried."

Kevin's image vanished from the main holoscreen right after he said those words. Multiple beeps greeted Xttra's ears. His eyes darted to a secondary holoscreen. Sensors tracked three new vessels. Each one was a Cassian dart. These vessels were closing in on the scout ship's position above the far side of Fengar.

Xttra liked his odds going up against a single dart. Tangling with four darts simultaneously produced no similar feelings.

"Hold your fire." Xttra signaled for Ohnro to pull his hand away from the trigger stick. "We're not on a suicide mission out here."

Ohnro scrunched up his eyes and nose and flung his left hand toward the windshield.

"You can't let him get away!"

"We don't exactly have a choice." An abrupt iciness tinged Xttra's words. "We're outnumbered here. Also, I have important questions that need answers."

The other darts took up safe positions around Kevin's vessel. All three ships bore no exterior markings like the first dart. Xttra could do nothing except watch as all four ships shot down toward a landing site inside a protected Fengar colony.

# 2

A shudder raced through Calandra from head to toe. Few things in this world produced this sensation within her body. Now she faced one of those awful triggers. Every word falling from Xttra's lips as he explained the entire situation only filled Calandra's soul with dread.

"You must tell them no." Desperation permeated her plea. "Please tell them no."

Xttra smashed his lips together and lowered his head. The fresh pain attacking Calandra deep inside washed over his face at the same time. He brushed back tears with his left hand and focused his deep blue eyes on her piercing green ones.

"I have no other choice."

Xttra clasped her left hand with a tenderness matching his voice. A scarlet silk glove, matching Calandra's dress, adorned her hand and covered her forearm up to her elbow.

"Their words to me were quite clear," he said. "Resume space missions full-time going forward or lose my rank."

Calandra shifted in her chair with an awkward suddenness. This night was supposed to mark a special occasion. One year to the day since they returned home from Earth. Healing from memories of their time on such an awful planet was still a daily struggle. With what she experienced, and its aftermath, she feared panic and anxiety were now permanent companions.

Calandra was not ready to see Xttra depart from Lathos again. He alone supplied a safe place from her fear, the only person who understood her trauma. Imagining what dangers awaited him among the stars made her mind and heart race at an equal pace. Some way must exist for him to buy more time. There had to be a higher Stellar Guard official willing to consider an appeal and overturn the decision.

Losing the man whom she loved counted as a gnawing fear Calandra did not want to face.

"I'm not ready for this." Tears rolled down her cheeks. "How can they expect either of us to be ready for this?"

Calandra's arms rested on the table before her. Xttra reached out and grasped her ungloved right hand with the same delicate touch he applied to the left one. He held both hands and gnawed on his bottom lip, visibly at a loss for words. She stared at Xttra and sniffed back her tears.

"You're still going to do it, aren't you?"

Her question sounded more confrontational than Calandra intended. It did not matter now. He must understand everything at stake here. A determined frown washing over his lips showed he did not get the message.

"What would you have me do? I put off the inevitable for as long as possible."

Xttra cast a quick glance over his shoulder at an elevated square floor near their table. Two dancers entertained the crowd with a traditional dance from the Rim Islands. Watching their agile dips and bends, executed at a rapid pace in harmony with each other's movements and background music, caused him to turn so he partially faced the dancers. Xttra slipped his right hand away from her left.

Calandra refused to let Xttra's rhetorical question go unanswered.

"Maybe now is the right time to consider leaving the Stellar Guard for good." She gave his other hand a gentle squeeze and spoke in a softer tone this time. "I want us to chart a new course. One leading to a long and happy life together."

Xttra turned and faced her again. His deep blue eyes matched his tightened lips, conveying his answer before he opened his mouth. She sensed a rift between them, and a tangible melancholy.

"You're asking me to walk away from everything I worked for so many years to achieve. That's a heavy sacrifice to demand from me."

Calandra snapped her other hand away from his hand. She straightened up in her chair. Her green eyes hardened into a piercing glare.

"Sacrifice? You want to discuss sacrifice?"

Her left arm lay motionless on the table. Calandra tugged at the glove on her hand, drawing the fabric on each finger forward. Xttra cast his eyes down at the table. Those eyes grew wider.

"What are you doing?"

Calandra ignored his question and continued pulling the fabric away from her hand. The silk sleeve slid down her forearm while the hand remained frozen to the table. At once, the fabric popped free.

Tears welled up in Calandra's eyes anew as she stared down at the limb. Black metal occupied space once claimed by flesh and bone. Fashioned to resemble a wrist and a hand with built-in rubber padding covering the palm and fingertips. The prosthetic arm served as a poor imitation of what she once possessed.

A cruel reminder of the cost of her journey to Earth.

Calandra gazed up at Xttra again. Tears glistened in his eyes, and he swallowed hard. She scowled and slapped the metal wrist.

"This is sacrifice." Her voice rose higher and grew sharper. "Do you see it? What I'm asking of you does not compare to what's been required of me."

Xttra buried his face in his hands for a moment and then let them trail down his cheeks. Calandra sensed several pairs of eyes focusing on her as the room grew quieter. She snapped her head to the side and glanced over at an adjacent table. Another couple sitting at that table quickly averted their eyes and stared down at plates holding partially eaten food. Calandra turned away and refocused her attention on Xttra.

He licked his lips as he met her gaze again.

"I know this ordeal has been rough for you. I'm so sorry. I wish I could snap my fingers and undo everything that happened to us on that awful planet."

"Neither of us can undo what's been done. This is real. And it's painful. And scary."

Xttra glanced down at Calandra's artificial hand and then closed his eyes for a moment.

"We can't afford to live in fear," he said. "No matter how much it hurts, we can't stop moving forward."

Calandra's frown deepened.

"That's simplistic advice. You didn't lose a hand."

Xttra straightened up in his chair. He answered her with a quick nod. His eyes darted to another adjacent table as he grew aware of other guests inside the club turning their attention to their argument.

"We'll get it working right soon. All we need is the right neural sensors in the hand and—"

"That's what my clan doctor has been telling us forever now." Calandra's fingers stayed rigid as she raised her left arm off the table. "My artificial hand is still no closer to functioning the way it's supposed to work."

Xttra ran a hand through his light brown hair and extended the other across the table toward her. He tried to muster a smile, but it remained partially frozen at the corners of his mouth.

"Things will work out in the end." Xttra worked to conjure up a reassuring tone. "Ahm will see to it. Hope isn't lost."

Calandra looked down at his extended hand and clasped it with her real hand. A lump formed in her throat. She wanted to believe what he told her. Countless setbacks painted a different picture.

"Hope never used to flee from me. Now it is sprinting to the horizon far from my grasp."

He gave her hand a gentle squeeze and painted a slight smile on his lips.

"I'll be safe. I give you my word. I already went to Fengar once without incident."

Calandra ripped her hand away from his hand again. Her heartbeat quickened at an increasing rate until it throbbed inside her chest.

"Why am I even bothering? My feelings mean nothing when it comes to getting your way."

She rose from the table abruptly and pushed her chair back with her right hand. Numerous pairs of eyes followed Calandra as she weaved past other tables and marched toward the door.

"Wait! Calandra! Come back!"

Xttra's voice bore a contrite tone. She did not care. Calandra did not bother to stop and turn or cast a brief glance over her shoulder. All her pain and fear should mean more than it obviously meant to him. She could not bear the thought of spending another moment inside this club. Dining and dancing. Pretending everything was normal.

Things were not normal. They never would be normal again. Not for her.

A steady drizzle from ashen clouds greeted Calandra as the main club door slid open. She stormed outside the building. Fresh puddles adorned minor dips on the stone walkway running along the front of the club. Water droplets trickled off a stone statue of a lupine mounted on a ledge above the door. They ran down the statue's erect triangular ears, oval eyes, and long snout before striking Calandra's forehead as she glanced upward. She brushed the raindrops away and started for their aerorover parked a few steps down the street.

A hand caught Calandra by her elbow as she turned to sprint down the walkway. Fingers gently wrapped around her arm.

"I don't want to talk about it any longer." Her voice grew soft enough that pelting raindrops threatened to drown it out. "Please take me home."

"I'm sorry. The mission started on Lathos. I had no idea pursuing an escaping vessel would lead me out to Fengar."

Calandra spun around to face Xttra again. A renewed fire surged through her eyes.

"You had no idea pursuing another ship would take you into space? Do you think I'm that naïve?"

"Someone had to intercept that Cassian dart. My scout ship was the nearest one when the call went out. What was I supposed to do?"

Calandra looked at him stone-faced while blinking back raindrops trailing down to her chin.

"Do you always need to be the hero?"

"What do you think would have happened if I ignored the communicator?" Xttra snapped. "Or said no? Do you think my superior officer would have embraced my resistance?"

Calandra dropped her head and closed her eyes. She knew exactly where such a scenario led. He was right. Fresh tears rolled through the cracks between her eyelids and mingled with raindrops already forging a path down her cheeks.

"I don't want you to die." Calandra's voice grew quieter as she contemplated the weight of her own statement. "I want us to grow old together. How can we do that if you continue to risk your life in space?"

Fingers brushed across her cheek. Calandra raised her head and gazed into Xttra's deep blue eyes. She could not tell if tears also mingled with the raindrops running down his cheeks, but his trembling lips signaled she was finally getting through to him.

"I never contemplated this decision in those terms," he said. "Losing you would destroy me. I can't put you through a similar ordeal."

"Does that mean what I hope it means?"

"It means I will do whatever it takes to guarantee a long, happy life together." Xttra curled a finger through a lock of her auburn hair. "You're my wife. I love you. If putting you first means keeping my feet on the ground, then that's what I'm willing to do."

He drew Calandra into his arms. Her eyes closed tight at the same moment their lips met. Calandra embraced him tighter as their lips pressed together. When she pulled back again, a smile appeared on his face.

A similar one now also adorned her own lips.

"I love you too."

Xttra clasped her right hand and led her back into the club away from the rain. They stopped just inside the main door, and he turned to face Calandra again. His free hand trailed down her cheek a second time.

"What do you plan to do?" she asked.

"I'll meet with my superior officer first thing in the morning and request reassignment as an instructor at the academy. If I can't lead missions myself, at least I'll get to mold future pilots who do."

Calandra sensed a slight crack in his voice as he said those last words. Giving up a dream was not easy, but Xttra made a choice to do it for them. His unselfish act in that moment reinforced why she chose to marry him when they came back from Earth. No other man could ever unite with her as a soulmate as Xttra did.

She circled her real arm around his back and planted another kiss on his lips.

"Thank you," she whispered.

Calandra slipped her right hand back into Xttra's left hand. The couple went back inside the main ballroom where they dined and danced together until pale twilight transformed into shadowy night.

# 3

Xttra drew in a deep breath and pressed his eyes shut. His heart thumped a few beats faster as he stood before the door to the simulation arena. Coming here already seemed like a futile gesture, but he had to do it anyway.

For Calandra's sake.

Xttra promised her he would appeal for reassignment to a different role within the Stellar Guard. One that kept him on Lathos. With her.

A horizontal beam of blue light fell on his face and crossed over his eyes. Once it passed his chin, a small sensor above the door emitted a pair of beeps.

"Welcome, Ttra Oogan."

A half-frown sprang onto his lips as his eyelids popped open again. It made no difference how many times he heard the automated greeting, Xttra never grew accustomed to how the artificial voice mispronounced his name. The same thing happened at every Stellar Guard training facility. Always dropping the first letter on his first name without fail.

He plodded down a corridor toward an instructional chamber. Dull yellow light reflected off his skin from the low ceiling. It cast a grainy glow on the polished volcanic stone floor. Similar dark stones covered the walls and ceiling. The whole corridor reminded Xttra of a tunnel winding downward into a narrow mine.

He approached a second broader door at the end of the corridor. Another beam of blue light fell upon him, and the door parted. When Xttra stepped inside, a spray of sand smacked him in the jaw and mouth. He instinctively raised his arm to cover his eyes and spit out sand residue coating his teeth and tongue.

Two junior officers hunkered down behind a smoldering aerorover ahead. One drew an eliminator. She peppered blue laser bolts across the hull of another crashed vessel resembling a Confederation short-range fighter. The junior officer used a detached aerorover door as a makeshift body shield. The other officer crawled around the rear of the vehicle and raised an armored sleeve. He intended to fire razor discs once he obtained a clear shot at an unseen target concealed behind the wrecked enemy vessel. Stray bolts blasted sandy terrain around both vehicles, throwing up more plumes like the one that first greeted Xttra.

"Halt simulation! Cease fire!"

Both junior officers lowered their weapons and sprang to their feet. The detached aerorover door clattered to the ground. They snapped their heads toward the instructional chamber entry door and fixed their eyes on Xttra. He ignored both junior officers and gazed up at an observation room window overlooking the chamber.

"What warrants interrupting this training session, Master Pilot Oogan?" The same voice spoke again, sounding gruffer this time around.

"I must speak with Commander Mikkah. It's urgent."

"Commander Mikkah cannot be disturbed. I'll tell him you stopped by, and he'll get back to you once—"

"I'm not leaving," Xttra said, cutting the voice off. "So, you'll have to continue your training session around me."

He folded his arms and raised his chin. His blue eyes hardened into a stony glare, never moving for a second from the window. Commander Mikkah never bothered to answer his arca vox all morning. Xttra refused to let an obstinate underling put him off now.

A heavy sigh and a muffled curse greeted his declaration. Another door, leading from the observation room down to the chamber, slid open a minute later. A bald man with broad shoulders stepped into the chamber and approached Xttra. His Stellar Guard uniform matched Xttra's apart from displaying a commander's insignia on front instead of a master pilot's insignia.

Mikkah narrowed his eyes and scowled.

"This isn't the best time, Xttra. Make it quick."

"I'm here to request a reassignment."

He raised an eyebrow and cast a skeptical glance at Xttra. Mikkah shook his head.

"We've already debated this more than once. Resuming space missions is mandatory."

"I haven't forgotten what you said."

"Have you forgotten the consequences of turning down assigned missions? Are you determined to get stripped of your rank and scout ship?"

Xttra rolled his eyes and sighed. He kicked at a patch of sand near his feet. Mikkah spoke to him as though he were a child. He understood the sacrifice awaiting him by going down this path. The commander did not need to hammer it into his skull.

"I'm well aware of the path that lies before me." His tone with Mikkah grew rougher. "Things change. I'm willing to step down as a master pilot."

"You're willing to throw away your career?"

Xttra cocked his head at Mikkah and scrunched his face. He harbored no intention of resigning from the Stellar Guard. Hearing the commander draw that exact conclusion without a second thought only stirred up annoyed feelings inside his mind.

"I want to shift gears and become an instructor at the academy. I'm certain you can find a spot for me there."

"No."

Mikkah turned away as though he intended to start walking back to the observation room. Xttra circled around him and cut off his path. He folded his arms a second time.

"What do you mean no?"

"I can't toss aside one of the best master pilots in the entire fleet just because his wife got inside his head."

Xttra felt heat rising under his collar. His muscles tensed and he grew as rigid as a statue.

"Do you understand what Calandra endured on Earth?" he snapped. "Do you understand what I endured? You haven't walked the same path we walked. I pray to Ahm you never walk it."

Mikkah's frown deepened. He stared down both gawking junior officers standing near the smoldering aerorover. Each officer averted their eyes. The commander refocused his attention on Xttra and pointed at the observation room.

"Inside. Now."

Xttra swallowed hard and followed Mikkah inside. The door sealed behind them with a whoosh. They stepped inside a glass elevator and Mikkah pressed a button for the top floor.

When the elevator door closed again, a fire enveloped his deep brown eyes.

"Do you understand what I've done on your behalf?" he asked. "I put my career on the line to save yours after what happened on that alien planet."

Xttra pinched his lips together and scowled. He did not crave a reminder of those long hours he spent inside the tribunal chamber. Waves of frustration washed over him while judicial officers debated his fate. They dismissed Xttra's account of attacks from hostile Earthians and Doni's treachery. Rather than consider evidence he shared with an open mind, the judicial officers seemed eager to blame Xttra for everything that went wrong, impose a stern punishment, and never speak of the whole episode again. He could do nothing beyond watch helplessly.

To his credit, Mikkah intervened and vouched for Xttra's record in the Stellar Guard and his character. He saved each survivor of the expedition to Earth from whatever dark fate brewed within the minds of the judicial officers. Now, it seemed as though Mikkah took personal offense at Xttra's decision to change course.

"Look, I'm not trying to be confrontational about this." Xttra's tone softened a bit. "I've done some soul searching and decided I need to consider what's best for me and Calandra together. This is the way forward."

The elevator door opened. Both men stepped out. Mikkah stopped in his tracks, turned, and faced Xttra. His eyelids snapped shut and a curt nod followed.

"Instructor, huh?" His eyes popped open again. "I hate to lose you in the field. On the other hand, I can't think of a master pilot more qualified to train other pilots. Your experience is invaluable."

A relieved smile crept across Xttra's lips.

"Calandra will be thrilled to hear this news."

"We'll make the switch right after you've completed your upcoming mission."

His smile vanished as fast as it appeared.

"No. Wait a minute." Xttra threw out his hands as he made his plea. "I want to make this change now. Today. Not after 'one final mission.'"

Mikkah shook his head.

"It's out of my hands. I'm sorry, Xttra. Your crew will meet with the Thetian delegation on Fengar as ordered."

"What do you mean it's out of your hands?"

Mikkah extracted a trique from his pocket. A small holoscreen popped up from the middle of the triangular gadget when he pressed a green-lit button to activate it. Lines of text appeared on the screen. Xttra recognized the Stellar Guard insignia at the top. The commander pulled up a report, but he had trouble deciphering all the words while only seeing the report from the backside.

"I have direct orders from the Minister of Space Exploration and Defense himself. The chief sovereign wants you specifically to take on this mission."

Xttra knitted his brows together and drew in a sharp breath. This qualified as an unexpected revelation. An unwelcome one as well.

"Why me?" he asked, voicing the first question that popped into his mind.

Mikkah shrugged.

"I just follow orders. I don't analyze them."

Xttra could not allow himself to embrace a similar attitude. Experience taught him to keep his eyes open when a situation seemed amiss.

This was one of those times.

***

Bo'un crumpled his lips into a puzzled frown. His reaction only reinforced to Xttra that his own suspicions concerning what Mikkah said earlier were warranted.

"Do you suppose the Earthian is right? It feels like much more is at stake here than tracking down a stolen shield emitter."

Xttra did not know what to think as he stared at a holoscreen tracking a life support system diagnostic. Nothing about this situation made sense in his mind. He could not imagine their chief sovereign insisting on him personally taking the lead on resolving a matter of such minor importance.

Xttra glanced over at his longtime weapons officer and simply shrugged.

"All I know, Bo'un, is Commander Mikkah ignored my request for reassignment until this mission is over."

Bo'un's eyes widened. His fingers traced over jagged scars covering the right side of his jaw and he brushed back his deep brown hair.

"Wait, what? You asked for reassignment?"

"I did." Xttra refocused his attention on the holoscreen. "The Stellar Guard granted my request. This upcoming mission will be our last one together."

A heavy silence permeated the scout ship's bridge. Bo'un drew closer to the station where Xttra sat and knelt by his chair. He made no effort to hide a disappointed frown overtaking his face. Xttra gnawed on his lower lip while he searched for the right words to justify a decision that not only altered his life, but the lives of his crew.

"When did you plan on telling the rest of us?" the weapons officer finally asked. "How long have you been planning to do this?"

Xttra turned away from the holoscreen and faced Bo'un a second time.

"It's a decision I've been agonizing over since we escaped from Earth," he said. "Calandra is struggling to heal from the trauma she endured there. I need to be with her. Help her. I can't do that if I'm always in space and she's alone on Lathos."

Bo'un nervously rubbed the same jagged scars again and his light gray eyes locked on a distant invisible point. If anyone understood Calandra's pain, Xttra knew he did. Bo'un's own survival bordered on being a miracle. No one aboard their scout ship genuinely believed he would ever come out of medical hibernation. A massive wild Earthian animal—which Kevin called a bear—inflicted so much critical damage while mauling him.

"That place changed all of us," Bo'un said, his eyes settling back on Xttra. "And not for the better."

Xttra answered him with an abrupt nod. He did not suffer any life-altering injuries like Calandra. Yet scars covered his mind and soul. Every moment from when their ship touched down amid the Earthian mountains until it blasted away from that wretched planet festered inside him like an open wound. Bleeding and oozing. Slowly infecting every part of him.

Two sequential beeps signaling the diagnostic's completion interrupted Xttra's thoughts. Life support systems still operated within acceptable functional parameters. Xttra hoped the diagnostic would uncover a hidden problem, giving him a credible excuse to delay the mission. He had checked every scout ship system now.

All functioned normally.

"Why us? Why are we the ones designated to pursue our Earthian ally at all costs?"

Xttra answered Bo'un with a blank stare. He had no clear answers. His official report did not include a mention of Kevin by name. Nor did he recount what Kevin told him concerning the former prime oracle.

None of it added up in his mind.

"We better dig a little deeper before we meet up with the Thetians," Xttra finally said. "If there's actual substance to Kevin's claims, we need to know before we get ourselves mired in a dire situation."

He rose to his feet and walked over to the main helm console. Xttra snatched up his trique lying loosely atop the console.

He pressed a button lit with blue light in a bottom corner on the triangular device. The trique holoscreen showed a detailed Stellar Guard report on the shield emitter prototype. Xttra pressed the blue button again to scroll past the report. A new holoscreen replaced the earlier one. This screen showed blank space apart from a long, empty horizontal box.

Xttra pressed down on a second blue-lit trique button in the opposite corner.

"Search for 'Prime Oracle Valadius accident.'"

A beep followed. Two words popped up on the holoscreen a few seconds later.

Restricted access.

Xttra scrunched up his face and shot a questioning look at Bo'un. Why would information related to a former prime oracle's demise aboard a spaceship merit restricted access? If Kevin's earlier revelation was indeed rooted in facts, such a turn of events only troubled him.

Xttra was not alone in feeling that way. A stoic frown now graced Bo'un's lips.

"Is this some sort of trap?" he said. "Something about all of this isn't connecting together for me."

Xttra nodded while continuing to stare at the holoscreen. He licked his lips and his heart raced faster. Bo'un's suspicions made sense. A nagging feeling washed over him. Someone intended to set a trap for the surviving members of the expedition to Earth.

Who was their next target?

# 4

Both eyes popped open unbidden. Calandra blinked a few times and sighed. Darkness shrouded her bedroom, broken in random places by faint moonlight peeking from behind borders of the bedroom window shade. She felt a sharp tug on the blankets. Xttra tossed and turned, eyes still closed. Calandra gazed upon him for a moment, wondering if she should rouse him from his slumber. She decided against it and sat up.

Calandra quietly swung both legs over the side of the bed and rose to her feet. She snatched up a robe from a nearby chair and wrapped it around her sleep clothes. Calandra peeked back at Xttra upon reaching the bedroom door. He now lay still, only partially covered by their Sapinoa hair blankets.

Her destination was their kitchen. Calandra opened a transparent door to their chiller. A blast of frigid air from inside the narrow vertical chamber brushed across both cheeks. Troubled thoughts bombarded her mind as she retrieved a stout bottle filled with glacier water from an upper shelf. Xttra shared unwelcome news after returning home the previous evening. His efforts to get reassigned from his upcoming mission failed. Calandra did not conceal her disappointment when he recounted his conversation with Commander Mikkah. Still, she did not blame Xttra for how things unfolded. Her husband showed his willingness to sacrifice for her and for them as a couple. That meant so much to Calandra.

A different nagging feeling kept her awake now. Why did the Stellar Guard push so hard for him to fulfill this specific mission? It made no sense to her. What was so important that they refused to consider sending any other master pilot out to the Fengar colonies?

Calandra set the glass bottle down on the kitchen table and retrieved a small chalice from a nearby cabinet. She glanced down at her left arm. The artificial fingers remained rigid and lifeless. Calandra longed to pick up more than one thing at a time again. One simple activity, among many, she took for granted when she had two working arms. She sat at the table and poured water into her chalice. Calandra sipped from the chalice. Her eyes drifted over to her arm a second time.

Those stiff unmoving fingers mocked her. Each one serving as a cold reminder of everything she lost.

Her arm. Her innocence. Her former life.

The Earthians bore sole blame for events leading her to this point. An Earthian doctor inserted pieces of metal in her arm, which Kevin called screws, to hold her broken bones in place. Those screws were supposed to stabilize her forearm while each bone mended. Instead, the tiny metal pieces caused a bone infection while she lay in hibernation during the return voyage to Lathos. The infection brought on a worsening fever soon after they landed in Luma.

An image clawed into her mind. That single image hardened and sharpened as it ripped open old scars into fresh wounds.

A bandaged stump.

Calandra sank down against her pillow in her hospital bed when she first noticed the altered limb resting there by her side.

She shook with sobs. Her clan doctor warned her they could do nothing to save the arm. If they did not amputate the infected part of the limb, she would die. Nothing he told her did enough to prepare Calandra to cope with a sudden loss of her arm.

"I'm so sorry, sweetheart. I'm so sorry."

She gazed up through tear-filled eyes. Tears also rolled down Xttra's cheeks. Calandra's lips trembled, and she extended her unaffected arm toward him.

"Why would Ahm let this happen to me?" Her words grew choked with sobs. "With everything I've been through and with all I've endured. Why this? Why now?"

She did not want to confront a hard truth. She hesitated to admit part of the blame rested with her. Calandra ignored her brittle bones in her zeal to go to Earth and it cost her.

Xttra said nothing. He simply crouched down by her bedside and embraced Calandra. Her remaining arm circled his back, and she clung to him while they both shed more tears together.

"Can't sleep either?"

Xttra's question jerked Calandra out of her thoughts. She snapped her head toward him. His slight brown curls were a bit disheveled from laying on a pillow for so long. A small smile adorning his lips morphed into a concerned frown when he laid eyes on her face.

"What's wrong?"

Calandra set down the chalice and brushed her fingers across her cheek. Tears greeted her fingertips. She quickly brushed them aside.

"I'm okay. Well … as okay as I can be, I guess."

Xttra straightened out his sleeveless sleep shirt and pulled up a chair next to her.

"What's on your mind? You can tell me."

She gazed into his deep blue eyes and then let her eyes trail downward. His eyes drifted to the same spot, and then he quickly glanced upward again. Calandra did not need to say a word. Her husband discerned those same unwanted thoughts overtaking her mind.

"We'll find a way to get this new limb working like your old arm. I give you my word."

An annoyed feeling crept out from shadows lingering inside her. Calandra heard the same vow before. Making promises over a situation beyond his control did not soothe her feelings. Still, when Xttra grasped her right arm and caressed her forearm with his fingers, she understood he meant well. He only wanted to comfort her troubled soul. Calandra allowed a faint smile to appear at last. She nestled her head against his shoulder.

"Sometimes I wonder if we'll ever be allowed to gain lasting happiness. It seems as elusive as a shadow, forever out of reach."

Xttra circled his other hand around her shoulder.

"We are masters of our own fate. No force on this planet or in the whole galaxy can take that away from us."

"I want you to be right. I want to feel something else again besides sadness and anger. I don't want to worry about you not returning home."

Calandra closed her eyes tight as he wound his fingers through a lock of auburn hair that fell against her cheek. Being nestled in his arms felt so good. She did not want the feeling to end.

"I want you to stay so much." Her voice dropped to a near-whisper. "Thinking about you going to Fengar never filled me with dread in the past. Now I can't break free from this awful sensation."

"I'm worried too. Something about this mission doesn't add up."

Xttra's tone perfectly matched the concern embedded in his words. Calandra popped open her eyes again, leaned forward, and turned to face him.

"What doesn't add up?"

Xttra gnawed on his lip and cast his eyes at swinging lights hanging above their heads. Each fixture formed a teardrop shape and connected to a single black rod suspended from the ceiling. He stared at the lights for a moment before finally shaking his head.

"I don't know if I should share this. It's technically restricted information. I never included it on my official mission report."

Calandra narrowed her eyes and tilted her head. Those cryptic words aroused instant curiosity.

"What is it? You know you can always trust me. I won't tell anyone else."

Xttra lowered his head and locked eyes with her a second time. Fear radiated from each one.

"I chased an old model Cassian dart to Fengar on my most recent mission. My orders were simple. Intercept an unidentified saboteur fleeing with stolen technology. Then I disabled the dart's secondary thrusters and spoke with the pilot. Everything I thought I knew about my mission turned out to be wrong."

"What do you mean?"

"Kevin was the pilot."

Calandra's eyes widened and her mouth dropped open. Her heart began racing until it shook her entire chest. There had to be another explanation. Kevin Riley was no saboteur. He saved her life on Earth. He sacrificed everything to help them escape.

"Kevin is no traitor," Calandra insisted. "Nor a thief. He would never risk his freedom over some gadget."

Xttra answered her with a slow nod.

"That's just it. I'm convinced someone wanted me to believe we were chasing a common thief at all costs."

"Why? What do they have to gain?"

"Kevin claims he found evidence that Valadius lives."

Calandra pressed her lips into a slight frown and shook her head. His claim was a mistaken one. What Kevin said could not be possible.

"Our chief sovereign reported that he died," she said. "A scout ship recovered the prime oracle's transport, adrift along with his body. His burial rites were broadcast to every man, woman, and child in Ra'ahm."

"I know." Xttra's gaze shifted to a copy of the *Book of Ahm* in the adjacent room. It lay on a small table flanking a couch. "We both witnessed the same rites. We both heard the same tragic news about the flare."

Calandra was still a child when tragedy befell Valadius. Her family mourning his sudden death formed one of her earliest memories. A solar flare sent out a radiation burst that bombarded his transport's hull. At the time, the prime oracle had set out on a quick journey to the Fengar colonies. He intended to minister to colonists belonging to the Order of Ahm.

It shook citizens of Ra'ahm to the core when their spiritual leader died so tragically. Delcor urged the rest of the Council of Oracles to waste no time and ordain a new prime oracle. The successor to Valadius was a fervent ally of Delcor and his clan during the Separatist War.

Calandra recalled how her grandfather, Janthore, stepped down as first minister only a year after the prime oracle perished. He never gave a reason for why he resigned from his high office. She suspected her grandfather could not cope with the tragic death of a prime oracle of Ahm he knew personally.

"It must be a mistake." Calandra said. "If he didn't perish, an oracle taking his place would have been unlawfully chosen."

Xttra rose from his chair. He walked over to twin glass doors leading to a small balcony and gazed out across Luma's skyline. A smattering of lights enveloped the old city, chasing away nighttime shadows. Calandra scrambled off her chair and joined him at the balcony door. His eyes remained fixed on those same city lights as she slipped her right hand into his left hand.

"If Kevin is right, and our former prime oracle lives, you know what this means."

Calandra closed her eyes and nodded. She completed in her mind those words Xttra left unspoken.

If true, this revelation would mean their chief sovereign lied to every man, woman, and child in Ra'ahm. It also would mean a usurper now led the Order of Ahm. If their chief sovereign deceived an entire nation on this matter, what other secrets would he keep hidden? Why did her grandfather resign from his service?

"They gave me a choice Calandra." Xttra turned and gazed into her eyes again. "Accept this mission and track down Kevin on Fengar. Or resign from the Stellar Guard."

A crease formed in her brow as Calandra's eyes now drifted over to the Luma skyline. Xttra could not do what they asked of him. Learning the Stellar Guard demanded he track Kevin down and bring him back as a prisoner sickened her. Unlike his fellow Earthians, Kevin had honor. Turning their backs on a friend in his hour of need was not an option.

"You can't do it," she whispered. Calandra lowered her head and cast a pleading glance at Xttra. "I owe my life to him. You have to save Kevin."

"I will not harm him. You have my word."

Xttra drew her into an embrace and planted a tender kiss on her lips. Calandra soaked in his kiss and tightened her embrace of him. Their lips lingered for a moment until she opened her eyes again and drew back a step.

"Pray for me," he said. "Pray this mission does not send us down a path neither of us wants to travel."

Fear squeezed Calandra like an invisible hand. Sleep would now elude her until Xttra returned home from Fengar and told her what he found.

Then, at last, he could stay.

# 5

Fengar never exuded a welcoming vibe during Xttra's past missions to the large moon. Still, touching down on the lunar surface this time around put him on edge more than usual. He pondered what he should say or do if he and his crew found Kevin inside the Thetian trade colony.

Calandra was right to be concerned for their Earthian friend's safety. An unshakable feeling gripped Xttra that someone set a trap for Kevin, and he narrowly avoided springing it. A plume of dust kicked up around the lower section of the hull as his scout ship touched down on a landing pad. Remnants of a recent lunar dust storm.

A square slot in a protective transparent dome over the pad sealed shut again. Xttra released a deep sigh while shutting down the primary thrusters.

He glanced over at Ohnro.

"Where exactly are we supposed to meet with these Thetians again?"

Ohnro squinted and tapped at a small holoscreen hovering above his console.

"Our destination is a shipping port west of the landing pad," he said. "The Thetians claim they have a reliable contact there with information on where the Earthian went and who he's working with."

Xttra nodded. "Let's gear up and go."

Their safety harnesses released, and they rose to their feet. The door leading into the cargo bay opened with a whoosh. Once he rose from the pilot's chair, Xttra wheeled around and fixed his eyes squarely on his crew.

"Let me make this clear: If we find Kevin, we bring him back alive. If you shoot or slice him, I'll personally bring you before a tribunal."

Talan shot him a disapproving look. The others simply nodded. Xttra cocked his head over at the navigator and a crease formed in his brow.

"Do you have a problem with my orders, Talan?"

Talan scratched his thin brown beard. His green eyes stayed in the same rigid gaze.

"What if he shoots first? You want us to capture this Earthian traitor while locking us in virtual restraints."

Xttra scowled at him.

"Kevin is no traitor. He saved my wife's life and helped us escape from the clutches of hostile Earthians. Follow my order."

Talan rubbed his hand down his cheek and nodded. He marched over to the weapons locker.

"Understood. I hope you know what you're doing."

His hardened glare told Xttra they did not actually reach a mutual understanding. Xttra joined him at the locker and cracked an annoyed half-smile.

"I know what I'm doing more than a navigator barely a year out of the academy."

Xttra bound armored sleeves to both forearms, cinching the ebutoka leather straps tight under each arm. He filled belt pouches with stun pebbles and Cassian fire shells to reinforce his usual eliminator. In addition to outfitting himself with standard Stellar Guard weaponry, Xttra also grabbed a mounted pulse cannon. This gave him a useful stun weapon for subduing Kevin without causing serious or fatal injuries.

Other ebutoka leather straps connected the pulse cannon to a metal plate that wrapped around the shoulder. A charging chamber sat atop the plate and a stout barrel protruded from the chamber opening. Xttra plucked a small remote off a locker shelf. Two stationary buttons, a sliding modulator, and a rolling ball functioned as a control panel for pulse cannon operations. One stationary button activated the weapon and the second released an electromagnetic bolt. The modulator determined voltage in each bolt before release. The rolling ball raised or lowered the barrel and aimed it at a specific target. Pulse cannon bolts held enough juice to short out communication equipment and laser-based weaponry on contact.

Ohnro lowered the ramp leading out from the cargo bay's lower hatch. Xttra turned and gave a friendly salute.

"Take care of my ship while we're gone. Run a diagnostic. Make sure no traces of lunar dust from outside are clogging anything important."

Xttra, Talan, and Bo'un walked down the ramp, leaving Ohnro, Sarianna, and Tressek behind to watch the scout ship. The ramp raised again after the trio stepped onto the landing pad.

"Keep your eyes and ears open," Xttra said, mostly intending his comments for his inexperienced navigator. "You can purchase instant trouble in a place like this."

Entering the shipping port impressed upon Xttra anew the difficulties they faced with limiting distractions in this place. Bright metallic containers of all shapes and sizes occupied tons of space.

This expansive storage area soon yielded to an equally sprawling market. Spending enough time inside a Thetian trading colony offered a quick path to experiencing sensory overload. Rows of booths decked out with colorful lights and displays stretched out in all directions. Merchants and traders flocked to this market to sell goods or barter because they drew patrons from the Fengar colonies, Lathos, and many other planets and moons within this sector of the galaxy.

Xttra's eyes drifted to a booth displaying handcrafted tools and weapons fashioned by ancient cave dwellers on Thetia. One weapon that drew his eye resembled a smooth stone ax with a spear shaped pointed head.

Stolen artifacts. A telltale sign of Thetian pirates.

He turned away and scanned a row of booths on the right end of the market. No sign of Thetian military delegates anywhere.

"Bo'un, get out your arca vox and have Ohnro double-check the coordinates. I think we're in the wrong place."

Silence greeted Xttra's order. He glanced over his shoulder and saw no sign of his weapons officer or navigator. Bo'un and Talan had vanished among a stream of patrons examining and purchasing goods.

Xttra sighed and pulled out his own arca vox. Before he pressed a button to activate the holoscreen, Bo'un let out a distinct shout. Xttra snapped his head toward a booth on the row directly across from him. He saw his weapons officer seize Talan by his shoulder and pull him away from the booth.

Talan had wandered over to a booth filled with cages housing exotic pets. He wrenched free from Bo'un's grasp and reached out his hand toward the nearest cage. It housed a long slender animal covered in short coarse brown hair. The animal had spindly arms and legs, a flat elongated head, and small beady eyes.

Xttra knew a russakin when he saw one. What did Talan think he was doing?"

Bo'un also thought the navigator had lost his mind.

"Don't touch it," he said. "You're asking to get bitten."

Talan laughed and gave him a dismissive wave with his other hand.

"I used to own a pet russakin. They're harmless."

"Harmless isn't how I'd describe one," Bo'un replied. "Leave it alone."

Bo'un reached out to grab his arm again and pull him away from the cage. Talan shook his hand off a second time and stuck his fingers between the slats. The russakin flickered a forked tongue at him and growled. At once, the creature bared its fangs and lunged forward.

Talan screamed and jerked his hand out of the cage. Two fresh holes in his flesh bore witness to this Russakin's temper. The punctured skin took on a purplish hue and started to swell.

"You fool!" Xttra snapped.

He charged toward the booth holding assorted caged animals. A mixture of growls and frightened cries came from neighboring cages around the russakin. Bo'un and Talan simultaneously turned toward Xttra. He activated his arca vox in mid-sprint and brought Sarianna up on the holoscreen.

"We're heading back."

She raised an eyebrow at him.

"So soon?"

"No Thetian delegates are waiting for us at the designated coordinates and Talan offered his fingers to a captured russakin."

Sarianna rolled her eyes.

"You're kidding me, right?"

"Afraid not."

Xttra glanced up at Talan again. The navigator cradled his injured hand. Sweat already formed on his brow and his breaths started growing heavier.

"Get the anti-venom ready," Xttra said, focusing his attention on Sarianna again. "We're still close enough to get him back to the scout ship before his muscles and nerves go completely numb."

She nodded. The medical officer's image vanished from the holoscreen a few seconds later. Xttra shoved the arca vox back inside his chest pouch. Bo'un grabbed Talan by his uninjured arm and marched him away from the animal cages.

BOOM!

A sudden loud blast reverberated through the market. Sparks and shards from shattering overhead lights flew in all directions. Screams from random patrons and merchants followed. Xttra dropped to his knees. He pinched his eyelids shut and pressed both hands tight against his ears. When he opened his eyes again, the entire market had plunged into darkness. Emergency lighting along the market floor activated near Xttra. It cast a darkened azure glow over him.

"This feels like an ambush." Xttra scrambled to his feet and faced Bo'un and Talan again. "Let's fly."

The trio sprinted toward a walkway connecting the landing pad and shipping port. At once, laser bolts rained down from a stack of shipping containers on Xttra's left side. He dove to the ground and crawled between rows of containers directly behind him.

"Get Talan to the ship." He motioned toward the landing pad. "I'll draw their fire."

Bo'un and Talan dropped down closer to the ground while Xttra activated his mounted pulse cannon. Three electromagnetic bolts blasted from the barrel in quick bursts. Each one rippled through an elevated metallic gray container and support beam in front of him. His crew members took advantage of the window

Xttra opened and made a dash for the landing pad. Laser bolts rained down from amid the shipping containers again. Each one targeted Xttra's new position among the shipping containers on the opposite side.

Xttra extracted his thermal tracker from his chest pouch. A heat pattern matching a human or humanoid alien popped up on the screen. They crouched behind a container on the highest row. Xttra adjusted the angle on the pulse cannon's barrel to match their position and fired a new volley of electromagnetic bolts.

These ones reached their intended target. A loud groan followed when the second bolt struck. Xttra glanced down at his tracker. It now showed the same heat pattern collapsed on a support beam behind the container. The shooter had not fallen from their position above him.

*They're alive*, Xttra thought. *Good. That gives me a chance to interrogate them once I revive them again.*

He retracted the pulse cannon, returned the remote to his chest pouch, and scrambled to his feet. The tracker emitted a beep. Xttra fixed his eyes on the holoscreen again. Three other heat patterns now appeared on the screen. Each one drawing closer to his position.

This situation just kept growing worse.

"Surrender now."

Xttra followed the sound of the gruff voice and turned to his left. Three people approached him, all clad in Thetian military uniforms. He raised both hands and the thermal tracker.

"There's been a misunderstanding," Xttra said. "I'm here to meet a Thetian delegation. I'm pursuing a Ra'ahm saboteur we suspect is hiding in this trade colony."

The nearest Thetian gave him a stern glare.

"You attacked a trade market and caused mass panic. You're in our custody until we sort this out."

The other Thetians each grabbed an arm and ripped the tracker out of his hand. They restrained his limbs before Xttra could unleash the arm saber hidden inside his right armored sleeve. The remaining Thetian took a cloth strip and blindfolded him.

Grainy darkness blanketed Xttra's eyes while his captors prodded him forward. He peppered the Thetians with questions. They refused to say a word. A mechanical hum greeted his ears after a few minutes of walking. His captors pushed him forward up a ramp. Once he cleared the ramp, he heard the same hum as it closed behind him.

"Sit down," a gruff voice ordered. The same voice from when the Thetians first made their presence known.

Both Thetians let go of his arms. One gave Xttra a hard shove in the back. Then a hand seized his blindfold and wrenched the fabric off his eyes.

"Good work, Xander," a new higher-pitched voice said. "That didn't take long at all."

Xttra turned and found himself standing face-to-face before a short woman with curly black hair, high cheekbones, and violet eyes. She owned the distinctive brow ridge, throat gills, and webbed fingers of a Thetian.

"Can we all settle down for a bit, so I can explain what's going on?" Xttra said. "I'm trying to track down –"

"You will speak when I'm ready to hear your words."

The Thetian woman thrust her arm toward a chair. He followed her order and took a seat. Xttra gave his surroundings a once-over and realized they brought him onto the bridge of a small ship.

Clear vertical tubes filled with water, each spaced a few steps apart, adorned the walls. Each tube was the width of an average person. Three stations faced an expansive windshield at one end of the bridge. A pair of stations angled between helm and windshield featured small consoles. A vertical glass sheet rose from the middle of each console and a single chair sat behind the console. The remaining station was the helm itself. It featured a longer console with a single chair for the lead pilot. Numerous buttons, switches and panels filled the length of the console and it lit up with blue and red lights.

The Thetian woman snapped her fingers at Xttra to draw his attention to her. She stood before his chair and rested her hands on her hips.

"I am Kyra Riso of the Thetian Field Brigade." Her eyes darted down to the Stellar Guard insignia on his uniform and back to his face. "You can't stroll in here and disrupt our market without facing consequences."

Kyra snapped her head over to the helm. Xander, one of the Thetians who marched Xttra onto the ship, had taken a seat at the helm console.

"Any word from the brigade outpost on the other side of the port?" she asked.

"We've lost contact with ground communications." Xander stared at his console and tapped a panel lit with red light repeatedly with his index finger. "We might have to reboot the entire system."

"Are you certain?"

Kyra couched her question in a suspicious tone, as though she did not believe what her own eyes told her.

"As certain as Fengar orbits Lathos."

"Fine." Kyra narrowed her eyes and cast a glance back toward Xttra. "You know what to do, Cavac."

Xttra narrowed his eyes in turn. A suspicious frown crossed his lips. Before he said a word or moved a muscle, a series of metallic snaps followed. Bands slapped down across Xttra's ankles and wrists. All four limbs were now bound to his chair. Xttra jerked at his new restraints with vigor as the horror of his situation hit him full force.

These Thetians intended to make him their prisoner.

# 6

Xttra refused to take his eyes off his restraints. Those metallic bands had to own an inherent weakness he could exploit to free himself. Xtrra counted only four Thetians. Dispatching each one and escaping to his scout ship did not present unrealistic odds for success. He wore new flex armor and armed himself with enough weaponry earlier to get the job done.

First, he needed to uncover their agenda. These Thetians did not ambush him for fun. What purpose drove their actions?

Kyra now stood over at the helm. Xttra knew he needed to draw her attention and trick her into divulging their plans. Figuring out why these Thetians went to the trouble of laying a trap for him on Fengar ate at him.

"My planetary leaders won't stand for this," he said. "Thetia and Lathos are at peace. Imprisoning a Stellar Guard senior officer without cause will be construed as an act of war."

Kyra slapped her hand down on the helm console and marched over to his chair again.

"Don't act so dramatic. You don't have an upper hand here, no matter how much you wish you did."

Xttra cracked a smirk and shook his head.

"Take a look around. This is my solar system." He made no effort to hide the smugness in his voice. "You're a long way from Thetia. There's no part of Fengar where you can hide from the Stellar Guard for long."

Kyra cocked her head at him, and a knowing smile spread across her lips.

"Is that a fact? I know everything I need to know about Lathos. The same is true with you, Xttra Oogan."

Xttra's eyes grew as wide as plates. A chill crawled up his spine. His heart now shook violently as though a hammer repeatedly struck it.

"How do you know my name?"

"I know much more than a name. I soaked up many details of your life while watching you and your beloved Calandra over the course of several weeks."

She leaned over him and rested her palms on top of his bound forearms. Kyra drew close enough to his face for him to smell the fragrance she wore. Her scent reminded Xttra of soli flowers, a plant that grew in abundance in the Cassian Mountains. The same mountains bordered the Cassia Province which formed part of the Confederation of Northern Tribes.

Did these Thetians journey to Lathos and operate as hidden spies in Ra'ahm? That scenario did not seem possible. Still, Kyra's fragrance told him they had not stayed exclusively on Fengar.

"Who are you? Why have you been spying on me?"

"You possess critical information you can offer us. Information unavailable through normal channels."

A crease formed in his brow.

"What information?"

"Simple." Kyra straightened up and circled the chair where Xttra remained bound. "You're going to take us to the planet you call Earth."

Xttra clenched his jaw and jerked against the metal bands holding his arms and legs in place.

"I will never set foot on that planet again!"

"You'll cooperate with our wishes. That is if you ever want to see your wife again."

"Are you threatening me?"

Kyra stopped and thrust an index finger at Xttra.

"No threats. Only a promise."

Xttra swallowed hard and licked his lips. His thoughts turned to Calandra. Did agents in league with these Thetians infiltrate Luma? Was she safe? Fear, like a clawed hand, squeezed his heart in its tightening grip.

"What did you do to Calandra?"

"Nothing. She's perfectly safe at home inside your apartment in Luma—for now."

Panic tightened his throat. Xttra struggled to keep his breathing calm and steady and felt certain Kyra sensed each of those tightening breaths. If only he somehow wriggled a hand free and retrieved his arca vox, then he could warn his crew and instruct them to take Calandra into hiding at once.

His crew.

A new horrifying thought bubbled to the surface. Did these Thetians also ambush his scout ship?

"What happened to my ship and crew?"

"They're in the same place you left them," Xander said, glancing up from the helm. He hunched over the console while checking data on a small screen. "Our only aim was to capture you."

Xttra shot him an icy stare.

"You'll never get away with this. The Stellar Guard does not shy away from doling out justice to Thetian scum. They will find you. Count on it."

Kyra laughed. Contempt radiated from her face like sunlight.

"The Stellar Guard? Seriously? Your precious military won't find us in a thousand years once we leave Fengar."

"You can't stay hidden forever. You're all fugitives now. No way will the Thetian military, or your planetary council, jeopardize peaceful relations with Lathos so you can save your skins."

"You're making a bold assumption, Xttra Oogan."

"And what assumption is that?"

"What makes you think Thetian leadership knows what's happening here?"

Xttra pressed his lips together and drummed his fingers on the end of the armrest. Her sarcastic attitude and contempt annoyed him, but it also might play into her divulging the information he needed at some point.

"You are Thetians."

Kyra smirked and shook her head.

"This is a Thetian ship. We are not Thetians."

Xttra's face contorted into a puzzled expression. At once, Kyra peeled off her brow ridge and throat gills and tossed them aside on the floor of the bridge. She then slid the webbing off from between her fingers like a glove. Other crew members followed suit and removed all Thetian features from their bodies. His eyes widened as they all revealed their true appearance.

"Who are you?"

"We are from the Confederation."

Pride swelled in Kyra's voice as she made that revealing declaration. Heat rose under Xttra's collar. Their knowledge of him and Calandra, and ability to spy on them, all made sense. Confederation officials were unable to examine the Earth probe Calandra discovered before he seized possession of the interstellar object in the Ice Belt. Now they had abducted him in a desperate bid to outdo Ra'ahm, following Xttra's first contact expedition to the Aramus system.

"You stole the Earth probe out from under one of our deep space vessels nearly two years ago," Xander said. He turned and directed a pointed glare at Xttra. "Now we're setting everything right."

Xttra answered him with an incredulous stare.

"What do you hope to accomplish by going to Earth? What does the Confederation of Northern Tribes gain from visiting that wretched planet?"

"A new trading partner. A new military ally. Who knows? We'll work out all those crucial details once we meet with the Earthian leaders."

Xttra lifted his chin and cracked an enigmatic smile. These Confederation fools had no clue what awaited them on such a dangerous planet. They would be fortunate to escape with their lives.

"Good luck. You'll need every bit Ahm will grant you."

A scowl deepened on Kyra's lips. She took a step forward and grabbed him by the chin. Her fingers pressed into his jawbone.

"Your cooperation is not optional."

Kyra's eyes lingered on his own for a few seconds longer. Xttra refused to blink or flinch. These Confederation setaworms could not entertain even a momentary thought they were intimidating him. She finally relaxed her grip on his jaw and stepped back from the chair. Kyra flashed an annoyed smile.

"What we want is simple," she said. "You will give us the coordinates for Earth inside the Aramus system. Then, you'll help us contact Earthian political and military leadership so we can form an alliance."

"You already know which star Earth orbits," Xttra replied. "Why do you need me to chart a route for you?"

"Believe me. You were far from our first choice."

"Is that a fact?"

"I wanted the Earthian you brought back on board. But he proved much too elusive for our agents."

His ears perked up at her mention of Kevin. Finding him drove the whole purpose behind Xttra's mission. He now worried what fate overtook his Earthian friend. Did he remain on Fengar? Or flee to another place altogether to escape the clutches of both Confederation and Ra'ahm leadership?

Kyra drew closer to the chair again, hunched over Xttra, and loosened the straps on his mounted pulse cannon. Then, she ripped it—metal plate and all—off his upper arm and shoulder. The Confederation agent pointed the cannon's barrel straight at his chest.

"Where did you conceal the remote controlling this pulse cannon?"

Xttra shrugged. His lips formed into a half-smirk.

"In all the excitement out there, I must have dropped it among the shipping containers. Maybe you should step outside and look around."

Kyra glowered at him. She set the pulse cannon on the floor and snapped her head toward a station ahead of the helm.

"Search him, Cavac. We don't have time to play games with this ictus bug."

A stocky man with hair shorn down to a dark fuzz approached him. His appearance stood out from the other Confederation crew members. Both hands were overlayed with a metallic shell that extended under his uniform sleeves. A thumb-sized cube-shaped neural processor jutted out from his left temple. An ocular implant filled his right eye socket. The implant continuously shifted or turned based on how much light and movement it sensed around Cavac.

Xttra scrunched up his face.

"You're a melder aren't you? Just my lucky day."

Cavac scowled. His natural eye dropped into a half-squint. The ocular implant remained wide open. It shifted and spun while focusing on Xttra. Gazing at the implant sent a shudder through him. The melder scanned Xttra from head to toe, dropping his chin and slowly raising it again as his gaze moved upward. When Cavac reached Xttra's chest pouch, his natural eye opened wide again.

"Found it."

He thrust a hand inside the pouch and drew out the pulse cannon remote. Xttra's eyes darted down to his chest and back up to Cavac. An unsettling toothy grin emerged on the melder's face. He stepped away from the chair, turned, and tossed the remote over to Kyra. She thrust up her left hand and snatched it out of the air.

Kyra pressed a button to activate the pulse cannon. She hoisted it off the floor and aimed the barrel squarely at Xttra's chest.

"Now your flex armor underneath your uniform might protect you from an electromagnetic bolt." She flashed a knowing smile as she spoke. "But I'm guessing it will amplify the bolt's effects. Do you want to test my theory out? Or will you give me the coordinates for Earth?"

Xttra knitted his brows together and glared at her.

"Use your brain. Find the planet yourself, like I did."

"Do you think I'm bluffing?"

"You wouldn't expend so much time and energy in capturing me simply to kill me."

An electromagnetic bolt leapt from the barrel and slammed into his chest with sudden ferocity. Xttra clenched his teeth and let out a pained moan as the bolt spread across his chest like electrically charged webbing. It vanished a few seconds later.

His eyes widened and Xttra panted. Kyra was crazy. She needed him alive. That bolt could have killed him. Had he miscalculated their need for him?

"I knew I was correct," Kyra said. "Now, if I leave this on the stun setting, I can keep going for a while. Do you think you can do the same?"

Xttra's stare hardened and deepened. He spit on the floor in front of her.

"Wow. You are one stubborn Ra'ahmian fool."

She fired a second bolt in the same spot as before. Xttra pinched his eyelids shut and clenched his teeth a second time. The electric charge startled him with the same abrupt energy as a chill enveloping his body after diving into a mountain lake. When this second bolt finally dissipated, Xttra panted much harder than the first time.

Kyra lowered the barrel and rested the pulse cannon against her hip.

"You have the power to make this stop. Give us the Earth coordinates. Simple solution. Your choice."

Xttra lowered his head. He didn't like his odds of withstanding the pain a third bolt promised to bring.

"I'll tell you." His voice devolved into a hoarse whisper. "I'll tell you what you want to know."

Kyra set the pulse cannon on the floor again and snapped her head at Cavac. She motioned for him to draw closer to the chair a second time.

"Take down the coordinates. I'll get us off this rock so we can power up the hyperlight engines and go."

Xttra refused to make eye contact with Cavac as he approached. His worst nightmare had been set in motion and no options remained for him to stop it.

He was returning to Earth.

# 7

Calandra's heart sank when Bo'un's image popped up on her arca vox. His deep frown and concerned eyes told her something awful had occurred. She did not need to be an oracle of Ahm to sense it involved Xttra.

"I wish I came to you bearing better news." Bo'un adopted an apologetic tone from the moment he opened his mouth. "After everything you've endured, you don't deserve this."

"Don't deserve what? Bo'un? What happened?"

"Your husband was taken prisoner on Fengar."

Calandra sank back against the cushions on her couch. Her throat tightened and tears welled up in her eyes. She brushed them away with her forearm.

"How did this happen?" A distinct tremor gripped Calandra's voice as she forced herself to ask a painful but necessary question. "Who took him as a prisoner?"

Bo'un cast his light gray eyes downward.

"I have no idea. Our meeting with the Thetian delegation turned out to be a trap. We were ambushed inside the shipping port at the Thetian trade colony."

"Ambushed?"

"Someone fired laser bolts at us. We made a run for the scout ship and became separated from Xttra on the way. He never rejoined us."

"No! … No." Calandra's lips trembled, and her voice cracked. "This was supposed to be his last mission."

Bo'un raised his head. A fresh look of determination rested on his scarred face.

"I'll find him," he said. "I'll track him to the ends of this galaxy if that's what it takes. I give you my word."

Calandra let her eyes drift away from the holoscreen. Numbness blanketed her whole body. Someone snatched Xttra away from her without warning. All Calandra could do was watch helplessly while her life crumbled like aging bricks into a ruinous heap. Why did Ahm keep allowing so many terrible events to unfold?

Fresh tears ran down both cheeks. Calandra sniffled and refocused her gaze on the holoscreen.

"Did you contact the Thetians?"

"I did. All I learned is they lost contact with one of their spaceships and its crew after unidentified attackers boarded the vessel."

Not knowing who abducted him or where they took him filled Calandra with fear. It crawled along her spine and seeped into every cell along the way. Tremors gripped her hand, and her eyes formed a half-squint as she tried to hold back more tears from forming.

"Please bring him home," Calandra said. "I don't know what I'll do without Xttra here, safe with me."

Bo'un answered with a slow nod. He had also grown teary-eyed at this point.

"Whatever it takes, I'll bring him back. I promise."

His image vanished from the holoscreen. Calandra set down her arca vox on the table. Her face contorted. Tears burst forth anew a second later. Calandra buried her eyes in her right hand and sobbed.

He was gone. Xttra was gone.

Stolen from her.

*Why?*

That one question scratched and broke through to the surface. What did anyone gain from abducting Xttra? He wielded no political power. His authority within the Stellar Guard did not extend beyond commanding his own scout ship. What happened to him made no sense.

A small furry body rubbed up against her leg. Calandra pulled away her hand and cast her eyes down at the floor. Bella stood on her back paws and stuck her front paws on Calandra's right knee. The little cala cocked her head to the side. Her wide unblinking yellow eyes stared up at Calandra's tear-stained face.

"Hi sweetheart." Emotion choked her voice. "I'm so glad you're here right now. I don't want to be alone."

Calandra dropped her hand and stroked silvery gray fur adorning Bella's head. The cala closed her eyes and bumped her snout and whiskers against that same hand. An audible coo greeted Calandra's ears.

Before she entered hibernation during the journey to Earth, Calandra wondered if Bella would still remember her when she returned home to Lathos. She always heard and read how calas only had short-term memories. Naturally, Calandra expected Bella to be skittish and elusive when she paid Alayna a visit soon after losing her arm. Bella defied those expectations. Her beloved cala sprang from her nest when Calandra opened the door, scurried down the smooth senosa wood post holding it aloft, and bounded straight toward her. For Bella, recognition was both instant and permanent.

Did Bella mourn her absence during their year apart? Did the absence of her familiar face or her familiar scent haunt the cala? Those questions gnawed at Calandra after their reunion. Alayna, of course, spent considerable time and energy doing everything possible to keep the little animal happy and healthy. Still, no one ever expected her to fully replace what Bella lost—even temporarily.

Calandra pulled her hand away from her pet. Her eyes wandered over to a sculpture sitting on a shelf mounted against the opposite wall. The sculpture depicted a spherical compass. Light grey stone, washed in a purple dye, formed the sphere. A single spindle jutted out from each end. Words circled the equator, spelling out a familiar saying drawn from pages in the *Book of Ahm*. Calandra knew each word by heart. This sculpture symbolized the traveler's compass and offered a promise to lost and lonely travelers. If a traveler accepted Ahm as their only guide, they would find the true path leading to his holy dwelling.

*Xttra will not become lost. I will bring him home.*

She rose to her feet. This resolution breathed a new determination into her body and soul. Calandra marched over to the closed balcony doors and gazed upon fraxa trees lining the streets below her apartment. Budding scarlet leaves shook as a gust of wind swayed their parent branches. Her eyes traced the Luma skyline beyond the window and soon focused on an ornate box-shaped building. A broad domed tower rose from the middle. Twin spires adorned the top.

Their chief sovereign would be inside that building tomorrow to address the Ra'ahm National Assembly. Gaining an audience with him would be Calandra's first step to rescuing Xttra.

***

Nerves and muscles quivered in unison as Calandra climbed steps leading to the main doors of the national assembly chamber. She drew a deep breath and worked to soothe her agitated mind. Still, her efforts did little to dissipate worried feelings swarming over her like a colony of agitated Ictus bugs.

How would their chief sovereign receive her plea? Would he react with anger or show indifference? Calandra wondered how much an individual master pilot's abduction truly mattered to him when compared to a larger picture.

Stone pillars flanked each main door leading into the chambers. Statues depicting a solitary mokai bird with raised wings sat atop each pillar. She glanced up at the nearest statue. Hardened stone eyes probed her, reaching deep into her soul. Their inanimate gaze unnerved Calandra further. No kindness dwelt in the eyes towering above her, only a fierce wildness. She squeezed her fingers around her thumb, suppressing tremors that threatened to break free.

A narrow line of blue light passed over her face while a guard at the doors scanned Calandra from head to toe. The light blinked red when it reached her arms.

"You're carrying a metallic object."

The guard shot a stern frown at her. A hand scanner wrapped around his palm hovered above Calandra's left arm. She returned a pained glare toward him.

"It's only my artificial hand. Nothing to worry about."

"Let's see it."

"I promise you I bear no weapons."

"Let's see the hand."

Calandra bent her elbow upward and peeled off the glove covering her hand and forearm. She shook the fabric at the guard.

"Here you go!" she snapped. "Happy now?"

The guard studied each exposed metallic bone, wire, and rubber pad for a moment. His expression finally softened, and he shook his head.

"Apologies. You're free to enter."

The guard opened one of the doors. Choice words Calandra wanted to say to him bubbled up in her mind. The way he gawked at her arm tore at her. Pity blanketed the guard's face. She wanted none of it. She deserved better than drawing morbidly fascinated stares followed by averted eyes whenever she caught gawkers looking at her. Calandra jammed the glove back over her artificial hand and stretched the fabric across her forearm to reduce unwanted attention.

Clacking from multiple shoes echoed through a broad main hall leading to the assembly floor. Marble columns lined both sides of the hall. Busts of famous Ra'ahmian political and spiritual leaders topped each column. A larger-than-life-sized portrait of Delcor, their chief sovereign, loomed over doors leading directly to the assembly floor. The painting depicted him dressed in his regal official uniform. His right hand displayed a ring bearing a symbol identifying the House of Cirkoy—their chief sovereign's ancestral clan.

Calandra veered off before she reached the assembly floor doors and climbed a winding staircase leading to a second-level balcony. Assembly protocols did not permit Ra'ahm citizens to enter the floor itself without an invitation from an assembly member, their chief sovereign, or one of his designated representatives. The balcony overlooked the assembly chamber, and offered a spot where Calandra hoped she could draw their chief sovereign's attention as he addressed the assembly.

A glass door slid open before her with a whoosh. Calandra stepped out on the balcony. She leaned against the edge and rested her arm on a smooth stone railing.

Their chief sovereign sat in an ornate chair mounted atop a small platform occupying the north end of the chamber. Staggered rows of chairs perched behind half-oval tables formed a half-circle facing his platform. Each matching table and chair had been hand-carved and molded from the finest senosa wood. Soft sapinoa hair covered cushioned backs and seats on the chairs. Calandra counted 73 chairs while her eyes drifted across the chamber. 72 members drawn from 12 districts in the northern province and 12 districts in the southern province formed the National Assembly. District governors, appointed to that office by their chief sovereign, selected three assembly representatives in each district. A polished white stone platform occupied a central position inside the chamber. The round platform filled floor space between the assembly members' seats and the chief sovereign's seat. An engraving of a giant flying mokai bird—the national symbol of Ra'ahm—adorned the platform floor.

A small bell emitted sequential chimes. At once, Delcor arose from his chair and approached the central platform. He climbed a set of narrow stone steps and planted himself in the center of the platform. Their chief sovereign thrust his arms skyward. His eyes hardened into a determined stare.

"What we do today shapes what tomorrow brings."

Several heads bobbed up and down throughout the chamber. Delcor paused and answered with a satisfied nod of his own.

"We cannot stand idle against any threat to our great nation," he continued. "The Confederation mocks our values and freedom. Their agents seek to destroy what the servants of Ahm decreed must exist forever."

His words struck a chord with Calandra, dredging up a once-forgotten memory. Xttra once told her how a Confederation vessel attacked his scout ship near an Ice Belt planetoid when he first retrieved the Earthian probe she discovered. Did agents from the Confederation of Northern Tribes orchestrate his abduction from Fengar? Such a scenario seemed more plausible the longer she mulled over it.

The rest of the chief sovereign's speech to Ra'ahm's legislative body coalesced into a blur while Calandra bowed her head and pondered her options. A full-scale rescue operation must be launched before Xttra vanished forever. How could she convince their chief sovereign to sign off on this plan of action and throw the necessary resources behind bringing it to pass?

At once, the chamber grew silent. Calandra lifted her chin and cast her eyes down at the central platform. Delcor paused and had turned to face the balcony where she stood. An unbroken stare fell upon her. Calandra swallowed hard and said nothing.

"The cost of doing nothing is too great," their chief sovereign finally said, resuming his speech. "We must secure our borders and eradicate threats to our internal security. If you support these measures I propose, the rising generation can know peace where our generation endured war."

Thunderous applause reverberated through the chamber. A customary call for votes on his proposed border strengthening measures followed. Not a single assembly member raised their voice in opposition. Delcor gave an approving nod once all votes were cast and stepped off the platform. An entourage of ministers and guards followed him toward a side door leading outside the chamber. Calandra took their departure as her cue to exit from the balcony. She conquered the winding stairs at a brisk pace. If she hurried, Calandra counted on catching their chief sovereign before his guards ferried him back to his palace.

"Calandra Menankar? I thought it was you. I must say I'm surprised to find you here."

She paused on the bottom stair and turned to face the voice greeting her. Delcor approached the staircase, still flanked by his guards. Calandra froze. Now that she had her desired audience with their chief sovereign, her heart thumped at an increasing pace and her tongue choked out the words she wanted to say earlier.

"Never met an astronomer who also took a deep interest in politics," he said. "Their eyes focused down here instead of out there."

Calandra's eyes darted between Delcor and his guards. He snapped his head toward them and waved them back. The guards withdrew a few steps from him.

"I suppose you did not come to this place simply to listen to my speech," Delcor said. "What compels you to seek me out?"

She cast her head down and focused her gaze on his feet. He wore shoes made from fine ebutoka leather.

"My husband is missing."

"Xttra Oogan?"

"I received word he was taken prisoner on Fengar. He vanished from a Thetian trade colony without a trace."

Silence greeted Calandra upon her revelation. She pinched her eyes shut and sucked in her lower lip. Calandra exhaled slowly and lifted her chin. Her eyes popped open again.

"I need your help, my sovereign. I need to find him and bring him back home."

Delcor answered her with an unblinking stare and stony expression. His gray eyes drilled down into her as though probing for some hidden object. Calandra silently scolded herself for even bringing her plight to his attention. Their chief sovereign ruled a nation of millions. She was so naïve to assume one master pilot's tragic abduction merited his undivided attention.

"Our chief sovereign cannot concern himself with such matters. You should take your request to the proper Stellar Guard channels where it belongs."

Calandra snapped her head toward a minister standing behind the guards. She narrowed her eyes, and a deep frown grew on her lips once those dismissive words left his mouth. Not one of these people cared about Xttra. Still, she refused to let their indifference sway their chief sovereign against her.

He would care.

Calandra promised to make such an outcome certain.

"What if agents from the Confederation abducted him?" She took a stab at the most plausible scenario in her mind, one calculated to rouse action from their chief sovereign. "Can we allow Xttra to fall in their hands so easily and give them free access to interrogate him?"

"Why would the Confederation care about a single master pilot?" Once again, the same minister interjected his opinion unbidden, and unwanted. "Your hubris is shocking. Our chief sovereign has greater priorities—"

Delcor turned and raised a hand without saying a word. The minister fell silent. Calandra felt a measure of relief at not hearing more of his equally disagreeable voice and words.

"This is indeed a grave matter if what you say is true," their chief sovereign said. He turned and faced her again. "What makes you convinced that Confederation agents have abducted him?"

"Because Xttra led our mission to Earth," Calandra said. She tugged at a cuff on her white silk shirt as she talked. "A Confederation deep-space vessel tried to steal the Earthian probe I originally discovered before we retrieved it from the Ice Belt. Since they couldn't obtain the probe, it makes sense for them to target the highest-ranking surviving member of our expedition to Earth and glean information from him."

Delcor closed his eyes and rubbed his chin while he pondered her words. The minister he silenced earlier fixed an annoyed glare on Calandra. She returned his glare with one of her own. Her eyes and expression softened as soon as she noticed their chief sovereign's eyes crack open again.

"We cannot allow the Confederation to succeed in their design," Delcor said. "I will send my best agents out to Fengar to track him down. We will go straight to the Confederation Emperor himself if necessary. Xttra Oogan will return to Lathos."

Calandra bowed.

"Thank you, my sovereign. I am again in your debt."

He flashed a brief smile and answered her with a briefer nod. Delcor resumed his walk past the staircase as his guards and ministers caught up to him. The group soon vanished down a nearby hallway. Calandra stood on the bottom stair and rested her right arm on the handrail as she watched him leave.

A small smile finally sprouted on her lips. Now wheels were in motion. Soon enough, Xttra would be back home and safe with her once again.

# 8

Everything about the red planet fit the definition of ordinary with exactness.

Sam wished for a fresh sense of wonder and excitement to wash over him. Instead, a bland numbness seeped into his bones. He quietly shook his head while gazing out of a small, tight window on the Orion spacecraft. Up close, Mars hardly merited exploration.

Or colonization for that matter.

"Have you ever seen such an incredible sight?"

An enthusiastic voice tinged with a Louisiana drawl cut through Sam's thoughts. He glanced over at his pilot. A wide grin plastered her face. The same expression also crossed the commander's lips. Both Norah and Cliff reminded him of kids tearing off wrapping paper on Christmas morning and beaming upon discovering the exact presents they begged to receive from Santa.

Sam shrugged.

"I've seen much more incredible sights." He paused and gazed at the far side of Mars again. "Back on Earth."

Norah pursed her lips. Sam glimpsed at the pilot a second time. Her smile had melted into a slight frown.

"Don't be a wet blanket," she said. "We're making actual history out here. Nothing could be more exciting."

Every time he heard those words, Sam couldn't resist rolling his eyes. Making history. Yeah, right.

Many years spent working for NASA, and now the Earth Defense Bureau, trained him to approach hype with skepticism. Every new mission would change the world until nothing changed. Sending small probes and manned missions to tinker around in the safer parts of the solar system held no joy for him.

Sam knew what lay beyond their own neighborhood. It ate at him, chipping away his soul with the persistence of water droplets escaping from a leaky pipe. Their chance to uncover answers to life's most persistent questions had already arrived. Earth opened a door to a much wider universe not so long ago.

Then the bureau slammed that door shut.

*We blew it*, he thought. *Our first contact with a peaceful, intelligent race and we blew it.*

His eyes drifted back to the red planet growing larger on the horizon. How could building a colony on Mars ever seem relevant or important when compared with the opportunity to build a friendship with beings from a world orbiting a distant star? Earth would not get a second chance to do it right and Sam refused to forgive himself for contributing to his planet's failure.

"Entering low orbit around Phobos. Only a stone's throw away now."

A joyful fervor dripped from Cliff's words. The Orion's engines incorporated technology reverse engineered from salvaged alien vehicles. This meant no longer blocking out anywhere from six to eight months to reach Mars. Still, those advancements only reduced their journey down to 60 days. Spending two months stuck inside a cramped spacecraft with three other people indeed felt as painfully long as it sounded.

"How much longer till we can dock with the space station?" Sam asked.

Cliff glanced at him with a weary expression mirroring a patient parent enduring their noisy child asking the same irritating questions again and again during a long road trip.

"Trust me, we're closer than you think."

Sam flashed a bemused smile at him.

"I'm not trying to get under your skin. I'm just dying to step out and stretch my legs."

"We all want to stretch our legs," Norah replied. "I'm personally counting down the minutes until I can step out of the space elevator and get back to the colony."

Sam leaned back in his chair, nodded, and released a deep breath. Going down to the surface also topped his list. Mars had not shaken off the boring and lifeless vibe from when he first laid eyes on the planet. Still, visiting the colony's base camp sure beat the hell out of riding in a cramped spacecraft for two months.

Images from conceptual 3-D models flooded into Sam's mind when he finally laid eyes on the Phobos Space Station. None of these design phase models did justice to the finished product. The station offered a breathtaking sight while circling an otherwise drab Martian moon.

Two dual horizontal cylinder modules made up the heart of the Phobos Station. One module rotated at one-half G and the other at one-tenth G, combining to create enough artificial gravity to offset a natural microgravity environment. Two shorter vertical cylinders bisected the midsection of each horizontal module. Two modules functioned as laboratories. A third acted as a service module. The fourth and largest module functioned as a residential module for the station's occupants.

Multiple flat arms housing solar arrays jutted out from each end of a steel and aluminum truss. The long vertical truss ran across the top of the pressurized modules. A single thick cable stretched from a counterweight only a short distance from the space station and plunged down through the Martian atmosphere to the planet's surface. Carbon nanotubes formed the cable, which served as a space elevator designed to transport raw materials from the station to the nascent colony.

"I've already claimed my acre of land on Mars." Norah cracked a broad grin when she said those words. "That Groupon deal I bought in grad school a few years ago is finally paying for itself."

Sam cocked his head at her.

"You seriously bought an acre of Martian land? On Groupon of all places?"

"Sounded like a fun idea at the time," Norah replied. She snapped her head toward him and winked. "And it turned out to be a shrewd investment."

Sam cracked a smile and chuckled. Scooping up a bunch of land on Mars never popped into his mind when pondering real estate investments to pursue.

Norah maneuvered the Orion spacecraft into a docking position with the airlock leading into the service module. Sam tugged on his helmet to test its fit. All the training he went through to prepare for this trip to Mars did nothing to reduce his nervousness about potential mishaps with his spacesuit. If anything, he grew more nervous when he started thinking about all the potential dangers lurking outside their spacecraft.

Sam's legs were a bit rubbery upon standing up for the first time in ages. He thrust out his hand and steadied himself against the back of his chair. Cliff and Norah led him through the airlock and into the space station. Once the hatch sealed behind the group, Sam popped his helmet off and drew in a deep breath.

He flashed a relieved smile.

"You don't know how good it feels to finally see new surroundings for the first time in two months."

"I understand. Better than you think."

Sam cocked his head toward the other end of the service module. A man sporting a thin reddish-brown mustache and tightly cropped hair approached the small group. He extended his hand.

"Sergei Ivanov. Welcome to the Phobos Station."

Sam shook his hand and added a quick nod.

"Sam Bono. It's a pleasure to meet you, Sergei."

His eyes darted around as Sam gave the interior of the service module a quick once-over. Those eyes settled on a series of open laptops mounted against the opposite module wall. Sam sauntered over to the nearest screen. Even with the presence of artificial gravity, his steps across the module bordered on bouncy hops. He tapped on the touchscreen and scrolled through aerial Martian landscape photos.

"So where did you uncover this mysterious object?" Sam snapped his head back in Sergei's direction. "The Earth Defense Bureau couldn't wait to get out here once we were briefed on your report."

"A Martian rover first detected anomalous signals inside a cavern, 13 kilometers from base camp," Sergei explained. "Rudra directed the rover to go inside. Sure enough, we found an object producing the signals."

Sam raised his eyebrows and shot a sideways glance at an aerial photo on the laptop screen.

"Did you figure out what we're dealing with yet?"

"No. It is as we reported earlier. I have never seen anything matching this object."

Norah nodded.

"That's why Cliff and I were dispatched to bring you back to Mars." She turned and glanced at Sam. "We were told you have valuable experience in dealing with aliens and alien technology."

Their confidence in him flattered Sam. He did not want to reveal he was the bureau's second choice to go to Mars. Sam only left Earth when Paige Beck ended up being unavailable to take the assignment. He cursed his bad luck and wished she drew the short straw instead of him. Paige's expertise made her more qualified to deal with this situation from the start. She had experience dealing with multiple alien races, while he had only been involved in one major extraterrestrial encounter.

"We moved it from the cavern four days ago," Sergei said. "Isolated it inside a manned habitat unit."

Sam answered him with an unblinking stare. He squared his shoulders in the cosmonaut's direction.

"You did what?"

"We could not wait. A global dust storm covered the planet for many weeks. Once the storm cleared, we decided we must use that window for retrieval before it closed again."

A scowl formed on Sam's lips.

"I relayed specific instructions before I left Earth for you all to leave the object untouched until I arrived here." He jabbed an index finger at Sergei. "How will we work together on this project if you won't listen to me?"

Sergei sighed and shook his head.

"You Americans are too uptight. We did not break or ruin anything. We used a special robot to extract the object from the cavern and bring it back to base camp for further research."

Sam stood with one hand on his hip, the other clutching his helmet. His stare continued unbroken. This trip was not off to the best start. Russians routinely beat Americans to the punch in numerous space exploration and colonization endeavors. How did the Earth Defense Bureau expect him to come here and take charge if the cosmonauts were determined to do whatever they wanted to do anyway? Sergei's eyes hardened into a fierce stare as the silence continued. Finally, after a few tense seconds, Sam pursed his lips.

"Let's hop in the climber and find out what we've got down there on the planet."

***

Taking a trip on a space elevator felt unlike anything else Sam ever experienced. He rode a bullet train when he visited Tokyo. Riding inside a climber to the Martian surface made any bullet train seem as fast as a puttering old tractor by comparison. Their pill-shaped climber zipped down the carbon cable at 300 kilometers per hour.

Still, in astronautical terms, a one-way space elevator trip from the vicinity around Phobos to Mars took around 20 hours to complete. Sam ran out of discussion topics with Sergei and Norah near the halfway point of their trek. He passed time inside the climber studying photos stored on the laptop he took with him from the Phobos Station. Sam wanted to transfer the batch of images to a smaller device but that was not possible out here. His smartphone routinely dropped calls in his backyard back home in Houston. He jokingly asked Norah if she thought the Wi-Fi would be working in the colony. She laughed at his question and said nothing else.

The robot took many photos of the object it retrieved from the cavern. Those images did not reveal much. To Sam, the object resembled a long box with each corner cut off to form diagonal edges. Reddish-brown dust and soil caked the outer surface. No doubt countless dust storms battered it over an indefinite period. This object only drew their attention when a rover exploring around the cave detected an artificial power source emanating from inside the cave.

When the Earth Defense Bureau received a report on the rover's findings, it was enough to entice bureau authorities to send Sam to Mars and learn firsthand exactly what the colonists discovered. They were convinced they stumbled upon an extraterrestrial artifact. Sam took a more skeptical approach before heading to the lifeless husk of a planet.

*The rover's sensors collected inaccurate data*, he told himself. *This will only turn out to be a huge waste of time and money.*

A Martian colonist stood on the mobile docking platform when the space elevator finally arrived at its destination. They waved at the climber as it touched down on the platform. The climber door opened. Sam, Norah, and Sergei all filed out.

"Sam Bono."

Sam extended his hand. The waiting colonist stared down at the hand and hesitated for a moment before finally shaking it.

"Dr. Bao Mei. Does this mean we can do some real research at last?"

Sam's eyes widened. He backpedaled a couple of steps. Her icy tone caught him off guard.

"The Earth Defense Bureau has direct oversight on this colonizing mission." Norah jumped to his defense before Sam even said a word. "You already know it. Furthermore, our discovery is in their wheelhouse."

Mei glanced over at their base camp before turning and facing him again a moment later. A protective visor kept Sam from seeing her eyes, but he still sensed a hidden, hardened stare digging down into his soul.

"Fine. Let's get on with this."

She turned toward base camp again. Before Mei stepped off the docking platform, she jerked her head around and faced him a second time.

"Let's be clear on one thing. This colony is a global partnership. Mars is not an American territory."

Sam threw up his hands.

"I'm not looking to start a pissing match. We all have the same goal here—to learn exactly what you folks found inside that cavern."

Mei answered with an abrupt nod and continued her walk from the platform back to the colony's base camp. Sam sighed and snagged the laptop before closing the climber door. He hoped this did not foreshadow endless arguments ahead with the scientist.

A series of interconnected manned habitat units formed the base camp. Each unit resembled a cylindrical drum rising three stories from the ground like a tower. Four spindly legs jutted out from individual drums. Each leg stood an equal distance apart to supply stability amid rocky terrain. Small polycarbonate windows peppered exterior walls on each unit. An outer layer composed of regolith and an inner layer composed of polyethylene formed the outer walls. These dual layers combined to protect colonists from intense ultraviolet radiation. Specialized robots constructed all building materials on site using 3-D printers.

Sam followed Mei and the others into the unit nearest to the mobile docking platform. It housed the colony's main laboratory. Once inside, he got his first close-up peek at what the colonists extracted from the cavern. The mysterious object rested against an interior lab wall on a white tarp. Small piles of dust and soil covered the tarp around the bottom end of the object. A curly haired man in a dark sweatshirt crouched down in front, sweeping away dust with a broad brush.

"Rudra," Norah said. "Our liaison from the Earth Defense Bureau is here."

He straightened up and turned to face Sam. Safety glasses covered his brown eyes. Rudra set his brush down, smoothed out his rumpled sweatpants, and extended a hand.

"Welcome to Mars. I'm Dr. Rudra Adarsh."

Sam shook his hand and nodded.

"Sam Bono." His eyes drifted back over to the object. "So, what have you learned so far?"

Rudra cracked an eager grin.

"I don't want to get ahead of myself, but I think we may have uncovered an extraterrestrial object."

Sam raised his eyebrows.

"Extraterrestrial object?"

Rudra pointed to a laptop resting on a nearby white desk built into a matching lab wall. Sam glanced down at the battery depleted laptop resting in the crook of his other arm. A sheepish feeling washed over him for grabbing it from the Phobos Station when he realized the exact same information was down here. Sam set down the laptop on a nearby shelf and walked over to the other computer. He hunched over the keyboard and brought up data culled from the retrieval robot's sensors.

Sam's eyes grew as large as plates while he studied the data. He gave a low whistle.

"Am I reading this right? You detected organic matter inside the object?"

"That's what the scans revealed," Mei said. She popped off her helmet, revealing short and flat black hair, and set it down. "We're cleaning it up to see if we can safely open the object and find out what's inside."

On cue, Rudra snatched up his brush and resumed cleaning. Sam removed his helmet. His eyes trailed the brush up and down as it crisscrossed the object's surface.

A mere mention of organic matter sparked his curiosity. Did the object house an alien? Such an idea seemed so far-fetched only a few years ago. After meeting extraterrestrial visitors in Utah, though, Sam had no difficulty believing this thing housed alien

DNA or even a living alien. The prospect of making such a discovery thrilled him. It turned a trip into Mars a more worthwhile pursuit than he first imagined.

"Is that what I think it is?"

Sam snapped his head in Norah's direction. Her helmet was off now, and she knelt by the side of the object. Sam squinted at the same spot. A blue button-sized dot blinked where Mei dislodged a patch of soil.

"Is that a light?" Sam asked.

A puzzled look adorned his face. Sam drew a few steps closer. As he gazed at the light, an unexpected thought struck him. The colonists uncovered a piece of advanced alien technology. One question remained.

If this was an alien gadget, what purpose did it serve?

Sam removed his thick glove and grabbed another brush. He raised his arm and started cleaning near the top end of the device. Along with Rudra and Mei, Sam worked feverishly to clear away Martian dust and soil. Each brushstroke revealed more surface details.

At once, Norah gasped.

Her left hand clamped down on his shoulder.

"That looks like a window."

Sam followed her finger and cast his eyes to the same spot where she pointed. A hint of glass peeked out on the surface. He concentrated his brush in that area. More glass rose from beneath the dust shroud. Sam parroted Norah's surprised reaction once he laid eyes on what the uncovered window revealed.

An alien lifeform.

# 9

From the moment he laid eyes on the alien lifeform, Sam's heart pounded with a steady drumbeat. Dirty glass partially obscured whatever alien species lay inside the object. Still, the few visible details were enough to make fresh goosebumps pop up all over his arms and legs. This lifeform resembled nothing Sam had ever seen outside of a nightmare buried in a dark hidden corner of his subconscious mind.

Their face owned some humanoid features, and their body matched an adult human in size. Whatever lay inside did not resemble any human in other key aspects. Odd bony ridges trailed along brows and cheekbones. Sharp ends belonging to massive fangs protruded from underneath the creature's upper lip. Waxy reptilian scales melded with ordinary pale human-like flesh around each bony growth.

"Why in God's name does it look like that?"

Palpable fear permeated each word in Sergei's question. No satisfying answer popped into Sam's mind. He doubted anyone else inside the habitat unit could produce one.

This creature—whatever the hell it was—embodied the scariest connotation of the term 'alien.'

"Is it alive?" Sam asked.

Mei's eyes darted between him and the humanoid creature. She swallowed hard.

"God, I hope not."

Rudra continued brushing away dust and dirt from the glass and both sides of the object. More blinking lights grew visible in newly cleaned areas. It resembled a high-tech isolation tank. Sam wondered if the alien inside had been cryogenically frozen. No signs of freezing were present on its visible flesh. Did the device preserve the alien in suspended animation or deep hibernation? He could not imagine why any alien species would go to all the trouble of sealing this odd-looking alien in a futuristic coffin and dropping it inside a random cavern on Mars.

Digital symbols became visible in clear panels above some lights. Sam knelt in front of a panel and squinted at a string of symbols. They bore an eerie familiarity. He recalled seeing similar symbols two years earlier, inside a crashed alien vessel salvaged from a ravine in Utah.

An alien vessel from a planet called Lathos.

Did this mean this creature hailed from the same planet? Sam closed his eyes and shook his head as he chased that theory from his mind. The odds against such a scenario were astronomically high. A more plausible explanation for the symbols must exist.

"What is it? You're starting to look like someone who's seen a ghost."

Norah's question pierced his thoughts. Sam's eyes snapped open again. He paused for a moment and drew in a deep breath before glancing at her over his shoulder.

"I recognize these symbols." Sam tapped on a transparent panel displaying a few symbols. "We found similar ones on a small alien craft we recovered near Salt Lake City two years ago."

Norah's eyes grew wider. They darted between the glass exposing the alien's face and Sam.

"You've encountered this alien species before?" Annoyance and concern blended into her question. "When did you plan on sharing this news? This isn't a detail you keep to yourself."

Sam tossed up his hands in protest.

"Whoa. Wait a minute. I never said I encountered a creature like this one. The aliens I met resembled humans, apart from some minor differences. They looked nothing like ... well, whatever this species is."

Rudra rose to his feet a second time and brushed Martian dust off his pant legs. His eyes drifted over to the same digital symbols and his lips pressed into a perplexed frown.

"Can you translate the symbols?"

Sam shook his head.

"I never actually learned what any of them meant."

Rudra pursed his lips and let out a sigh. Sam started to regret bringing up his earlier experiences with aliens. His revelation only fostered a lingering annoyance inside the room.

"Conducting a thorough set of thermal imaging scans will tell us if the alien here is dead or alive," Rudra said.

Mei cocked her head toward him. She remained in a kneeling position while carefully cleaning off dust around buttons, lights, and panels.

"And what if it is alive? Do we try to wake the alien and talk to it?"

Sam's eyes drifted back to the alien's face. It showed closed lids. This simple fact splashed relief over him like a cool spray from a waterfall. Forget about seeing the alien's eyes. Sam did not want those eyes to see him. A nagging feeling told him someone sealed this being inside this tank for a wise reason. Until the bureau opened the device under safe and controlled conditions on Earth, he had no desire to revive the alien from a deep slumber if it truly remained alive.

"We're not waking it." Sam finally said, casting a glance down at Mei. "Not here. Not on Mars. If that alien is alive, we're transporting it back to a secure facility on Earth before we do anything else."

***

Waiting for the lab computers to complete detailed scans took much longer than Sam expected. He eventually left the lab and walked through a covered tunnel into a neighboring habitat unit. Standing around in the lab and staring at the alien only made his heart race faster than a stock car circling an oval track. It did no good to work himself up over an odd-looking alien in stasis before they recovered any firm data.

Sam fished out a deck of cards and some poker chips from an overhead bin inside a small activity lounge. He tossed cards and chips on a round white table circled by orange hardback chairs. Norah peeked her head inside the room just as Sam settled down on a chair. Once her eyes fell on the cards, she cracked a broad smile and brushed back a short strawberry-blonde lock of hair.

"Deal me in."

Sam waved her forward and tossed five cards on the table. Sergei also joined them after the first hand. Neither were a match for Sam. The cosmonaut shook his head in disbelief after losing a fourth straight hand.

"I did not realize we were tangling with a poker genius here." Sergei flashed a disbelieving smirk. "You're trying to take every last ruble to my name."

Sam leaned back and clasped his hands behind his head. He cracked a satisfied smile of his own while Norah dealt a new hand.

"What can I say? When you grow up in Vegas, knowing how to gamble becomes second nature."

Norah rolled her eyes and laughed.

"Enlighten us, oh wise one."

Sam soon found himself sharing a story of how he sneaked into a casino with his best friend Simon back in high school. They used phony ID cards to get inside but drew unwanted attention after Simon won $500 on a slot machine. He and Sam did an impromptu celebration dance near the winning machine. A pair of burly security guards showed up a few minutes later and asked to see their IDs. Soon enough, a large hand wrapped around Sam's arm and marched him off the casino floor. The guards shoved both him and Simon outside the main doors and told them not to come back.

"I became determined to get back inside that casino when I turned 21," Sam said, wrapping up his story. "Learned every poker trick and strategy I could find, so I'd break the house and stick it to them."

"I'd say your research is paying off," Norah replied. "You're cleaning us out without breaking a sweat."

A knock interrupted their conversation. Sam glanced up. Rudra stood inside the doorway.

"So, what's the word? What did the scans reveal?"

Rudra peeked over his shoulder at the short tunnel leading back to the laboratory door. He faced Sam again and shook his head. His frown spoke volumes.

The scans did not turn up welcome news.

"Our thermal imaging scan detected body heat and an active heartbeat," Rudra said. "The alien is alive."

Sam dropped his cards on the table and rose from his chair. He silently hoped the alien would turn out to be dead. The scan's findings troubled him. Some unknown party made a special effort to keep this strange-looking humanoid alien alive—and hidden. Why? What purpose did it serve to conceal it on Mars?

All eyes in the room settled on Sam. He pinched his eyelids shut and bowed his head while weighing the options before him. Leaving this alien here on Mars was out of the question. Finding and ending threats to Earth functioned as the Earth Defense Bureau's primary mission. Sam's instincts told him this alien fit those threat parameters to a tee. Bringing it back to a secure bureau facility stood out as the only practical alternative.

"Only one thing left to do now." Sam opened his eyes and fixed his gaze on Rudra. "We need to load the alien tank into the climber and prepare to transport the alien back to Earth."

Norah gave both men a sideways glance.

"Are we sure that's a wise idea? I understand Earth Defense Bureau protocol. But I also think taking this alien creature off Mars is risky."

"Risky?" Sam repeated. He snapped his head in her direction. "How is it risky?"

"What if it wakes up from stasis?"

Sam's throat tightened while he contemplated her question. What if this alien indeed did awaken during the long return flight to Earth? He had no clue how to combat a potentially hostile alien in tight quarters while millions of miles away from civilization. No one living in the tiny Martian colony had the right training to deal with such a frightening scenario either.

"We'll need to rig up something to keep that object sealed during the trip home," Sam said. "I'll see what Cliff and I can figure out after I return to the Phobos Station."

At once, an alarm sounded through the habitat unit. Sam glanced over at the wall and spotted a flashing red light. Norah's eyes grew as wide as plates. She sprang up from her chair.

'That's not good," Sergei said.

He rose from his chair and simultaneously sprinted through the open doorway with Rudra. Sam and Norah followed hot on their heels. They arrived in the laboratory a few seconds apart.

Mei stood back against the opposite wall from the object holding the alien. Lights flashed more rapidly than before along the sides. Air hissed from a growing crack as a door in the device began to open.

"What did you do?" Rudra shouted.

Mei shot him an icy stare.

"Nothing," she said. "I don't know what happened. One of us must have triggered a fail-safe while cleaning the device."

The door lifted away from the rest of the device. A loud gasp followed. The humanoid creature's eyes cracked open. Sam gulped. They looked startlingly like human eyes, only with more vibrant blues in the iris. Strange clothing made from metallic fabric adorned the alien's body. It resembled a uniform.

A cold sweat formed on Sam's brow. He licked his lips and backed up a few steps. The alien's eyes narrowed, and a puzzled expression washed over its face. It stepped down on the floor and turned its head while taking in new surroundings.

"The alien seems disoriented," Sergei said. "Maybe if we show we are not a threat, everything will be fine."

He took a few deliberate steps forward and offered his hand to the strange-looking alien. Sam felt his throat tighten anew. His legs grew as rigid as tree trunks. What was Sergei doing? They needed to seal off this room and quarantine the lab, not try to make new friends.

"We aren't here to hurt you." Sergei adopted a soothing tone as he held his hand out toward the alien. "We want to be friends."

The alien stared at Sergei's hand. Both eyes narrowed and it uttered a guttural growl. At once, the alien seized his wrist.

A sickening crack followed.

Sergei screamed. Other screams from other voices inside the room joined his pained cry. His wrist dangled like a cooked noodle at an odd angle. The alien snapped both bones into two separate pieces.

"Oh God!" the Russian shouted. "Seal off the lab!"

The alien grabbed him by his throat with its other clawed hand and wrenched him off the ground using only one arm. Sergei kicked at the alien's shins in a futile effort to free himself. Each claw pressed harder against Sergei's flesh until blood spurted out from around the alien's fingers. It flung Sergei against a wall like a limp stuffed animal. The cosmonaut left behind a jagged trail of blood as he slid down to the floor.

Sam pressed his hand against his mouth to keep from vomiting. He scrambled toward the exit. One fact became clear above any other consideration.

They could not let this murderous alien escape from the lab at any cost.

# 10

Sam glanced over his shoulder as he sprinted toward the door connecting the underground tunnel with the habitat units. The alien charged after him and the other fleeing colonists. Norah backed against a table and threw a microscope right at the creature's head. It ducked and directed a hissing growl at her.

"Get to the door!" Sam shouted. "Hurry!"

Rudra made a mad dash for the door while Mei tossed an empty beaker at the alien. The beaker bounced off the creature's shin and shattered. Multiple shards scattered across the floor. The alien caught up to Mei and Norah just as they reached the door. A long bony stinger shot out from a small hole at the left wrist. The alien grabbed Mei by her shoulder and yanked her backward.

"It's got me!" she screamed. "Get it –"

A violent cough choked out her words. Mei spit out blood a second later. The stinger's pointed end burst through her left breast. Norah cried out and reached her hand toward Mei. Rudra grabbed her by the other arm and pulled Norah back. The alien drew out its stinger and then rammed the same arm forward once again.

This time, the stinger burst through Mei's ribs on the right side of her chest.

She fell to the floor after the creature retracted its stinger a second time. Mei's empty eyes and gaping mouth remained frozen in a permanent state of terror.

"Hurry!" Sam urged them forward with his hand. "We need to seal off the room!"

Rudra pulled Norah backward into the tunnel just as the alien reached the doorway. Sam pushed a steel door toward the creature. It thrust an arm between the edge of the door and the jamb. Sam dug his shoulder into the door and gave a shout as he pressed forward.

"Help me seal this thing inside!"

Norah and Rudra rushed forward and joined Sam at the door. The alien jabbed its stinger into Norah. She cried out and fell backward, cradling her wrist. Blood seeped between her fingers from a fresh puncture wound. Sam and Rudra gave the door one final hard push and crunched steel against the alien's arm. It grunted in pain and wrenched the arm backward. Rudra slammed the door shut and spun a wheel embedded in the middle, locking the door in place.

Sam heard a groan behind him. He wheeled around and spotted Norah sitting on the tunnel floor with her back pressed against the wall. Tears streamed down her cheeks. Norah clenched her teeth. Her left hand clutched her right wrist where the stinger penetrated flesh. Blood oozed out from under her palm.

"I think it went clean through my wrist." Her tear-flooded eyes darted upward and fixed on Sam and Rudra. "Oh God, I haven't felt this much pain since I tore my ACL while skiing in Colorado."

Sam knelt in front of Norah. He gently pried away her hand. A nickel-sized puncture wound adorned her wrist. Surrounding tissue took on a purplish hue and had become swollen around the wound. Rudra hunched over to also get a closer look at her wrist. He shook his head when he surveyed the damage the alien creature inflicted on Norah.

"I think that alien released some venom into your body," Sam said. "Your wrist is quite swollen."

Norah sniffed back a few tears. Her arms trembled when she stared down at the wound.

"Will I die?"

Rudra stared wide-eyed at Norah for a moment. A resolute frown finally graced his lips.

"Not if we can help it," he said. "We'll find a way to extract that venom."

Sam rose to his feet. He clasped Norah's uninjured wrist and helped her stand again.

"We better track down a first aid kit and patch you up," he said. "The sooner we disinfect and close up your wound, the better."

Violent pounding on metal greeted their ears a second later. A low sustained growl soon followed. The door did not budge from its hinges, but everyone inside the tunnel backpedaled a few steps anyway. Sam scoured both tunnel walls, hoping to spot a control switch or button capable of drawing out the lab's remaining oxygen once activated. He did not want to find out how long the door would stay sealed under the alien's continued assault. If it broke down the door and entered the tunnel, they faced bleak odds for outrunning the feral creature and reaching the next habitat unit alive.

"Can we vent the oxygen from the room?" Sam turned and glanced at Rudra. "Expose the laboratory to Martian atmosphere?"

Rudra shook his head. He cast a worried glance over his shoulder at the sealed door.

"We designed these units to be airtight. Those walls and windows are thick and durable. It would take considerable force to breach one."

Sam furrowed his brow and glanced at Norah again. Her breaths came in shallow bursts, and she clenched her teeth while cradling her injured wrist. His eyes widened and he jerked his head back in Rudra's direction.

"Do you have a mining vehicle equipped with a drill designed to bore through the rock?"

"Of course." Rudra answered him with a quick nod. "We used it to mine and collect regolith for the walls."

"I'll take care of Norah," Sam replied. "You better track down the mining vehicle and drill through the outside wall. Let's make sure this alien doesn't make it out of that lab alive."

Rudra nodded again and darted ahead into the neighboring habitat unit. Sam clasped Norah's uninjured arm above the elbow, and they sprinted behind him. None of the group dared look back even as growls, shouts, and banging emanated from the lab at a higher volume. Sam and Norah slipped past a now-open second steel door and Rudra sealed it behind them once both were safely inside. He spun the wheel, locking it in place.

"That should buy us a little time while I bring back the mining vehicle," he said. Rudra spun around and faced Norah and Sam. "I'm really hoping that thing isn't strong enough to break down two of these doors."

Norah pinched her eyelids shut again and let out a whimpering groan. Sam's eyes darted to her wrist and back to Rudra. They needed to do something fast to dull Norah's pain, draw out any lingering venom, and stitch up the oozing puncture wound in her wrist.

"Where are your medical supplies?" Sam asked.

"We have a small medical station above us on the next level," Rudra replied. "There should be enough surgical equipment, medicine, and bandages to care for Norah short-term."

Norah opened her eyes again. Fresh tears coursed down each cheek. She bit down on her lower lip for a moment and stared up at Sam.

"Hurry! I don't know if I can handle this pain for much longer."

Sam gave her a sympathetic nod. He waved at Rudra.

"Good luck. Keep us posted on your progress."

They parted ways and Sam led Norah to a covered staircase by the exterior wall. The staircase wound along the wall like a giant snake. It led into rooms corresponding with each story of the habitat unit. Their destination occupied a compact second level room. Essential equipment common to a typical medical clinic on Earth packed the small medical station.

Sam directed Norah to a nearby bed. She sat on the edge, still clasping her injured wrist. He slapped on a pair of sterile surgical gloves and scoured nearby cabinets and drawers for supplies and equipment. Sam eventually filled a tray with a scalpel, sutures, gauze, bandages, ointment, and a small bottle of rubbing alcohol. He set it on the bed next to Norah.

"This may sting quite a bit." Sam unscrewed the cap from the rubbing alcohol bottle. "I'm sorry."

Norah nodded and bit down on her lower lip. She pulled away her hand and exposed the wrist. It had grown more swollen and discolored since he first examined her wounded limb in the tunnel. Sam shook his head.

This was not a good sign at all.

He hunched over the wrist, tilted the bottle, and splashed a few drops of alcohol directly on the wound. Norah unleashed an ear-piercing scream. At once, she swung her right forearm and belted him in the abdomen. Sam gasped. He doubled over and staggered backward. The bottle slipped from his hand and crashed on the floor. Alcohol sprayed across the tile, leaving a fresh shallow puddle near the bottle's landing spot.

"Holy shit!" He snapped, glaring at Norah. "What are you trying to do to me? I know your wrist must hurt like hell, but I can't help you if you attack me while I'm treating your wound."

A definite anger burned in her steely eyes as Norah stared him down. Her chest heaved up and down while hard, angry breaths escaped her lips. Then, within a few seconds, her breathing slowed to normal, and her expression softened.

Norah glanced down at her wrist, then back at Sam. She swallowed hard. An apologetic frown washed over her lips.

"I'm sorry. I don't know what came over me. I felt this animalistic rage once the alcohol touched my wrist. It was the weirdest thing."

Sam pressed his hand against his stomach and drew in a deep breath. He nodded and approached the bed a second time.

"Luckily, you only knocked the wind out of me for a moment. I'm fine now. I hope you're better too."

Sam threaded sutures through the broken skin and closed the now sterilized puncture wound. Once he finished stitching up Norah's wrist, he opened a small tube of ichthammol ointment. Sam smeared the pungent black goo over swollen tissues around the sealed puncture wound. He wrapped gauze bandages around the wrist and taped the gauze firmly in place.

"That should offer a quick fix for the moment," Sam said. "I'll consult with our medical officials back on Earth, once I check in with the bureau, and see what else needs to be done for your wrist."

Norah stared at him wide-eyed. She gently rubbed her bandaged wrist, trying to massage away pain from that injured limb.

"Is the ointment going to work? Will it draw out whatever is infecting my wrist?"

Those same questions rolled through Sam's mind. No satisfying answer materialized for either one.

"I hope so."

Norah cast her eyes at a circular window above their heads on the opposite wall. Polycarbonate glass let in some natural light while also blocking tons of dangerous UV radiation from entering the structure. The window itself occupied a spot high enough on the wall to prevent anyone from seeing much of anything other than a narrow patch of dusky Martian sky.

"Cliff will freak out when he hears what happened to us down here."

Cliff.

Sam forgot entirely to alert Cliff and the others still on Phobos Station concerning their situation down here. He needed to warn them to not travel to the Martian surface under any circumstances. Mars must remain off-limits until Rudra neutralized the confined alien.

# 11

Each time she gazed upon the portrait, the image before her eyes offered a painful reminder of everything Calandra lost.

She perched on a stool before a broad canvas woven from dried kerval skin fibers. Sky blue paint dripped from the end of her brush. A drop splashed on the canvas, landing on a pair of billowing white clouds. Calandra took brief note of the errant paint and laid the brush down on a narrow rectangular table flanking her stool. Her eyes drifted back to the opposite wall. She raised her chin as they settled again on the portrait hanging before her.

Xttra's dark blue eyes seemed so warm and real. As though he were standing inside the cozy studio with her, watching Calandra add another painting to her growing collection. She released a deep sigh and fresh tears rolled down both cheeks.

It almost seemed like a lifetime ago when Calandra hesitated to share her talent with Xttra. A small smile graced her lips when she recalled how he learned about her artistic side. Xttra only became aware her painting of him existed following a slip of the tongue from Alayna.

Calandra introduced him to Alayna three weeks after she began dating Xttra. Her best friend flashed a warm smile upon meeting him for the first time inside Calandra's apartment. She clasped his wrist in traditional Ra'ahm fashion.

"You're right. He is cute." She cast her eyes over at Calandra. "I approve."

Alayna's sudden declaration caught Calandra by surprise. Both of her cheeks grew warm. Calandra had no doubt they sported a new shade of crimson matching the leaves that adorned fraxa trees lining the streets outside her apartment.

Xttra cracked a grin at both women.

"I'm flattered."

"You certainly live up to your portrait."

He raised an eyebrow as soon as those words passed between Alayna's lips.

"Portrait?"

Calandra waved her hand at her friend in a cut-it-out motion. She instantly dropped the same hand to her side when Xttra's eyes darted over in her direction. His smile grew wider by the second.

"Did you create a portrait of me?"

Calandra looked down and away at the floor. She wished to find a hiding spot where he could not pursue the matter further. Calandra did not want Xttra to think she was obsessed with him. How embarrassing! And what if he did not like her painting? What if he did not think she made him look flattering?

"I painted ... a painting of you." Calandra hesitated to confirm Alayna's revelation even as she forced herself to make eye contact again. "It's in my studio ... in the other room."

"Cool. Can I see it?"

"I don't know if it's quite ready to show—"

"She'd love for you to see it," Alayna said, impeding her final attempts to keep her artwork hidden. "Trust me. You'll love it."

Calandra gulped and answered with a nervous nod.

"Of course. I'll show you right now."

Xttra reached out and clasped Calandra's hand as she started forward. Feeling his fingers intertwined with her own did not produce the calming effect he intended. Her heart pounded harder with each step toward the studio.

Calandra slid the door open and all three popped inside the small room. Xttra's eyes at once darted to the exact spot where her portrait of him hung on the wall. Her own eyes stayed glued to his face, watching and waiting to see his reaction.

Xttra stood in silence for a couple of minutes, soaking in each detail captured on the kerval skin canvas as though examining his face in a mirror. When his eyes drifted back to Calandra, they beamed with happiness.

Xttra planted a tender kiss on her lips.

"I love it," he said, pulling back again. "You made me look great. Captured me perfectly."

Tears rolled down Calandra's cheeks as she stared at the same portrait now. If it were possible to trade the painting in exchange for feeling Xttra's touch and warmth again, she would do it in a heartbeat. She would trade every painting she owned if that single action would restore him to her life.

Days blended into weeks without any positive news on the search for Xttra. Bo'un contacted her with periodic updates and did his best to offer hope amid a lack of results. Still, he struggled to uncover solid evidence surrounding Xttra's fate.

*He is alive,* she told herself. *He's still alive. I just need to be patient. He is alive. He'll find his way back to me.*

Xttra was out there somewhere among the stars. Ahm watched over him. She pleaded daily for him to work a miracle and bring Xttra home.

Calandra wiped her tears away with a small square cloth. She sealed the open paint jars again. Finishing this painting needed to wait. Troubled thoughts made concentrating difficult, and her art suffered. The panorama of rocky cliffs overlooking crashing ocean waves she sought to capture became difficult to hold in her mind. It felt a little like grasping a wriggling orange spinefish after a while.

Bella lay curled up on one end of the couch, nestled next to a cushioned arm. Neither eye opened as Calandra entered the living room. Her paws and whiskers twitched while she peacefully slumbered. Calandra slumped down a short distance from the diminutive cala and snatched up her arca vox from an end table.

Working an arca vox had grown difficult since getting an artificial limb. The neural stimulator in her hand refused to read and respond correctly to nerve impulses, making her left arm virtually useless. Simple tasks like contacting someone on her arca vox took on added complexity. Calandra had to uncurl each finger with her opposite hand and press them flat just so she could rest the arca vox on her palm. She was slowly adjusting but could not do it with the unthinking speed that she did before her injury.

She entered five digits into three clear crystal panels near the bottom of the circular pad. Each number popped up in the corresponding panel, backlit by a yellow-green light. A holoscreen popped up from a port on the top end of the arca vox. It cast a blue-white glow that tinged her fingertips. This day would be the day Bo'un finally shared some good news. Calandra told herself this same thing every time she contacted him over the past few weeks.

Bo'un did not appear on the holoscreen. Only three words. Three awful words flashed before her eyes, mocking Calandra's pain, and crushing her hopes of receiving good news.

Out of Range.

Calandra pressed down on the lowest crystal panel and ended the transmission. The holoscreen vanished. Bo'un must be off world. She hoped this time it meant he found a promising clue at last. His efforts to track down Xttra only turned up one dead end after another. Every Thetian official he contacted denied knowledge of Xttra's whereabouts. Officials from other Fengar colonies proved equally unhelpful. Judging by how Bo'un described these encounters, none acted particularly concerned or showed empathy toward the awful situation Xttra faced or her own tragic ignorance of his whereabouts.

Calandra punched in a new set of numbers on her arca vox. A holoscreen materialized a second time. The image of a woman around her age, with black curls falling to her shoulders, appeared a few seconds later.

"Hi Calandra! You caught me at just the right time."

Alayna wore her usual energetic smile. Seeing that smile always sparked a twinge of joy inside Calandra as soon as she laid eyes on her friend.

"Can we talk? I'm having one of those days again."

Alayna's smile dimmed as she discerned the sadness and pain afflicting Calandra. She nodded.

"I'm always here for you. You know that."

"I do."

"You need to get out of that apartment for a night. And I have the perfect idea for what we can do."

Alayna snatched up an object offscreen. A second later, she held up a pair of large diamond-shaped tokens between her thumb and index finger. Calandra scrunched up her eyes and nose when she saw the tokens.

"Slotball? You told me you swore off slotball matches forever after what happened with Titus."

"There's no rule telling us we can't go to the arena and cheer against him."

Calandra finally cracked a small smile. Heckling that jerk until their voices fled offered a fun way to give her troubled mind a reprieve.

Titus started out looking like a good match for Alayna. They first met during a fan celebration hosted by Luma Central - one of three elite slotball teams based in the capital city. Calandra and Alayna attended the fan celebration together. Titus approached them after mistaking Alayna for another woman he knew from his home village on the Serranta Islands. Their encounter sparked an extended conversation and led to a date the following evening.

Titus and Alayna bonded through a ni'amo rite only a month later. This ancient Serrantan custom let two lovers symbolically join their souls into one soul in preparation for a future marriage rite. Both Titus and Alayna received a tattoo of a ni'amo symbol encircling their navels when the rite concluded.

Calandra suspected things were amiss a few weeks after the rite when Titus became elusive toward Alayna about his post-match activities in other Ra'ahm cities. She urged her friend to uncover what he was doing in her absence. Alayna did some snooping and uncovered a message on Titus' arca vox while he excused himself during a date. The message came from a second girlfriend who lived in Birshana.

Alayna shed countless tears over the ensuing days after kicking Titus Grogg out of her apartment and cutting him out of her life. Some outside observers would no doubt characterize it as petty to go and cheer against him at slotball matches three years later. Especially since Titus had passed his prime as an athlete. From Calandra's perspective, however, it offered effective therapy for Alayna. She resolved to support her friend in anything designed to help her feel better after enduring such an awful, heartbreaking moment in her life.

Calandra met up with Alayna less than an hour after their conversation ended. She arrived outside her apartment in a custom aerorover. Her vehicle sported narrow retractable wings with a more prominent curve than the ones on Xttra's aerorover. Its sleek cylindrical frame, splashed with a dark green hue, was also narrower on each end. Alayna's aerorover also included an open stall with a protective mesh in the rear cargo space. She had it designed and installed specifically for transporting Bella during Calandra's absence. Other features bore similarities to Xttra's aerorover. Same half-circle windows on each door. Same dual bucket seats.

Alayna flew the aerorover toward the Nectura River. Calandra let her eyes drift downward when their vehicle neared the river. Sunlight gleamed off the surface of those lazy waters. A small fishing boat sailed upstream toward a harbor on the southern bank. Across the expansive river, a massive arena overlooked the northern bank. Calandra cast her eyes skyward. The sun already began to dip behind the peaks of the Aurora Mountains.

"This is the popular place to be tonight," Alayna said.

Calandra gazed down again. The aerorover circled above the arena while Alayna searched for a suitable landing spot. Little available space remained on the senosa tree-lined landing platforms flanking all four sides of the arena. This meant one thing. A longer walk to the arena than she anticipated.

"Is Luma Central challenging one of the Sendala teams?" Calandra asked. "There's a bigger crowd here than usual."

Alayna nodded. "Of course."

They joined a burgeoning crowd pressing toward the main arena entrance after finding a landing spot on a northside platform. Bronze statues of notable Luma Central slotball athletes formed a semicircle ahead of two giant doors serving as the front entrance. A polished stone path cut between two statues at the top of the semicircle. Calandra craned her neck upward and gazed at the nearest statue as she and Alayna walked past. The statue showed a slotball athlete in full uniform gripping a passing stick. A determined glare and scowl decorated the statue's metallic face.

"Fate dictated we meet at this moment in this place."

Calandra stopped in her tracks and snapped her head in the direction of the voice. It came from a white-haired woman wearing a long black skirt and a sleeveless blue top. Bracelets woven from senosa bark adorned both wrists. Small charms dangled on tiny hooks from each bracelet. Each charm featured an embedded gem surrounded by a shiny metal frame with an engraved symbol from the ancient Aracian alphabet.

"A diviner? Just what we need."

The white-haired woman cast a scowl at Alayna when she caught the sarcastic tone infused into her words. She painted on a smile again and quickly refocused her attention on Calandra. Her eyes trailed down Calandra's emerald long-sleeved lace shirt and finally settled on her gloved left arm hanging down at her side.

"I sense tragedy in your life," the diviner said, glancing briefly up at her. "You search for meaning and your true purpose."

Calandra stiffened. Her first instinct told her to check the glove. Did this diviner see the components of her artificial hand outlined in the fabric? Immediately, Calandra started wondering how many other random strangers headed into this slotball match were staring at the same limb. Her eyes darted around, trying to catch other sets of eyes gawking at her.

Alayna turned around and marched up to the diviner. She stopped once she had placed herself as a protective barrier in front of Calandra.

"Who are you?"

"I am Ominade. I reveal secrets of the eternal world."

Alayna flashed a rare frown.

"Well, Ominade, why are you bothering my friend?"

The diviner widened her eyes and gasped. Ominade pressed her hand to her chest and backed up a couple of steps, exaggerating each step for dramatic effect.

"You wound me, child. What I discern must never be tossed aside as worthless." She cast her eyes over Alayna's shoulder and stared right at Calandra a second time. "Holy voices from the eternal world compel me to share their message with you."

"I think you're a no-good—"

Alayna stopped in mid-sentence when Calandra clasped the back of her arm and shook her head. She turned and faced the diviner. Calandra's green eyes turned cold and grew more piercing than usual.

"I don't want your message. Your kind preys on desperate people to gain riches. You neither serve Ahm nor speak for the divine creator."

Ominade folded her arms and tilted her head. She tried to match Calandra's own unblinking stare but let a wry smile creep on her lips. Seeing it only made Calandra shudder inside. This diviner knew exactly what she was all about and did not care one bit.

"I sense what you treasure most was taken from you." Ominade cast another glance down at the gloved arm and then met Calandra's eyes again. "My message holds the key to restoring what is now lost."

Calandra's throat tightened. A tremor charged up her spine. One word popped into her mind.

*Xttra.*

Was this self-styled diviner connected to whoever abducted Xttra from Fengar? Did she know where they had taken him? Calandra needed answers. If this woman knew those answers, she needed to stop being cryptic and help her find her husband.

"What have you done with him?"

"Who?"

Anger flashed through Calandra's eyes.

"You know who I'm talking about. You say you're a diviner. Go ahead and divine."

Ominade pressed her lips tight. Her eyes darted around. Other slotball fans stopped and started gathering near the statue where Calandra, Alayna, and the diviner stood. Whatever boldness Ominade possessed earlier, it fled from her now.

"Not here. What I reveal must be for your ears alone."

"Tell me now." Calandra seethed. "Tell me what you know. I deserve to know too."

Ominade pulled a charm from one of her bracelets and cast it at her feet. Calandra bent down to snatch it off the ground. When she looked up again, the diviner had already turned away and now walked briskly in the opposite direction from the statues.

Alayna clasped Calandra's shoulder.

"Should I alert some city guards to pursue her?"

Calandra stared hard at Ominade's long white hair cascading and bouncing down her neck as she blended into the crowd. She bit down on her lower lip and shook her head.

"No. I ... I just want to watch the slotball match."

Alayna draped her arm around Calandra as she stuffed the charm into her pocket. Her friend did her best to lift their mood once they entered the arena and found their seats. Calandra cracked a broad smile when Alayna started sharing chants she created to hurl at Titus during the match. The chants were equal parts funny and clever.

A boisterous long horn reverberated through the arena, signaling the start of the match. At once, a multi-colored ball launched from a starting circular slot and spit out into an open chute at a blistering speed. The ball was only the size of Calandra's fist. Helmeted attackers from Luma Central and Sendala Coast launched down parallel outer tracks alongside the chute. They swung down passing sticks designed to scoop up the slotball from a laser-guided inner track. Each passing stick had small black netting woven on one end to prevent the slotball from hitting the ground.

The Sendala Coast attacker scooped the slotball off the inner track and charged out into the open field on his skates toward the Luma Central end slot. Titus skated in front of the attacker to barricade his path and intercept a pass. The attacker dished it off to a waiting teammate and lowered his shoulder. He plowed straight into Titus and knocked him flat on his back. A chorus of boos exploded from the crowd.

Calandra and Alayna unveiled one of their chants.

"Titus Grogg chopped like a log!"

They both laughed with as much enthusiasm as they showed while chanting. Calandra could practically feel glares from surrounding slotball fans focusing on her, but she did not care. She needed this diversion.

Calandra's eyes trailed from Titus as he scrambled to his feet and back into the action. She gazed over at the crowd of fans gathered on the other side of the synthetic scarlet grass field. At once, her muscles stiffened, and her breathing quickened.

Ominade stood among the crowd.

Staring back at Calandra and Alayna.

"That diviner followed us inside the arena." Calandra frantically tapped Alayna on the shoulder with her right hand. "I see her directly across from us."

She pointed in the same direction. Both women turned to look at Ominade. By this time, the diviner recognized she had drawn unwanted attention. She abruptly turned and marched toward the exit.

Calandra pulled out the diviner's charm from her pocket and stared at the Aracian symbol. One thing had become certain. She needed to investigate this symbol and the diviner, so she could learn if Ominade played a role in Xttra's disappearance.

# 12

Cliff had no intention of letting this drop. Sam guessed this exact scenario would unfold from the moment he informed him of everything that happened earlier. Emotion overrode reason and protocol once Cliff learned of Norah's condition. He watched the video chat request signal linger on the screen for a second longer before clicking on the button to allow Cliff to vent again.

Sam tried again, with a firm tone, to dissuade the colonist from undertaking what he knew occupied his mind when Cliff popped up on the video screen.

"We've been over this three times now," Sam said, cutting him off. "Norah needs to be isolated until I can determine if an alien pathogen has infected her."

Anger radiated from Cliff's eyes. His face hardened into a stony stare.

"You can't expect me to stay away when she needs me by her side. I love Norah. She means the world to me. Let me help her."

Sam sighed. Cliff knew the Earth Defense Bureau protocols for situations like this one. They could not risk carrying a potential disease back to Earth. Until her blood tests turned up negative, that meant isolating Norah, Rudra, and himself from everyone else on Phobos Station. Sam sympathized with Cliff's desire to do something to help his partner. But he also refused to further jeopardize their lives and safety beyond what already happened.

"I wish none of us were in this situation," Sam said. "I'd love nothing more than to hop on the space elevator and get the hell off this rock. But this is our cross to bear for the moment."

Cliff slammed his fist on a console next to the laptop screen. Sam flinched at the sudden noise.

"This is our cross to bear? That's what you have to say to me? Good God! Do any Earth Defense Bureau officials possess actual human feelings or are you all robots housed in flesh?"

Sam threw up his arms.

"What do you want me to say? Coming down here is too dangerous. Just stay on Phobos Station if you don't want to get sent back to Earth for good when this is all said and done."

Cliff mashed a button on his laptop keyboard. The screen flickered and his image vanished a second later. Sam sighed again and rubbed his hands across his eyes and cheeks. Why was Cliff so determined to make things tougher than their current state? His hands were tied, and he damn well knew it. Sam did not want to ponder what repercussions lay in store if he made an exception to quarantine protocols.

Earth had already dealt with enough pandemics on its own. No need to introduce another extraterrestrial pathogen into the mix.

A slight groan greeted his ears. Sam glanced over at Norah. She lay on a twin bed pressed against a wall inside her living quarters. Two blankets covered most of Norah's body, leaving only the injured wrist, her head, and her neck visible. Her eyelids remained closed. A promising sign. The sedatives were working. They bought him time to figure out what else to do to lessen whatever pain still afflicted Norah.

Sam walked over to her bedside. He ran a handheld digital thermometer over her forehead. The thermometer displayed a temperature of 38.1 degrees Celsius. A mild fever consistent with fighting off an infection.

Exactly as Sam feared. An alien virus or toxin invaded her system. Her body cranked up the temperature to burn out the invader.

If venom or a pathogen indeed infected Norah, killing the alien and studying its corpse offered the best path for effective treatment. Then, Sam would have a chance draw venom from the stinger and Rudra could run some tests. If all went well, they would cobble together an anti-venom antidote on the fly and stabilize Norah enough to return her to Earth for further medical treatment.

Sam cast his eyes at a circular window above his head. Rudra had not checked in for a while since leaving the habitat unit to track down the mining vehicle. He wondered if the scientist's attempt to breach the outer walls had been successful. Sam double checked and triple checked the door leading into the tunnel connecting to the laboratory while Norah remained sedated. He found no evidence the alien had breached the other habitat unit and escaped into the tunnel.

For now, he found himself stuck in a desperate waiting game with no exit.

*Where is Rudra? He should have checked in by now.*

These thoughts gnawed at Sam. He marched over to the laptop sitting outside Norah's living quarters. Sam planted himself on a short stool in front of the screen. It displayed both Coordinated Mars Time and Coordinated Universal Time back on Earth. The clock showed Rudra had been absent for 33 Martian minutes.

Not a good sign.

Sam pulled up the video screen and tried to connect with Rudra through his helmet camera. Static popped up at once on the screen. It took a minute before a grainy video feed broke through and he saw the colonist. A clear protective visor shielded Rudra's face. A protective suit and helmet encased his body. Video feed from his helmet camera had a definite shaky-cam vibe as the mining vehicle's wheels bounced over rocky Martian terrain.

"How's Norah? Ran ... some trouble ... engine seized up for ..."

Rudra's voice mirrored the choppy quality of the video feed. Sam clicked on the video call settings and adjusted the feed to try to buffer out the static.

"Where are you, Rudra? How close are you to the laboratory walls?"

"Five minutes ... I hope ... works."

"Me too. Check back with me once you punch a hole through the regolith. We'll need to retrieve the alien creature's body once it has been neutralized."

Rudra nodded. The video feed cut off again a second later. Sam clasped his hands behind his head and pinched his eyelids shut. How would he explain everything that happened on Mars to Director Marks at the Earth Defense Bureau? This simple mission had turned into a complicated nightmare.

Two years had passed since the debacle in Utah. Sam counted himself fortunate to keep his job with the bureau after so many things went wrong during that first contact situation. The odds did not favor him this time. Two dead colonists and another one battling a serious wound and a potential pathogen.

Under his watch.

Sam had considered taking early retirement once he returned from Mars. Now, the bureau would take the choice out of his hands. His career as he knew it would meet an end. General Daly gave him some latitude. Marks, his successor, viewed every situation through a no-nonsense accept-all-responsibility lens.

*If I'm finished, at least I can go down swinging and save Earth from this alien threat.*

Sam tried to comfort himself with this thought as he rose from his stool. He walked over to a porthole in a center column running down the center of the unit. The column housed a hydroponic garden serving as a primary food source for the colonists. He rubbed a green leaf between his fingers. Everything would work out. Rudra was on the verge of boring a hole through the walls. They would neutralize the alien creature. Things were going to become normal again down here.

Peace would return soon enough.

On the other hand, what happened if the aliens who left this creature on Mars returned? Did they have sinister plans formulated for a direct attack on Earth?

*Don't think about that right now*, Sam told himself. *One problem at a time.*

Two rapid beeps greeted his ears. Sam sprinted back to the laptop screen. Rudra popped up—his video feed still choppy. Drilling noise alternated with heavy static.

"What's the word?" Sam asked. "Have you breached the walls yet?"

Rudra tapped a gloved index finger on a screen inside the mining vehicle. He glanced up at Sam and nodded.

"The computer shows the drill penetrated both wall layers." Rudra's eyes darted back to the other monitor. "That alien should suffocate within two or three minutes."

"Understood. I'll meet you down at the lab."

Sam made his way over to a locker and donned his specialized Mars space suit. A heads-up display popped up once he snapped his helmet in place. It displayed critical data ranging from life support status to environmental conditions. A camera and microphone embedded inside the helmet allowed Sam to be seen and heard through his protective gear.

He plodded down to the ground level and exited through the airlock. Sam cast his eyes toward the Sun hanging low on the horizon. Sunset approached. Wispy clouds laced traces of water ice diffused violet hues into the usual butterscotch colored Martian sky. Back in his NASA days, Sam studied Martian sunsets in photos sent back by rovers. Seeing one in person seemed a little surreal. No matter how many times he gazed out at the horizon, it never quite sank in that this same sun journeyed across blue skies back home. The Sun appeared so much smaller here, resembling an alien star revealing itself to Sam for the first time.

Rudra exited the mining vehicle just as Sam reached the building perimeter. He waved to Sam and beckoned for him to join him at the airlock leading into the lab. Sam embraced Rudra and gave him a couple of hearty pats on the shoulder.

"I started to wonder what happened to you out here," he said. "You were out of contact for over a half-hour."

Rudra shrugged.

"Sorry about that. The mining vehicle's solar power reserves were depleted. The engine seized up twice. Didn't think I'd make it over here."

Sam cast his eyes at the habitat unit's outer wall.

"You made it here and you drilled the hole. That's what matters."

"Indeed. It's only a few meters wide, but deep enough to get the job done."

Sam's eyes darted over to the fresh hole. Rudra drilled a nice circular chunk out of the regolith wall. Patching up the hole and repressurizing the unit would be simple enough for the colony robots to do once he and Rudra cleaned out the dead bodies and sterilized the laboratory. Sam shuddered as scenes from the brutal deaths of Sergei and Mei unfolded in his mind a second time.

What would become of the Mars colony? Sudden tragic deaths were bound to scare participating Earth governments and underscore dangers facing future colonization missions. Would Russia and China pull out from Mars and yank their contribution to colony funding? Sam was not convinced his own government would keep the colony going. The United States could not keep untimely deaths of Martian colonists out of the public eye, especially with high-profile global media coverage surrounding this colony from day one. Learning the fates of Sergei and Mei would only precipitate calls by opponents to cut funding and scrap the colony.

Sam did his best to shut those concerns out of his mind as Rudra opened the airlock. His focus needed to center on their immediate problem—gathering the dead alien and loading it on the space elevator to send back to Phobos Station for further study. No question remained on what threat it presented to humans. Now they needed to learn how to effectively combat these aliens if others from the same species showed up on Earth at some point.

The lab door still hung on its hinges. Bulges and dents from repeated assaults pockmarked the steel. Yet, the alien did not dislodge the door. Chaos reigned inside the lab. Broken and overturned equipment lay scattered across the floor. Lengthy cracks decorated lab walls. Sergei's corpse and Mei's corpse remained in the same spots where they had fallen. An eerie silence blanketed the whole lab now.

"Where's the alien?"

Sam jerked his head toward Rudra. The same question popped into his mind. His eyes darted from wall to wall. He spotted only two dead bodies inside the lab.

No sign of a third one anywhere.

"This isn't possible." Sam faced Rudra again and shook his head repeatedly. "Exposure to carbon dioxide atmosphere should have killed that thing."

Rudra lifted his head and cast his eyes at an air duct on the ceiling. Sam let his eyes trail in the same direction. A gaping hole blanketed a spot formerly occupied by a vent cover.

"The alien created an escape route before I drilled," Rudra said. His eyes stayed glued to the ceiling. "Damn. I never expected it to be this smart."

"How in the world did it escape? It should be dead. No oxygen is left in this unit."

"That's not entirely accurate."

Sam lowered his head at the same time as Rudra. He cast an unblinking stare at the colonist.

"What do you mean? Unless the alien somehow breathes carbon dioxide, there's not a snowball's chance in hell it can survive oxygen deprivation."

Rudra pressed a gloved hand against his helmet and peered back up at the ceiling.

"We have an automatic failsafe inside the unit. In case of containment breach in the lab, all remaining levels are sealed off from this level."

Sam's heart sank as he pondered the implications behind Rudra's words.

"So, what you're saying is a deadly alien is alive and roaming an upper level in this unit?"

"Exactly."

Sam crossed his arms, each hand gripping the opposite upper arm. His breathing quickened. This redefined worst case scenario. If the alien were smart enough to escape the lab, they had no way of knowing how much damage it could still inflict.

"Do you have explosives?" Sam asked. "Or any combustibles to spark a large fire?"

"A fire won't burn without oxygen."

"Plenty of oxygen is left on the upper levels where the alien is hiding."

"Isn't burning down the habitat unit risky?"

"We're running out of options. We can't evacuate Norah until we get back conclusive evidence an alien pathogen isn't infecting her. And the longer this alien lives, the slimmer our own odds for survival become."

Rudra tossed up his hands.

"Fine. Let's try your plan."

Sam and Rudra tracked down explosives the colonists used to blast regolith in mining operations. They attached a payload of explosives to a small robot. Then, after unsealing a door leading from the lab into the outer staircase tunnel, Rudra tucked the robot and explosives under one arm and entered the tunnel.

"Wish me luck," he said.

Sam saluted him.

"Godspeed."

Rudra turned and started climbing stairs leading to the upper levels. Sam closed the door behind him. He switched on a laptop and brought up multiple video screens. One screen connected to a video feed from the robot. A second screen showed the feed from Rudra's helmet camera. Other screens showed feeds from cameras on each level of the manned habitat unit.

Sam's eyes darted from screen to screen as he hunched over the laptop, searching for any visible sign of the alien creature. Dimming sunlight allowed immense shadows to spring up across each level. Burgeoning darkness only complicated his efforts to spot the alien inside whichever room where it skulked.

"See anything on the second level?" Rudra asked.

Sam squinted at the corresponding screen. Nothing showed in the light or shadows.

"I don't think the alien is in there. Try the next level."

Feeds from both cameras bounced a bit as Rudra trudged up the stairs with the robot. Sam's eyes drifted upward to the third level room camera. At once, he spotted movement within the shadows. His heart began pounding. He straightened up and instinctively jumped back from the screen.

"I see it. Third level."

Rudra paused outside the door. A worried sigh greeted Sam's ears.

"Let's do this. Arming the explosives now."

He flipped a control switch attached to the payload and set the robot on the ground. A digital timer clicked on, and numbers appeared. 60 seconds. Rudra spun the wheel and cranked open the door leading into the room.

"So far, so good."

He activated the timer. The robot rolled past the open door with the speed of a remote-controlled toy car. Sam drew a deep breath and clasped his hands together. This would work. This had to work. He had no alternative ideas on how to destroy this alien threat if their current plan failed.

Without warning, a chair flew from across the room. It struck the robot and knocked it over on its side. Sam froze. His muscles tensed up and his eyes stayed glued to the screen. The alien ran forward and scooped up the robot. It glanced down at the digital timer and turned to face Rudra.

"Get out of there!" Sam shouted. "Get back here now!"

Rudra backpedaled from the door and stumbled into the tunnel wall. The alien snarled and charged toward him. It hurled the robot and explosives straight at Rudra. Both objects hit him in the breadbasket, and he let out a pained grunt. The impact sent Rudra tumbling down the closest stair as the alien pulled the door shut again.

BOOM.

Shockwaves rocked the staircase. A fireball ripped through the length of the tunnel. Shards of polyethylene plastic rained down from the tunnel walls on the stairs. The visor on Rudra's helmet cracked like an eggshell and his video feed cut off a second later. The robot's video feed also stopped in the explosion.

Sam sank to his knees. His eyes widened and his mouth hung open. He began panting and quickly slammed his fist against the floor. Twice they had tried to outsmart this alien and failed both times. Now Rudra joined Sergei and Mei in a growing list of casualties on this mission.

Sam closed his eyes for a moment and tried to calm his breathing. He did not want to die on this god forsaken planet. Little hope of creating a different outcome for himself remained.

He could not risk hopping inside the climber with Norah and riding up to Phobos Station in her condition. And the alien already resisted two attempts to kill it. Only one course of action remained for him and Norah. He needed to warn the Earth Defense Bureau about what happened here. Then, Sam had to destroy all escape routes from Mars.

If dying on this barren planet ended up being his fate, he damn well would make this murderous alien share the same fate.

# 13

No sign of a planet showed up on the sensors when the stolen Thetian vessel dropped to sub-light speed. Kyra frowned and furrowed her brow.

"These are not the coordinates for Earth." She cast a hard stare over her shoulder at Xttra. "Why do you insist on lying to us?"

Xttra shrugged and did his best to suppress a smile threatening to break free from the corners of his cracked and bleeding lips. He was not entirely successful.

"I could have sworn this is the place. If we keep looking around, we'll stumble upon it eventually."

Xander whipped out a melter from a holster on his belt. He pointed the weapon right at Xttra's face and rested his finger right in front of the trigger, ready to press it at a moment's notice.

"His usefulness to us has vanished as far as I'm concerned." Xander practically growled each word. "Let's just put him out of our misery."

Kyra thrust an index finger at him and shook her head with vigor. "I'm not done with him yet."

"I'm picking up a small object on the sensors," Cavac said. He turned and glanced at the others from his seat at the navigation console. "We're closing in on its location."

An asteroid popped into view only a few seconds later. The space rock matched the chief sovereign's palace in size. Another asteroid, roughly the size of an aerorover, bisected the larger asteroid's path. It bounced off the larger asteroid. A small explosion followed.

Jagged chunks of rock spiraled in all directions. Some broken rock shot straight at the vessel.

Kyra's eyes widened.

"This is not good."

She pushed the steering stick to the left as far as it would go. The ship veered in the same direction and slid out of the broken asteriod's path, avoiding a collison with only a moment to spare. It continued spiraling past the outer hull until finally fading from view.

"We need to move away from these asteroids before they tear my ship apart." Kyra's tone grew more annoyed. "Maybe letting that particular scenario play out doesn't bother you, Xttra. But it should."

Xttra bit down on his lower lip to suppress a momentary chuckle from growing into a full-fledged laugh. He did not care what happened to anyone aboard this Thetian ship at this point, including himself. The path ahead of him led to limited destinations, and none were favorable. These Confederation fools intended to kill him once he no longer served a useful purpose. Xttra knew it. And if they reached Earth, then a bunch of hostile Earthians would track them all down and torture or kill everyone. Either way, he considered himself a man marked for death.

*What about Calandra? Can you give up like this, knowing she is searching and praying for you?*

Guilt splashed over his mind with the suddenness of a foaming wave crashing onto a beach at high tide. Xttra could not accept defeat now. No one had killed him yet. He used his training and intelligence to escape from worse situations than this one. Whatever the cost, he had to pay that price to return home to the woman he loved.

A low continuous beep echoed throughout the bridge. Kyra glanced over at the navigation console.

"That's not an asteroid proximity alert," she said. "What's our status?"

Cavac looked up from a star chart displaying coordinates for Aramus, the yellow sun anchoring the Earthian system. He flashed a confused frown at her.

"I think we're picking up some sort of distress signal. Navigational sensors indicate a signal is originating from a small rocky planet beyond this band of asteroids."

"Distress signal?" Kyra rubbed her chin with her hand as she pondered broader implications behind Cavac's revelation. "If that signal is from the Earthians, helping them might offer a perfect path for us to earn their trust."

Xttra fixed his eyes on the restraints binding him to his chair. Everything about this alleged distress signal screamed trap to him. These Confederation fools were free to risk their own lives for no good reason. But he vowed to not travel down the same path for Calandra's sake. Someone needed to add a dash of common sense into the equation before they undertook reckless and deadly actions to forge an alliance.

"You can't trust the Earthians," Xttra said. "This is a clever ruse. Nothing more."

Kyra dropped her hand and glared at him.

"You spare no effort to paint these aliens as insects sharing a single mind focused on destroying other life in the galaxy. I refuse to believe it."

Xttra clenched a fist. A tight-lipped frown crept over his mouth. Kyra obviously regarded him as nothing more than a perpetual liar. Why would he deceive them about the Earthians' true nature?

"I visited their planet and barely escaped with my life," he snapped. "Not one of you can say the same. This whole expedition is nothing but a fool's errand."

The Confederation pilot rolled her eyes, answered him with a dismissive wave, and faced forward again.

"Chart a course to the small planet, Cavac. We're going there whether our master pilot here likes it or not."

Xttra closed his eyes and shook his head. A realistic scenario for gaining control of the Thetian ship and returning to Lathos must exist. He only needed to concentrate on forming a workable plan to extract himself from this mess.

He opened his eyes again and stared at the restraints binding his wrists to the chair. Xttra studied each metallic band, like he had already done multiple times during their trek to the Aramus system. He searched for an exploitable weakness in the metal or a way to trigger a release mechanism from inside the bands.

When he glanced up from his restraints again, a small red planet loomed before their ship on the horizon. Kevin once told him the planet's name on their return trip to Lathos. It slipped Xttra's mind now. All he remembered is his scout ship sensors detected small vehicles sending transmissions from the surface and other signs of a colony. Everything that happened on Earth afterward compelled him to skip visiting the planet before returning to Lathos and following up on that sensor data.

"I'm now picking up a communications signal with the distress signal." Cavac's voice pierced Xttra's thoughts. "Definite audio transmission."

"Patch it through the ship's internal speakers," Kyra replied. "Let's see if we can discover what it says."

Garbled static filled the bridge a few seconds later. Xttra squinted and cocked his head toward the speaker above his chair. Cavac and Xander both worked to clear static from the audio transmission and isolate any voices. Thetian communication filters proved effective in cleaning up the transmission enough to where Xttra could pick out actual words.

He recognized the language. Earthian.

It used the same phonemes as the language Kevin spoke, a language he called English. Kevin taught him how to speak and understand English during their return journey from Earth to Lathos.

"What are they saying?"

Xttra's eyes drifted from the ceiling back to Kyra. Her violet eyes locked on him like a pair of laser bolts zeroing in on their next target.

"Do you recognize the words in the message?" she asked. "Is it an Earthian call for help? Enlighten us."

Xttra lowered his head and released an anxious sigh. Their suspicions were correct. The voice belonged to an Earthian and indeed carried a distressed tone. Still, Xttra remembered where the last Earthian messages they intercepted led. He had no desire to take a return trip down that path.

"Translate it and find out."

Xttra lifted his chin and cast a defiant stare at Kyra.

"What did you say?"

"Translate the message yourself. You want to understand their language? Decipher their words on your own like my crew and I did."

Kyra turned away and let out a shout. She slammed her hand down on the console before her.

"Ryollo!"

Immediately, a burly bronze-skinned man emerged on the bridge and marched over to Xttra's side. A single thick braid of black hair extended from his scalp down to his shoulders. They needed no introduction. Ryollo monitored the hibernation pods after their ship left Fengar bound for Earth. He already worked Xttra over once for information, presumably under Kyra's orders, after awakening him from a pod. Drying blood on his cracked lips offered a token reminder of their encounter.

"Stick him back inside a pod until he decides to be a little more cooperative with us."

"My pleasure."

Ryollo narrowed his eyes, and a stern frown graced his lips. He unlatched the metal restraint covering Xttra's right arm and seized his wrist. Xttra swallowed hard and shook his head with vigor. No chance he would let these Confederation fools place him back in hibernation this close to Earth.

Survival required being awake and alert.

"I'll tell you what you want to know," he said. "Just don't stick me back in that pod."

Kyra studied his face for a moment as though she were genuinely torn on what to do with Xttra. Her eyes finally drifted over to Ryollo, and she nodded at him.

"Good. You're speaking my language now."

Xttra wrenched his hand away from Ryollo's grasp and stretched out his fingers. He studied his forearm. Only his Stellar Guard uniform sleeve and underlying flex armor covered it now. Kyra stripped off both armored sleeves before Ryollo stuck him inside the hibernation pod earlier. Xttra gave her credit for being smart enough to confiscate his weapons. With access to his arm saber or razor discs, he liked his chances of subduing all four Confederation officers and taking control of the stolen Thetian ship with minimal resistance.

"You can take the other restraint off his wrist." Kyra turned and addressed Ryollo again. "But keep the restraints on his legs secured for now."

Ryollo followed her instructions at once and unlatched the other restraint encircling Xttra's left arm. Xttra stretched out the fingers on his left hand in the same manner as the right hand earlier. He rubbed both hands over his eyes and down his cheeks.

"It sounds more like a warning than a call for help," Xttra said. He let out a long sigh and leaned forward in his chair. "The message is directing other Earthians in the vicinity to stay away from Mars."

"Mars?" Kyra repeated.

"That's what the Earthians call this planet."

"Why?"

"I don't know why they call it Mars. An Earthian is better suited to answer your question than I am."

"That's not what I asked. Why are they sending out a warning? Does the message specify the reasons for it?"

Xttra planted his elbows above his knees and rested his chin in his hands while he listened to the voice on the transmission.

"An attack. Two dead. One injured. Alien creature has broken containment."

"Alien creature? That would mean …"

Xander trailed off before finishing the thought. Xttra sensed a definite tremor in his tone. Fear etched into every line and crevice of Xander's face. Color drained from Kyra's cheeks.

"What?" Xttra's eyes darted back and forth between the two Confederation officers. "What does it mean?"

"It means we need to land on this 'Mars' and investigate this attack." Kyra's tone grew more subdued. "We can only hope this isn't what I fear it is."

Xttra wondered why she was being so cryptic. Learning an alien creature attacked Earthians on the small red planet caught him by surprise. His scout ship sensors detected no signs of life here during the earlier expedition to Earth. Then again, Xttra was first to admit he had limited knowledge of what secrets the Aramus system held.

Myths and wild tales occupied more space in his memory than verified facts about what lay beyond Earth itself. Still, a random attack from an unidentified alien creature produced more reasons to stay away rather than investigate.

Cavac charted a course for the small red planet called Mars. Xttra stared ahead unblinking and dug his fingers into the armrests of his chair. Their insistence at diving in without careful consideration to rescue some unknown Earthians seemed equal parts foolish and dangerous.

Soon, Mars appeared on the horizon. Two small moons orbited the planet. A small ribbon shaped cable extended from near a space station orbiting the near moon down to the planet's surface. Xttra's eyes became glued to both objects. Earthian technology had advanced enough for them to build colonies within their own solar system. Fear crawled up his spine as he pondered the implications of their colony building.

How soon before the Earthians made their way to other planets outside the Aramus system? What would they do to Lathos if they ever figured out how to reach his home planet?

"I've traced the distress signal's point of origin," Cavac said. "It originated from the planet's surface. I'm uploading the signal coordinates to the helm control screen now."

Xttra jerked his head toward the main holoscreen before Kyra. New symbols and numbers flashed on screen. She leaned forward and studied them for a bit before nodding.

"Who's ready to save some Earthians?" she said, cracking a grin specifically aimed at Xttra.

The Thetian ship shot toward the planet's equator, plunging through the thin atmosphere. Minimal tug from inertial and gravitational forces affected Xttra, and not simply because of internal dampening fields. Mars' small mass meant it exerted much weaker gravity than Lathos, Earth, or any other habitable planet where he landed his scout ship.

They began their descent on the dark side of the planet. Stars pockmarked the blackened sky. Three cylindrical towers rose from a barren plain below the ship. Interior and exterior lights lit two fully formed towers. Multiple vehicles surrounded a third partially constructed one, which remained darkened. Dozens of solar panels dotted the plain, extending out in a northward direction from the towers.

"Check out the environmental readings." Xander tapped a finger on the holoscreen hovering above his station console. "Sensors show only trace amounts of oxygen and a below freezing air temperature."

Kyra scrunched up her face.

"Why do Earthians want to put a colony here? This place isn't remotely habitable."

Xttra had a good guess for the reason behind it.

"They don't have faster-than-light technology to power their spaceships," he said. "They can't leave their solar system and reach a neighboring star in their lifetimes. Praise Ahm."

Kyra shrugged. "Maybe we'll have to help them out."

Xttra shot her a dumbfounded look.

"They don't need that sort of help."

She answered him with a dismissive laugh. Xttra felt uncertain if the Confederation pilot kept willfully pushing his buttons or if she truly intended to ignore all his warnings. Her reaction burrowed under his skin like a setaworm digging through freshly broken soil. Giving the Earthians a key to unlock the door leading to deep space travel was a terrible idea.

Kyra steered the ship toward a flat spot only a short walk from the nearest lit tower. Plumes of reddish dust kicked up around the landing gear as it pressed against rocky soil. The main engines groaned as Xander powered them down. Lights from the front of the ship flooded the ground ahead, creating a walking path to the structure from the belly of the ship.

"Let's suit up," Kyra said. "Xander and Ryollo you're with me. Cavac, stay here and monitor the ship."

She sprang out of her chair. The other Confederation officers also rose from their chairs. Xttra plastered a smug grin on his face and fired off a mock salute—an Earthian gesture he learned from watching Kevin.

"Enjoy your trip."

Kyra marched up to his chair and glowered at him.

"You're coming with us."

Xttra shook his head slowly.

"Nah. I'm better off on this ship. Easier to stay out of the line of fire here."

"You can suit up or go outside the ship in your present state and become a frozen corpse. Your choice. But you're coming with us, one way or another."

Xttra's smug grin melted from his lips. Kyra jerked her head toward Xander. He turned and clicked a button on his console. Both leg restraints unlatched at once from around Xttra's shins. His first instinct was to knock Kyra out and sprint toward the armory to grab the first weapon he laid eyes on. Kyra sensed his intentions before he thought to move from the chair.

She whipped out a Confederation speargun from a side holster and pointed the barrel at his chest.

"Don't even think of hatching an escape plan."

Xttra's heart sank a bit, and he raised his hands after a moment's hesitation. Xander marched over to the chair. He seized his right arm and yanked him to his feet. Xttra glared at him and ripped the arm away from his grasp.

"Do I at least get a weapon for self-defense?"

Kyra burst out laughing.

"You must think I'm the biggest fool on Lathos. I'm not letting you near a weapon or any object you can turn into one. I don't need to be an oracle to know how that scenario would play out."

Xttra frowned. Xander gave him a hard shove and marched him from the bridge down an adjacent corridor. Once inside a cargo room, the Confederation officer snatched two Thetian spacesuits from a storage locker. He tossed one at Xttra's feet.

"Put this on."

Xttra cast his eyes down at the spacesuit and back up at Xander.

"You still have a chance to turn back, you know. Why risk your life for Kyra? What do you get out of it?"

Xander took his turn unholstering a speargun.

"Put the suit on."

Xttra raised his hands a second time.

"I'm putting it on. Stay calm."

He slipped into the suit while comparing Xander's face to ebutoka droppings under his breath. Once Xttra snapped his helmet in place, Xander waved the speargun at him and forced him to face the wall. The Confederation officer quickly donned the other spacesuit while Xttra faced away from him.

"Move."

A hard object poked Xttra in his shoulder. He turned and plodded out of the cargo room with Xander trailing a few steps behind him. They soon joined Kyra and Ryollo at the ship's exit hatch. Both Confederation officers had also donned Thetian spacesuits.

Ryollo opened the hatch door. Xttra gazed down at the lowering ramp. His heart jumped into his throat. An unarmed prisoner about to face Earthians. Who knew what their true intentions were?

His fate rested in Ahm's hands now.

# 14

A deep sense of foreboding gripped Xttra after entering the cylindrical tower. No trace of any Earthians on the module's bottom floor. So quiet and empty inside. A place as desolate as death itself.

"Where are the Earthians?"

Kyra's voice carried a worried lilt revealing to Xttra that the eerie silence did not trouble him alone. No signs of a violent struggle were present inside the module. Xttra wished he had a thermal tracker on him as he studied the room. The tracker would detect body heat from hidden Earthians and solve this mystery in a hurry. No visible hiding places jumped out at him.

This room reminded him of an activity room. A small round table, surrounded by three chairs, occupied space near the middle of the room. To the right, he spotted a long bench bordering a garden box filled with various leafy green plants. Two stationary machines with pedals and seats flanked the left side of the garden box. A row of waist-high cabinets topped by an empty counter lined a wall left of the table. Green vines and other similar plants climbed a central vertical column.

"My sensors show a mix of oxygen and nitrogen similar to Lathos," Xander said. "The air is breathable."

Xttra smirked.

"I would've never guessed after seeing Earthian plants everywhere."

Kyra turned and scowled at him. She extracted a thermal tracker from among her gear and started scanning the room for signs of life.

"Why are these plants so green? I've never seen anything quite like it. Such an unusual color for plants. And I don't see any red plants anywhere."

Xttra remembered he harbored the same question as Kyra when he visited Earth. He and Kevin discussed plant colors back when his Earthian friend first set foot on Lathos. Kevin told him green vegetation grew all over his home planet because of photosynthesis. Xttra imagined differences existed between his home sun and Aramus—Earth's sun—at an atomic level to cause a universal difference in colors on the two worlds.

Of course, he kept this theory to himself. These Confederate setaworms could conduct their own research as far as he was concerned. Xttra was in no mood to volunteer information.

"I see two heat patterns," Kyra pointed at the ceiling. "On an upper level of this module."

Xttra surveyed the room, searching for an access door. He spotted one on the north wall, directly opposite from the airlock where they entered. The metallic door featured a single circular window near the top, a central wheel embedded below the window, and a vertical handle off to the side running parallel to the wheel.

"Over there." He pointed at the metallic door. "I think that one leads to the upper levels of this structure."

Xander and Kyra took point as they approached the door. Ryollo sidled up next to Xttra to prevent him from making a run for the ship while their backs were turned. Xander tugged on the wheel. The door refused to budge.

"They must not want visitors," Kyra said. "Too bad. They're getting some anyway."

She extracted an Aracian cutter from a pouch on her belt. This type of cutter differed from the Ra'ahmian cutters Xttra and other Stellar Guard officers used. It did not feature a volcanic glass blade augmented by a blue laser or a polished stone handle. This cutter had a wider black metallic handle with four finger holes that slid down to each knuckle. A thin vertical black rod with a sharpened tip rose from the center. Micro ports on each side cast a white laser around the rod to form a blade.

Kyra plunged the cutter's laser blade between the door and the door jamb. She pulled her left hand down in a straight line, cutting through locks sealing the door. When the cutter passed the door handle, Kyra yanked on the handle and the door popped open without any trouble. She switched off the device and returned it to its former place on her belt.

"That's better," Kyra said.

They filed out of the room onto a winding stair. It traveled in a gentle winding arc upward from one level to the next. The stair wound around the outer perimeter of each room like a corridor. More small circular windows dotted the upper walls.

Xttra again considered making a break for the ship while the others were distracted. He quickly squashed those thoughts when he realized his chances for survival were not realistic. Not only was he unarmed, but he had no way of knowing what added risks lurked on the Earthian compound. Better to face down those risks in the company of his Confederation captors.

For now.

A small beep sounded on Kyra's thermal tracker. She glanced down at the screen and held up a hand signaling the others to halt.

"One heat pattern is moving away from the other. It's closing in on our position."

Xander rested a hand on his speargun. Ryollo did the same. Xttra frowned, wishing he had his eliminator, a Cassian fire shell, or some other weapon for self-defense. He hung back behind Ryollo a couple of steps.

Soon, a head peeked out from behind a circular wall hugged by the corridor. An Earthian. He laid eyes on the group in the corridor and instantly pulled back behind the wall. Xttra did not get a clear look at his face before he disappeared again. Still, something about his appearance seemed vaguely familiar.

"You aren't taking us alive. And I promise I won't let you reach Earth either."

The Earthian's brave words did little to mask a frightened tone in his voice. They outnumbered him and he knew it. Xttra wondered how quickly Kyra and the others would turn on the Earthian once they learned about his hostile intentions.

Kyra glanced over her shoulder at Xttra and motioned him forward.

"Your turn. Tell us what the Earthian is saying."

Xttra hesitated. He glanced side to side before taking a few steps forward.

"The Earthian thinks we're attackers."

"Tell him we intercepted a distress signal originating from this planet, and we've come to rescue him and his fellow Earthians."

Xttra raised his hands and walked toward the wall where the Earthian concealed himself.

"We don't want to hurt you," he said, switching his words to the Earthian dialect he learned from Kevin. "We are visitors from a different star system. We intercepted your distress signal and came here to Mars to help you."

"Mars?" a confused tone arose in the Earthian's voice. "Where did you learn the name of this planet? And where did you learn to speak English?"

"This isn't my first trip to this region of space."

The Earthian poked his head out and furrowed his brow. He wore no helmet and sported short brown hair, graying at the temples. His face looked so familiar.

"Let me see your face." He pointed to Xttra's helmet. "The air in here has enough oxygen. You're safe."

Sensor readings on his visor confirmed what the Earthian claimed. Environmental conditions inside this tower supported life. Xttra reached up and popped his helmet off. He tucked it under his left arm. The Earthian's eyes grew as big as plates.

"Xttra Oogan? That's not possible."

Kyra and the others did not understand anything else the Earthian said in his native language up to this point. But they instantly recognized Xttra's name sewn among those other words.

"How does this alien know your name?" Kyra said.

Xttra scowled. His eyes hardened into an angry stare. He knew exactly which Earthian scum stood before him.

Sam Bono. An Earth Defense Bureau agent.

"Simple," Xttra said, without looking back at the Confederation pilot. "This Earthian helped slaughter my crew and injure my wife."

Xttra lunged forward before anyone else said a word. He swung a fist and struck Sam in the upper jaw. Xander and Ryollo sprang forward and seized both of Xttra's arms. They wrenched him backward before he could tackle Sam and crush his windpipe. His helmet clattered to the floor. The glass visor narrowly avoided cracking on contact with the smooth surface.

"Calandra lost an arm because of your worthless alien race! You want our help? I'd sooner see you all die."

Xttra wriggled with the tenacity of a freshly caught Serrantan mudfish, fighting to break free from the two Confederation officers restraining him. They had pinned him against the floor. Sam closed his eyes and rubbed the spot where Xttra landed his blow. When he opened them a second time, a distinct sadness swam in each one. Sam licked his lips and frowned.

"I'm so sorry, Xttra. I wish I could go back and undo everything we did to you and to her."

"Apologies don't restore a lost arm."

"You're right. Maybe I don't deserve to live. But there are billions of people on Earth who don't deserve to die. If the creature I battled here escapes to my homeworld, countless lives will be in jeopardy."

Kyra tapped Xttra's shoulder with her foot. He shot an angry glare at her as well.

"Are you going to translate for us? That is your purpose for being here."

"Program a translator and talk to him yourself." Xttra shifted back to his normal language. "I want nothing to do with this Earthian."

He finally wrenched himself free from the grasp of the other two Confederation officers. Xttra snatched his helmet off the floor, jumped to his feet, and stormed down the corridor toward the ground level room.

"Record the Earthian's words and instruct Cavac to remotely program our translators with his language," Kyra ordered. "Once they're ready to go, see what you can find out from him."

Xttra refused to glance back at her, Sam, or the others. He kept a steady brisk pace until crossing through the open doorway into the ground level room. A hand tugged on his left shoulder. Xttra stopped and wheeled around. Kyra stood alone in the doorway, her helmet now off and tucked under her arm the same as him.

"You better be prepared to shoot me," he snapped. "I will not help that worthless pile of Ebutoka droppings."

"Why?"

"I don't need to explain myself to you. You're willfully blind to the danger facing us."

"So that's it? You want to abandon these Earthians to whatever dark fate awaits them on this barren planet?"

Kyra directed an accusing glare at Xttra. Her tone was consistent with a commander taking a soldier to task for deserting their post.

If the flames burning inside Xttra's eyes could ignite real sparks, they would have reduced the entire structure to ashes. Kyra could never fathom exactly what he and Calandra experienced at the hands of these aliens while exploring their planet.

The Earthians did not deserve salvation.

"They purchased their fate. I'll leave them to it."

Xttra waved his hand dismissively. He turned away from the Confederation pilot and started walking back to the module airlock.

"You don't get to decide which lives matter and which ones are worthless," Kyra shot back. "You're not some distant, unseen immortal being holding the fate of this galaxy in your hands."

Xttra stopped but did not turn back to face her again. He let out an angry sigh.

"Let's see how you feel after the Earthians do to you what they did to me and my crew."

"How would Calandra feel?"

Xttra tilted his head at her. Kyra should count herself fortunate he did not have a weapon handy.

"What did you say?"

"You heard me."

"Don't you dare bring her into this." Xttra stabbed a finger at her. "You have no clue how she would react in this same situation."

"I don't claim to know your wife personally." Kyra folded her arms and continued to stare him down. "But I have seen and heard much from you both during our surveillance. She does not strike me as one who would wish death upon a single innocent Earthian. She would still fight to save them all even after everything she's endured."

Xttra pressed a fist into his other hand and pinched his eyelids shut. Her words formed a sharp blade that dug deep into his soul. Xttra hated to admit it, but those words rang true. Calandra stopped him from shedding Sam's blood during their first encounter with the Earthian. She appealed to his conscience and subdued Xttra's anger. No doubt existed within his mind a similar scenario would unfold if she were here now.

"Will you come back willingly? Or do I need to make the decision for you?"

Xttra opened his eyes and, at once, saw Kyra's speargun aimed straight at his helmet. His throat tightened and his breathing quickened. Once a spear head exited that wide barrel, it would punch a massive hole through the helmet and his arm for good measure. Those laser-reinforced spear edges were famously lethal in their ability to slice through flesh and bone. Even flex armor did not slow spearguns down.

"You win. I'll cooperate."

Kyra's frown melted from her lips, and she lowered the weapon. She pointed it back at the corridor and waved him forward. Xttra had to keep telling himself to do whatever was necessary to survive for Calandra's sake. Somehow, they would reunite on Lathos. He just needed more time to map out a workable escape plan.

# 15

Calandra's eyes traced each curve and swoop on the symbol repeatedly as the charm rested in her palm. Ever since returning home from the slotball match, this lone ancient letter dominated Calandra's thoughts and danced inside her eyelids as she drifted off to sleep.

Why did the diviner leave this charm with her?

Did she intend to communicate a specific message?

Calandra became convinced those actions masked a hidden purpose beyond making money. Ominade approached her alone among fans gathering to watch the slotball match. After their encounter, she kept spying on Calandra from a distance until drawing unwanted attention to herself and leaving.

These events must hold a deeper meaning. This could not be a simple random occurrence. Calandra refused to write it off as coincidental. When rays from the morning sun peeking over the horizon fell upon her closed eyes, she resolved to figure out what it all meant.

Once fully awake, Calandra set the charm down on a table before her in her living room. She snatched up a trique from the same table. Maybe taking a glance at ancient Aracian letters and studying traditional meanings for each symbol would offer enlightenment. Give her clues to illuminate Ominade's cryptic words and actions.

Calandra searched for the charm symbol in the public archives. An identical symbol—resembling a vertical line intersecting a horizontal diamond—popped up on the holoscreen along with other symbols forming the ancient Aracian alphabet. Each symbol's traditional meaning displayed underneath the corresponding symbol, written in the Confederation Universal language. The charm symbol's meaning struck her.

Hidden knowledge. Power.

Her eyes drifted down to the charm and back to her holoscreen. Calandra tilted her head and stared at the Aracian symbol. How did this connect to Xttra and his abduction? Something with tangible substance lay hidden before her eyes. Perhaps it was nothing. Maybe her desperation pushed her into pursuing a fool's dream.

Calandra sighed deeply and dipped her chin to her chest. She set the trique down in its former spot. Fear and grief twisted her mind. Every thought had grown so muddled. Calandra desperately sought to uncover the smallest hint of evidence pointing to more than a random act of violence. She wanted to learn what agenda precipitated Xttra's disappearance and uncover a way to track and rescue her husband.

So many months passed without any positive news or leads. She sensed Bo'un neared a point of ending the search and moving forward with his life when they last spoke on the arca vox. Calandra refused to quit. Her soulmate remained alive and trapped in some unknown corner of the galaxy. Deep in her soul, she knew this scenario was real. She vowed to devote every particle of energy inside her to bringing him home.

Bo'un was finished.

It had to be her.

Calandra's eyes fell upon a clear gem embedded in the center of the charm. A purple stone. It shimmered when sunlight struck the gem at exactly the right angle.

Purple.

Her eyes narrowed and lips tightened as Calandra peered at the gem. Why did the diviner pair it with this specific symbol? Gem colors and lettering always conveyed the same meaning in a shared charm. Diviners did such a blending on purpose to reinforce specific messages to their patrons. Red hues traditionally represented power and knowledge among Ra'ahmian acolytes of esoteric teachings within the Order of Ahm. Purple stood for spirituality and leadership.

Calandra snatched the charm off the table a second time and laid it inside her artificial hand. She teetered near the edge of the couch cushion and turned the charm over in her hand. Metal pulled away from the gem on one side, leaving a sliver of open space. That meant it did not form part of the original charm.

She dumped the charm back on the table again and marched into the kitchen at a brisk pace. Calandra rifled through a drawer and found a small ice chipper. She grasped the dronden wood handle and returned to the charm. Calandra wedged a needle-like metallic point between metal and gemstone. Soon, the gem popped loose from the surrounding metallic casing.

Calandra's mouth dropped open.

She plucked the gem off the table. A micro port was now visible on one end. It owned the correct shape and size to insert into a holocaster.

This was no ordinary stone. Ominade gave her a storage crystal. Why did this scenario not cross her mind before now?

Calandra sprang to her feet and retrieved her holocaster from her bedroom. The square pad owned a matching micro port along its bottom edge. She sat on the couch again and plugged the storage crystal into her holocaster. A holoscreen popped up a few seconds later. Ominade's image graced the screen.

"Greetings, Calandra Menankar."

Calandra's eyes widened upon hearing her name. A tremor gripped her entire spine and her throat tightened. How did the diviner know her name? Neither Calandra nor Alayna shared their identities with Ominade during their encounter outside the slot-ball arena.

"I know much about both you and your husband. My knowledge is not coincidental. We have watched you from a distance since your return to Lathos."

Calandra pressed a button on her holocaster. The diviner's image froze on the holoscreen. Her mouth hung slightly open, and her eyelids drooped in equal measure. A lump formed in Calandra's throat as her eyes traced the still image.

Who were these people spying on her and Xttra? What purpose did their actions serve? Calandra cast her eyes around the room. Perhaps a hidden gadget in her apartment recorded her image and words at this moment. If it did, these hidden spies now realized she had uncovered their crystal.

She pressed the button again and resumed playing back Ominade's recorded message.

"The survivors of the Earth expedition are now a growing threat to the chief sovereign. Your lives are in grave danger, Calandra. His ruthless cunning and wrath have no limits."

Calandra stared unblinking at the holocaster. Her life in danger? From their chief sovereign? No. This was a lie. Confederation propaganda.

"What happened to Doni Zell back on Earth sealed your fate and Xttra's fate," Ominade continued. "Delcor practices patient vengeance. He is working to isolate and destroy you all one by one. I know this is difficult for a granddaughter of a former first minister to hear, but I speak the truth."

Calandra fidgeted with an auburn lock that had fallen to her right cheek. Her breaths grew quicker and shallower. What did this woman know concerning Doni's fate? Every survivor from the expedition to Earth received strict orders while inside the Stellar Guard tribunal chamber to not publicly discuss what Doni did on that alien planet. His treachery embarrassed military and government leaders alike. Their chief sovereign himself disavowed Doni's actions and apologized for sending him to Earth.

Why would their chief sovereign change his mind a year later and put together a plot to kill them all as Ominade claimed? Such a scenario made no sense to her. And it did not track with what she observed during her interactions with Ra'ahm's ruler.

"Delcor believes you uncovered his crimes." Ominade spoke as though she anticipated Calandra's doubts while recording this message. "Doni played a pivotal role in precipitating those same crimes. He's become convinced you murdered his long-time friend and ally. Delcor will stop at nothing to exact his version of justice and prevent his crimes from being exposed."

Calandra pinched her eyes shut and shook her head. Nothing Ominade said seemed real. Their chief sovereign admittedly was a strict and passionate ruler. But he fought alongside his father Bathal in freeing their nation from despotic brutality endured under the Confederation of Northern Tribes. She remembered what her grandfather Janthore told her as a young child about Confederation oppression. All Ra'ahm clans owed an eternal debt to the chief sovereign for winning the Separatist War.

He was a national hero.

"We can save you, Calandra. We can save both you and Xttra. You deserve to learn the same truths your Earthian friend uncovered."

Her eyes popped open again. Calandra stared hard at the holoscreen.

Kevin.

A suspicious vibe gripped her. If Ominade forged a connection with Kevin, her acquired knowledge started to make more sense. Learning Kevin was at odds with their chief sovereign did not surprise Calandra in the smallest degree. It fit with the course her friend charted on his life path since settling on Lathos. Kevin had no faith in the benevolence of the chief sovereign and never did. His experiences with treacherous Earthian governments poisoned his mind against authority.

"Come to my shop bordering the street markets in Luma Flats," Ominade said. "Tell no one and bring no one else with you. I have more to share—meant for your eyes and ears alone."

The diviner extended a hand toward an unseen recording device and her image vanished from the holoscreen a second later. Calandra leaned forward and stared unblinking at the blank holoscreen.

Meet with her alone?

Not a chance.

Calandra knew better than to trust a random stranger. Especially one with intimate knowledge of her. She needed a familiar, trusted face at her side. A friend also skilled with a weapon if anything should go awry. Journeying to Earth taught her to never jump into situations unprepared. Not everyone owned good intentions toward her.

Reaching out to Alayna sprang to mind. Calandra dismissed that thought soon after it appeared. Alayna did not own a weapon as far as she knew. Only one choice made sense in this situation.

Calandra rose from the couch and walked into the bedroom again. Bella stirred in her nest for a moment when she entered the room, then settled back into a deep morning nap. Calandra snatched her arca vox off an end table by the bed and activated the communicator.

This time she hoped it would connect with Bo'un.

A holoscreen popped up. Bo'un's image followed only a few seconds later. Seeing his scarred face lifted a huge weight off her. If the weapons officer had not answered, Calandra would have exhausted her limited options for finding meaningful help. Bo'un cracked a friendly smile once he saw her on the other end of the arca vox.

"You have impeccable timing," he said. "I just returned to Lathos. Landed at the shipyard after dawn."

"I need your help."

"Of course. Name it."

"Can you get away from the Stellar Guard for a couple of hours today?"

"That shouldn't be a problem. What's happening?"

Calandra's eyes darted to the storage crystal still inserted in her holocaster and back over to her arca vox holoscreen.

"I think I uncovered evidence that can lead us to Xttra. I need to meet with someone near the street market in the Luma Flats district."

Bo'un's eyes lit up when she spoke these words. His smile broadened and he answered Calandra with an approving nod.

"What time do you want me to swing by and pick you up in my aerorover?"

With Bo'un on hand as a temporary bodyguard, Calandra did not want to waste another second. Tracking down Ominade and learning exactly what information she possessed concerning Xttra's whereabouts became her top priority.

"Come to my place within the hour if you can arrange it," she said. "The sooner we can shed some light on what is happening, the faster we can find my husband."

# 16

An energetic crowd of patrons swarmed the street markets when Calandra and Bo'un arrived at their destination in the Luma Flats district. She felt unsure if this portended a good or bad omen. Large crowds made it easier for spies to move around the premises unnoticed while watching her and Bo'un. Yet, those same people would be less inclined to do anything sinister with so many eyes and ears around.

Pleasant music greeted her ears when Calandra stepped out of the parked aerorover. Two street musicians danced on a street corner directly ahead of the vehicle. Both musicians played a syri'nai—a musical instrument featuring nine hollowed out, polished senosa sticks bound together with ebutoka leather straps. Each stick forming the syri'nai increased in length from the one preceding it, supplying a variety of pitches to the performer. Younger Ra'ahm musicians preferred the ancient sound, look, and feel of authentic senosa syri'nai over modern synthetic versions. A call back to their ancestors who first crafted these instruments.

Several street market patrons gathered around the musicians to watch and listen to their performance. Bo'un and Calandra circled behind this small cluster of patrons and rounded the corner. A narrow street paved with smooth interlocking polished stones lay ahead. Covered stone booths lined each side of the street. Each booth featured three walls and a built-in counter facing the street. Merchants displayed their goods on wooden shelves lining the walls, in hanging baskets, or inside rotating circular cages suspended on long thin chains attached to the booth's ceiling.

"Are these street markets usually this crowded in the morning?" Bo'un asked. "This is more hectic than a typical market on Fengar."

Calandra shrugged.

"Never been much of a street market patron," she said. "When I have free time, I'd rather not waste it on purchasing whatever trinkets or gadgets a local merchant is peddling that particular day."

She cast a sideways glance at a booth displaying shiny moldable spheres. Several spheres hung on a rope suspended from a canopy supplying shade to the booth. A blue sphere on the middle of the rope drew her eyes. It resembled one her mother and father gave to as a gift when she was still a child. Calandra stopped and gazed at the spheres. She smiled, recalling her excitement at receiving such a wonderful gift. Calandra devoted countless hours molding her sphere into whatever image entered her mind. Animals. Faces. Planets. All found temporary life on the sphere. It opened a door to a lifelong love of art.

"I think I found it."

Bo'un's voice snapped Calandra's thoughts back to the task at hand. He stopped several steps ahead of her and stared at a cylindrical shop topped with a pyramid shaped roof. The shop occupied a spot near the corner at the end of the narrow street. A small square sign hung from a horizontal metal pole extending out above the shop door. Slender shiny chains connected sign to pole at each upper corner. Calandra studied the sign. It displayed a common diviner's symbol, painted in silver and white lettering, and set against a black background. Such contrast in coloring made the symbol pop out. It gave an impression of being backlit by an unseen light source embedded within the sign.

"This definitely resembles a diviner's shop from the outside," Calandra said. "Let's see if Ominade is inside."

A metallic whoosh greeted her ears as the front door slid open. Chimes rang out signaling their arrival inside the shop. Two patrons on the left side of the room stood before a rotating cylindrical pole dotted with hooks. Pendants and rings made from black volcanic glass dangled from each hook. Both patrons briefly looked over at Calandra and Bo'un before turning their backs again to examining a specific pendant.

Wood squeaked. Footsteps followed. Calandra cast her eyes toward stairs ascending into the room from a spot on the opposite wall. Ominade soon appeared in the open doorway and brushed back her long white hair hanging loosely above her shoulders. A smile burst forth on her lips when she laid eyes on Calandra and Bo'un.

"Welcome travelers! Are you prepared to learn secrets the eternal world seeks to share with you?"

Bo'un turned and rolled his eyes at Calandra. Her feelings matched what she saw in him. Listening to typical diviner nonsense did not serve her true purpose for coming to this place.

"You know exactly why we're here."

Calandra dug the storage crystal out of her pocket. Ominade raised her eyebrows when her eyes fell upon the crystal. She signaled to an assistant standing near a medium-high shelf displaying assorted vials and beckoned him forward.

"See to our patrons' needs. I must meet with our new visitors alone."

Her assistant nodded and walked over to the pendants and rings. Ominade started toward the doorway she came through earlier.

"Follow me to my divining chamber."

Calandra and Bo'un exchanged incredulous looks. He sighed and followed the diviner. She did the same. Calandra's brief time in the shop had done nothing to erase her skepticism. Diviners were all cut from the same cloth. They peddled impossible answers, wishful dreams, and useless gadgets to desperate people without enough sense to know better.

Once Calandra stepped through the doorway, a distinct whoosh followed behind her. She snapped her head toward the sound. A metal door now blocked the path behind her. Overhead lights and smaller lights embedded on the wall above each stair automatically activated. Calandra now noticed the stairs led down into a narrow tunnel when she faced forward again.

"The magnetic locks will keep unwanted guests from bothering us," Ominade said, glancing over her shoulder.

"Magnetic locks? Unwanted guests?"

Calandra stiffened and froze on the stairs. Did this diviner intend to make them her prisoners? Similar thoughts must have crossed Bo'un's mind. His hand dropped down to a concealed eliminator on his belt.

"Relax, Bo'un. No need to shoot anyone. You're in no danger down here."

His eyes grew as wide as small plates.

"How do you know me?"

Ominade flashed a knowing smile.

"I've made it my business to become familiar with all survivors from the secret expedition to that alien planet called Earth."

Calandra eyeballed her suspiciously.

"Why are you spying on us?"

Ominade turned away without answering and marched down the rest of the stairs. Bo'un gazed at the magnetically sealed door for a moment. He finally shrugged and started walking forward. Calandra stayed a step behind Bo'un. Letting him be a buffer between her and Ominade seemed like a wise idea. Calandra did not trust the diviner, and, unlike Bo'un, she neglected to bring along a weapon for self-defense.

"I told you to come here alone." A distinct sharpness tinged Ominade's voice. "Extra eyes and ears divulge sights and sounds not meant to be shared."

"That saying isn't relevant here," Calandra said. "I'm not trusting my safety to a stranger."

Ominade shot a scolding look over her shoulder at her. She let out a sigh.

"Child, I intend no harm on you. Quite the opposite. I want to save you from the designs of the chief sovereign."

Doubt flashed through Bo'un's eyes as they narrowed. He shook his head at the old woman, treating her words as outlandishly false.

"Designs? What designs?"

"All will be revealed in time. Follow me."

The diviner turned away and walked down an arched hall. A single row of pale yellow-white lights lit each wall. Multiple ancient Aracian letters painted in black ran parallel above the lights. Colorful glyphs imbued with symbolic meaning among diviners were interspersed among the letters. Calandra paid only scant attention to the diviner artwork. Ominade's continued insistence on being cryptic rather than giving straight answers tested her patience. Still, she needed to see this through and find out what the diviner knew or claimed to know.

Calandra and Bo'un followed Ominade down the hall at a deliberate pace. It eventually opened into a square chamber. A backlit curtain hung suspended over the back wall. Calandra peered at the edges of the purple curtain, trying to discern the source for the light peeking out from behind the edges. A small round table and chairs—all made from painted senosa wood—sat a few steps away from the curtained wall. Little rectangular metal blocks lay scattered across the table's surface. Each block had an Aracian letter carved into its face.

"You're not actually a diviner, are you?"

Calandra shot Bo'un a puzzled look. He motioned to the right side of the chamber. Her eyes drifted to where he pointed, and she stared in disbelief.

Crystal screens lined the wall along with input terminals. A workstation and chair sat below the screen. Two active holoscreens hovered above parts of the workstation. Calandra's eyes darted from screen to screen. Each one showed multiple locations in Luma. On one screen, she recognized the apartment building where she and Xttra dwelt.

"You are a spy. Are you a Confederation agent?"

Ominade wheeled around as soon as Calandra unloaded her accusation. She laughed like a parent hearing a child make an outlandish statement. Calandra despised that sort of laugh.

"I'm certainly no diviner. Nor am I aligned with the Confederation."

"Then who are you?" A cold sharpness infused Calandra's question. She did not relish being made a fool. "Why this charade? Why go to the trouble to make me think you're a diviner?"

Ominade brushed back her white hair. She directed Calandra and Bo'un to the small table.

"For your protection and mine." Ominade pulled on a long cord woven with ebutoka hair and drew back the curtain behind the table. "An aging Animo Islands rebel masquerading as a diviner does not draw attention from eyes and ears loyal to the chief sovereign and his agents."

"A rebel?"

"Indeed I am."

"From the final days of the Separatist War?"

"That's when my cause took root."

Calandra's heart started to race again. This was not real. What Ominade said could not be real.

Whispered rumors going back to her childhood told of an underground rebellion against their chief sovereign. A remnant band of freedom fighters who felt betrayed by one they painted as an authoritarian ruler. These rebels were fleeting shadows skulking in hidden places. Striking out like tenacious ictus bugs and retreating again.

Assassinations. Robberies. Sabotage.

Their illicit criminal activities only swayed hearts and minds of regular Ra'ahm citizens to oppose their cause.

"The Animo Islands do not exist," Bo'un said, pulling Calandra from her thoughts. "Only the ignorant and ancient call them by that name. Everyone knows those islands are called Delcor's Islands."

Ominade glared at him.

"In your lifetime, yes." Her tone grew annoyed. "Yet, your chief sovereign seized my homeland after he seized power. Delcor imposed his name on our islands to erase our identity while his troops simultaneously crushed all who opposed him."

Tangible pain dripped from those words. Fear gnawed at Calandra deep within her bones. Surely, their chief sovereign could never be capable of such brutal actions.

She cast her eyes toward the drawn curtain. The wall directly behind the curtain retracted to reveal a half-cylinder chamber wide enough to admit a single adult human. A circular platform rested on the bottom end of the chamber. Narrow vertical lights, matching Calandra's forearm in both width and length, lined the chamber walls from floor to ceiling.

She shot Ominade a puzzled look.

"What purpose does this chamber serve?"

Ominade stepped on the platform. She stretched out a hand to Calandra.

"What you're seeing is a virtual imaging chamber. A useful communication tool which I obtained from Peleusian traders."

Calandra approached the virtual imaging chamber. She ran her right hand over an embedded light.

"What does this do that an arca vox can't already do while taking up a fraction of the space?"

Ominade blew out her cheeks and sighed. She stepped down from the platform. Each light switched off once she was outside the chamber again. Calandra figured they must use a hidden motion sensor.

"An arca vox is not a secure communication channel," Ominade said. "I needed a channel Delcor's agents can't monitor easily."

Calandra turned and faced the fake diviner. Concern washed over her face anew.

"Your message said both Xttra and I were in danger. I'm convinced you know what happened to my husband. Who abducted him? Where did they take him?"

Ominade raised her eyebrows and tilted her head.

"What makes you think I have answers to those questions, child?"

"Then why did you ask me to come here?" Calandra's voice climbed a few decibels to match her rising anger. "I want to bring Xttra home. If you can't help me achieve that goal, then you cannot help me."

Ominade walked past Calandra and Bo'un without making eye contact. Both turned and instinctively trailed her with their eyes. She approached the table and grabbed one of the blocks scattered across the surface.

"My goal is to open your eyes." Ominade turned and faced her again. "I want the survivors of the Earth expedition to keep surviving. Your lives are also precious to those beyond your own clans."

Calandra and Bo'un exchanged puzzled glances. She appreciated the old woman saying her life held value. But Calandra wanted answers, not platitudes.

"Open my eyes?" she repeated.

Ominade sauntered over to her and held out the block. When Calandra extended her right hand, the aged rebel nestled the block inside the palm and closed her fingers around the device.

"This is your connection to me and other brave souls assisting me," Ominade said. "Press down on the engraved symbol. It will send out a signal and alert us to contact you."

Calandra opened her fingers again and studied the symbol. It resembled a four-pointed star, each point extending outward in a standard compass direction, surrounded by a circle of light. The symbol represented hope within the Order of Ahm. She stuck the block in her pants' pocket and gave Ominade a questioning gaze.

"I will do what I can to uncover the whereabouts of Xttra Oogan," Ominade said. "It is up to you to learn why Delcor seeks to end your lives."

"You told me Doni's death placed us in danger. Why?"

"Doni belonged to an inner circle of conspirators who maneuvered Delcor into power to secure their own place as the new ruling class of Ra'ahm."

Ominade snatched up another block from the table and handed this one to Bo'un. A crease formed in his brow, and he scrunched up his face at her.

"Our prime oracle gave our chief sovereign his blessing as the rightful successor to his father. He rules over Ra'ahm by the will of Ahm."

A scornful laugh greeted Bo'un's assertion. Ominade shook her head and pivoted to face Calandra.

"Valadius decided to withdraw his blessing to rule when faced with crimes Delcor and his inner circle committed," she said. "His gesture came too late to do any real good. Delcor held a firm grip on power, and he decided to end the prime oracle's life before Valadius could expose his evil deeds."

Calandra's eyes widened. Her throat tightened and her heart pounded against her ribs. Ominade did not hide behind multiple cryptic statements this time. Her words were clear.

Heresy.

Calandra fought the urge to cover her ears. Did the tragic accident where a solar flare killed Valadius never occur? Did their chief sovereign try to murder the highest leader within the Order of Ahm?

What she said could not be real. Everyone in Ra'ahm knew Delcor was beyond reproach.

"How can I trust what you're saying?" Calandra asked. "It goes against what I've been told my whole life."

Ominade pulled a chair away from the table and motioned for her to sit there. Calandra did as she directed. Then, the rebel marched to the opposite side of the chamber and pressed down a raised panel embedded in the chamber wall. A lit drawer popped out. She scooped out an unseen object and nudged the drawer back into its former place.

"I'll show you I'm your ally by presenting you a gift. Something you've sought but have not obtained."

Calandra narrowed her eyes and crinkled her nose. Gift? What gift? She looked up at Ominade's closed hand. Her frustration had nearly reached a boiling point. Why must she be so continually cryptic about everything?

Ominade plopped into a chair across from Calandra.

"Lay your left arm across the table. Remove the silk glove concealing its true nature."

Calandra started to extend her left arm. She stopped and pulled the limb back.

'Why?"

"Just humor me for a moment, child."

Calandra shot a puzzled look at Bo'un. He shrugged. She sighed and followed the fake diviner's instructions. Calandra tugged at the fabric covering her metal wrist and hand until it popped free of the limb.

Ominade leaned forward and opened her hand. A single crystal, equal in size to a thumbnail, rested inside the palm. Nano wires ran through the length of the crystal. Calandra recognized the device as a neural stimulator. Her clan doctor implanted one into her artificial hand and it malfunctioned from day one. His efforts to obtain a working replacement for Calandra led nowhere as weeks soon became months.

In her mind, she stepped away from herself and watched the surreal scene unfold as a detached observer. A rebel woman who should not exist. Telling her things which could not be true. One who brought her no closer to finding Xttra. Yet she claimed she could help fix her arm? Still, a desperate flicker of hope shined through clouds of doubt.

Hope for her arm. For hidden knowledge. For Xttra.

Ominade opened a slot in the back of the metal hand housing the neural stimulator. She popped out the old crystal and inserted the new one in its place.

"Try it out." Ominade glanced up at her as she sealed the slot again. "See how it works."

Calandra pinched her lips together and stared at her left hand. So many times, before now, she willed her fingers to move. Nothing ever happened. Her brain was willing. Her neural sensors were weak. They formed connections too scrambled to send correct signals to her brain. That's what the best specialists told her.

This time around it was different.

Her index finger uncurled. Then her thumb wiggled.

Calandra raised her head as she moved all her fingers at the same time. Tears streamed down her face. Her hand worked.

Praise Ahm. It finally worked.

"Now you have tangible evidence I want to help you," Ominade said.

Calandra flashed a grateful smile amid her tears. For the first time in a long time, she felt whole again.

# 17

Sam's eyes darted from Norah's room back to the alien visitors standing before him. Only two stayed behind in the corridor when Xttra stormed off in anger and a female alien pursued after him. Both aliens removed their helmets after seeing their fellow aliens do the same. They stood before Sam, their eyes fixed squarely on him and the open doorway leading into her room.

Neither alien said much since the others left. Not that it mattered much anyway. Sam never heard enough of their alien language when first exposed to it back in Utah to translate even their most basic words and phrases into English. Confusion washed over him anew when the two aliens spoke to him. All Sam did is answer with a blank stare and an occasional shrug. His own attempts to communicate also led nowhere fast. Both aliens only responded with confused expressions.

Sam let out a relieved sigh when Xttra and the other alien rounded the corner. Both tucked their helmets under one arm. The female alien held a pair of small gadgets in her other hand. Both devices appeared oddly familiar to Sam. They resembled wireless earbuds with two open ends. She handed the gadgets to the other aliens standing with him.

The female alien turned toward Sam and pointed to her own ear where a similar gadget already rested.

"These are translators," she said. "They convert your Earthian language into my language and vice versa so we can understand each other."

Of course. It clicked in Sam's mind now. Xttra and the other aliens who came to Utah used the same gadgets to aid in communication. This would make explaining his situation so much quicker and easier—especially given Xttra's understandably hostile feelings toward him.

"I'm happy we can finally talk to one another." Sam extended his hand. "My name is Sam. Sam Bono. As you correctly guessed earlier, I am from Earth."

The female alien glanced down at his outstretched hand. She also extended her hand but clasped his wrist instead of shaking hands.

"I'm Kyra Riso. I hail from the Confederation of Northern Tribes on my home planet of Lathos."

"Lathos?" Sam's eyes darted over to Xttra and back to her again. "The same planet as Xttra? I'm surprised to see your people show up in our solar system a second time."

Kyra cast a sideways glance at Xttra. A wry smile crept across her lips.

"His people and my people are not the same people."

"You mean your planet is divided into multiple nations the same as Earth?"

Kyra raised her eyebrows at his question.

"So, Earth is home to multiple nations and tribes like Lathos? Fascinating. Is your nation the dominant power on your planet?"

"The United States is one of—"

"Why did you send out a distress signal? Is this another trap like the probe you sent to Lathos?"

Sam and Kyra simultaneously snapped their heads toward Xttra. A hardened scowl dug into his lips. One hand rested on his hip while the other grasped his helmet cradled inside his elbow. Xttra cast a glare at Sam with his piercing deep blue eyes.

"I sent out no distress signal." Sam stepped back and raised his hands. "I activated a warning beacon and transmitted a message to the Earth Defense Bureau."

"Warning beacon?" Kyra repeated. Concern flashed through her violet eyes.

"An alien creature attacked us and, for now, is stuck inside another manned habitat unit. It killed three colonists and injured another one."

Xttra's scowl morphed into a bitter smile. He shook his head.

"Deathtrap. Exactly as I predicted."

"Be quiet." Kyra narrowed her eyes and jabbed an index finger at him. "We are helping these Earthians—whether you like it or not."

She glanced back at Sam after dressing down Xttra, her face still awash with concern.

"What happened to this alien creature who attacked your people? Where did you say you trapped it?"

Conflicted feelings stirred inside him. Sam welcomed a rescue from his current situation. Norah's condition did not show signs of improvement. Encountering these aliens now opened a door for her to get much needed help. Surely, they owned the technology and knowledge to help her. On the other hand, Sam hesitated to involve them in such a dangerous situation. Here was the second chance to build a relationship with a friendly alien race he wished for. Putting their lives at risk to fix his own mistakes could cement permanent hostilities between Earth and the distant planet called Lathos.

"We should cut our losses and leave Mars at once," Sam finally said. "No sense sticking around here and putting your lives on the line."

Kyra directed a questioning glance at the other two aliens accompanying her and Xttra. One shrugged at her. The other said nothing.

"If there's a dangerous creature lurking around here, shouldn't we destroy it?" She asked, glancing back at Sam. "Before it reaches your planet?"

Sam frowned. He did not appreciate her insinuation that he and the Mars colonists had done nothing to remedy the problem.

"We already tried to kill that creature twice. It escaped death both times. What more can you do that I haven't already done?"

Kyra matched his frown with one of her own. She crossed her arms and let out an exasperated sigh.

"Don't get defensive. I'm offering our help here."

"I get that. I really do. At the same time …"

Sam trailed off before finishing the sentence. He already saw enough of the alien creature's destructiveness firsthand to not want to risk another confrontation. Evacuating and destroying all habitat units from orbit offered a better strategy at this point.

"I have tons of experience dealing with exotic alien species." She turned and pointed to both aliens standing with her and Xttra. "So does Xander. So does Ryollo. So does Xttra. We can fix your problem if you'll let us."

Sam turned and gazed at Norah through the open doorway. Her eyelids remained closed. The sedatives he pumped into her system were still working their magic. Putting an end to this lingering menace would allow him to focus his energies on finding a way to flush the pathogen from her body. Sam supposed the alien visitors owned knowledge or medicine he could employ toward that end. Refusing their help was not worth the risk.

"I'll take you inside the ruined lab." Sam wheeled around and faced the four aliens again. "I suggest you bring whatever weapons you have."

Kyra pressed her hand against a holster on a belt circling a protective spacesuit she wore. Her suit bore a sleeker design closer to normal clothing than any spacesuit Sam had seen manufactured on Earth.

"We're always prepared," Kyra said.

Sam ducked inside Norah's room and snatched his helmet off a counter. He snapped it in place and the aliens all followed suit.

"When do I get a weapon? Confronting a dangerous creature unarmed isn't as fun as it sounds."

Sam cocked his head at Xttra. His statement seemed odd. Until Sam's eyes drifted down to Xttra's belt line. Then, for the first time, he noticed the absence of a belt stocked with weapons that adorned the waistlines of the other aliens.

"Wait a minute." Sam tapped Kyra on the shoulder. "Why is he unarmed?"

"For his own protection. And ours."

Sam narrowed his eyes and scrunched up his face as he connected the dots.

"Are you saying Xttra is your prisoner?"

Xttra flashed a bitter grin at him.

"Good observation. Took you long enough to connect the dots. No way in Ahm's name I'd come back to your solar system by choice."

Sam turned back abruptly and crossed his arms.

"If he is your prisoner, I demand you release him at once. There can be no friendship between my planet and your planet unless Xttra is set free."

Kyra wheeled around as soon as those words left his mouth. A crease formed on her brow and her lips twisted into a deep frown.

"What? You don't realize how dangerous he is."

Sam answered her with an unblinking stare.

"He isn't dangerous. Not to me. Not to Earth. These are my terms. End of discussion."

Kyra snapped her head toward Xttra. A satisfied grin washed over his face. He added an exaggerated slow nod. She scowled harder, first at him and then at Sam.

"You're making a terrible mistake."

Sam did not understand her animosity toward Xttra or reluctance to accept the terms he set out. Perhaps reasoning with Xttra himself would produce a favorable outcome.

"I trust you," Sam said, while turning to face him. "I promise here and now to help you return home if you help me."

Xttra laughed and shook his head.

"How can you make such a promise? How can I trust you? Your people tried to destroy me and my crew when I came to Earth."

"I'm sorry for what we did. I will do what I can do to repair the damage, even if it takes me a lifetime."

Xttra glanced down at the floor while pondering Sam's words. When he locked eyes again, a solemn expression replaced his earlier cocky grin.

"Even if I believe you, how can you guarantee these Confederation setaworms won't go back on their word once we're out of your sight again?"

"I'll find a way to keep you safe," Sam replied. "Even if that means enlisting every Earth Defense Bureau agent under my direct supervision to protect you."

He extended his hand toward Xttra.

"Do we have a deal?"

Xttra stared at the outstretched hand for a moment. He finally clasped Sam's wrist in the same fashion as Kyra did earlier.

"I'll hold you to your promise, Earthian."

Sam smiled. "Please call me Sam."

Kyra and the other two aliens fumed in silence, glaring at Xttra. Sam wondered what animosities existed on their planet to create such a sharp divide between their respective peoples. He wanted to find a way to bridge the divide. For now, there were bigger fish to fry.

"Follow me," Sam walked past the four aliens down the corridor. "The tunnel leading to the building where we isolated the alien creature is this way."

He led the group down through the corridor and into the habitat unit's lower level. Sam opened an access door to an underground tunnel connecting both habitat units. Kyra removed an unusual gadget from a pouch on her belt once they entered the tunnel. Sam had never seen anything like it before.

The square gadget matched an average human hand in size. A crystal screen occupied the top two-thirds on one side. Below the screen sat a silver rolling ball flanked by a single button on each side. Kyra switched on the gadget and the screen lit up with a blue-white light. A grid appeared across the screen. Five red blobs popped up a few seconds later. Each one formed a humanoid shape.

"What is that thing?" Sam asked.

Kyra glanced up from the screen at him.

"Thermal tracker," she said. "It detects body heat patterns. If our alien creature is hiding somewhere inside the building ahead of us, we should have no trouble pinpointing its location."

Sam's eyes wandered down to the thermal tracker again. Remorse gripped him. If only they had access to a similar device on the premises when Rudra tried to plant explosives earlier. It would have saved his life.

Sam cranked the wheel and opened the lab door. Dim lights brightened to normal levels once he stepped inside. He flinched and averted his eyes from the sprawled-out corpses of Sergei and

Mei after stepping through the doorway. Those same dead bodies did not escape the aliens' attention.

Xttra froze in his tracks and pressed his hand against his helmet visor.

"What in Ahm's name happened in here?"

A shudder went through Sam as their last moments replayed in his mind. He rubbed the back of his neck and swallowed hard.

"The alien creature attacked us before we could escape from the lab." His voice quavered a bit while he recounted the trauma that brought this whole nightmare to life. "It cut down both Sergei and Mei without breaking a sweat."

"Where did it come from?" Xander cast his eyes around the lab. "This planet isn't capable of sustaining life. Based on what our ship sensors told us anyway."

"The colonists found a high-tech capsule or tank in a cavern before I arrived here," Sam replied. "The alien creature was in stasis inside when they first brought the tank in here."

Kyra snapped her head toward him. Her eyes had grown as wide as plates.

"Stasis?" she repeated. "Where is this device?"

Sam pointed to the tank. It had not moved since the alien exited from the device earlier. The open door hung suspended in the same spot. Piles of soil and dust on the white tarp beneath the tank lay undisturbed. Kyra and Xttra converged on the device only a few seconds apart. Xttra stooped down and examined the lights and buttons running along the side.

He turned and cocked his head at Sam.

"You said you found this device here on this planet."

Sam nodded. "That's the whole reason I came here from Earth.

"This is a hibernation pod." Xttra turned away and studied the device again. "From Lathos, judging by the looks of it."

Sam's eyes drifted over to the other three aliens. Each one now stood as rigid as tree trunks, with eyes locked on the hibernation pod. Fear swam in those pairs of eyes and spread through their faces. Ryollo and Xander both drew weapons from their respective belts.

"No." Kyra's voice dropped to a near whisper. Her breaths grew more intense. "This can't be real. It isn't possible."

Witnessing her terror and fearful reactions from the other aliens caused a tremor to crawl up Sam's own spine. They already showed familiarity with the horrors this creature inflicted without laying eyes on it.

"Are you saying this alien is from your homeworld?"

Kyra ignored his question and started fiddling with the rolling ball on her tracker. Sam sidled up next to her and peered over her shoulder. Five red blobs appeared on the screen, same as before.

Her eyes darted from the tracker to the ceiling. At once, Kyra jerked her head toward Sam.

"You trapped the alien creature inside this building?"

"It's on an upper level without a spacesuit or helmet."

"Are you certain?"

"What do you mean? Of course, I'm certain."

Kyra glanced at her tracker screen a second time. Her lips twisted into a worried frown.

"Then I have some terrible news."

Sam stiffened like a board. He shot a glance at Xttra and spotted the same wide-eyed terror gripping his face. They all knew how to complete the thought she left unfinished.

"It escaped?" Sam finally found the words for the awful revelation that barged into his head. "How? How could it leave this habitat unit without dying?"

"Do you have additional spacesuits stored in this place?" Xttra asked.

"Of course, but I don't see how that's relevant," he replied. "This alien had some humanoid features. But it behaved like a wild animal. How would it know how to identify a spacesuit or have enough mental awareness to wear one?"

Kyra dropped her hand still clutching the tracker to her side and locked eyes with Sam. Anger flashed through those violet eyes.

"Simple. The creature was fully human at one time. And it came from Lathos—Ra'ahm to be exact."

Sam's mouth dropped open. He drew in a sharp breath and clasped his hands behind his neck. Her statement was the last thing he expected to hear concerning the hostile alien's origin.

# 18

What Kyra told Sam was a complete lie. Xttra refused to accept her claim. Nothing more than Confederation propaganda. He and his crew were the first people from Lathos to journey to Earth. If this alien creature who slaughtered Earthian colonists came from Ra'ahm, it meant so many things taught to him while serving with the Stellar Guard were categorically false. It also placed the longstanding travel ban to the Aramus system and Earth in a whole new light.

Xttra did not feel prepared to accept such an uncomfortable scenario. Kyra had to be wrong. He clung to this single thought and kept repeating it in his mind. He could not let these pieces of alternative history fall into place. He would not let them deceive him.

Yes, Kyra was wrong.

"Where's your evidence?" Xttra countered her with a blunt tone. "How can you claim this thing discovered in another star system came out of Ra'ahm?"

"It confirms what we knew about your chief sovereign," Kyra shot back, while giving him a sideways glance. "Delcor is a war criminal. This proves it."

Xttra folded his arms and drilled an unyielding stare into the Confederation pilot.

"Nothing more than a Confederation myth, dreamed up to give your people a reason to hate us and save face over losing a war."

"So, you're telling me the alien who attacked this colony came from your homeworld?"

Both Xttra and Kyra wheeled around and faced Sam. They shouted simultaneous conflicting answers at him. A distressed and puzzled look washed over his face.

"Why would someone from your planet put such a dangerous creature here on Mars?" Sam's voice percolated a quiet anger. "What did you all intend to do to Earth?"

Kyra frowned and raised the tracker. She studied the device as though she hoped the thermal sensor readings had changed in the last minute or two. Xttra glanced over at the device. Only five red blobs showed on the screen. Same as earlier.

"Earth had nothing to do with it." Kyra said. She raised her chin and locked eyes with Sam again. "You were never meant to find this creature. Neither were we."

Sam's eyes drifted over to the open hibernation pod and back to her.

"What do you mean? This whole ordeal was some sort of sick accident?"

Xttra cast his eyes toward the ceiling. He let out an angry sigh. Kyra spared no effort to poison the Earthian's mind against him and Ra'ahm. At once, he spotted a video camera mounted on the upper corner of a wall. Xttra smiled. The Earthian surveillance device would expose her lies.

"I see one of your surveillance devices in the corner." Xttra refocused his attention on Sam. "Did you make a visual record when you opened the pod earlier?"

Sam cast his eyes toward the camera in question. They quickly darted back to a laptop—an Earthian computer—sitting on a nearby workstation.

"Yeah, I can dig up a saved feed from earlier," he said. "Give me a second to find the right file."

Sam planted himself on a short stool in front of the laptop. Multiple square windows popped up on the screen. Each one showed a live video feed from a different room inside the building. Xttra marched across the lab and took up a position behind Sam. He scrutinized various feeds over the Earthian's shoulder. Dim lighting in other rooms allowed nocturnal shadows to conquer territory. Darkness obscured corners and angles within each room in question, making it difficult to see any specific lifeform inside.

Soon, Sam found a recorded feed for the room they currently occupied. He cued it to an earlier time and started replaying captured images. Xttra kept his eyes glued to the screen once the pod began opening. A humanoid alien stepped out of the pod. He swallowed hard and bit down on his lower lip after getting a clear view of the creature. Scales and bony ridges along the brow and cheekbones blended with human flesh.

The non-human features reminded Xttra of a dochu—a flying nocturnal animal on Lathos. How was such a blending possible? Dochu and people were not supposed to be able to be genetically combined in this manner. Their biological codes were incompatible.

Two distinct species with few common traits.

One Earthian on the feed extended a hand toward the creature. Without warning, it snapped the Earthian's wrist in half and seized him by the throat. Xttra jumped back with widened eyes. His breaths devolved into shallow rapid bursts.

"Is this still Confederation propaganda?"

Xttra snapped his head toward Kyra. She flanked Sam's other side, peering at the same images. Terror consumed her face in equal measure. Xttra shook his head slowly over and over.

"This can't be real."

Kyra's violet eyes shifted from wide to narrow in a flash. They burned hot with rage as a new scowl formed on her lips.

"You can't deny the proof before your eyes. Not only is this real, but it's also evidence Delcor committed a major atrocity among my people."

Sam paused the video feed. He turned around on the stool and greeted both with an intense frightened stare.

"What did he do?"

"He partnered with scientists from a planet called Rubrum to engineer a legion of hybrids just like this creature running loose in your colony." A trembling lilt infused Kyra's words. "Delcor unleashed his hybrids in two Confederation cities bordering Ra'ahm during the final weeks of the Separatist War. They slaughtered more than 10,000 soldiers and civilians in a matter of days, forcing the Confederation to beg for peace."

Sam's mouth dropped open. He clasped his hands over his helmet.

"Rubrum? Oh God. This can't be happening again."

Kyra gasped and stepped back.

"You're familiar with Rubrum?"

He nodded slowly.

"They attacked Earth almost 15 years ago. Invaded a small town in Texas. Murdered hundreds of our people. Abducted what survivors remained and performed nasty genetic experiments on them. We only stopped the invaders after destroying the entire town."

Xttra bowed his head and pressed his gloved hand against his helmet visor. This whole situation had to be a sick nightmare. He knew aliens from Rubrum reached Earth at some point after Doni lied about an alliance with them to turn the Earthians against him, Calandra, and Lance. Still, he had no clue about the atrocities they committed on Earth. Until now. The Earthians' hostile reaction to their expedition suddenly made more sense.

Still, tying this hybrid back to Ra'ahm and the chief sovereign made no sense to him. More than 40 years had passed since the Separatist War ended. Even if Kyra's allegations were true, how did this hybrid survive locked inside a hibernation pod this whole time? Where did it get food and water? Xttra never heard of a hibernation pod storing enough nutritional reserves to last over four decades without an outside source replenishing those reserves. Surely, the hybrid's muscles and organs would have broken down during such a long hibernation period until it perished from malnutrition.

Xttra raised his head again. He motioned to the open pod door. Xander and Ryollo stood on opposite sides of the pod, examining it.

"We better take this pod back to the ship and run some scans. That should give us a clearer idea of where the hybrid came from and how a hibernation pod ended up in this solar system."

Kyra closed her eyes and sighed.

"The hybrid's origin is clear to everyone in this room—including you. Why do you want to waste our time?"

"I found some holes in your theory," Xttra shot back. "I want actual proof. Not your version of proof."

Sam sprang to his feet.

"Your research can wait. Finding the alien hybrid is our priority. If you can't find any sign of it on your thermal tracking device, we better figure out where exactly it's lurking around here before it can cause any more damage."

Ryollo looked up from his spot hunched over the pod interior and shrugged.

"Maybe the hybrid died on its own. You should check for a corpse on your alien gadget."

"It's called a laptop and, no, I can't see anything," Sam said. "All lights run on motion sensors to conserve energy. Nothing has triggered the sensors on the upper levels."

"Dead bodies can't move," Ryollo replied.

Sam responded with a cold stare.

"Thank you, Captain Obvious," he snapped. "Minimal lighting probably means no alien. But I'm not sending anyone else to check out the upper levels. Already lost one colonist—"

A persistent beep interrupted Sam. All eyes turned toward Kyra. She dug into a pouch on her belt and brought out an arca vox. Cavac's image appeared on a holoscreen. Seeing his ocular implant on a holoscreen made Xttra shudder anew.

"I detected an alien ship landing outside the colony," he said. "Touched down a short distance from our ship. What should we do?"

Kyra looked up from the holoscreen at Sam.

"Were you expecting some more visitors?'

Sam gave her a sideways glance. An alarmed expression overtook his face again. Xttra felt uncertain if it came from learning another ship landed outside the Earthian colony or from seeing Cavac's melder visage.

"No, I'm not. Can he send us a picture or video of the other ship from his current location?"

Kyra repeated the request to Cavac. He nodded and his image vanished from the holoscreen. A new image occupied the screen a few seconds later. Sam's eyes narrowed and a deepening frown formed as he studied the ship's image.

"I recognize it. That's our prototype deep space vessel docked at the Phobos Station."

"Phobos Station?" Xander repeated.

"What in the hell does Cliff think he's doing?" Sam snapped, ignoring the question. "I ordered him to stay up there until I got the situation down here under control."

"Cavac, where is the pilot of the Earthian vessel?" Kyra asked. "Is he still with the ship?"

Cavac's image reappeared. He glanced off screen for a moment and then his eyes refocused on her.

"No. The Earthian left his vessel. Sensors indicate he entered the neighboring building."

Sam slammed a gloved fist into his other hand.

"That damned moron is here to take Norah away."

Xttra tilted his head at Sam.

"Norah?"

"She's an injured colonist," he replied. "Suffered a punctured wrist when the hybrid attacked us. I need to stop him from what he intends to do."

Sam turned and started for the tunnel door.

"Wait!" Kyra thrust up her hand. "Where is she now?"

"Back in the other building, under sedation." Sam did not bother to look back. He kept cranking the wheel to reopen the door. "She's supposed to remain under quarantine. And he knows it."

Quarantine?

Xttra did not like the implications behind that piece of news. He had taken his helmet off inside the other building. Did the Earthian expose him to some alien disease or toxin? He sprang forward and caught up to Sam right as he opened the door.

"Why is your fellow Earthian quarantined?" Xttra jabbed his finger in the same direction as the tunnel. "When were you planning on sharing this nugget of information with the rest of us?"

Sam turned and glowered at him.

"I had more pressing concerns. Listen, can we save this impending argument for later? Every second we waste hashing this out is another second for Cliff to do something incredibly selfish and stupid."

"What is he trying to do?"

"Take Norah back to Phobos. Or possibly Earth."

"How did she puncture her wrist?" Kyra asked. Her question told Xttra she also suspected Sam purposefully withheld some critical details. "Does this have anything to do with the quarantine?"

Sam cast his eyes down at the floor and nodded.

"The alien hybrid, as you call it, jabbed a giant stinger from its forearm through her wrist. I did what I could to treat the wound, but the surrounding tissues swelled up and she's had a fever ever since."

Kyra froze and stared at him with widened eyes and trembling lips. Her expression perfectly mirrored the dread crawling up through Xttra's whole body. This situation rated much worse than exposure to a simple disease or a toxin.

"Retrieve Xttra's weapons, Cavac, and bring them to me at once," she said, glancing down at her arca vox again. "We'll need every bit of help we can get in here."

"But I thought you told us—"

"Ignore my earlier order."

Cavac answered with a reluctant nod. Both his image and the holoscreen vanished a second later. Kyra raised her head and looked over at Xander and Ryollo.

"When Cavac gets here, help him load that pod into the ship. Xttra and I will take care of things here."

Sam's eyes widened.

"What's going on? What are you planning to do?"

Kyra simply shook her head and said nothing. He crossed his arms and stared at her, probing for an answer with his eyes. The Confederation pilot glanced away from Sam and stuffed her arca vox back inside its pouch again.

What could she say? Xttra understood the frightening reality they now faced. But he also had no clue how to frame what they needed to do in terms the Earthian would accept.

Norah had to die. Immediately.

# 19

Calandra curled one finger after another on her artificial hand. A radiant smile spread across her lips and reflected in her eyes. To see the metal hand finally working like a real hand brought indescribable joy. So much pain and anguish washed away like an unanchored boat in a swollen current. The storm receded and sunlight finally pierced ashen clouds smothering her soul.

A functioning neural sensor made everything feel normal again. She felt the fingers and thumb pressing together when she closed the artificial hand. If she grasped an object with the hand, she experienced a similar sense of touch as with her natural hand.

Warmth. Cold. Roughness. Smoothness.

Her artificial hand experienced every sensation as though real nerves now sent signals to her brain.

No doubt Xttra would feel equally thrilled. They both prayed long and hard for this outcome. Calandra longed to share this life-changing moment with him. His absence created an emptiness within their apartment. A void that taunted her and refused to recede.

She picked up the small metal block Ominade imparted to her earlier from an end table near her bed. Calandra sat on the bed and studied the block, turning it over in her hand. The black colored symbol stood in stark contrast to the rest of the block's metallic luster.

Hope.

The symbol meant hope.

What message did Ominade intend to share with her?

Calandra's thumb hovered over the symbol. If she pressed down on it, Ominade or one of her fellow rebels would contact her again. Or so she promised.

She could not bring herself to follow through with that action. Calandra set the block back down in its former resting place. Ominade unveiled a startling number of unbelievable revelations to her and Bo'un. If what she said was indeed the truth, it shattered everything Calandra believed about their chief sovereign, her own grandfather, and the Order of Ahm itself.

*I can't reject her claims without question,* Calandra thought. *I need more information. If what she says is true, then evidence must exist somewhere to confirm what she said.*

Her first instinct was to go grab her trique and do a basic search through the public archives. Calandra glanced over at the device sitting on a small shelf on the other side of the room. She did not rise from the bed to retrieve it. If their chief sovereign truly had something to hide, she would not find it in such an open place.

No. It became clear where Calandra needed to turn.

She needed to dig into the Central Archives. And she could not do it alone. Calandra sprang to her feet and grabbed her arca vox from the same table where Ominade's block rested.

Alayna flashed a bright smile as soon as her image popped up on the holoscreen. It grew more pronounced when Calandra shared the news about her arm.

"Let me see it in action. Move those fingers."

Calandra obliged and wiggled the fingers on her artificial hand. Alayna pressed her hand to her mouth. Tears trickled down her cheeks. She wiped her eyes with a cloth and the smile returned.

"This is a joyous day!" Alayna said. "One we both hoped for. We need to celebrate."

Calandra matched her friend's happy expression with a radiant smile of her own.

"I love the sound of that idea."

"Today."

Calandra's smile dimmed and she pressed her lips together. She hesitated to speak the words lingering in her mind, uncertain of how to reveal her true motive for contacting Alayna. Should she draw her friend into her quest and force her to share this burden?

That question gnawed at her mind because she did not want to create trouble for Alayna. Still, her search for Xttra threatened to reach a permanent impasse without involving her friend in the search. Alayna worked for the Central Archives and Calandra had no means of gaining access to specific information inside the archives without her help.

"Is something wrong?"

Alayna's question pierced through her thoughts. Calandra cast her eyes down and drew in a deep breath.

"I hate to ask this, but I need a huge favor from you."

"Name it."

"I'm not sure how to put this—"

Alayna laughed.

"You're acting like your whole life hinges on this single favor."

Calandra answered her with a silent worried glance. Alayna's smile dropped off her lips.

"What's going on? What aren't you telling me?"

"I encountered that diviner … again." Hesitation gripped Calandra's voice. "She shared information that … concerns me."

Alayna buried her face in her hands and then rubbed them down her nose and mouth. Concern filled her eyes as she focused on Calandra again.

"Self-professed diviners only create endless trouble in their wake. You're smart enough to not entangle yourself with one."

"Ominade isn't a diviner."

A knowing smirk crawled across Alayna's lips.

"Really? Could have fooled me."

"She's actually a rebel from Delcor's Islands."

Alayna froze and stared wide-eyed at her once those words left Calandra's lips. Her thumb caressed a small starlight tattoo on her opposite wrist. An uncomfortable silence grew between the two friends.

"She told me things about our chief sovereign that scare me," Calandra said, finally cutting through the silence. "I need to know the truth."

Alayna shook her head.

"No. I can't do what you're asking me to do."

"You're the only one who can help me." Desperation seeped into Calandra's voice. "You have access to restricted records inside the Central Archives which I can never see as a visitor."

"Do you realize how much trouble I'll create for myself if I take you inside there with me?"

"You can tell them we're collaborating on historical astronomical data research with the observatory. Or something else."

Alayna mashed her lips together and cast her eyes downward. She sat rigid on her chair, not saying a word. Calandra felt constrained to make one final appeal to her.

"Please. I'm begging you as a friend."

Her friend finally glanced up again and answered Calandra with a reluctant nod.

"I'll do it. Meet me inside the main lobby at the Central Archives tomorrow morning."

Alayna reached out an arm and her image vanished from the holoscreen. Calandra felt some relief at enlisting her help. Now she had a real chance to finally verify Ominade's claims for herself.

***

Calandra attacked steps leading to the Central Archives entrance at a brisk pace. Gray stone pillars flanked each side of the main doors. The staggered square building towered over her like an inanimate monstrous giant, filled with front-facing windows serving as a swarm of transparent eyes.

Alayna stood inside the lobby only a few steps beyond the main doors. She waved as soon as Calandra cleared the top step. Both main doors parted with a whoosh and Alayna ushered her inside. She greeted Calandra with a nervous smile and an embrace.

"I secured an access stamp for you," Alayna said, after pulling away again. She dug into an ebutoka leather pouch hanging from a strap strung across her chest. "This will let you go through all checkpoint sensors beyond the main floor."

The access stamp resembled a thin oval disc with ancient Ra'ahm lettering occupying one side. Each letter had more elongated swoops than their more familiar modern counterparts. Calandra studied the lettering, trying to make sense of their meaning.

"Hold out your right wrist."

She did as Alayna instructed. Calandra flinched. She glanced down at her arm as Alayna pulled away the disc. Each letter bled from the stamp and settled on her skin, taking on the appearance of a translucent tattoo.

Calandra shot a wide-eyed look at her friend.

"What did you do?"

"Relax." Alayna stuffed the blank stamp back into her chest pouch. "It's designed to only last a day. The stamp will vanish within 28 hours."

She turned up a cuff on her shirt. A stamp with similar letters graced Alayna's right wrist. Her heartbeat slowed from a gallop to a steadier, nervous rhythm brought on by a fear of discovery. Calandra recalled seeing such a stamp on Alayna's wrist in the past, although she never paid it a second thought. She simply assumed Alayna wanted another clan tattoo to match the one already imprinted on her left wrist.

Calandra followed Alayna between twin polished stone columns. Vertical rows of embedded circular lights ran down the middle of each column. Those lights blinked yellow as she passed. Once the lights detected the stamp on her wrist, yellow morphed into white. This same process repeated as Alayna led her between other columns. Finally, they reached a room housing a collected record depository.

Glass doors vanished with a whoosh when Calandra and Alayna reached the depository entrance. Rows of horizontal cylindrical lights sprang to life on each wall when they entered the room. Towering shelves filled with parchment, metal plates, and bound books of varying shapes and sizes dotted the room from wall to wall. Calandra's mouth dropped open as her eyes bounced from one shelf to another. Studying all the knowledge contained inside this vast depository would take a full year, even if she spent entire days doing nothing else.

She followed Alayna to a central column set apart from a shelf. The column matched Calandra in height from its base to top. A square pad resembling a holocaster topped the column. Embedded control buttons were further down the column, only a short distance below the pad. Alayna pressed a button and a blank holoscreen appeared atop the column a few seconds later.

"What exactly are we searching for in here?" Alayna glanced over her shoulder. "You know, that isn't already accessible in the public archives?"

Calandra fixed her eyes on the holoscreen. She teased a slight frown that threatened to turn into a larger one.

"I need to pull up every scrap of information I can find on Valadius."

"The former prime oracle?"

"Indeed. I was told the official familiar narrative is not the real story."

"Do you believe that?"

"I believe Xttra was abducted from Fengar, in part, to stop him from tracking down a friend of ours who fled Lathos after uncovering evidence Valadius still lives."

Alayna cast a glance back at the depository entrance. Tangible fear flashed through her sharp brown eyes.

"That's impossible. We all heard about the flare. We all witnessed his burial rites. My family shed so many tears on that day."

"Kevin told Xttra the same things Ominade shared with me. Where smoke billows into the air, flames are always present somewhere near."

Alayna opened a drawer on the side of the column and removed a pair of black scrolling gloves. Glowing circular spots equal in size to a Ra'ahm coin adorned each fingertip on both gloves. She tossed a right-handed glove to Calandra and kept the left-handed one for herself.

"We better get to work in that case."

Alayna slid her hand inside her scrolling glove and cinched it tight. She enlarged the holoscreen with her glove and touched a scrolling symbol in the upper corner. The symbol matched the same one inscribed on the charm Ominade gave Calandra. She entered the name Valadius into a search box. Images of the former prime oracle popped up on the screen. Alayna split the holoscreen into two separate screens.

One image showed Valadius raising his hands and addressing a crowd while standing atop a short tower outside the walls of the main temple of Ahm in Luma. Another showed him laying his right hand upon the bowed head of a young man to bless him. A warm smile adorned his face in both images.

Calandra scrolled past images of Valadius speaking on her holoscreen until she finally reached an image of his adrift transport. She clicked on that image and words materialized below. Each word resembled narrow three-dimensional blocks on this holoscreen instead of flat letters on a page. It was an official report detailing how a solar flare engulfed the prime oracle's transport and the aftermath of the accident.

Calandra's eyes trailed the words as she kept scrolling. Midway through the report, she let out a sudden gasp. Calandra jabbed her index finger at the holoscreen. The scrolling words froze. Her breaths grew shallower. Fear billowed inside her with the suddenness of a rolling storm cloud.

The Stellar Guard found no bodies on the vessel.

This could not be real.

Calandra shook her head as she continued reading the report. It detailed how an escape vehicle was missing when Stellar Guard officers boarded the transport. No traces of the prime oracle or any other passenger were anywhere on that vessel.

"He's alive." Calandra's voice barely rose above a whisper. "I can't believe it. Valadius lives."

Alayna pivoted toward her and studied the report for herself. The same fear gripping Calandra soon drew her into its grasp. Her lips trembled and she swallowed hard.

"Why would our sovereign lie about this?" Alayna said. "There must be a different explanation."

Calandra stared at the holoscreen. She fiddled with a lock of her hair brushing against her cheek. What was the prime oracle's true fate? Why did he abandon the transport in the first place?

"Oh no. What did our sovereign do?"

Calandra glanced over at Alayna's holoscreen. Her friend shook her head and pinched her eyes shut. She pressed her hand against her mouth. The holoscreen displayed a letter inscribed on a metal plate, culled from a chronological list of historical documents. It bore an official seal from Valadius. The letter's time stamp showed he sent it out three days before his reported death. His correspondence went to the first minister.

Her grandfather, Janthore.

Calandra's eyes trailed each word on the holoscreen, and she mouthed what she read as she dug into the letter.

*Honorable First Minister Janthore:*

*I send you greetings and salute you as a brother in the Order of Ahm, our Divine Creator. Peace be with you and clan Menankar this day.*

*With a heavy heart, I write to inform you that I must withdraw my blessing upon Delcor to act as ruler of this great nation. Our sovereign committed unspeakable crimes that are unforgivable in the eyes of Ahm. Evidence of these crimes has come to my attention and holy words I have received constrain me to support Delcor no longer in his office.*

*I invite you to meet with me upon my return from Fengar. We will discuss this situation further and consider options for a successor.*

*Valadius*
*Prime Oracle of Ahm*

Tears brimmed in Calandra's eyes and splashed down her cheeks. Ominade's charges against Delcor were true. Worse yet, her own grandfather knew their chief sovereign had done awful things. And he did nothing about it. Was he complicit in those same unspeakable crimes the prime oracle referenced in his letter? How much did her mother and father know about his activities as first minister?

"We have to keep searching. We need to find out what the prime oracle learned."

Calandra's words were meant for herself as much as for Alayna. No matter how painful it ended up being, she had to uncover the truth.

Her eyes refocused on her own holoscreen, and she scrolled through more records from the first minister's office. Reports. Letters. Speeches. No further clues surfaced as Calandra worked backward from the date her grandfather received the letter from Valadius.

"We better wrap this up," Alayna said. A rising fear seized her voice. "I don't know how long we can get away with searching these records before someone decides to check on us."

Calandra shook her head and kept her eyes locked on the holoscreen.

"We won't get another chance to do this."

She reversed directions and scrolled forward until she came to the same letter Alayna uncovered. Calandra paused and cast a glance over her shoulder. No one else had come inside the room to check on them. Yet. Calandra let out a relieved sigh and continued scrolling.

Finally, after a few minutes, she spotted an official memo from her grandfather. It did not say who received the memo, but the message instantly caught her eye.

*Assassination plot?*

> *Captured rebel claims to have evidence implicating our chief sovereign in orchestrating his father's assassination. Disturbing accusation that seems impossible. Still requires due diligence. Must interrogate her further on the matter.*

Calandra stared at the time stamp on the memo. Her grandfather recorded it only one week before he abruptly stepped down from being first minister. She never understood why he left Lathos and never came back. Now the puzzle pieces were locking together.

If their chief sovereign plotted his own father's assassination so he could take over as Ra'ahm's ruler, such an action qualified as an unspeakable crime. Perhaps her grandfather feared for his own safety after he uncovered evidence of said crime.

"Now that we know these things, what do we do?"

Calandra turned and faced Alayna. A numb shock adorned her friend's face as she blurted out the question. No satisfactory answer sprang into Calandra's mind. A new sensation also washed over her as she processed these revelations.

For the first time since leaving Earth, Calandra feared for her own life.

# 20

Norah's head still throbbed when she cracked open her eyes. The entire room swam as sedatives lingered in her system. She squinted and clenched her teeth. Her throat had grown dry and scratchy. The inside of her mouth had become dried out like someone stuffed it full of cotton while she slept. Norah licked the roof of her mouth, trying to stimulate saliva.

"Good God! What have these bastards done to you?"

A hand tenderly touched her shoulder. She glanced over at the gloved hand with half-closed eyes. Cliff stood at her bedside, hunched over her with an angry frown plastered on his lips.

"What's going on?"

Norah barely mumbled the question before stopping to clear her throat. Both wrists ached. Her eyes drifted downward. A thick gauze bandage covered the puncture wound on her right wrist. Jutting out below the gauze, a narrow bulge had formed on her forearm. Norah snapped her head over to the opposite wrist. A similar sized bulge had formed in a corresponding spot on the underside of her left forearm. Both wrists ached in the area around each bulge. The bulges were hardening like stones beneath her skin and pressed against her wrist bones.

Her hands were in no better condition. Fingernails on both hands had grown oddly elongated and misshapen. Each one resembled animal claws more than human fingernails. Norah's hands started to tremble while she stared at them.

"What's wrong with my arms?" Her voice cracked as she shifted her gaze upward. "What's happening to me?"

Cliff stared straight ahead at her. He visibly strained to keep his worried eyes from drifting down to her arms. His face grew flushed.

"I don't know," he said. "We'll find a way to fix whatever's wrong. Whatever's infecting your body, we'll undo the damage. I promise."

His trembling lips shined a light on Cliff's hidden thoughts. She must resemble a ghoulish monster to him.

Disgusting.

Frightening.

Already, Norah sensed changes in her body not limited to her arms. Her fingers traced over the lines and contours of her face. It did not feel how a face should feel. Her back and legs also felt different. Her teeth felt different. Some had grown tight and uncomfortable like when she wore braces. Others were loose. Norah's first instinct was to find a mirror and see what was wrong. But she dreaded uncovering whatever changes a mirror would reveal to her.

Norah closed her eyes and shook her head.

No. This was a sick nightmare.

She was still Norah. The same woman who spent summer days going on long bike rides down colorful nature trails. The same shy girl who curled up on her couch with an engrossing mystery novel while sheltering from rainstorms pounding her Louisiana home.

*I am still human. On the inside.*

Norah clung to that thought. She treated it like a life preserver keeping her from sinking beneath turbulent waves forever.

"I undocked our deep space vessel from Phobos Station." Cliff cast a nervous glance over his shoulder as he shared this news. "I know the Magellan's still an untested prototype, but it's also our only feasible option for getting back to Earth in a workable timeframe."

Norah also peeked over his shoulder. No sign of Sam anywhere outside the room. She wondered what became of him. Judging by his agitated body language, Cliff did not have permission to travel home.

"Where did Sam go? If he discovers you breached quarantine—"

"Sam Bono doesn't need to know anything. That bastard tried to lock you away from me. I love you way too much to sit above that damned moon and do nothing."

Cliff removed one of his gloves and caressed her cheek. Norah pinched her eyes shut for a moment as tears rolled out. She clasped his hand, mirroring the gentle touch imparted to her. His devotion touched her deeply. A relationship first blossomed when they started this colony together. But now those feelings seemed deeper, more real than at any other time.

"Let's get you out of here," he said. "We'll find a doctor back on Earth who can help you. And who is willing to help you."

Cliff marched over to the doorway and peeked around the wall down into the corridor. Norah swung her legs over the side of the bed and stood on her feet. A wave of dizziness smacked her. She blinked rapidly, pressed her hand against her temple and drew in a deep breath.

"I think the coast is clear." Cliff cocked his head back at her. "Grab your suit and helmet. If we hurry, we can reach the Magellan before Sam discovers what we're doing."

Norah slipped into her spacesuit and fastened her helmet in place. Sudden sharp pains burst through all four limbs. The medicine Sam gave her earlier had worn off. She formed both hands into fists and cried out. Norah squeezed her fists tight and drew in a deep breath.

"I'm not changing," she whispered. "I'm still human. I'll stay human."

Norah forced herself forward, joining Cliff outside her sleep quarters. They attacked the corridor at a brisk pace. Her natural heel to toe rhythm felt different now. It had become virtual leaps off her toes, her heels barely touching. Cliff raised his hand when they reached the communal area at ground level, signaling for her to halt before anyone spotted them. Before they saw her. Norah watched anxiously as he peeked around the wall. Cliff glanced back at her, nodded, and motioned her forward. She let out a relieved sigh and they dashed toward the door leading to the airlock.

"What do you think will happen when we reach Earth?" Norah asked between breaths. "If Sam contacts the Earth Defense Bureau and reveals my condition –"

"One problem at a time," Cliff said, interrupting her concerned scenario before she shared every worry swimming in her head. "As the old saying goes, we'll cross that bridge when we come to it."

Norah clenched her teeth again. Sharp pain overloaded her nerves. Her heart pounded and her throat tightened. She panted after the pain subsided.

"I hope the bureau doesn't blow up that bridge before we reach it."

Cliff shot a concerned glance back at her as he turned the wheel to unlock the door. Those bleak words unnerved him in a visible way that matched her own emotions. Norah wanted to believe everything would work out right in the end. Her frightened mind and her changing body told a different story.

At once, metal creaked from a door cracking open. Norah's heart thumped faster. Her throat cinched tighter, and her legs grew as rigid as wood posts.

Cliff had not popped open the door leading into the airlock yet.

"What in the hell do you think you're doing?"

Norah turned and faced the door to the tunnel linking the habitat units. A scowl adorned Sam's face, perfectly matching the angry tone present in his voice.

"I'm doing what needs to be done to help Norah—unlike you."

Sam shook his head and planted himself directly between Cliff and the airlock door.

"You can't break quarantine just because you feel like doing it. These rules are in place for a good reason."

"I'm taking her somewhere else where she'll be safer and still get the help she needs."

"And where exactly is this safer destination?"

Cliff crossed his arms and glared at him.

"It sure as hell isn't this god forsaken planet. Who else is still alive down here besides us?"

Sam shook his head and glanced over at Norah. His eyes widened as soon as they settled on her.

"Your face ... has changed," he stammered. "What's ... happening to you?"

Sweat beaded on Norah's brow. Her heart raced like a distance runner unleashing a final lap kick. Changes occurring in her body were growing increasingly visible to others. If she let Sam have his way, she would never return home. He seemed more concerned about covering his own mistakes than doing anything to help her.

Cliff was right. She had to flee Mars before it grew too late to fix the damage to her body.

"Get out of my way."

A low growl followed Norah's words. Sam held up his hands, forming them into a makeshift shield in front of his throat and chest. He drew in a deep breath.

"I'm not going to hurt you, Norah." Sam adopted a soothing tone. It did not fully disguise the trembling in his throat. "I want to flush out whatever alien pathogen is messing with your body. You want the same. Stay calm."

Norah heard more footsteps. She snapped her head toward the tunnel door. Two more people entered the room, both dressed in odd looking spacesuits. Each pointed a strange weapon at her.

That told Norah all she needed to know.

"Don't tell me to stay calm!" she snapped, looking back at Sam. "You're planning to kill me!"

Sam cast his eyes back at the tunnel. When he saw weapons pointed at her, he frantically waved a hand.

"Are you two out of your minds? Don't shoot her!"

Neither weapon budged an inch. The person nearest to her tilted their head at Sam.

"Don't be a fool. Your fellow Earthian poses a serious danger to all of us."

Earthian? Norah never heard that word in her life before that moment. Why did they use such an odd term to refer to her and Sam? Were they not from Earth?

They must be different aliens.

Yes, they were aliens.

Norah stared at the one who backtalked Sam. A woman. She resembled a human with stunning violet eyes. Did her human-like appearance mean these aliens disguised themselves to deceive them? Did they bear responsibility for planting the creature here who killed so many colonists and injured Norah herself?

Her fear only intensified as these questions flooded her mind.

"Please let me handle this situation." Sam turned around and faced both aliens. "Norah needs our help. Threatening her life isn't doing anyone any good."

"You don't understand." The other alien, a man with deep blue eyes, spoke this time. "You can't undo the changes happening to her. Neither can we. She'll become like the other hybrid who attacked you."

NO!

That was a lie.

Norah gazed at Sam and Cliff and pleaded for help with her eyes. She was human now and forever. Not the first stages of some awful humanoid creature like these aliens claimed.

Cliff fixed a hard stare on both aliens.

"If you harm one hair on her, I'll make sure you won't leave this colony unharmed."

Adrenaline pumped through every blood vessel. Norah clenched her teeth and breathed hard. She was fleeing Mars and going home, Sam and his new alien friends be damned. She charged forward and pushed Sam into the aliens' path. He collided with the male alien. Both tumbled to the floor. Cliff clotheslined the female alien with his left arm and knocked her weapon from her hand. It slid across the floor.

Norah plunged headfirst inside the airlock. Cliff followed behind her as both aliens scrambled to their feet. The female alien sprinted toward her weapon, scooped it up, and fired at the closing inner door. Norah flinched at the noise and backed up against the outer door. The inner door's metallic shell prevented any weapons fire from breaching the airlock.

Cliff popped open the outer door. He grasped Norah's hand and helped her to her feet.

"Let's hurry before they can catch us."

Norah sprinted side-by-side with Cliff toward the Magellan. The weaker Martian gravity made it easier to cover ground at a faster rate than running the same distance on Earth. Instead of struggling to keep up, she found herself edging ahead of her larger companion. Her helmet partially blocked her peripheral vision. Norah dared not look back to see if anyone had followed them out of the habitat unit yet. Her thoughts focused on running forward.

Reach their deep space vessel.

Take off from Mars.

"Halt!"

A rock exploded into jagged shards on her right side. Smoke and dust climbed from the remnants. Norah glanced back over her shoulder. An alien ran in full stride a short distance behind her and Cliff. He dug into a pouch on his belt, wound up his arm, and hurled what resembled a smooth round stone in their direction. The object sailed over Norah's head and landed between Cliff and the Magellan.

A sudden bright flash enveloped her face.

Norah shrieked and pressed her hands against her protective visor. Cliff let out a pained shout at the exact same moment. She stumbled and dropped to her knees. Open or closed, nothing except a blinding whiteness invaded her eyes. What sort of weapon did the alien use on them? Norah panted and lowered her head, fearing it had permanently blinded both her and Cliff.

Sight seeped back into her eyes with a gradual grainy focus. When she pulled away her hands again, a hand wrapped around her elbow and yanked her into a standing position.

"You're not going anywhere."

She ripped her arm away and wheeled around. The alien had caught up to them. It aimed an odd-looking pistol at her chest.

"This is Ryollo." The alien spoke in a gruff deep voice. "I captured the Earthians outside their spaceship. Bringing them back to our ship now."

Norah clenched her teeth and unleashed a fearsome shout. She tackled Ryollo and knocked his weapon out of his hands. The alien landed face-first on the ground. Norah grabbed the back of his helmet and slammed Ryollo's head into partially exposed rock. The protective visor covering his face cracked like an eggshell from the force of impact.

"Help!" he shouted. "One of the Earthians—"

Norah mounted his back and wrenched the helmet off his head. Ryollo started gagging uncontrollably upon exposure to the carbon dioxide filled air. She wrapped her gloved hands around his neck and squeezed tight. Norah bared her teeth. A front tooth fell out inside her helmet and a partially exposed new fang peeked out from the empty socket.

Ryollo flailed his arms and hunched his shoulders. He tried to buck her off his spine. Norah tightened her grip. Blood dribbled through his teeth and out of the corners of his mouth. Gurgling noises followed. The alien's eyes grew glassy. His arms and torso stopped thrashing.

Norah finally relaxed her grip. Ryollo slumped to the Martian soil. His now empty eyes fixed on partially exposed regolith a few inches from his bloodied mouth.

She instinctively pressed her fingers to her visor. The loose tooth rattled around inside. Other teeth had grown loose in her gums. Soon, they would suffer the same fate. Tears splashed down from her eyes. Norah wanted to hide herself from everyone—including Cliff.

How could anyone look upon her now and see anything besides a monster?

Monster was an apt descriptor now. She choked the life from that alien to avoid capture. Norah had never so much as hurt a bug in her whole life before that moment. But a feral rage seized her once she felt threatened. It first set upon her when Sam treated her puncture wound. Only strong sedatives subdued that awful feeling. Her animalistic rage and strength grew more pronounced as her body kept changing.

"This isn't me," she whispered. Norah tried to calm herself with deep calculated breaths. "This isn't me. Oh God. I need help. I need help."

"What in the hell happened here?"

Norah cast her eyes upward. Cliff stood on his feet again, shaking his head. She did not know where to begin explaining the full story.

"The alien tried to attack us. I fought him off and removed his helmet."

Shock enveloped Cliff's face.

"You killed him?"

"I was defending myself." A trembling lilt infused her words. "I thought he chased us down, so he could kill us. I didn't mean to do it."

Cliff extended his hand. Norah grasped it and he pulled her up from the ground.

"Let's get inside the ship before anyone else catches up to us out here."

Neither one looked back or said another word about the dead alien as they climbed aboard the Magellan and started the engines. Nothing needed to be said. Norah kept reassuring herself she killed the alien in self-defense. She told herself she was no monster.

Not while she still had her mind and soul.

# 21

Xttra tumbled to the floor as Sam fell backward into his chest. Another thud against the hard floor greeted his ears. He cocked his head to the side. Kyra grasped the side of her helmet and shook her head. She pulled herself up into a kneeling position. Her speargun lay on the floor a short distance away. It popped out of her hands after Cliff knocked Kyra flat on her back when he leveled her with his forearm.

Sam groaned. Xttra shoved him off his chest and scrambled to his feet at the same time as Kyra. She dashed over to her speargun and scooped the weapon off the ground.

"Don't let them get away," Xttra said.

He scoured the floor for any sign of his eliminator. It flew out of his hand when Norah shoved her fellow Earthian into him. Two blasts rang out in quick succession. Xttra snapped his head toward the airlock. The Earthians had sealed the inner door behind him. Neither spear head Kyra fired penetrated metal, even with aid of laser reinforced cutting edges.

"That's reinforced steel," Sam said. He sat upright and drew in a deep breath. "Your weapon isn't punching a hole through the door."

Kyra shoved the speargun back inside her holster and stamped her foot.

"Wonderful. Those two have a head start on us. If they reach that ship before—"

"Does your prototype Earthian vessel possess hyperlight engines?" Xttra cut off Kyra in mid-rant. He wheeled around and faced Sam again. "Can your ship attain faster than light speeds?"

A worried frown crossed Sam's lips.

"We haven't field tested the technology on a manned vessel yet, but the bureau engineered the Magellan with the same capability for generating an artificial wormhole as the probe we sent to your planet."

Xttra glanced over Kyra. Her eyes widened at hearing Sam's revelation. She mashed down a button on the sleeve of her spacesuit.

"Two Earthians eluded capture and are fleeing for an Earthian ship. One's infected by hybrid biomaterial. Do not let them reach that ship under any circumstances."

"I'll track them down." Ryollo's voice crackled across her suit's internal communicator. "Xander and Cavac are finishing up loading the hibernation pod into a storage compartment."

"Report back when you've captured them."

Kyra peeked up at Xttra and Sam after pressing the same button a second time. She scowled. Her eyes drilled down into the Earthian.

"You put our lives at risk with your interference."

Sam raised his eyebrows and tilted his head at her.

"Say what?"

"That infected Earthian is turning into another hybrid before our eyes. She'll soon become like a wild animal and kill indiscriminately and without remorse."

"How can you say that?" Sam's voice climbed a few decibels. "Norah is the epitome of a gentle person. I shared a spaceship with her for two months. She doesn't have a single murderous bone in her body."

"Hybrid biomaterial changes both body and mind." Kyra marched over to the airlock door. "It stimulates chemicals that alter a sentient brain. Rubrum scientists who first created these creatures designed it that way."

"What do you mean?"

"Hybrids produce chemicals that stimulate violence and aggression. This causes them to attack like cornered wild animals and leave a trail of massive carnage behind."

Sam shot a concerned look at Xttra. He confirmed Kyra's words with a slow nod.

"Oh God. We need to help Norah."

"You can't save her." Xttra shook his head. A sad tone gripped his voice. "We need Rubrum bio code technology to undo the changes. None of us have access to that technology or know where to find it at this point."

Kyra cranked the wheel and popped open the inner airlock door. She stepped through the doorway and motioned for the others to follow. Sam cast his eyes to the floor and hung his head. He stood frozen in the same spot as though he had lost the will to even move.

"I wish a better solution were possible," Xttra said. "We don't have a choice."

Kyra paused outside the airlock's outer door. She tapped the same communicator control button on her forearm.

"What's your status?"

"This is Ryollo." His voice popped up a second later. "I captured the Earthians outside their spaceship. Bringing them back to our ship now."

Kyra gave an approving nod.

"Excellent work. We'll see you in a little while."

Xttra stepped through the outer door behind her. He surveyed the horizon. The mountains were still a silhouette against the sky. Streaks of pale morning light began to reveal themselves from behind the peaks. Operating in daylight would make it easier to explore the colony and flush out the remaining hidden hybrid. Xttra felt confident he would get the job done before a new sunset approached. The quicker he repaired this situation; the sooner Sam could honor his part of their agreement and help him return home to Calandra.

Kyra stopped and tapped on the side of her helmet. Xttra froze. He heard the same thing.

A desperate call for help from Ryollo.

"Help!" he shouted. "One of the Earthians—"

Static filled the communicator and then the sound stopped altogether. Xttra's limbs stiffened, and his heartbeat quickened.

"What happened now?"

He jerked his head around and saw Sam finally joining them outside.

"Something bad. I'm sure of it."

Kyra whipped out her thermal tracker. The screen showed three heat patterns near one another, south of their current position. Xttra joined her on a dead sprint toward the heat patterns. Sam struggled to match their pace and dropped back a few steps behind them. Two patterns soon moved away from the third one. Kyra and Xttra exchanged concerned glances.

Soon enough, an awful sight greeted their eyes.

A body sprawled out on the ground. Head uncovered. Their helmet, with a shattered visor, also lay on the ground a short distance away.

Kyra stopped and dropped to her knees in front of the body and brought her hands to her helmet. She cast her eyes toward Xttra and grimaced. She pinched her lips tight like she wanted to vomit even though she could not remove her helmet to do so.

His eyes trailed down to the exposed face.

Ryollo.

The Confederation officer's eyes hung open. Blood had seeped out from the corners of his mouth and down his chin. Purplish bruises covered his throat. No doubt existed in Xttra's mind that Norah choked every ounce of life out of Ryollo before he suffocated from exposure to the planet's toxic atmosphere.

Sam gasped as soon as he laid eyes on the ugly scene.

"Oh no. Cliff wouldn't do this. Norah couldn't have done it. Could she?"

Xttra wheeled around and stared down the Earthian. He scowled and stabbed a finger at the dead body.

"Now do you believe us?"

Sam quickly turned his head away. Like Kyra, he could not stomach the sight of Ryollo's fresh corpse on the frozen dry ground.

"This is a nightmare. What am I going to do?"

An explosive thunder shot out in all directions. Xttra and Sam were thrown to their knees, joining Kyra on the ground. The percussive blast sent out rolling soundwaves his helmet did nothing to absorb. Those vibrations permeated his body and shook him down to his bones. Dread seeped from his bones in response and joined the soundwaves in creating a rising panic.

They were too late to prevent Cliff and Norah from boarding their ship.

Xttra raised his arm and held it against his forehead. Flames from engine exhaust lit up the surrounding plain as though the bright morning sun had already arrived. Plumes of red dust shot upward and outward around the vehicle. The Earthian ship lifted off the ground and barreled toward the upper reaches of the thin Martian atmosphere.

A hand tugged on his arm. Xttra glanced upward.

"We need to go." Kyra pointed to the sky. "We can still catch the Earthians and bring them down before they reach the upper atmosphere if we hurry."

Their situation afforded them no time to retrieve Ryollo's body or provide him with a proper burial rite. The shaking ground jostled his body into a more natural pose, like Ahm himself foresaw this would be Ryollo's final resting place and the Confederation officer was making himself at home. Xttra wanted to protest Kyra's abandonment of her comrade, but he knew he would do the same in her situation.

He had already done the same.

Xttra scrambled to his feet and joined her on another sprint—this time to their ship. He glanced back over his shoulder. Sam's attempts to keep pace were as futile as before. Once again, he lagged several steps behind Xttra and Kyra.

"Bring our main systems online," Kyra shouted into her communicator between heavy breaths. "Plot an intercept course for the Earthian ship."

Their ship's ramp started lifting off the ground once she and Xttra set foot on it. Sam had to take an unexpected hop to clear the edge of the ramp before it ascended too high. He stumbled forward a couple of steps when he landed but managed to stay on his feet.

"Wait for me." The tone in Sam's voice grew cross. "Don't leave me behind."

Xttra glanced over his shoulder and scowled.

"Then do a better job of keeping up with us."

"Get me a better spacesuit like yours and it won't be a problem."

Sam mumbled his complaint. Loud enough to draw Xttra's attention, but not loud enough to provoke a reaction from the others.

Lights embedded in the ramp switched off once it retracted and the door sealed tight against the hatch. Kyra dashed to the pilot's chair. Xttra and Sam found seats at the back of the bridge.

"Strap in. I'm going to push this hard."

Kyra fired the main thrusters. A loud whoosh went through the bridge and the engines whined as they sprang to life. The Thetian ship lifted off the ground and then barreled upward from the colony perimeter. Sam dug his fingernails into both armrests and pressed his back tight against his chair. His eyes widened and he started to dry heave. Xttra smirked. The Earthian clearly had no prior experience with lightning-fast launches.

Kyra snapped her head toward Cavac at navigational controls. She flashed an anxious frown.

"How long before we reach the Earthian vessel?"

Cavac's ocular implant shifted and pulsated as he surveyed the other ship's projected route on his main holoscreen.

"Six minutes."

"Good. Let's bring those setaworms down."

Sam's eyes darted from the main navigational holoscreen to the pilot's chair.

"Wait a minute," he said. "You can't destroy that ship. That's our only working deep-space prototype."

"Would you rather have a murderous hybrid attacking Earth instead? Your call."

Kyra did not bother to look back at Sam. The chill in her voice told Xttra exactly what she thought of the Earthian's protests. Xttra hated to admit it, but she was right. Again. He also favored destroying the deep space vessel. They needed to kill the hybrid before others followed. Also, if they delayed the Earthians from striking out beyond the Aramus system for a few more years, all the better.

"How about you just cripple the engines and leave the ship adrift so we can salvage and repair it later?"

Xttra rolled his eyes and looked away from Sam. He hoped Kyra was not giving serious weight to keeping the Earthian vessel intact.

"Fine. You've got your wish."

Xttra scowled and shook his head. Once again, Kyra let her desire to form an alliance with Earth cloud her judgement.

"Thank you," Sam replied.

"Tell us where to target the wormhole generator," Kyra tapped an index finger on the weapons holoscreen. "We'll cook their engines and strand them in orbit around this planet."

Twin red lines wound across the navigational holoscreen. One denoted their ship. The other one tracked the Earthian vessel. Xttra's eyes stayed glued to the holoscreen, watching while the distance between both lines grew narrower.

Sky yielded to space. Soon, the Earthian ship came into visual range. It resembled a drum topped by a cone shaped cap. Four long thin rectangular arms filled with solar panels jutted out from the rear of the spacecraft. Xttra spotted no visible weaponry as they approached.

"What sort of weaponry does your Earthian vessel carry?" Xander glanced over his shoulder at Sam. "And how do we neutralize those weapons?"

Xttra shifted in his chair and gazed at Sam as well. Images flooded his mind of weaponry used on him and his crew during their prior expedition to this solar system. The Earthian attack vessels used tracking missiles to crash their aerorovers.

"Railguns. Missiles. Mines."

Sam ticked each weapon he mentioned off on his fingertips. Xttra bit down on his lower lip. Some things about the Earthians never changed. Their violent natures were on display again. A prototype deep space vessel. Brimming with tools of destruction.

"You better activate some defense shields." Xttra said, turning toward the helm. "Or else this will be a short pursuit for all the wrong reasons."

Kyra glanced over at Xander and gave him an abrupt nod. Her assistant pilot toggled a pair of switches at his console and pushed a small lever upward. A protective energy shell enveloped the outer hull.

"Where is the wormhole generator?" Kyra asked.

A shockwave rippled through their shield. The entire bridge quaked and sent vibrations through Xttra's chair. An alarm blared on the bridge.

"They're firing on us," Xander said.

Kyra frowned and unleashed an irritated sigh.

"I know. I'm not blind. Lock on their weapons and blast them with our plasma cannon."

She wrenched her steering stick to the opposite side. The ship dipped downward. Another explosion. A second shockwave. More tremors followed. Xttra wondered why Xander was taking so long to fire back. Running the Thetian weapons systems should not carry such a high degree of difficulty.

"I can't take much more of this."

Sam locked his fingers into a death grip on his seat's armrests a second time.

"Neither can our ship," Xttra replied.

Bolts shot out from the plasma cannon. One hit a rear solar arm. A cloud of solar panel shards burst from the arm. Another bolt grazed the underside of the hull, leaving a black scorch mark.

At once, a long barrel popped out of a port on the underside of the Earthian vessel. A bolt blasted back at their ship and struck the energy shell. Ocean wave-like ripples formed in the shield and the entire shell dissipated within a matter of seconds.

Lights and holoscreens blanked and shut down across the bridge. Darkness washed over the entire ship.

Kyra slammed her fist on the helm console.

"An electromagnetic blast. We're dead in the water."

Everyone watched helplessly as a small wormhole formed ahead of the Earthian vessel. It shot forward into the wormhole before it closed again.

"How long before that ship reaches Earth?" Xttra asked, peering at Sam.

"The Magellan only generates stable wormholes long enough to permit long distance subluminal travel for a few minutes," he said. "But it's still long enough to shave a journey from Mars to Earth from several months down to a few days or less."

A series of running lights blinked on across the bridge. Xttra unloaded a relieved sigh. The Thetians had equipped their vessel with a secondary power system shielded from electromagnetic pulses. At least, they would not remain stranded above Mars until restoring primary power.

"Secondary power is online," Cavac said. He turned and faced the helm. "What are your orders?"

Kyra peered down at the planet's atmosphere below the ship. She closed her eyes and pinched the bridge of her nose.

"We're heading back to the surface," she said, opening her eyes again. "We still haven't accounted for the original hybrid. And I'll feel better about pursuing the other vessel to Earth once our primary power systems are back in working order."

Kyra pointed the nose of the ship toward the atmosphere and began their descent back to the colony. Xttra questioned if they had enough time to dispatch the hybrid still on Mars, repair this ship, and reach Earth before the infected Earthian did.

His instincts told him the odds were not going to end up in their favor.

# 22

If Kevin were here now, Calandra imagined how he would react to the startling information she uncovered inside the Central Archives. Her Earthian friend raised a warning voice on multiple occasions during the months prior to Xttra's abduction. She wished she had listened instead of dismissing his words as growing out of homesickness for Earth.

Kevin grew increasingly restless after settling in Ra'ahm. Calandra first took note of his agitated state on the day she married Xttra. He shifted in his seat and his eyes darted about during their marriage rite.

Calandra noted Kevin's discomfort in her peripheral vision. She devoted the bulk of her attention to Xttra as they knelt before opposite sides of a polished stone altar and faced each other. Staring into her soulmate's deep blue eyes on that day brought her such deep joy. He flashed a warm smile as he clasped both of Calandra's outstretched hands over the altar.

Kevin sought them out soon after the rite concluded to offer his congratulations. He dug into his pocket and placed a small square box in the palm of Calandra's artificial hand. The box was composed of senosa wood chips stitched together. She glanced down at it and flashed a bright smile at him.

"A gift? How thoughtful of you! This is wonderful."

Kevin returned the smile.

"It's for both of you. Open it up."

Calandra pulled off the lid with her natural hand. A pair of gold-colored rings lay inside the box. Simple bands with no jewels.

"Back on Earth, couples exchange rings as part of their wedding ceremony. The rings symbolize two uniting as one. I know exchanging rings is not a marriage tradition here on Lathos, but I thought you'd both appreciate the symbolism."

Xttra picked up a ring and turned it over in his hand. An appreciative smile crossed his lips.

"We'll cherish this gift."

"Put it on Calandra's ring finger." Kevin pointed to his own ring finger. "And then she takes the other one and puts it on your ring finger."

Xttra slid the ring on Calandra's right hand, and she mirrored his action. His arm circled her back, and he drew Calandra in to share a tender kiss. When their lips parted again, she stepped back and clasped Xttra's hand with her natural one.

Kevin partook in the celebration following the rite. Calandra sought him out when she spotted him trying to leave the temple grounds unnoticed. His troubled body language during the rite still weighed on her mind.

Calandra flashed a joyful smile at him as she and Xttra caught up to him before he reached the walls.

"I'm so happy you could share this special day with us. You may not be part of our clan by blood, but you are a part by friendship."

"I wish all your people were as welcoming. I can't shake the feeling I'm being watched."

Kevin turned and peered over his shoulder after saying these words. Calandra and Xttra exchanged puzzled glances. She raised her eyebrows in concern and gazed at their Earthian friend.

"I know how difficult it is adjusting to a new planet." Calandra tried to adopt a reassuring tone. "Some people in Ra'ahm have never met a real alien. Don't worry about them. Lathos will feel like home soon enough."

Kevin gave his best attempt at responding with a sincere smile, but he could not disguise the worry swimming in his eyes.

"I spent enough years in the US Army to recognize when someone is spying on me," he said. "I don't think your chief sovereign wants me to feel 'at home' here."

Xttra's smile turned into a half-frown.

"What are you saying?"

Kevin licked his lips and shook his head. He rubbed his hand down part of his left cheek.

"You know what I'm saying. Delcor sees my presence as a threat to him. This isn't the best time or place to dive into it, but I've got some evidence I want you to see. I'm not making this up."

Calandra dismissed his claims, even after he later shared the compelling evidence he gathered. She refused to believe their chief sovereign was capable of the actions Kevin alleged. She thought her Earthian friend had been deceived by Confederation propaganda. Now, as she recalled his words, she wished she had given what he said more serious weight. He did his best to warn them. Neither she nor Xttra chose to listen. What she found in the Central Archives seemed to confirm what Kevin shared. Those unwanted revelations shook Calandra to the depths of her soul.

She stepped out on her balcony and leaned against the railing. Calandra cast her eyes toward a telescope stationed in front of a wooden chair on the left end of the balcony. So many nights she spent gazing into the sky, wondering where Xttra was among those stars. What would he do if he were here now? How would he deal with the uncomfortable facts she uncovered? Loneliness gripped Calandra more than usual on a night like this one. If only he were here so they could face this together.

If only she knew where to look for him.

Her eyes drifted upward, first toward Laxa and then settling on Fengar. Both moons shone bright while hovering above peaks of the Aurora mountains.

"Please help me find him," she whispered. "Ahm, please bring Xttra home."

Calandra's eyes drifted down and settled on her artificial arm. It rested on the railing. She drummed her fingers and studied each one as they moved. Why did her clan doctor struggle to obtain a fully functioning neural sensor? Weeks bled into months without him making progress on that front. Yet, Ominade supplied her with exactly what she wanted and needed on the spot.

The whole ordeal aroused her suspicions now. Did her clan doctor intentionally deceive her? Calandra wondered if someone wanted her to focus on struggling with a defective artificial hand rather than taking note of the world around her. She did not want to yield to paranoia. Still, the thought someone would purposefully put her through this ordeal ate at her.

What right did they have to toy with her life?

She turned and faced the balcony doors. Calandra stared through the glass at the contact block Ominade gave to her earlier. The block sat on an end table next to the couch. It silently beckoned to her to reach out and probe deeper. Find more answers. The ancient letter engraved on the block symbolized hope.

Hope for a better world.

That's what Calandra needed. She needed to create a better world. For herself and Xttra. A world where they could be together again.

Calandra walked back inside her apartment and pushed a button on an artificial candle occupying a spot on the end table. A glass covering shaped like a flame topped the candlestick. Dim white light from a luminal shaft flickered on inside the glass. It gradually grew stronger until flooding the room. She snatched up Ominade's block and pressed down on the letter.

It began glowing around the edges.

Calandra studied the block, wondering what would happen next. Ominade said she or one of her fellow rebels would make contact. How? She dismissed using an arca vox in their conversation earlier, labeling it an unsecured communication channel.

This all seemed insane. Calandra's eyes fell on her arca vox resting on the table in front of her couch. She should contact Bo'un or Alayna. Or speak with her parents and press them to discuss the real reason her grandfather resigned his office and left Lathos.

A knock came at her door. Calandra cocked her head toward the door. Who would pay her a visit at such a late hour? She set the metal block down on the table again. Calandra hesitated to move, standing fixed to the same spot next to her end table.

Knock.

She tiptoed to the door, trying not to make audible footsteps. Calandra pressed a square black button on a panel affixed to the wall bordering the door. Visual and thermal sensors sprang to life on the other side. A little screen embedded in the panel showed a stocky freckle faced man standing in the hallway. Calandra scrunched up her face and released it into an annoyed frown. She opened the door. It slid into a slot with a whoosh.

"This isn't an ideal time for a visit. What can I do for you, Dal?"

Dal brushed back his blond curls from his forehead and grinned.

"I just finished watching an exciting maniogo race and since I happened to be in the neighborhood, I thought I'd come over and check on you. See how you're holding up."

"There's no maniogo racing in this district. That's more of a Luma Flats activity."

"My definition of neighborhood is a bit broader than your definition, I guess."

Calandra sighed. A distinct robust aroma greeted her nostrils. She sniffed and twisted her mouth. Uzakian Ale. Laced through Dal's breath.

"Go home. Sleep off your excess ale."

Dal laughed and shrugged.

"I only had half a jug." He held up his thumb and index finger. "Just a small amount."

Calandra glanced over her shoulder and back at him.

"You should have contacted me on my arca vox if you wanted to chat. Why are you actually here?"

Dal rubbed his hand down his face.

"We miss you at the observatory."

"That's sweet."

"I miss you at the observatory."

Calandra gulped.

"This isn't going where I think it's going, is it?"

His piercing blue eyes trailed down past her neck. Calandra instinctively draped her arm across her chest. Dal stumbled a bit as he looked downward before catching his balance.

"I've always wanted to date you but never had the courage to ask. You're so warm, happy, and—"

"Dal, I'm married. You know that."

He squinted while trying to peek over Calandra's shoulder into her apartment.

"Where is your husband anyhow?"

"Please go home."

She stepped back and raised her arm to seal the door. Dal's eyes trailed over to the limb. He cracked a broad grin again.

"Your new arm seems to be working fine. Tell me, why haven't you returned to the observatory yet?"

Calandra jabbed a finger at him.

"Leave. Now. Or should I alert city guards to come escort you out of here?"

Dal threw his hands up and gave her a grouchy stare.

"So sorry to bother you. May Ahm smile upon you."

Calandra sealed the door again as her former colleague stumbled down the hall toward the elevator. She sighed and buried her face in her hands. Dal visiting her in a drunken stupor did not register as a life event she needed to experience at this moment.

Two beeps sounded from the sensor panel in rapid succession. Was Dal outside the door again? When did her apartment suddenly turn into a sky tram station? Calandra stepped back and glared at the screen. An unidentified person with a hood covering their head stood outside her door. Their back faced the wall.

Calandra opened the door a second time.

"Seriously, Dal, if I have to keep telling you to leave me alone ..."

She trailed off when her visitor turned to face her and threw back his hood. Calandra's mouth dropped open when she laid eyes on his face. Her legs stiffened and became rooted to the floor like tree trunks.

Kevin stood before her.

# 23

A tidal wave of questions flooded Calandra's mind. She spoke none into existence. All she did was stare at Kevin. This bordered on impossible. A lucid dream simulating reality without being real. He fled Lathos. Efforts to track him down led to Xttra's abduction in the first place. Now her Earthian friend stood before her as though nothing had happened over the past few months.

"Hello, Calandra."

Kevin greeted her with a warm smile. She blinked rapidly and drew in a deep breath.

"Xttra told me you fled to a dissident colony on Fengar. I never thought I'd see you again."

"Life takes you down unexpected roads."

"You left without saying a word."

"What was I supposed to say?" Kevin frowned and shoved his hands inside the pockets of a deep brown jacket covering his light gray uniform. "'Guess what? Old Delcor wants to assassinate me because I got the goods on him, so I'm blowing this popsicle stand. Peace out.'"

Calandra stared at his hands while he made an Earthian gesture he referred to as air quotes. A confused look washed over her face when she made eye contact with him again.

"Why would you blow a popsicle stand? What is a popsicle stand? Peace out? Huh?"

"They're common Earth expressions. In other words, I didn't feel safe sticking around."

An urge to chide Kevin for his flippant attitude blossomed inside Calandra. She brushed it aside. He had every reason to not bid her or Xttra farewell before he fled from Ra'ahm.

Calandra insisted Kevin let his imagination take control of him and quickly dismissed his concerns during their most recent conversation. Xttra's reaction proved no better. He downplayed everything Kevin learned concerning Delcor's crimes. Pangs of guilt sprouted within her as she recalled that whole episode. He had every right to feel hurt and distrust both her and Xttra going forward. Kevin sacrificed his old life on Earth for their sake. They did not stand by him when he was right.

Calandra was better prepared to listen now after what she and Alayna uncovered in the Central Archives.

"I was wrong to ignore your earlier warning," she said apologetically. "I hope you can forgive me. I believe you now, for what it's worth."

Kevin's smile returned.

"I wasn't mad at you. You've known nothing except Delcor's regime your whole life. I guess I couldn't expect you to reject the cult of personality surrounding him overnight."

Calandra stepped forward without saying a word and wrapped her arms around Kevin. Her arms passed through his body. She gasped and stepped back a few steps. Calandra stared at him with unblinking eyes and trembling lips.

"Are you—"

"I'm not a ghost, if that's what you're thinking."

"Then, how ... what happened to you?"

"I'm not standing outside your door in the literal sense. Some cool high-tech equipment is making it possible for me to be here."

High-tech equipment? Calandra wheeled around. Her eyes fell on the glowing block inside her living room. It pulsated more brightly than before Kevin showed up. She turned to face him again and pointed back at the block.

"Did that device beam your image here?"

"More or less. Your block sends a signal to a corresponding block on my end. Then, I activate a virtual imaging chamber, step inside and, poof, here I am."

"How can you see me?"

"Your contact block casts a particle field filled with light waves not visible to human eyes. When it broadcasts a signal back to my end, the imaging chamber picks up the signal and recreates everything inside the particle field. This lets me see my surroundings and move anywhere within the field."

"That's ... amazing."

"It resembles an Earth technology called virtual reality in some respects, only this is actual reality here."

Her eyes drifted over to the sensor panel. He showed up on the screen like a flesh-and-blood person. Still, the sensors detected no thermal data. Kevin amounted to nothing more than a projection. He felt more real, though, than anything she had ever seen on a holoscreen. His voice did not emanate from the block. His body was not partially transparent. He stood before her with the color and dimensions of a solid tangible person.

Calandra beckoned to him. Kevin walked through the doorway, and she sealed the door behind him.

"If you're not here physically, where are you exactly?"

"A safe place. Far from the reach of Delcor's agents."

Calandra frowned. He answered her question without really answering her question.

"How do you know Ominade?" she asked. "Did she track you down like me?"

"I first met her one day after finishing my usual morning run near my old apartment. She's quite an unusual character but, damn, she's plugged into what's actually going on around here."

Calandra nodded. Admitting Ominade spoke the truth made her heart heavy. She still did not want to believe people she once trusted fed her a lifetime's worth of lies. What she uncovered with her own eyes forced her to accept that the chief sovereign and other Ra'ahm leaders were lying.

"Now you work for her."

"I want to help others learn the truth about Delcor. Ominade offers the best avenue for making that possible."

Calandra turned and walked to her studio. Kevin followed on her heels.

"What is her goal? Insurrection? Revolution? I'm not sure I'm comfortable getting involved with such things."

Kevin pinched his lips together and shook his head.

"Your life has changed forever. It doesn't matter if you like it or if you want it. You can't run away and hide from this new reality."

Calandra opened the studio door. She turned and beckoned him to join her inside. After Kevin entered the studio, Calandra marched straight up to Xttra's portrait on the opposite wall.

"I've never once hidden since this ordeal began." She tapped the bottom of the painting while turning back to face him. "Xttra is still missing. Weeks and months pass by without a word. Yet, I persevere and fight to find him."

Fear filled Kevin's eyes as he stared at the painting of Xttra. He licked his lips and rubbed his hand down the side of his neck.

"Xttra is missing?"

"Didn't Ominade tell you? Abducted from Fengar. While attempting to track you down no less."

Kevin lowered his head and gazed at the floor.

"I had no idea." His voice grew quiet. "Calandra, I'm so sorry. I didn't mean for such an awful thing to happen. I tried to keep you both out of this mess."

"It's not your fault."

She stepped away from the painting and turned around, squaring her shoulders toward Kevin.

"Bo'un thinks someone set a trap," Calandra continued. "He's probably right. My original theory was Confederation agents abducted Xttra and took him back to your home planet because he stopped their first contact with your world."

Kevin wrenched his head upward. His eyes widened.

"Earth? You think someone took him back to Earth?"

"Now, after learning what I learned at the Central Archives, I don't know what to believe." Calandra ignored his question. "I feel like I'm starting over in trying to learn what became of him. Maybe the chief sovereign just wanted to—"

Her voice stuck on that word. Calandra could not finish the thought resting on her tongue. The chief sovereign would not murder Xttra.

Would he?

"What did you find out in your archives? Is this why you sent a contact signal to Ominade?"

Calandra swallowed hard and closed her eyes. Repeating aloud what she read in those records caused her to experience distress anew.

"I learned the same things you learned." She opened her eyes again and shook her head. "Our chief sovereign tried to murder the former prime oracle and may have assassinated his own father. The worst part is my own grandfather uncovered evidence proving he did these things and turned a blind eye."

"That's not all I learned."

A crease formed in Calandra's brow.

"What do you mean? What else did you find out?"

"Your former prime oracle is alive."

She tilted her head at him. Her eyes blinked rapidly, betraying her lingering disbelief in Kevin's revelation.

"Where is he? Xttra told me before his abduction you claimed to have evidence Valadius is alive. If you do, where has he been this whole time?"

Kevin turned without saying a word and marched out of the studio. Calandra scrambled after him, wondering where he was going. He stopped in front of the balcony doors and thrust his index finger at a night sky lit by dozens of visible stars.

"Beyond this solar system. Hidden in a place called the Land of the Three Suns."

Calandra's mouth fell open. She pressed her hand to her lips and stepped back from him. Her eyes drifted from Kevin over to a copy of the *Book of Ahm* laying on the end table flanking her couch.

"Are you familiar with such a place?"

She nodded without looking over at Kevin. Calandra walked over to the table and picked up the *Book of Ahm*. She cracked open the cover and thumbed through thin pliable metallic pages.

"Only from what I've read in the *Book of Ahm*. The Land of the Three Suns is an ancient land of refuge on a secluded world placed among hidden stars by Ahm himself. Only pure and humble souls are allowed passage to this land."

Calandra stopped on a page referencing the Land of Three Suns within the book. She walked over to Kevin and showed him the open page. He leaned forward and studied the words, written in the Confederation Universal language, as she steadied the book in her hand.

"I always assumed it served as an allegory for Ahm's dwelling in the eternal worlds," Calandra said. "Are you saying such a place actually exists?"

Kevin raised his chin and nodded.

"It does. And I can show you exactly where this so-called ancient refuge is located."

"Show me."

Kevin motioned for her to follow him and passed through the closed balcony doors. She cringed. Calandra understood he came to her apartment as a virtual image, but it still seemed uncomfortably strange to see him passing through solid objects. Calandra set down the *Book of Ahm* in its former spot on the table and joined him out on the balcony a few seconds later.

"You know where to find the Sun—my home sun—in your telescope over there, right?"

Calandra cracked a wry smile.

"You know you're talking to an astronomer, right?"

"How could I forget?"

She sauntered over to the telescope and removed the cap covering the lens. Calandra pressed a button on the side to activate an adjacent holocaster. It rested on a platform fused to a metal band circling the bottom of the telescope. A holoscreen popped up over the holocaster, displaying a three-dimensional image of distant stars barely larger than dots of light. Her telescope pointed to a section of sky directly above the Aurora Mountains.

Calandra adjusted the settings on the telescope and rotated the lens toward the southern sky as she peered through it. Soon, a faint speck of yellow light appeared on the holoscreen. Aramus formed the end point on a zigzag constellation incorporating several other stars.

"There you go. Aramus." Calandra leaned back from the telescope and glanced over at Kevin. "Now what?"

"Back on Earth, we had a constellation called the Southern Cross," he said. "It was visible in the southern hemisphere of my planet. A pair of pointer stars directed where to find the constellation in the night sky. I know the layout of the stars is different here on Lathos, but it shouldn't be radically different from Earth."

"What am I looking for?"

"A bright star pointing to the Southern Cross. The stars form a pattern matching this symbol."

Kevin pressed one index finger against the other. He held one finger vertical and laid the other horizontal across the vertical finger's knuckle. Calandra studied the symbol Kevin formed with his fingers for a moment and turned back to her telescope.

Aramus vanished off the holoscreen as she moved the telescope lens and zeroed in on the new coordinates. When Calandra pinpointed the approximate spot Kevin described, images from multiple faint stars hovered above the holocaster.

Three faint stars.

Calandra pulled away from the telescope and leaned back in her chair. She rested her chin in her hand as she stared at the three faint balls of light on the holoscreen. The triangular shape they formed resembled the image inscribed in the book's pages. This seemed too surreal. That ancient refuge detailed within the *Book of Ahm* was no mere legend.

"I can't believe it," she said, glancing up at Kevin again. "I'm actually seeing the Land of the Three Suns with my own eyes."

"On Earth, we called the brightest star Alpha Centauri," he said. "This is the closest star system to my home solar system. There's no doubt in my mind you'll find Valadius living on a habitable planet orbiting one of those three stars."

Calandra turned and gazed at the three distant stars again. She crossed her arms as she studied the holoscreen image. Her brows knitted together. A disconcerted scowl formed on her lips.

"Why did he flee? He should have stood tall and shined a light on our chief sovereign's crimes. The prime oracle had the power to expose him. And he had the responsibility to take that action."

"Do you really think he could have stood against Delcor and succeeded?"

"He is—or was—the spiritual leader of Ra'ahm. Who else would the people believe?"

Kevin shrugged.

"I can't answer that question for you. Overthrowing a dictator never comes easy. Back on Earth, it usually took a war to do the deed."

"What do I do now? If I'm truly in danger—"

"I can connect you with an underground refugee network. They helped me escape from Ra'ahm. They'll do the same for you."

Calandra rose from her chair and walked over to the balcony railing. She leaned against the railing. Kevin joined her at the railing as she gazed at the Aurora Mountains on the horizon.

Worry splashed over her face like a billowing ocean wave. Luma was home. Ra'ahm was home. Could she leave the only home she ever knew, her family and friends, and never return? It amounted to another sacrifice Calandra felt unprepared to make.

Still, if their chief sovereign truly counted her as a threat, who knew what measures he would take against her? Calandra's time on Earth taught her in a painful fashion to never assume things could not take a quick turn in a bad direction.

"Once we get you safely out of Luma, I'll help you find Xttra again," Kevin said. "We'll track him down together."

Calandra turned and faced him. Tears rolled down both cheeks.

"Thank you."

Kevin smiled and saluted her. His image vanished a second later. Calandra cast her eyes at the balcony doors. The contact block inside her apartment ceased glowing and resumed its normal appearance.

# 24

Xttra stared at the images playing on his holocaster. Despair squeezed his heart with sharp talons and became etched on his face. He longed to be with Calandra again. See her bright smile. Feel her warm embrace. Her absence cast a never-ending cloud on his life. It haunted him when he closed his eyes or even if he kept them open.

He gazed upon the visual record of their marriage rite. These images occupied the most treasured position among the records detailing their adventures together stored on his holocaster.

Calandra's natural radiant beauty shone even brighter on that day. She dressed in a traditional clan dress for the rite. Her violet dress wrapped around her body and fell to her ankles. A lace sash bound the dress together at the waist. Matching gloves extended to the elbow on both arms. A thin circlet woven from fresh flowers adorned her head, nestled amid Calandra's auburn locks.

Xttra tried to match her with his high-collared forest green tunic—his clan's traditional wedding attire. Both her dress and her beauty overshadowed what he wore. Not that he minded.

Xttra could not take his eyes off his beautiful bride as she approached the smooth stone altar. Her green eyes sparkled, and her smile was breathtaking. It lit up the room more than sunlight shining through long vertical windows adorning the temple walls. They knelt on opposite sides of the stone altar and faced each other. Both stretched their arms across the altar. Xttra grasped her hands and matched Calandra's joyful smile.

A high cleric stepped on a square platform adjoining the altar. He adjusted the top of his robe around his neck and smiled indulgently at the young couple.

"Ahm, our divine creator, smiles upon you this day," he said. "Two souls intertwined in love. Companions becoming one in his eyes."

The high cleric recited the words of the marriage covenant. He admonished Xttra and Calandra to pledge love and devotion to each other above all others. Then, he promised their union would ignite a candle flame that never dims, become calm waters that guided their vessel to safe harbors, and grow into a sturdy tree sheltering them through all seasons.

"Do you bind yourself to accept this covenant with Ahm and each other this day?" the high cleric asked after finishing his recitation.

Xttra glanced up at him and nodded. He fixed his gaze upon Calandra again.

"This day and forever, I pledge to be one with Calandra as her husband."

Calandra mirrored his actions.

"This day and forever, I pledge to be one with Xttra as his wife."

The high cleric gave an approving nod. He laid his palm upon the crown of Xttra's head, and he bowed before Calandra. Then, the cleric did the same with her. She also bowed her head before Xttra.

"In the eyes of Ahm, you are joined as companions in this life and in the eternal worlds."

Calandra and Xttra both lifted their heads again. They simultaneously leaned over the altar and shared a tender kiss to seal the marriage rite.

Tears swam in Xttra's eyes while he relived these memories. Being apart from her tormented him more than anything else he experienced during his current ordeal. These many months apart had to be equally excruciating for her, not knowing what became of him.

"How long have you been apart from her? This must be really tough on both of you."

Xttra sighed when Sam's intruding voice greeted his ears. He brushed away the tears and pressed a button on his holocaster. The holoscreen vanished. These memories were meant for his and Calandra's eyes alone, not some unwelcome Earthian who had tried to kill them and did not value privacy.

"What do you want?"

Xttra did not bother to look at Sam when he posed his question. He abruptly rose from his chair inside the crew sleep quarters and shoved the holocaster back inside his chest pouch.

"Kyra thinks we've got a lock on the other hybrid. We're gearing up to go back inside the habitat unit."

Xttra wheeled around and faced Sam.

"Is that it?"

Sam cast his eyes at the floor and licked his lips. An uncomfortable silence formed between them. Xttra folded his arms and his eyes hardened into an unbroken stare.

"A penny for your thoughts?" Sam finally said. He lifted his head and locked eyes with Xttra. "Sometimes it helps to share what's on your mind."

"Why would I want some worthless Earthian coin? I don't want to talk to you."

"Why?"

Xttra answered him with a dismissive scoff. His annoyed scowl returned a second later.

"I don't trust you."

Sam's eyes trailed down to the pouch where the holocaster rested and back up to him again.

"I'm trying to do better this time. Please give me a chance to make things right between us."

"How can you ever make things right?" Xttra's voice climbed a few decibels as anger wrapped around him. "Calandra will never be the same. I'll never be the same. We came to your wretched planet as peaceful explorers and were lucky to escape with our lives."

"I'm sorry. What we did to you has haunted me nonstop since you left Earth."

Xttra tossed up his hands and flashed a sardonic grin.

"All better. Say it one more time. Maybe your next apology will bring back my crew members your people slaughtered or restore Calandra's arm to her."

Sam turned away as a frown deepened on his lips and headed for the exit.

"Hopefully, I can convince you to forgive me at some point. I don't want bad blood to exist between us Xttra. Or between your planet and Earth."

Xttra clenched his fist and pressed it into his other open palm. He bit down on his lower lip. An urge to hurl a large object at the Earthian bubbled up inside him.

He released a deep sigh, tightened the straps on his armored sleeves, and headed back to the bridge. Kyra struck him as an impatient and cunning woman. Xttra decided to head off a potential confrontation before one had a chance to materialize and take part in hunting the hybrid without argument. He did not trust Sam's ability to enforce the truce and release he brokered earlier.

Kyra gave Xttra a cursory glance when he rejoined the others on the bridge.

"How long before our primary power systems are up and running again?" She asked, looking back at Cavac.

The melder studied a power control terminal on the back end of the bridge. Cavac had laid out an assortment of tools before him to fix or replace components fried from the electromagnetic blast.

"No more than two hours. Hopefully, I can get us fully online again within an hour."

"Excellent. The rest of us will dispose of that hybrid still lurking around this colony."

She turned and faced the others.

"Let's make this quick before the hybrid can do any further damage."

Kyra whipped out her thermal tracker and entered the cargo bay. Xttra, Xander, and Sam filed in after her. Xttra snapped his helmet in place as the door leading to the bridge sealed behind him. He cinched his armored sleeves tight over his arms a second time. Xttra normally did not wear these weapons with a spacesuit and worried about their fit around the bulky protective material. Still, it gave him quick access to both his razor discs and arm saber if the hybrid somehow ambushed him.

Xander opened the rear hatch and lowered the ramp. Pale yellow-white rays from the distant rising sun flooded the red rock plain before the ship. Xttra's environmental readings on his visor displayed correctly. He drew in a deep breath and followed a step behind Kyra and Xander as they approached the habitat units.

"I'm detecting a definite heat pattern," she said. "Our hybrid is inside the same building where the infected Earthian made her escape."

"I was afraid of that," Sam shook his head as he opened the airlock's outer door. "I didn't think we could keep it trapped inside the other unit for much longer."

She turned and glanced at him.

"It isn't getting out of this one as long as everyone here follows my lead."

Xttra rolled his eyes. He silently vowed to take charge once they finally cornered the hybrid. His odds of survival were better that way.

Sam sealed the outer door behind them and opened the inner door. The shell bore deep blast marks and crinkled metal in spots Kyra's speargun struck earlier. An eerie quiet permeated the ground level of the structure.

"Where is it?" Sam's voice barely climbed above a whisper. "There's limited space in this place where the creature can hide."

Kyra pointed to the ceiling.

"One level directly above us. Keep your eyes and ears open. These hybrids are all genetically designed to be killers."

Xttra's eyes darted from wall to wall. Even with thermal trackers at their disposal, an apprehension enclosed him and squeezed his nerves like an unseen hand. Blind corners peppered the inside of this building. What if he ended up on the wrong end of a surprise attack from one of these hidden spots?

The foursome rounded the first blind spot in the corridor leading from the ground level to the next level. Pale sunlight hit green leaves on plants from a vertical garden climbing up a central interior wall. The wall formed a half-circle around a small room serving as living quarters for a single colonist.

"My tracker shows the hybrid is on the other side of this wall," Kyra said. "Circle around and approach the room from opposite directions."

She motioned Sam and Xander to go left. Xttra stayed with Kyra on the right. They circled around the wall and stopped in front of an alcove. It held a padded bench set against a thin wall. A glass block window flanked one side of the wall and a sealed door flanked the other side. The door employed a recessed handle for opening and closing but had no visible lock or keyhole.

"Is this door locked?"

Kyra whispered her question to Sam, trying not to tip off the hybrid inside the room to their presence. He shrugged. She sighed and motioned to Xttra and Xander as she unlatched her holster. All three drew their sidearms. Xander and Kyra brandished spearguns. Xttra brought out his eliminator.

"Obliterate that thing," Kyra said.

All three opened fire at the same time. Spear heads ripped holes through the glass block window. Shards of glass popped out and blanketed the floor. Laser bolts punched other holes through the alcove wall and door. Fresh scorch marks and tiny plumes of smoke peppered both objects once they finally stopped firing.

"Let's crack that door open now," she said.

Xander unlatched the Aracian cutter from his belt. He jammed the laser-reinforced blade between the door and the jamb and sliced through the locks. Xttra reached down and pulled a stun pebble from a pouch on his belt.

"Better safe than sorry," he said.

Xander and Kyra cast their eyes at the stun pebble and stepped back. Xttra approached the door, now riddled with holes, and tossed the stun pebble toward a bed inside the room. He turned and pinched his eyelids shut. A blinding flash emanated from the open doorway. No panicked screams nor growls followed the bright blue-white light discharging from the micro ports.

"Is the alien creature dead?" Sam whispered.

"If it's still alive, that hybrid is one tough –"

Xttra paused after he stepped through the door. An overturned bed and chair greeted his eyes. Both obscured sight lines inside the room. Holes from laser bolts and spent spear heads pockmarked each one.

"Where is it?" Xttra snapped his head back at Kyra. Fear crawled into his eyes. "Where is it hiding?"

Kyra whipped out her tracker. Xttra turned and studied the displaced furniture again. His eyes trailed over both bed and chair, and across the floor, while he searched for a blood trail or other signs of the hybrid's location inside the room.

"I'm picking up a heat pattern behind—"

A low growl cut Kyra off. Xttra lifted his head. The chair flew straight at him. He threw up his forearm and it struck his elbow, knocking him to the floor.

Xttra landed on his side. He scrambled to his knees just as the hybrid wrenched off a helmet. The creature bared fangs and snarled as it charged at him.

"For the glory and liberty of Ra'ahm!"

Those words slithered out of the hybrid's mouth at the same moment a stinger made from bone popped out from its forearm. Xttra pressed a button on his armored sleeve, unleashing his arm saber. He ducked his head to avoid the stinger and punched the saber upward.

His aim was true.

The hybrid groaned and clutched its belly when Xttra withdrew the blade again. Dark red blood seeped out between the creature's fingers. Kyra and Xander fired their spearguns. Two laser-reinforced spear heads punched new holes in the hybrid's chest and right leg.

It staggered backward. Xttra rose to his feet. He grabbed the hybrid by the shoulder and plunged the saber straight into its chest. The volcanic glass blade ripped through the creature's heart like worn fabric. It let out a violent cough and fresh blood dribbled down its chin.

Xttra retracted the saber and shoved the hybrid backward. It stumbled to the floor and let out a loud gasp. The creature's eyes became empty, and its muscles stopped twitching a second later.

"That was a close call." Sam's voice trembled even as he tried to express relief. "I started having flashbacks to the attack I survived in the lab."

Xttra turned around and blasted an immediate scowl at the others.

"It was a closer call than it needed to be," he snapped. "Were you all waiting to see if the hybrid skewered me before taking action?"

"Everything happened so fast," Sam replied.

Xttra stabbed an index finger at him.

"You didn't even fire a weapon!"

Xander answered him with a dismissive wave.

"You survived. We survived. Quit whining about it."

He turned away and walked out of the alcove. Xttra lowered his eyebrows and clenched his jaw. A few choice words sat on the tip of his tongue. He bit his tongue and resisted a growing urge to unload a new verbal jab at the Confederation setaworm. It did not merit risking his tenuous freedom.

"Get back here."

Xander stopped and turned around as soon as he heard Kyra's order.

"We need to haul this hybrid back to the ship and stick it inside the pod it came from," she said. "This is our proof Delcor did what we always suspected he did."

Xttra tore a strip off a sheet still partially attached to the overturned bed and cleaned the remnant blood off his saber blade. He retracted the saber back into its resting place inside his armored sleeve. His eyes drifted over to the hybrid's now-lifeless face.

As much as it pained him to admit it, Xttra could no longer dismiss what Kyra said as mere Confederation propaganda. The hybrid echoed a popular Ra'ahm battle cry from the Separatist War before attacking him. It saddened and terrified Xttra to realize the chief sovereign was indeed capable of such atrocities.

His throat tightened and sweat beaded along his scalp as more unwelcome thoughts swarmed his mind. A different feeling of terror gripped him now. Delcor must have instructed one of his minions to lay a trap for Kevin and then for him. If that were the case, Calandra faced grave danger. And he was not there to protect her.

Xttra licked his lips and pinched his eyes shut. Concerns over her fate blanketed his mind like a dense fog. He needed to return to Lathos before time ran out.

To save Calandra.

# 25

Calandra checked the contact block periodically, waiting impatiently for an update from Kevin. Night turned into day and into night again without a word from him or Ominade. Their silence ate at her. Should it take this much time to connect her with their underground refugee network?

She tried to channel her troubled thoughts and energy into painting. Her unfinished panorama of rocky cliffs overlooking a vast ocean mocked those efforts. The contrast between shadow and sunlight on the farthest cliff did not strike the balance Calandra wanted. She tinkered around with hues, tints, tones, and shades. Yet, the scene she wanted to portray still did not evoke a brightness and hopefulness she sought.

Calandra set down her brush, still tipped with fresh paint, and closed her eyes. She exhaled slowly and rubbed her hands over her cheeks. Beautiful scenery did not rise to the surface easily in a mind swimming in fear.

How was Alayna handling this situation?

Calandra had not spoken with her friend since the day they uncovered evidence of the chief sovereign's crimes. Alayna's usual happy-go-lucky attitude degenerated into a fearful somberness after they left the Central Archives together. She said only a few words and had grown teary-eyed when they parted company after a hasty embrace.

Calandra walked from her studio to her bedroom and grabbed her arca vox. She punched in the contact code for Alayna. The holoscreen remained blank for a minute before flashing a message.

Not Available.

"It's me." Calandra said, pressing a crystal panel and recording a message. "I want to know how you're feeling. Let's talk when you get a minute."

She lowered the blank holoscreen again and set her arca vox back on a table next to her bed. Calandra started toward the door but stopped after taking a few steps. She turned back and stared at her arca vox.

Multiple beeps rang out from the communicator. Calandra dashed over and scooped it up. She raised the holoscreen.

"Alayna, it's so good to—"

Calandra stopped mid-sentence. The image on the holoscreen did not belong to her friend. She found herself looking at a youthful man with a skinny brown beard and pointed nose.

"Who are you?"

"Apologies. I assumed you remembered me."

"Should I?"

"I'm Talan."

Talan? His name sounded familiar to Calandra. She had no clue why it did. They never met or interacted on any prior occasion she remembered.

"We met at the Stellar Guard shipyard a while back." Talan flashed a warm smile to try to ease the growing awkwardness. "I serve as the navigator on your husband's scout ship."

Calandra closed her eyes and nodded. That's why he seemed oddly familiar. Xttra introduced her to his new assistant pilot and navigator on the same day he told her he resumed taking planet-based missions from the Stellar Guard. He introduced his new crew members to Calandra to ease her apprehension about him returning to active service.

"I do remember you now." She opened her eyes again and returned a polite smile. "It feels like a whole lifetime has passed since we met."

"All we've gone through sure makes it feel that way."

"What can I do for you, Talan?"

He paused and licked his lips.

"I don't know if Bo'un told you this, but I'm assisting him with searching for Xttra. I've hit a wall and could use your help."

"My help?"

Calandra lowered her eyebrows. Bo'un acted as her lone contact on Xttra's crew up to this point. He had not delegated communication to anyone else. This all seemed a little unusual.

"Is something wrong with Bo'un?" She unloaded another question before Talan made any effort to answer the first one. "Why isn't he contacting me?"

Talan scratched his left ear and glanced off-screen.

"He's taking care of an urgent matter." He redirected his eyes to her. "I can't delve into any specific details. I'm sure you understand."

Calandra did not understand why he gave such an evasive response to a straightforward question. She knew Bo'un at least as well as Talan did. If something bad happened to him, she deserved an honest answer.

"So, why do you need my help?"

"We found a merchant who has extensive off-world contacts with Thetian traders. Took some digging to find her. But there's one little snag."

"What snag?"

"The merchant isn't comfortable meeting with any Stellar Guard officers. She will only speak to you."

"Why only me?"

Talan shrugged and cast his eyes off-screen again. Calandra furrowed her brow. Why did he keep looking away from his holoscreen? The Stellar Guard officer acted like a person convinced they were under surveillance or taking orders from some unseen party.

"I realize I'm asking for a huge favor from you here, but I agreed to set up a meeting." Talan returned his gaze to her again. "The merchant wants to meet at her shop in Luma Flats at her normal closing hour."

Calandra's heart sank. Luma Flats? She did not feel safe trekking out to that part of the city alone at such a late hour. Even with her artificial arm in proper working order, unease washed over her at the prospect of flying an aerorover alone. Calandra last piloted one before journeying to Earth a couple of years earlier.

"Going alone isn't such a wise idea," she said. "Maybe I can bring my friend Alayna along?"

Talan leaned forward and raised his brows.

"Alayna?"

"She's helped me so much through this ordeal. I'd feel better with her around."

Talan shook his head.

"I … I don't know."

He hesitated and paused for a moment. Talan cast his eyes at the ground. Calandra did not like the direction of this conversation.

Too many unknowns. Too much risk.

"I understand why you're nervous." He looked at her again. "I do. But this merchant only agreed to meet under the specific condition she meet you alone."

"I don't like this. You haven't told me anything about her—including her name."

"Listen, I can monitor you from a distance and make sure she doesn't do anything suspicious. I'm counting on you. If I didn't have to involve you—"

Calandra rubbed her cheeks and let out a defeated sigh. Talan had forced her into a corner, and she did not like it one bit.

"Fine."

Talan flashed a relieved smile.

"Good. I'll let her know you're heading to her shop."

"What's her name? What do you know about her?" Sharpness tinged her questions. "If I'm agreeing to do this, I deserve a little more information."

"Of course. Her name is Zatoriah. I don't know much more beyond what I told you. But I can send directions to her shop and her image over to your arca vox, or your trique if you prefer."

Calandra nodded.

"Sounds good. I'll be in touch."

Talan's image vanished from her arca vox. Calandra sat on her bed and stared at the blank holoscreen. A creeping anxiety spread through her body like a web. Something about this situation did not add up. Perhaps her imagination only conjured up unfounded fears, but Calandra did not want to dismiss them out of hand.

She entered the contact code for Bo'un on her arca vox. Talan claimed he was unavailable to talk. Calandra had to find out for herself. A blank holoscreen greeted her eyes. Two dreaded words followed.

Not Available. Just like Alayna.

Calandra released a deep sigh. Why were the people she needed to talk to all unavailable at the same time? She glanced at a clock. Many shops in Luma Flats would be closing soon. If this merchant had an actual lead on Xttra's whereabouts, she owed it to herself to at least investigate. Still, making a trip to her shop at such a late hour called for taking precautionary measures. Calandra snatched up an eliminator Xttra gave her for self-defense after their return to Lathos. She stuffed the weapon inside a pouch she slung across her chest.

Calandra sealed her apartment door and hurried down to the aerorover. She flashed a brief smile when she opened the driver's side door and climbed inside. If Xttra only knew she was flying his prized classic aerorover in his absence. Mortified would not begin to describe his reaction. Xttra squashed every attempt anyone made to fly his aerorover in the past.

She distinctly remembered how he reacted to Kevin's desire to jump in the driver's seat and go cruising around Luma. Xttra shook his head with vigor right after the suggestion left Kevin's mouth.

"Not a chance. No one flies this aerorover except me."

Kevin rested his hand on the aerorover hood and cocked his head at him. He smiled.

"C'mon dude. I promise I won't wreck it. You can't tease me by showing off this beauty and then refuse to let me try it out."

"You've never flown an aerorover before. I'm not letting your first time be with this one."

"I learned to fly your scout ship on the fly. And we all made it back to your planet here without any trouble."

"That's a whole different animal."

Kevin pressed his hand against his chest and cast his eyes over at Calandra, pleading for help. She laughed.

"Remember how you showed me that Earth car you spent tons of time restoring? How would you feel about somebody else driving your car around?"

Kevin leaned back and gazed up at the sky. His eyes drifted down to her again and he nodded.

"When you put it like that, I see your point." He laughed, admitting defeat. "No way I'd let either of you behind the wheel of my Mustang."

Calandra released a heavy sigh as those memories faded back into the shadows of her mind. Her thoughts refocused on the task ahead of her in the present. Having Kevin, Bo'un, or Alayna by her side on this trip would ease troubled thoughts from bombarding her with relentless energy.

An electrical whoosh surged through the aerorover's interior when Calandra started the engine. She pushed down the control knob and raised both wings. Then she pulled the knob back toward her and retracted all four magnetic wheels against the vehicle's belly. Once it lifted off the ground, Calandra pushed the same knob forward and the aerorover zipped away from its parking spot outside her apartment.

Sky traffic was minimal at this late hour. Only three other aerorovers were near Calandra as her vehicle zoomed over treetops. Hanging lamps ran parallel to streets below the aerorover. Each lamp held two clear globes on a single metal rod bisecting a stone column. The lamps alternated with trees and served as a natural boundary between streets and sidewalks. Hanging lamps offered Luma residents enough light for travel at night without blocking visibility of stars from city streets. They also provided useful reference points for reducing the risk of mid-air collisions with trees or other aerorovers.

Beeps emanated from Calandra's chest pouch. She gnawed on her lower lip and shook her head. Of course, someone would try to contact her on her arca vox while in mid-flight. Her guess was Alayna. Calandra kept both arms glued to the steering controls. A conversation with her would have to wait until she and the aerorover were back on solid ground again.

Calandra pinpointed the shop where she was supposed to meet Zatoriah and landed along an adjacent street. More beeps emanated from her arca vox. She drew it from her chest pouch and raised the holoscreen.

Bo'un's image popped up.

"I'm happy to see you," Calandra said. She opened the aerorover door and stepped out. "I wish you were here to help me."

"What are you doing exactly? Maybe I can spare a few minutes."

"I just flew an aerorover out to Luma Flats. I'm meeting with a merchant you tracked down who has a lead on where we can find Xttra."

Bo'un twisted his lips into a half-smile and scrunched up his eyes and nose.

"I didn't track down a merchant. I've made zero progress since we met with that fake diviner."

Calandra paused at the street corner. Zatoriah's shop overlooked another street corner directly across from her. Lights were still on in the front window. A pair of patrons opened the main shop door and stepped out.

"You mean to tell me you didn't talk to a merchant named Zatoriah?"

"No. Who said I did?"

"Talan contacted me and claimed you both found her while investigating Xttra's abduction."

Bo'un's eyes widened. A concerned frown quickly washed over his lips.

"Talan hasn't been assisting me with anything. When did he speak to you?"

"Less than an hour ago. He told me he was contacting me on your behalf."

"This is bad." Bo'un swallowed hard. Fear laced through his words. "Get out of there now, Calandra. You're in serious danger."

Calandra's heartbeat quickened. Her mouth dropped open. A tremor raced through her limbs.

"What are you saying?" Her voice trembled as she forced the question out of her mouth.

"I suspected an infiltrator joined this crew and arranged for our ambush on Fengar. Talan confirmed it by contacting you. You're walking into a trap."

Her eyes darted back to the shop. The patrons who exited earlier had turned a corner and disappeared down a side street. Now, a woman with tightly cropped platinum blond hair stood on the shop steps. She stared straight at Calandra.

Zatoriah.

"I see the merchant now." Calandra's voice dropped to a whisper. "What do I do?"

Bo'un peeked over his shoulder as though he heard someone behind him on his end.

"Act natural and leave. Return to your apartment. I'll get over there as fast as possible."

She answered him with a silent nod. His image vanished from the holoscreen. Calandra slipped the arca vox back inside her chest pouch. Her fingers wrapped around the eliminator handle.

"Wow. This is the wrong place." She raised her voice while slowly backpedaling toward the aerorover. "I'm so bad with directions."

A crease formed in Zatoriah's brow. Her metallic gray eyes stayed locked on Calandra.

"Stay right where you are," she called out. "I can help you find your way."

Calandra waved her off with her gloved arm.

"I'm fine. Really. Don't worry about me."

The aerorover door popped up in her peripheral vision. Calandra gave it a sideways glance. At once, Zatoriah withdrew a weapon from her belt. Calandra mirrored her action, withdrawing the eliminator from her pouch. The merchant's eyes trailed down to the weapon in her hand, and she shook her head.

"So, a hotshot astronomer thinks she can put a laser bolt through me? You're out of your element here."

Calandra's throat tightened and her heart pounded even harder. Zatoriah already knew her identity. She uttered a silent prayer to Ahm, pleading for deliverance. Her mind screamed at her to kill the woman, but she could not compel herself to pull the trigger.

"Good riddance," the merchant said.

Zatoriah clicked the trigger on her sidearm. A small spark formed at the barrel. Nothing else happened.

The laser bolt did not discharge.

A relieved sigh escaped Calandra's lips. She opened the aerorover door and dived inside the vehicle. Zatoriah smacked the barrel against her open palm and cursed at the weapon. Calandra tossed her own eliminator on the passenger seat, strapped herself in, and got the aerorover airborne.

The merchant fired her weapon a second time. Same result. It had malfunctioned completely. Calandra threw the control knob forward. The aerorover zipped away from Zatoriah and her shop.

Her heart kept pounding with a relentless beat. Talan laid a trap for her. Zatoriah planned to shoot Calandra dead once she crossed the street.

What if he did the same with Alayna?

NO!

Calandra needed to rescue Alayna before it grew too late. Her life faced equal danger.

She made a sharp turn and sped toward Alayna's apartment overlooking the Nectura River's northern bank. Calandra licked her lips and pushed the aerorover speed past her normal comfort levels. Her thoughts drifted back to her inability to connect with Alayna's arca vox earlier. Did it reveal an omen Calandra overlooked? Was her friend safe?

*Please be safe. Ahm, please protect her.*

She repeated this desperate thought while making a sharp descent toward Alayna's apartment. Calandra parked along the street a short distance from the building's main doors. She grabbed the eliminator and scrambled out of the aerorover.

Calandra wrenched her arca vox out of her chest pouch after she entered the building. She sprinted toward the elevator while punching in Alayna's contact code. A holoscreen appeared, displaying the same message as earlier. Calandra punched in the code a second time after entering the elevator. No image replaced the message. Two words suspended on the holoscreen mocked her.

Not Available.

She raced out of the elevator before the door fully opened. Panicked, heavy breaths escaped through her lips as Calandra sprinted down the hall toward the apartment. Why did Alayna not answer her arca vox? This was so unlike her. She never repeatedly skipped an opportunity to chat like this.

An open door greeted Calandra.

No sign of forced entry.

She slowed her pace as she reached the doorway. Calandra peeked her head inside and surveyed the outer edge of the living room, searching for any sign of Alayna.

"Alayna? Where are you?"

Calandra stepped through the open doorway as she called out to her friend. No answer. Not so much as a voice, or footsteps, or any other discernable sound signaling human activity.

"We need to flee from here. Someone tried to kill me, and I think they might also be after you."

She rounded the corner, her eyes darting in multiple directions. When Calandra approached the kitchen, she froze. Her arca vox and eliminator simultaneously dropped from her hands to the floor. Calandra cried out and pressed her natural hand to her mouth. Tears sprang forth from her eyes.

Alayna lay crumpled on the floor.

A hole from a laser bolt was in her neck.

# 26

Calandra sank to her knees and shook with sobs. Tears coursed down both cheeks. Her breaths devolved into quavering bursts. This was not real. It had to be a dark twisted fantasy. She wanted to wake from this nightmare.

Alayna's eyes were cold and empty. Her face forever frozen with an expression of pained shock. Blood had pooled around her gaping mouth.

Executed like a dangerous traitor.

Calandra was powerless to do anything to stop it from happening. What if she had stopped here earlier? Would she have made a difference if she checked on Alayna earlier in the day?

She pinched her eyelids shut and grabbed a handful of the carpet woven from ebutoka hair.

"You didn't deserve this." Calandra barely forced the words out between sobs. "I'm so sorry."

She blamed herself for what happened. Calandra dropped Alayna's name in her conversation with Talan before learning his true intentions later. Did he pull the trigger? Was that ruthless pile of Ebutoka droppings responsible for ending Alayna's life?

Calandra's eyes popped open again. She snatched up her eliminator and arca vox from the floor and pulled herself to her feet. She drew deep breaths and stuffed both objects inside her chest pouch.

"Talan won't get away with this," Calandra seethed. "He'll face justice. I'll see to it."

She wiped away tears moistening her cheeks. Her eyes darted from wall to wall in both the kitchen and living room. Calandra studied both rooms, searching for any clues implicating Talan as Alayna's assassin. Her narrow escape from Zatoriah convinced Calandra that he, or someone in league with him, planned to kill both her and Alayna that evening.

Footsteps.

Calandra stiffened upon hearing other sets of feet enter the apartment. Her heart pounded anew. Someone either tracked her to Alayna's place or they were already waiting for her here and came out of their hiding place.

"Stay right where you are."

Her breaths sped up into shallow fevered bursts. She turned her head incrementally toward her shoulder, trying to identify who owned the gruff voice behind her.

"Don't move a muscle or we will blast you."

Two men wearing combat armor, helmets, and wielding melters soon flanked each side of Calandra. City guards. One guard on her left cast his eyes down at Alayna's body. A fierce scowl crawled across the guard's lips when he looked back at Calandra.

"You did this. You murdered this woman."

She shook her head with vigor.

"No. She's … she's my friend," Calandra's voice cracked as she denied the accusation. "I found her here. What did they do to her? If only I …"

Calandra trailed off. Tears brimmed in her eyes anew and she broke down sobbing a second time. The guard on her right seized her chest pouch and unlatched it at her shoulder.

"Wait! What are you doing?"

She instinctively extended her hand to grab the pouch. The city guard on her left quickly clamped a hand down on her forearm and jammed his melter up against her ribs.

"I told you not to move. Are you deaf?"

Calandra pinched her lips together and watched helplessly as the other guard hunted through her chest pouch. He drew out the eliminator and scowled at her.

"Found the weapon. She's our culprit."

She froze and stared at the two city guards with wide eyes and raised brows. They were convinced she murdered Alayna. Fear crawled up her spine. Her face contorted and her lips trembled.

Calandra walked right into a trap.

"No! I didn't do this. Alayna is my best friend. I found her like this."

Both guards shook their heads and glared at her.

"Your 'friend' was killed by a laser bolt. Fired from an eliminator." The guard holding her eliminator thrust the weapon in her face. "You have an eliminator in your possession. No one else is here."

He unhooked magnetic restraints from his belt and slapped them across Calandra's arms. The other guard produced a cloth pouch. Her eyes widened as he placed it atop her head and started pushing it down over her hair.

This was not normal procedure for city guards in restraining a suspected criminal.

"What are you doing to me?"

Calandra struggled against the restraints. The guard stretched the cloth bag over her eyes and nose. An overwhelming sickly-sweet aroma greeted her nostrils.

Maidron root extract.

A powerful sedative.

Liquified Maidron root soaked the cloth, and the pungent aroma filled her lungs. Calandra's eyes grew heavy. Voices of both guards faded from her ears as she slipped into oblivion.

***

Calandra pressed her hands to her face and let out a heavy sigh. Dizziness from prolonged exposure to Maidron root still gripped her, even as numbness in her extremities began wearing off. She blinked rapidly and tried to rise to her feet.

After several tries, Calandra kept her balance. Her eyes drifted from wall to wall as she carefully assessed unfamiliar surroundings. She found herself standing inside a sterile windowless cell. Horizontal lights hung from each wall, casting a pale white glow over the cramped room. Besides Calandra and a narrow metallic bench, nothing else occupied the cell.

A loud whoosh from a sliding door greeted her ears. Calandra turned toward the source of the sound. Both city guards who imprisoned her entered the room. Then, a third visitor entered through the doorway behind the guards. A short gasp escaped her lips before Calandra pressed her real hand to her mouth to stifle it.

Delcor stood in the cell with her.

He shot a disapproving frown at her and shook his head like a weary parent disciplining an unruly child. Calandra did not take her eyes off him for a second. Since when did he make personal visits to prisoners? Drawing an unexpected audience with the chief sovereign counted as a bad omen with all she uncovered about him.

"I expected better things from the granddaughter of my former first minister." His accusatory tone matched his expression perfectly. "Tell me, Calandra, what would Janthore say if he saw the mess you created for yourself?"

Calandra pinched her eyes shut for a moment, then opened them into a stony stare.

"I did not murder my best friend."

"Compelling evidence tells me a different story. You were carrying an eliminator. The same weapon, according to the city guards, used to kill Alayna Bocane."

"I found her already dead inside her apartment. You can check my eliminator yourself. I never fired it once."

Delcor clucked his tongue.

"I want to believe you. I want what you say to be true. But I also cannot ignore how you involved yourselves in nefarious activities before her untimely demise."

She raised her eyebrows at his accusation. How much did he know? Playing ignorant was her only hope.

"Nefarious activities? What are you insinuating here, my sovereign?"

He scoffed at her question.

"Stop pretending to be so innocent and naïve." Delcor started pacing in front of her and the bench. "It will not help your case. You and your friend accessed restricted records within the Central Archives. Did you think our image sensors would not capture you inside that room?"

A lump formed in her throat. Calandra sat on the bench and rubbed her natural hand across her chin. He knew everything she and Alayna did to uncover his crimes. Did his agents also monitor her and Bo'un when they paid a visit to Ominade? Were Bo'un and Ominade also in danger now?

"I just want to bring my husband home." Her voice cracked a little when she said these words. "I want to see Xttra again. I will not leave a single stone unturned in my search for him."

Delcor's eyes softened as he studied her. Calandra wondered if she reached him and cracked through his shell. It turned out to be nothing more than a mirage. Those same eyes hardened again as a twisted half-smirk formed on his lips.

"Your excuse does not sway me. No information related to Xttra Oogan's abduction is stored among those restricted records. You already know as much. Those are confidential records of the government of Ra'ahm."

His penetrating gaze pressed down on Calandra like an unyielding blinding light. She wanted to close her eyes, turn away, and transport herself to the other side of Lathos far from his reach. Calandra forced herself to hold her ground and keep eye contact.

She refused to let Delcor intimidate her any longer.

"Do you know how many months have passed since I have seen his face or heard his voice outside my own memories?" Calandra rose to her feet a second time. "Do you understand the pain, emptiness, and loneliness I feel? Can you grasp the desperation fueling me to find my soulmate and bring him home?"

Both city guards started toward her as Calandra's voice climbed in strength and pitch. Delcor turned to each approaching guard and abruptly waved them off.

"I understand pain. I understand loss. On a scale you cannot imagine. And it can come to your door."

He edged closer to her and quickly stabbed an index finger in Calandra's face. She flinched and backpedaled until her legs pressed against the bench.

"You should know better than to chase after seditious lies and rumors conjured by Confederation leadership. They never cease working to destroy me. They never stop opposing our freedom from their tyranny."

Calandra bowed her head and gazed at the floor. So many words rested on her tongue. Bold words. Harsh words. Passionate arguments designed to cut to their chief sovereign's soul and open his eyes. Such words would pierce like sharp blades. They would cut her down in the end. Not him. Calandra understood this much. Delcor made a determined effort to bury evidence of past crimes. Confirming her knowledge of those same crimes while in his presence would not end well for her.

She chose a different tactic.

"Why did my grandfather step down from being your first minister?"

Silence greeted her question. Calandra lifted her head and fixed her eyes on Delcor. A resolute frown washed over her face.

"Why did he leave Lathos? What drove him to leave behind family and friends, never to return?"

The chief sovereign shook his finger like a club at her.

"Janthore was a wise and pragmatic leader. He understood and embraced his role in aiding me with governing Ra'ahm. You should learn from his example."

"Why did he leave?" Calandra's lips trembled as she repeated the question. "Why?"

Delcor leaned closer and did his best to make himself tower over her.

"He understood compromises for the greater good needed to be made. The prime oracle's tragic fate crushed so many of us. Janthore was no exception. His desire to serve fled from him. We both knew he could not continue in his office. For his sake and his family's sake."

A tremor raced along her spine. Calandra swallowed hard and gazed upon the chief sovereign in stunned silence. The true implication behind his words became perfectly clear. He gave her grandfather a simple choice—self-imposed exile or die along with his entire family.

"I do wonder, Calandra, what choice you would make," Delcor continued. "What would you do if you faced the dilemma Janthore once faced? Would you share his pragmatic viewpoint?"

Calandra averted her eyes from his piercing gaze. She stared past Delcor's shoulder and noted satisfied smiles splashed on the faces of both city guards. Their reaction to his words mocked her internal despair. The path before her seemed too rugged to traverse. Ahm required a burden too heavy to bear.

The chief sovereign made her fate clear. Calandra had no other choice. She needed to do whatever was necessary to survive. For Xttra. For her family. Her life, like Ominade said, was precious. Too precious to let him snuff it out like a weakening candle flame.

Delcor claimed victory in this battle. She could not afford to let him win the war.

"I understand." Her voice grew quiet and defeated. "I understand my grandfather's decision now."

The chief sovereign answered her with an approving nod. He laid a hand on her shoulder. Calandra gave the hand a cursory glance but said nothing.

"You can have your old life again," Delcor said. "This incident tonight can disappear. You can go back to the observatory. Who knows? Ahm may smile on you and even bring Xttra back to you."

His words mocked her pain. The way he spoke told her he believed Xttra would never return to Lathos alive. Kevin was right. Her life had changed forever. Nothing she did, or Delcor said, would turn back time and chart a new and better path.

"Go back to the observatory," Delcor said. "Live a safe life quietly studying distant stars and planets. It will be better for you and the ones you love if you do."

Fresh unbidden tears splashed down Calandra's tear-stained cheeks. She answered him with a pained nod.

"Good. I hoped a little reasoning would sway you. I owed it to your grandfather to try."

Delcor paused and stared at her. She knew what she was supposed to say at this point. Words programmed into her reaching back into her childhood. Calandra wished her eardrums would shatter, so she did not have to listen to herself say these awful words. They tore her soul into pieces.

"May Ahm preserve you and lengthen your rule to match your days, my sovereign."

Calandra refused to look him directly in the face while she recited this expression. She had no clue how she would handle seeing Delcor wearing a satisfied condescending smile at her total humiliation.

"The evidence tying young Calandra here to her friend's murder is circumstantial at best," he said, turning to the city guards. "Return her possessions and release her from your custody at once."

Both guards bowed and opened the door leading out of the windowless cell. Delcor turned and peered at Calandra one more time with renewed sternness when he reached the doorway.

"I hope our next chat will be under much better circumstances," he said. "That, of course, hinges on you."

Calandra did not want to envision what a future chat with the chief sovereign would bring. She counted on not leaving his presence a second time with either her freedom or her life still intact.

# 27

Xttra stared at the lifeless hybrid while Xander and Kyra loaded its corpse back inside the hibernation pod. Questions clawed their way to the surface in his mind. He wished he could bury each one again and continue living in blissful ignorance about the past.

This hybrid offered unmistakable evidence the Confederation spoke the truth. Upon closer examination, he discovered the pod's surface bore an official seal of Ra'ahm. The hybrid's final words also confirmed its origin. What drove the chief sovereign to create these monsters? Did his agents stow this hybrid away in an alien solar system for use at a future time? Were hybrids lurking in other hidden corners of the galaxy, existing as a backup plan to keep Delcor in power?

Xttra glanced up from the pod. Sam stood on the other side, also staring at the dead hybrid. Concern and fear took root in his face. The Earthian shuddered and finally averted his eyes. It seemed bitterly ironic to Xttra how his entire world had turned upside down again because of another encounter with Earthians.

Xander rigged up a makeshift harness to keep the corpse from falling out of the vertical pod while Kyra sealed the pod door. Running lights along each side of the pod clicked from red to blue once the device enacted a fresh hibernation cycle.

"Hopefully, the same systems which preserved the hybrid in stasis will keep its body from decomposing during our return journey to Lathos," Kyra said. "We need the specimen intact if possible."

Sam turned and gazed at the sealed hibernation pod. His expression gave Xttra a distinct impression the Earthian expected the hybrid to spring back to life again and escape from the pod.

"How long was that hybrid inside this pod before we found it here on Mars?"

Kyra cast her eyes skyward.

"Since the end of the Separatist War. That means a hibernation period of at least 40 years."

Sam scratched his head.

"How did this alien survive so long? And how did this pod maintain sufficient power to preserve said alien on a barren planet?"

Xttra stooped down and examined panels above running lights on both sides of the pod. Each panel corresponded with specific functions ranging from life support to internal power.

"The pod's power cells generate energy from a small antimatter chamber," he said. "If the cells were fully charged when this pod was brought to this planet, they can supply enough life support power to preserve the hybrid in stasis for 100 years—but only with a steady supply of nutritional supplements, of course."

Sam's mouth dropped open.

"100 years? Are you serious?"

Kyra shot him a worried frown.

"It's clear to me Delcor hid this hybrid in your solar system for a specific purpose. The question now is if his agents hid more hybrids elsewhere."

Xttra did not want to ponder the scenario she put forward any further. Sleep grew hard enough without bringing other unwelcome thoughts into the picture. He anchored his mind on completing two specific tasks—chasing down and neutralizing the infected Earthian and returning home to Calandra before it grew too late. That left no room for tackling unseen problems elsewhere.

"How soon before we're flight-ready again?" Xttra straightened up and cast his eyes toward the bridge where Cavac continued making repairs. "Giving the Earthian vessel too much of a head start is asking for additional trouble later."

Kyra moved closer to a button connected to the ship's internal communications system and mashed it down. Cavac had already restored communications—along with a few other basic primary systems—before the others boarded the ship again.

"Do you have some good news for me?"

"I'm making steady progress." Cavac's voice crackled over the internal speakers. "Antimatter injectors and primary thrusters are back online. Thetians don't construct high quality ships, but at least their designs are simple to repair."

"Excellent. We'll meet you on the bridge."

Kyra turned and faced the others inside the cargo bay.

"We're back on track," she said, beckoning them forward. "Our hyperlight engines are at normal operating capacity again, so we should regain lost ground quickly."

Xttra flashed back to what unfolded for him and his crew when they first approached Earth. Language and technology barriers stymied their original efforts to communicate with Earthian leaders. Once they entered the planet's atmosphere, the Earth Defense Bureau sent attack vessels to shoot his scout ship down. Fears of a repeat attack flooded his mind.

He cocked his head at Sam as they entered the bridge.

"If we pursue the other vessel back to your planet, can you guarantee your fellow Earthians won't deploy attack vessels to shoot us down?"

Kyra stopped and wheeled around.

"Shoot us down?" she repeated.

Sam raised his hand and shook his head.

"Relax. If you set your communication systems to the correct frequency, I can talk to the bureau when we reach Earth and fill them in on everything."

Xttra narrowed his eyes and studied Sam suspiciously for a moment. The Earthian did not strike him as one eager to sacrifice his own skin to let his people destroy this spaceship. Then again, Xttra could not afford to ignore any plausible scenario when dealing with this treacherous alien race.

He turned and glanced at Kyra.

"If you want my advice, we should establish communications from a safe distance around the Earthian moon." Xttra pointed his thumb back at Sam. "His people are violent and reactionary. No need to purchase us more trouble than we're already facing."

Sam answered him with an annoyed frown.

"I promise you'll be perfectly safe with me aboard. Trust me for a change."

Kyra swung around and marched to the pilot's chair.

"Xttra is right," she said while settling into the chair. "It's not you who we doubt, Sam. We'll go to your planet's moon and stay in orbit until you contact your Earthian leaders before going any further."

Xttra, Sam, Xander, and Cavac all took seats on the bridge and strapped in for launch. Kyra fired the primary thrusters. The usual whoosh and hum greeted Xttra's ears. Primary engines seemed to be working adequately.

The red rock Martian surface receded from view as their ship barreled through the thin atmosphere's upper reaches. Kyra and Cavac extrapolated correct coordinates for Earth based on information Sam shared with the group. Cavac plotted a course to the Moon and the ship quickly jumped from orbit around Mars.

Were they too late to stop the Earthian vessel from reaching Earth? The question flashed through Xttra's mind as Mars receded from view. They lost an entire day while Cavac made repairs. If the artificial wormhole the other vessel created remained stable long enough, they might already be entering orbit or landing on the planet's surface by now.

What would the two rogue colonists tell their fellow Earthians? Would they trick Earthian leaders into attacking the Thetian ship before Sam had a chance to make contact and explain the situation? A reactionary Earthian attack against a ship not from their world was not unprecedented, and that knowledge only escalated a growing fear burrowing into every corner of Xttra's soul.

He lost track of how much time passed before the Moon appeared in visual range. Kyra slowed the main engines and guided their ship into orbit around the Earthian satellite. A loud beep from one of the sensors resonated through the bridge.

"I'm detecting a Ra'ahmian sensor array near the dark side of this moon," Cavac said.

Sam shot Xttra a questioning look.

"Sensor array?"

"How do you think we programmed your language into our translators?" Xttra replied. "We intercepted transmissions from your planet and fed your language through my scout ship's central computer."

"We can do the same thing here," Kyra said. She cocked her head at the navigation station. "Patch us into the sensor array, Cavac.

Feed the transmissions through the speakers, so Sam can help us pinpoint the necessary frequency to communicate with his people."

Xttra scoffed. A satisfied smirk popped on his face as he leaned forward in his chair.

"Ra'ahmian made sensor arrays are well protected. You can't just hack—"

"I patched into the sensor array," Cavac announced, cutting him off. "Looping the transmissions through the internal speakers now."

Distorted voices broken up by static blasted from the speakers. Xttra flinched and crinkled his eyes and nose at the sound. Cavac fiddled with a small knob on his console and the static lessened. Voices grew more distinct and refined. Each one spoke at a rapid pace. Xttra wondered if he should put a translator in his ear like the others. He recognized few of the words these voices said.

Xttra shot a puzzled look at Sam. The Earthian tilted his head, crossed his arms, and studied the nearest speaker above him.

"You picked up a signal from a Spanish-language TV broadcast," he finally said. "Keep trying."

Another transmission soon replaced the first one. Xttra sank back in his chair and nodded. This one used the same Earthian language as Sam. Two people spoke. One described an unseen Earthian dribbling a ball and running ahead of a second Earthian in an animated voice.

"I recognize some of these words," he said.

Sam looked over at him and smiled.

"Another TV broadcast. Sounds like we picked up an NBA game between the Lakers and the Warriors."

"Lakers and Warriors?" Xttra repeated. "Are those two Earthian tribes?"

"Basketball teams," Sam said, correcting him. "Basketball is a sport we play on Earth. A popular one. And I think we made it back from Mars in time to catch the NBA Playoffs."

Kyra snapped her head around.

"Let's focus on catching the infected Earthian."

Sam flashed an annoyed frown but said nothing. Both he and Xttra refocused their attention on listening to Earthian transmissions. They sifted through more signals filtering through the sensor array. One after another did not connect back to the Earth Defense Bureau. Xttra sensed tension building on the bridge. Irritated scowls and sharpened tones in the Confederation officers' voices only confirmed his suspicions.

"That's it!" Excitement infused Sam's voice. "We've picked up a bureau radio channel."

Xttra instinctively cocked his head at the internal speakers. A dry voice repeated multiple questions to an unidentified silent Earthian. He had no context for words spoken on the transmission, but the first Earthian's tone grew increasingly persistent.

Sam edged forward on his chair and tapped his fingers on the armrest.

"Can you match the transmission frequency? We need to communicate with the bureau and warn them the Magellan is headed to Earth."

Cavac nodded without looking at him. His eye and ocular implant remained fixed on a communications console bordering the navigational console.

"Already working on patching into your Earthian radio channel."

"How do I talk with them from here?"

Kyra glanced over her shoulder and beckoned him forward. Sam unlatched the safety restraints on his chair and approached the helm. He crouched down next to the pilot's chair.

"This activates the ship's external communicator." Kyra tapped a square green button on the helm console. "Press down on the button until it clicks, and it will open a communication channel. Press down a second time to release the button and sever the channel."

Once he adjusted the communicator to match the designated Earthian frequency, Cavac turned and gave Sam an abrupt nod. He reached over and pressed the button in the same manner Kyra showed him.

"Can you read me?" Sam rose to a standing position again. "This is Sam Bono from the Earth Defense Bureau. Patch my signal through to Director Marks at once."

"Sam?' A surprised husky voice finally answered after a minute of silence. "Where are you? Deep space tracking picked up your warning beacon from Mars a few days ago. We were readying a rescue mission."

"The threat on Mars is neutralized," Sam replied. "But a bigger threat remains."

"Bigger threat?"

"Alien venom infected one of our colonists. She and a second colonist stole the Magellan. They're headed to Earth."

"What?" Director Marks' voice climbed in pitch as he soaked in Sam's revelation. "We spoke with the Magellan pilot less than an hour ago and gave him permission to land."

Kyra's mouth dropped open and her eyes grew as large as plates.

"Are all Earthian leaders this dumb? Why would you do such a foolish thing?"

"Who is that?" Director Marks' voice grew flustered. "Where are you, Sam?"

"I'm onboard an alien ship orbiting the Moon," Sam replied. "Listen, you can't let the Magellan land under any circumstances. Send out drones. Fire missiles. Do what you need to do."

"For a simple medical emergency?"

Sam sighed and pressed his palm to his forehead.

"Whatever they told you is a lie. Norah Baker is becoming a hybrid, like the ones which overran Travis, Texas 14 years ago."

Silence greeted Sam. It continued long enough for Xttra to wonder if a glitch severed their communication channel with Earth prematurely. He hoped that was not the case. These violent Earthians would jump at the first excuse to shoot their ship down once it reached the planet's lower atmosphere.

"A Rubrum hybrid?"

Director Marks' question pierced the silence like a sharp blade. Xttra sensed a newfound terror couched in the Earthian's voice.

"A different hybrid laid waste to our Martian colony," Sam said. "Aliens from Lathos rescued me and helped destroy the first hybrid, but we were unable to prevent Cliff and Norah from taking off from Mars."

"Aliens from Lathos? Like the ones you encountered out in Utah?"

"I don't have time to explain all the details. We need to move fast. Where's the Magellan's current location?"

"It entered the thermosphere a little while ago."

"Understood. We'll try to intercept it before they cross the Karman line."

Sam snapped his head toward Kyra.

"The Magellan is entering Earth's upper atmosphere. Can you intercept it before it lands?"

Kyra stared at the helm thoughtfully for a moment while appearing to weigh scenarios in her mind. She finally glanced over at Sam and answered him with a confident nod.

"Faster than a cala scurries up a fraxa tree."

Sam gave her a puzzled look.

"What's a cala?"

Kyra turned and faced the helm again, ignoring his question. She fired the primary thrusters and the ship zipped out of orbit from around the Moon.

"What's a cala?" Sam repeated, this time looking over at Xttra for an answer.

An image of Bella popped into his mind. Xttra smiled as he thought of Calandra's treasured pet. She darted around the apartment with limitless energy at times and often got under foot along the way.

"A small, furry, and energetic Lathoan animal," he said. "Calandra and I keep one as a pet."

"You also have pets on your planet? Fascinating."

Earth grew larger on the horizon. Shadows partially cloaked the blue-green orb. The planet's natural beauty contrasted so powerfully with the ugly, violent natures of Earthians who called it home. Xttra tried to prepare himself mentally and emotionally for dealing with an inevitable return to Earth. Now, with their ship nearing low orbit, a mixture of fear, anger, and sadness besieged him. This swirl of emotion gripped him as tight as a mokai bird seizing fresh prey.

"Our sensors have locked on the Earthian deep space vessel," Xander said. "It's descending through the planet's upper atmosphere."

"Plot an intercept course," Kyra said, glancing over at Cavac. "Let's bring down that ship before it can land."

Cavac nodded and entered coordinates into the navigational computer. A new course targeting the Earthian deep space vessel popped up on the main helm holoscreen. Kyra tapped the route, highlighted in red, with her finger and then shifted the primary thrusters to a higher speed.

The distance between their ship and Earth fell away with blinding speed. Xttra studied the blue tinge of atmosphere with anxious eyes as their ship reached low orbital range. Images of Earthian attack vessels firing weapons flooded his mind. He refused to let himself assume they were safe with Sam on board. The presence of Kevin and his fellow soldiers offered no protection from lethal attacks while retaking his scout ship from Earthian leaders.

A loud beep echoed through the bridge.

"We have the Earthian vessel in visual range," Kyra said. "It's headed for a green land mass on the daytime side of the planet."

"That's North America," Sam replied. "My home continent. They're trying to land in the United States."

Kyra glanced at the forward station where Xander sat.

"What's our weapons status?"

"Thetian ion mines are at one-third power."

She shot him a disappointed scowl.

"Wonderful. That will have to be good enough."

Xttra turned his attention back to the windshield as their ship dipped below a bank of white clouds. At once, the Earthian vessel appeared below. It grew from a distant dot to a full-sized ship within seconds.

"Target the engines before they can fire their weapons again," Xttra said. "And activate our shields."

Kyra sighed.

"I know how to bring down a hostile vessel," she said. Her eyes remained fixed on the holoscreen before her. "If I want assistant piloting from you, I'll ask for it."

An energy shell enveloped the outer hull. Two ports opened and ion mines launched from the belly of their ship. Each mine resembled a giant metallic egg spiraling toward the Earthian vessel.

A pair of blinding flashes lit up the sky between the two ships. Flames and smoke billowed out from remnants of a solar arm and a secondary engine exhaust port on the left side of the Earthian vessel.

Kyra steered the Thetian ship closer until it was almost on top of the Earthian vessel. She dodged the cloud of smoke and flames and shot ahead trying to block the other vessel's descent path. Xttra's eyes stayed glued to the Earthian ship.

It veered off from its original trajectory and prepared to fire an electromagnetic blast at their ship. Xttra could visibly see the weapons and where they aimed. Kyra was ready this time. She entered a steep climb to dodge the shot. The Confederation pilot then began a descending turn and resumed chasing the Earthians.

At once, a smaller vessel popped into visual range. Xttra instantly recognized the cylindrical body and V-shaped tail. An Earthian attack vessel. It resembled one which tracked his scout ship and another that eventually shot down one of his aerorovers.

Panic flooded his eyes as he glanced over at Sam.

"Your people are going to shoot us down."

Sam gazed over at the same spot outside the ship where Xttra spotted the attack vessel. A worried frown graced his lips.

"Open a communication channel with the Earth Defense Bureau again," he said. "We need to move that drone out of our way."

A tremor shook the bridge. Flames and smoke billowed off from an impact point on the energy shell, sending ripples in multiple directions. Shell integrity held. No Earthian weapons breached their hull.

Xttra did not see from his vantage point if the deep space vessel or the drone, as Sam called it, fired on their ship. Either way, they were in considerable danger.

"I'll just get rid of your drone," Kyra said. "It's getting too crowded up here."

Sam threw up his arms.

"No! Wait! You can't do that."

She cast a sideways glance at him.

"Are Earthians inside the drone?"

"No. But that doesn't matter. Let me—"

"That's all I needed to know."

Sam's eyes darted toward the holoscreen Kyra used as a guide to retarget her weapons.

"You can't just blow up a US military drone."

"Watch me."

Another ion mine blasted from the belly of their ship. The mine spun straight into the drone's flight path. An explosion followed, turning the Earthian attack vessel into a sinking metallic ball of flames.

Sam scowled and sank back in his chair.

"This isn't sending a good message."

"Trying to blow our ship out of the sky isn't what I call a friendly message," Xttra replied. "It sure feels like a familiar one though."

Cavac spun his chair around and faced the helm.

"The Earthian vessel we tracked from the red planet is dropping in altitude. Estimated landing time based on current speed and trajectory is five minutes."

Kyra's frown deepened on her lips.

"Not if I can help it. Get that communication system with the Earthians back online!"

She angled the ship downward and shot toward the ground. An ocean coastline rose to greet their ship. Kyra pulled the ship within visual range of the Earthian vessel again. It veered away from the coastline and approached a forested area in a semi-spiral.

Bolts erupted from the plasma cannon. One missed wildly. Another clipped one of the still intact arms, leaving a cloud of solar panel shards in its wake. The Earthian vessel plunged into the forest. It plowed through branches while disappearing below the treetops.

"Pull back! You're going to crash into the freeway."

Panic gripped Sam's voice. Kyra sighed and pulled the steering stick toward her chair. Xttra glanced down at the ground outside the windshield. Two broad paved roads, divided by a narrow strip of grassy land, cut through the forested area. Cars dotted both roads. Earthian vehicles traveled west on one road and east on the other.

Several cars made sudden stops in both directions. Earthians jumped out of multiple vehicles and held up small rectangular devices aimed at their ship. Kevin brought a similar gadget with him, which he called a smartphone, when he came to Lathos.

"We better find a safe out-of-the-way landing spot before we draw further attention." Sam also fixed his eyes on the Earthians below the ship. "I'll get us some help to recover the crashed ship and check for survivors."

Xttra did not like the sound of Sam's promise of finding help after seeing an Earthian drone attack their ship. He had no wish to run into more Earth Defense Bureau agents—or soldiers—out here.

None could be trusted.

"Do you actually think they survived a crash landing?" Xander posed his question before Xttra had a chance to voice his concerns. "The odds are not in their favor."

"We can't make any assumptions," Sam replied. "This part of Louisiana will be placed under an emergency Earth Defense Bureau quarantine until this situation is fully contained."

# 28

Norah unleashed a ragged cough. Billowing smoke from the engines wafted into her nose and mouth. She blinked open her eyes and squinted at her surroundings.

Giant cracks ran through the cockpit windshield. The glass remained only partially intact following their crash. Norah turned toward her right shoulder. Cliff lay back against his chair. Both eyelids remained shut and his chin dipped down to his chest. Blood oozed from a fresh laceration across his hairline and trailed down his temple.

She popped off her helmet and cast it aside. Norah then removed her glove, extended the same arm, and tenderly lifted his head.

"Wake up." Her voice had grown strained like a person fighting a raging cold. "Please wake up."

Cliff let out a slight groan. His eyelids cracked open. A sudden cough followed. He gasped and pressed his hand against his chest.

"I guess it was too much to hope those aliens wouldn't catch up to us."

Norah answered him with a forlorn nod. She held out faint hope crippling their ship would slow the aliens down. It did not work out like either she or Cliff wanted.

She let her eyes drift down and settle on her hand. Norah recoiled and instantly let go of Cliff's chin. Her hand and lips trembled in equal measure while she stared at the limb.

Each finger now sported a jagged claw in place of a normal fingernail.

"I'm a monster." Tears splashed down Norah's cheeks anew. "What is this thing I'm becoming?"

Cliff lifted his arm and caressed a lock of her strawberry blonde hair resting against her cheek. One look into his eyes revealed his hidden fear to Norah. But he refused to acknowledge he owned any such feelings toward her.

"You're no monster." He mustered a pained smile between labored breaths. "You're still the same strong, gentle, and beautiful Norah I've always known."

Norah sniffed back tears and flashed a grateful smile. Cliff unlatched the safety belts holding him in place and popped his helmet off. She helped him rise to his feet. Cliff stumbled when Norah let go of his arm and pressed his gloved hand against his forehead.

"Wow. Still a bit woozy."

He worked to calm his breathing and steadied his other hand against the chair back while he stepped over the seat. A bird chirped beyond the cracked windshield. Norah froze. Her eyes darted back and forth as she tried to pinpoint the bird's location. She sniffed and turned her head slowly.

Norah licked her lips.

She had to find that bird.

"What are you doing?"

Cliff's question snapped Norah's thoughts back to the Magellan. She gazed at him and shook her head.

"I don't know what came over me. A bird chirped outside, and a sudden urge gripped me."

"Sudden urge?"

"I wanted to track the bird down and eat it."

Cliff's eyes widened at that revelation. Norah was embarrassed to admit such a desire even entered her mind. She lived on a strict vegetarian diet since her college days. Her heart told her to leave the bird alone, but a baser instinct compelled her to prey on the innocent creature once she stepped outside their vessel.

"Let's focus on getting you somewhere safe," he said. "We can figure out dinner after we're settled."

Cliff pressed his shoulder into the exit door and grunted as he forced it open. He pushed the dented and twisted metal aside, creating a narrow opening. Norah approached the edge of the door and peered down at the ground. The crash landing rotated the Magellan to a weird angle. This meant they would need to make an awkward jump down a few feet to reach solid ground.

She turned and cast a worried frown at him.

"Are you sure you can jump down from here without hurting yourself further?"

Cliff shrugged.

"We can't stay in here."

He crouched down, braced his hand against the edge of the door, and jumped. Cliff staggered as his feet hit the ground and rolled onto his hip. Norah gulped and took a running jump. She stuck the landing with the ease of a gymnast finishing a routine.

Norah extended a clawed hand and helped him to his feet. Cliff winced as he stood up and clutched his upper left leg. Worry flooded her eyes.

"Are you hurt? Can you walk?"

He answered her with an abrupt nod.

"I'll be fine. I'm more worried about your condition."

Norah struck out in front, and they started walking east through the forest toward Sulphur. Her eyes darted back and forth as they snaked past a nearby bayou. Every chirp from a bird or chatter from a squirrel amid the longleaf pines captured her attention. Norah's belly rumbled. Her tongue rolled over her lips. Such bad hunger pangs.

She needed to eat something.

Anything.

Cliff groaned. Norah stopped and snapped her head back at him. He moved with a noticeable limp as he pushed himself to match her pace. Heavy breaths escaped between his lips. Sweat beaded on his forehead and the muggy air was not the only cause. She turned around and dashed back to him.

"Are you sure you can keep walking with me?' Norah trailed her clawed fingers over his hair. "You don't look so good, honey."

Cliff painted a smile on his lips and nodded.

"I'll be fine. I promise. I just tweaked my hamstring when I jumped down from the Magellan."

Norah wrapped her arm around his shoulder and helped take the weight off the affected leg. She slowed her pace to account for Cliff's limited mobility.

The sun dipped low in the sky, lengthening shadows of surrounding longleaf pine trees, before they reached the forest's edge. Norah's hunger pangs grew more intense. Sweat trickled down her forehead while her feet pounded over uneven wild grass and lumpy soil. They had to be near Sulphur now. The Magellan crashed only a few miles outside her hometown. Helping Cliff keep weight off his leg made the journey go slower than she first expected.

Norah's eyes brightened. A wooden telephone pole peeked out from the treetops ahead of her. They had reached the edge of town. Now they could search for some food and, hopefully, find a kind stranger willing to offer them temporary shelter. She and Cliff needed time and space to track down someone who possessed the necessary knowledge to restore her body to its original human form.

Trees soon yielded to a grassy yard surrounding a long rectangular house. One end faced a one-lane asphalt road. The other end led back into the forest where they crashed. Water bubbled and churned inside an enormous stock pot sitting atop a portable propane-fueled burner in the yard. The burner was set up a few feet from a picnic table covered with a rough tablecloth.

Norah sniffed when she spotted the stock pot. Saliva moistened her lips. Her belly rumbled anew. She knew that pot brimmed with crawfish, potatoes, and corn without looking inside. Norah could practically taste the Cajun seasoning from the edge of the yard.

They had stumbled upon a backyard crawfish boil.

Cliff ducked out from under her arm and limped over to the picnic table. Norah's breathing intensified as she crept toward the stock pot.

Loud barks greeted her ears. She froze and jerked her head toward the back end of the house. A black Labrador stood behind a closed screen door, alerting the entire neighborhood to her presence.

Norah held out her hand.

"Be quiet," she pleaded. "Be a good dog."

Her eyes darted over to neighboring backyards and back to the screen door. No sign of any neighbors or the dog's owners yet.

Norah only wanted to grab a little food for her and Cliff and find a hiding place before any search parties tracked them down. That noisy irritating black lab dog had no intention of letting it happen.

"Be quiet, you stupid mutt."

A faint growl followed Norah's words this time around. The dog backpedaled from the screen door and barked even louder.

"Judd, can you go see what's bothering Meaux?" an unidentified woman's voice inside the house intercut the barking. "He won't quit yapping."

"I was just heading out to check on the crawfish."

A bald man with a trimmed beard, clad in overalls, popped open the screen door. The dog bounded past his burly legs and charged toward Norah. His barking grew more relentless. Judd's mouth dropped open when he laid eyes on her.

"Holy shit."

Her heart pounded as his dog Meaux closed the gap. A stinger popped out from the underside of her forearm. It mirrored the one that hybrid stabbed her with on Mars. She bared fangs and let out a savage growl.

Judd jerked his head toward the screen door.

"Grab my shotgun, Beth." Panic gripped his voice. "We got a … I don't know what the hell it is. You better come quick."

Norah lunged forward and snapped her teeth at the dog. Meaux backpedaled before her stinger came close enough to impale him. He kept barking as he backed away, before running off to hide.

"Good God. What in the hell are you?"

Beth stood at the open screen door behind Judd. Her hands trembled as she tried to load shells into a shotgun. An explosive rage gripped Norah from her head down to her toes when she laid eyes on the weapon. They intended to shoot her.

Not if she could help it.

Norah retracted the stinger and dropped to all fours. She galloped toward the couple and sprang off her feet as she reached Judd. The stinger popped out from her forearm a second time and she plunged it straight into his belly. Judd gasped. He clutched his belly and stumbled forward. Fresh blood oozed between his fingers. He staggered a few steps and fell face first in the grass.

Beth snapped the shotgun barrel back in place. Norah lunged at her and swatted the weapon out of the woman's quivering hands. She knocked Beth to the ground and perched atop her chest. Saliva dripped from Norah's mouth, and she panted. Her right hand wrapped around Beth's right arm and pinned the limb to the cement pad outside the screen door.

Beth kicked out her legs and jerked her shoulders, trying to free herself from Norah's grasp. She clenched her teeth and lifted her head off the ground. Tears streamed down her face.

"Please let me go. I don't want to die."

A fierce higher-volume growl escaped Norah's lips.

"Then you shouldn't have tried to shoot me."

She rammed the stinger into Beth's gaping mouth and out through her upper neck. The woman gagged and then fell silent as blood dribbled off her lips and down her chin. Norah stared at the lifeless body with hardened, feral eyes. At once, a hand grabbed her shoulder.

"Norah! What are you doing?"

She sprang to her feet and swung the bloody stinger around. Norah jabbed her arm forward without thinking. Cliff groaned. He stumbled backward and clutched a fresh puncture wound on his upper arm.

Norah blinked. Her eyes and brow softened. Both lips trembled and tears washed away the feral rage occupying her eyes moments earlier.

"I'm sorry," she sobbed. "I didn't mean to hurt you."

Norah retracted her stinger a second time and started toward him. He grimaced and backed up a few steps.

"You're changing so fast, honey." Pain bombarded both his arm and his words. "I don't think I can stay safe with you any longer."

Norah pinched her eyes shut and wiped away tears with her clawed hand. Why did she hurt Cliff? How could she do this to the man she loved so much? She did not mean to attack him. Her instincts drove her to lash out like a wild animal when she felt his hand touch her before she realized it belonged to Cliff. He never wavered from trying to help her from the time they fled Mars until now, even while everyone else wanted to put her in quarantine or simply kill her.

"I'm so sorry," Norah's eyes popped open again. "Please don't leave me. I don't want to be alone."

"You just murdered two people, Norah."

"They were going to shoot me. You saw it. I had no choice. I had to defend myself."

Cliff bowed his head. He bit down on his lower lip for a moment and winced. Norah's eyes trailed over his wounded arm. She grasped the limb and quickly ripped open his spacesuit around the area her stinger penetrated with her claws.

Norah pressed her hand to her mouth.

Purplish swelling already began forming in his flesh surrounding the puncture wound. She must have injected him with venom in the same manner that horrible alien creature infected her back on Mars. This meant an awful new reality faced them now.

Cliff would transform into a humanoid monster.

Just like her.

"You have to stay with me," Norah said. "You're going to go through the same changes as me. We have to keep helping each other survive."

He raised his head and stared at her. Tears brimmed in his eyes as he grew resigned to his new fate.

"What do we do now?"

Norah glanced at the darkening evening sky and back at him. Streaks of orange and red painted scattered clouds as the sun dipped toward the expansive horizon.

"Let's grab some food, find shelter, and figure out a plan in the morning."

# 29

Broken tree branches blanketed the ground surrounding the Earthian ship. Glass shards crunched under Xttra's boots as he drew closer to the vessel. A crumpled front end of the hull also bore witness to a sudden impact. As he studied the scene before him, Xttra wondered how anyone on board the ship survived such a crash.

Still, both Earthians survived based on evidence around the crash site. They found traces of hair and blood on seats inside the cockpit. Nothing in large enough quantities to point to life-threatening injuries for either colonist. That pointed to a frightening and plausible scenario in his mind. At least one Earthian deep in the throes of changing into a hybrid now ran loose somewhere in this forest.

Maybe two.

"We need to send agents from the Houston bureau office out here to clean up this mess," Sam said. "We'll probably need to rebuild the Magellan from scratch."

Xttra cocked his head at him and frowned.

"You should be more concerned Earthian hybrids are now loose on your planet."

"Hybrids?" Sam repeated the word like he misheard him. "Norah is the only infected one."

Xttra turned and gazed at the crumpled ship again.

"My guess is you have at least two hybrids on your hands now. The Earthian who helped her escape is no doubt also infected at this point. Dead bodies and new hybrids will multiply in equal measure as long as both remain alive."

Silence greeted Xttra's explanation. He rolled his eyes and wheeled around to face Sam again. The Earthian stared blankly ahead.

"You don't believe me?"

"Why are you jumping to such a terrible conclusion? We've seen no evidence Norah would or could infect Cliff. I spent two months alone with them on a spaceship. It isn't in her nature."

Xttra sighed. Sam adopted a far too trusting and naïve approach to this situation for his own good.

"We can walk away right now and leave the whole matter in Ahm's hands," he said. "Maybe he'll smile on your planet and solve your problem himself."

"Why are you being so sarcastic?"

"If you don't want our help capturing these hybrids, we won't force it on you."

"Do I have another choice?" Sam shook his head as though it pained him to say these words. "After seeing the damage already done back on Mars, I can't leave anything to chance. It's obvious what the future entails if we fail to track them down."

Xttra wiped sweat from his forehead across his armored sleeve. Weather conditions on this part of Earth were much more unpleasant than the area he and Calandra last visited. A stifling humidity hung in the air like a dense morning fog. It made his skin damp underneath his stellar guard uniform and flex armor. Now both were chafing. He withdrew a thermal tracker from a pouch on his belt and activated the device.

"Is your tracker picking up anything yet?"

Xttra glanced up at Kyra after she posed the question. She climbed down from the open hatch of the Earthian vessel and jumped to the ground. He shook his head.

"No one besides the three of us and ... wait."

Xttra raised his hand and signaled for everyone to be silent. Kyra whipped out her own thermal tracker from her belt. Sam stiffened and his eyes darted from tree to tree, trying to figure out what Xttra discovered.

A twig snapped. Footsteps followed.

Xttra's hand dropped to his belt line. He unlatched his holster and wrapped his fingers around the handle of his eliminator.

The footsteps drew closer.

"Identify yourselves."

Xttra turned in the same direction where he heard the voice. It belonged to an Earthian. His grip on his weapon tightened. No visible sign of the unidentified Earthian among the trees. That meant nothing. Even if he did not see them, they saw him.

"Tell me who you are first."

"We're agents with the Earth Defense Bureau."

The voice sounded gruffer this time. Xttra shot an alarmed frown at Sam.

"Relax, agent. I'm Sam Bono—field director from the Houston office. Lower your damn weapons and come out here in the open so we can chat face-to-face."

Three different agents popped out from hiding places among the trees. They holstered their pistols and approached the wrecked Earthian ship.

"Sorry, Mr. Bono. I didn't recognize you in that spacesuit." The lead agent, an Earthian man with dark curly hair and light brown skin, adopted a much more subdued tone. "We tracked the Magellan to these coordinates after it crashed."

"We also tracked it from a spacecraft," Sam replied. "Both colonists survived a crash landing and fled the Magellan. Have you uncovered any signs pointing to where they might be headed?"

The lead agent shrugged.

"We've enacted quarantine protocols throughout Calcasieu Parish. Our immediate goal is to prevent them from crossing out of Louisiana into Texas or escaping into a neighboring parish."

"That's a good start," Sam replied. He motioned to the two agents behind the lead agent. "Can you get me a phone and a car, Agent Wells? My alien friends and I need to cover ground inconspicuously and I want to stay in contact, so I can direct the bureau's search efforts."

Agent Wells stared past Sam's shoulder and his eyes settled on Xttra. A weary frown poked out from the corners of his lips. It did not offer a positive sign the agent trusted Sam or would follow his orders.

"Are you sure that's such a wise idea, sir?" he said. "You know the bureau policy on alien visitors. If they find out we're letting aliens traipse around in Louisiana—"

"I'm in charge here and they're assisting in this manhunt." Sam turned and pointed at Xttra. "These aliens are the only reason I came back from Mars alive and unharmed. I trust them with my life. There's no reason for you not to trust them."

Agent Wells' eyes drifted downward and settled on Xttra's armored sleeves. They trailed upward again until meeting his face. Xttra crossed his arms and returned a cold stare at the bureau agent.

"Have something you want to say to me, Earthian?"

He stood as rigid and motionless as a statue before Agent Wells. The bureau agent's eyes hardened, and he mimicked Xttra in folding his arms and refusing to move.

Sam sighed.

"We don't have time to start a pissing match. Carry out my request, Agent Wells, while we still have enough daylight left."

Agent Wells raised his arms and backed away. He turned away from them when he reached the edge of the tree line and relayed Sam's orders to the other two bureau agents. All three disappeared into the woods again.

"He's certainly a pleasant alien, isn't he?"

Kyra did a poor job of concealing the sarcasm couched within her words.

"Few of them are," Xttra replied.

She adjusted the range on her tracker. Sam strolled over to Kyra's position and stared at the screen. Heat patterns from random animals popped up, one after another, as the body heat sensor range spread out to cover a larger geographical area. It also picked up patterns from the departing Earth Defense Bureau agents as well as Cavac and Xander still aboard their ship.

"How much distance does your tracker cover?" Awe infused Sam's question. His eyes stayed glued to the tracker screen. "Seems like you're picking up quite a few animals out here."

"20 peds." Kyra glanced up from the screen. "At least with the newer trackers, anyway."

"Ped?"

Sam jerked his head up. He scrunched up his eyes and nose upon hearing that unfamiliar word.

"Standard unit of measurement on Lathos," Xttra said. "In Earthian terms, the tracker's range extends about 25 kilometers in any given direction."

His explanation did not do much to erase the confusion resting on Sam's face. The Earthian nodded and refocused his eyes on the tracker.

"And here I thought converting miles to kilometers was complicated," he mumbled.

Xttra scanned in the opposite direction. His tracker detected heat patterns from multiple small Earthian animals. He adjusted the tracker's sensitivity. The Earthians were larger, so Xttra realized he needed to block out irrelevant heat patterns. His adjustments boosted the tracker's range and the patterns changed. He detected two larger heat patterns moving east toward the border of the forest.

One still resembled a typical Earthian. The other exhibited characteristics more consistent with a hybrid.

"Found them." Xttra raised his head and wheeled around, facing Kyra and Sam. "Our Earthian hybrids are moving east out of the forest."

"Damn. I was afraid of that," Sam said. "They're heading into Sulphur. We need that car now."

"How many men, women, and children dwell in this Earthian village?"

"20,000? 30,000? I don't know the exact number."

Kyra pressed her hand to her mouth and shook her head. Xttra's heart started racing when Sam disclosed the population numbers. Nothing good could come from this development. Hybrids escaping into a small Earthian city offered a blueprint for a massacre.

He only hoped they reached this place called Sulphur before things spiraled out of control further.

***

A sign suspended between two brick posts bisecting a brick circle welcomed visitors to Sulphur. Xttra's eyes drifted from the sign over to an expansive Earthian burial ground across the road. Partially exposed tombs littered the ground. Each tomb matched an adult Earthian in site and were paired with single thick flat stones of varying shapes and sizes. A chill consumed his bones like a ravenous monster as Xttra gazed upon this burial ground. Nagging thoughts of sharing their fate dug at him.

Executing a Ra'ahmian hybrid on a barren planet like Mars offered a night and day contrast to tracking down an Earthian hybrid on their home planet. Even with the aid of advanced technology, they navigated unfamiliar surroundings among a mostly unfamiliar alien race. Xttra understood all too well how quickly hostile Earthians ambushed interplanetary visitors.

"Are you getting any signs of their whereabouts on your trackers?"

Sam glanced in the rearview mirror at Xttra. Both of his hands gripped the steering wheel. Kyra peeked up from her tracker screen and shook her head.

"So many Earthians are popping up around us. I can't get a clean lock on the hybrids."

Sam glanced over at her in the front passenger seat and frowned.

"In other words, we're literally searching for needles in a haystack."

Kyra crinkled her eyes and nose at him.

"What's a haystack? I'm not sure what you mean."

Sam returned an equally puzzled look. Then his expression changed when it dawned on him neither Kyra, nor Xttra, nor Xander owned a deep enough knowledge of Earth to understand what his saying meant.

"Sorry. It's a common expression among my people. It means we're searching for an object that's virtually impossible to find."

Xander, who shared the backseat with Xttra, gazed out the window.

"Conducting this search would be so much easier from our ship."

Kyra turned and furrowed her brow at her assistant pilot. A stern frown crossed her lips. Xttra did not fault Xander for making such a suggestion. His nerves were getting the better of him. He wanted to be in a safer place.

"How do you suggest we do that?" she said. "Our thermal trackers won't pick up anything useful from that altitude and you know it."

Sam drummed his fingers on the steering wheel as he weaved around the left side of another slower-moving Earthian car.

"Our best bet is to travel west toward the edge of town," he said. "That should thin out the number of people showing up your trackers and help us zero in on Cliff and Norah."

Sam made a sharp left turn when the paved road they were traveling on intersected with another paved road. Two sets of three lights housed in vertical casings hung from a horizontal metal pole running above the point where the two roads joined. Sam started his turn as the hanging lights changed from yellow to red. A loud noise blared from a car traveling down the opposite side of the road when he cut in front of the oncoming vehicle's path.

Xttra's eyes drifted down to his own tracker again. Red blobs showing heat patterns belonging to multiple Earthians and animals cluttered the screen. They were taking a panicked, disorganized approach to this search. A better path lay ahead.

He closed his eyes and puzzled over what he knew about dochus. The hybrid he killed on Mars owned a blend of dochu and human features. Dochu nests were abundant along the northern coasts of Ashmuth on Lathos' southern continent. These animals sought out caves, rainforests, and damp environments for shelter and food. If dochu biomaterial also infected the Earthian colonists as Xttra suspected, it made sense for them to seek food and shelter in a place with abundant water.

"I have an idea where they went." Xttra opened his eyes again and peeked up from the tracker. "Where is the nearest river or lake?"

Sam shrugged. "I'll have to adjust my GPS to see."

Kyra snapped her head at Xttra.

"What makes you think the Earthian hybrids are headed to a river or lake?"

"Think about it. The hybrid I killed had dochu biomaterial laced into its bio code. What's one thing we know about that species?"

"They love water."

"Exactly."

A subtle smile peeked out from the corners of Kyra's lips. The same revelation which entered Xttra's mind earlier also settled on her.

"We need to travel to whatever river or lake is nearest to where our trackers last detected the infected Earthians," she said, glancing over at Sam. "Our hybrids will build a nest in that area."

Sam's eyes darted over to his smartphone, mounted on the car's dashboard. It now displayed a map of a nearby river named the Bayou D'Inde. Several small unnamed lakes and ponds also cluttered the screen.

"I see a few ponds that would work as possible nesting places," he said. "This isn't narrowing it down much."

At once, a buzzing sound came from the smartphone. A series of numbers materialized on the screen. Two words—incoming call—appeared below the numbers. Sam furrowed his brow and quickly pressed a button on the steering wheel.

"Talk to me."

"We've got a lead on the infected colonists."

Xttra recognized the voice. It belonged to Agent Wells, one of the Earth Defense Bureau agents they encountered at the crash site. His voice came through a round silver and black speaker clipped to a visor directly in front of Sam hanging above the car's windshield.

"Where are they?" Sam asked.

"We patched into the Sulphur police scanner," Agent Wells said. "A frantic emergency call just came in from a local waterpark. Eyewitnesses reported two people get into a scuffle with a park employee. They described one as having inhuman features."

Xttra's eyes grew wider as Wells shared what he overheard on the police scanner. They had tracked down the infected Earthian colonists.

In one of the worst possible places.

"Where is this waterpark located?" Sam asked.

"Parrish Road."

Sam gasped.

"We're already driving on Parrish Road."

"Fortunate timing."

"We're on our way," Sam said. "Meet us outside the park entrance as soon as possible. And call in an emergency code to the bureau. Put a ranger team on standby just in case."

The car's speed increased as soon as the conversation ended. Xttra hoped they would not arrive too late to stop a massacre from unfolding.

# 30

Several Earthians were fleeing toward their parked vehicles when Sam turned into a paved lot outside the waterpark. Panic claimed ownership of their faces and bodies. The same fear seized Xttra's heart, no matter how much he tried to push it away.

He had a brush with death while battling the last hybrid. Fortune may not favor him in the same way a second time. All sentient beings believed themselves exceptional. Their natures made them see death as a distant menace unable to stake a claim until a detached future time. A part of him acknowledged the panicking Earthians were smart to flee. Yet, Xttra would never permit himself to join their flight. His sense of honor told him he must do his part to save innocent people—even on a planet he despised.

Their car skidded to a stop only a short walk from an iron fence. Xttra spotted one Earthian lying motionless on the ground only a few steps beyond the fence line. He frowned. They were already too late to save at least one person from these hybrids.

"Stay alert," Kyra said. "This is alien territory. Keep your eyes and ears open."

She flung open the car door and sprang off the seat. A black car sped into the paved lot right as Xttra climbed out of the backseat. Flashing lights adorned this new vehicle. Yellow lettering, spelling out police, covered the driver's side. The car's sudden appearance made him skittish. Xttra encountered Earthians driving similar vehicles once before. Those Earthians helped the Earth Defense Bureau capture him and Calandra when they tried to flee from the Earthian village called Hideout.

"What's the meaning of this?" Xttra poked his head back inside the car door. "Are these Earthians here to make us their prisoners?"

Sam narrowed his eyes and let out a frustrated sigh.

"Local police," he said. "You got nothing to worry about. Let me handle them."

Sam popped open his door and exited the car right as a door on the police car opened. An Earthian clad in a dark short sleeve shirt and black pants stepped out of the vehicle. Xttra's eyes were drawn to a bright gold badge hanging off the Earthian's shirt below his left shoulder. He also wore a belt with a weapon resting in a holster on his right hip.

He approached Sam.

"We got a call about an altercation here at the waterpark. Are you the ones who made the call?"

"You better let us handle this situation, officer," Sam replied. "This is out of your jurisdiction."

A fresh scowl appeared on the police officer's face.

"Who the hell do you think you're talking to? This is a police matter. Get back inside your vehicle and stay there until we need to take statements from—"

"We don't have time for this," Kyra said, cutting him off. "This situation will only spiral further out of control if we let those hybrids escape from this place."

The police officer jabbed his index finger at her.

"If y'all keep back talking, I'm gonna lock you up faster than a gator swims through a bayou."

Xttra cracked a sarcastic grin.

"Is that a fact? I count four of us and one of you."

He wheeled around and faced Xttra.

"Are you threatening me, son?"

"One threat deserves another."

"Enough!"

Sam pounded his fist on the hood of the Earth Defense Bureau car. Xttra and Kyra both flinched when flesh and bone struck metal and exchanged nervous glances. Neither had seen his temper flare to a degree rivaling this current outburst.

"I am with the Earth Defense Bureau." Sam locked his eyes squarely on the police officer. "This is a matter of planetary security. For your own safety, hang back and let us handle this situation."

The officer cast a sideways glance at their car. EDB adorned the side in bold block lettering, mirroring how the word police covered the side of his own vehicle. His brows knit together, and he sighed.

"Let me see some ID."

"What?" Sam cast a nervous glance toward the waterpark fence. "Are you serious?"

"Look at me."

All eyes turned to Xander. His fingers wrapped around a stun pebble, telegraphing his plan for the rest of the group who understood what he intended to do. Xttra quickly averted his eyes as Sam protested with a shout. A blinding flash followed a few seconds later. When Xttra opened his eyes again, the local police officer had dropped to his knees. He buried his eyes inside his hands while he cursed at them.

"Nice work," Kyra said. "Bind his arms and legs and shove him back inside his Earthian vehicle."

Sam just shook his head repeatedly, after opening his eyes again, while Xander carried out her orders. He bound the officer with restraints, shoved him across the backseat of his vehicle, and sealed the door behind him.

"Relax," he said, facing Sam. "Your fellow Earthian won't experience permanent blindness."

"That's not my main concern," Sam said.

Kyra and Xttra struck out in front, both holding thermal trackers. Xttra reduced the range on his tracker to encompass only the waterpark and immediate surrounding area. Three heat patterns popped up inside the park. All human or humanoid. One lay on the ground. Two others were still upright and moving.

Vivid orange and yellow streaks painted clouds flanking the Earthian sun as it dipped low on the horizon, foretelling the arrival of night. Retreating sunlight invited lengthening shadows to emerge from buildings, the perimeter fence, and odd towering structures inside the park he had never seen before. Xttra's eyes darted about as he passed through the park gate. Two Earthians lay in crumpled heaps on the ground. One, a lanky man, had half-open lifeless eyes and a blood-soaked shirt. The other, a petite woman, let out an anguished moan and went silent. Blood pooled out from under her chest.

Sam dashed over to her side and pressed his fingers against the woman's throat. He flashed a somber frown and shook his head.

"She's dead."

Kyra's expression hardened into a determined scowl.

"I'm closing in on one of our hybrids." Her voice barely rose above a whisper. "A heat pattern is climbing upward toward an enclosed tube ahead."

"That's a waterslide," Sam said. "Be careful. If they're around a slide, they will have the high ground against us."

She nodded and unholstered her speargun. Xttra simultaneously drew out his eliminator. Kyra glanced over at Xander and Sam and motioned for them to split off. She pointed at a building next to the main gates.

"Track down the hybrid hidden inside that building."

"The ticket office?" Sam replied.

Kyra nodded a second time. She stuck the tracker back in her pouch and tossed him an eliminator. Sam caught it with both hands and stared at the weapon.

"Let's end this right now."

Xander and Sam split off and headed toward the ticket office back door. Kyra and Xttra continued forward at a deliberate pace toward the structure Sam called a waterslide. Two of these structures stood near one another. One slide, built from yellow plastic, started from a high platform with guard rails and coiled toward the ground in a tight spiral. The tube straightened out near the bottom and stopped at the edge of a shallow pool. The second slide resembled a giant green tube winding over and under the yellow slide. It also straightened out before reaching the same pool.

Xttra carefully studied his surroundings as they neared the pool. It was not a natural pool. The water rested inside an artificial depression. A white pavement covered all sides and the bottom. Similar pavement blanketed the entire ground inside the fence.

He glanced down at the tracker. It showed a heat pattern on the stairs leading to the high platform at the start of the yellow slide.

"On the stairs." Xttra pointed skyward. "Block the hybrid's escape route."

Kyra crept toward the bottom stair, her speargun pointed straight ahead. A shot rang out. She crouched down and ducked behind a support beam. Xttra also ducked behind another support beam and stared upward. Cliff stood atop the platform, aiming an Earthian weapon at their position below. The weapon reminded

Xttra of Kevin's old rifle, only it featured parallel metallic tubes for high velocity projectiles instead of a single tube. His face showed distinct signs of developing hybrid features.

"You alien bastards don't know when to leave us alone," he shouted. "Get back in your spaceship and go back to your own damn planet."

"I plan to go home," Xttra replied. "Just as soon as we've dealt with you and your hybrid friend here."

He fired an eliminator bolt at the platform. It struck the surrounding railing. Cliff flinched at sparks spraying out from the metal. He ducked and swung his weapon toward the support beam. Xttra dropped behind the beam a second time.

At once, Kyra's arca vox beeped inside a pouch on her belt. She pulled it out and activated the holoscreen. A bouncing blur appeared in place of a distinct, solid image. Shouting voices blasted through the arca vox. Their words were partially muffled, but their fear came through loud and clear.

A door flew open. Both Xander and Sam sprinted from the ticket office. Sam haphazardly fired his borrowed eliminator while glancing back over his shoulder. Xander's right arm hung limp and his speargun was missing. He ripped a Cassian fire shell from his pouch, pressed the detonator button on top, and lobbed the cylinder back at the door. Blue-white flames ignited and billowed through the open doorway.

Exterior lights atop towering metal posts along the perimeter fence sprang to life. Other cars with flashing lights and sirens entered the paved lot outside the fence. Sam cocked his head toward the oncoming vehicles.

"We've got company," he said.

At once, Norah leapt through the wall of flame. She charged toward Sam and Xander with the determination of an angry sapinoa. A stinger popped out from her left forearm, and she bared jagged fangs. Her appearance was enough to induce a few nightmares. Kyra stepped out from her hiding spot behind the support beam and fired at the hybrid. The spear head's laser edge grazed Norah's right shoulder. She unleashed a fearsome yowl.

It did nothing to slow her down.

A second shot rang out from the platform above their position. An empty shell rolled off the platform and struck the ground. Kyra dived behind the support beam again. She winced and grasped her left arm. When she pulled her hand away, blood coated the palm.

"My flex armor didn't fully absorb the impact from that projectile." Her voice grew strained while she leaned back against the beam and clutched her upper arm again. "Blast that wretched thing off that platform."

Xttra peeked out from behind the adjacent support beam and fired multiple eliminator bolts in rapid succession. The first bolt struck the railing. The second one found its mark. Cliff clutched his left leg and let out a shout. He staggered toward the winding yellow slide and ducked inside the narrow tube.

Norah reached Xander and Sam before Xttra had a chance to impede her progress. She barreled into both men. The borrowed eliminator flew out of Sam's hand. All three splashed into a shallow pool below the slides.

Water churned around them as Xander struggled with Norah. With an injured arm, he proved no match for the hybrid. She plunged her stinger through his spine and shoved his head under the water. Xander kicked and flailed his arms trying to free himself.

Norah growled and only pushed him down further into the water, attempting to crack his skull on the bottom of the pool.

Xttra sprinted toward the pool, firing his eliminator. A fresh bolt struck Norah in the same shoulder Kyra grazed earlier, forming a smoking hole in both fabric and flesh. The hybrid howled in pain and shouted an unintelligible word at Xttra.

She raised Xander's head from the water and quickly snapped his neck. The Confederation officer splashed back down into the pool. His lifeless body now floated face down atop the water.

Cliff shot out from the end of the yellow slide and splashed down into the water right after the eliminator bolt struck Norah. He swam toward Sam while the Earth Defense Bureau official scrambled to reach the edge of the pool. Cliff caught Sam by his right ankle just as he scrambled out of the water.

Norah plunged deeper into the shallow pool and swam away from Xttra. He kept sprinting along the water's edge. She needed to pop out of the water to breathe soon. When the Earthian hybrid resurfaced, he would finish her off.

"Stop! Don't come one step closer."

Xttra stopped running and swung his eliminator toward Cliff. He had wrapped Sam up in a chokehold. The same eliminator Kyra lent to Sam earlier now pointed at his left ear. Small puddles formed around their feet.

"I will shoot him if you keep trying to kill us."

Cliff gave Sam an agitated sideways glance. A wry smile crept across his lips.

"Or maybe I'll make him endure the same ordeal Norah and I are enduring. And force your hand. You'll have no choice but to help us."

Xttra kept his eyes locked on the infected Earthian colonist, not flinching for a second.

"I found one simple flaw in your little scenario. I'm a faster and better shot than you."

Shouts outside the waterpark fence grabbed Cliff's attention. He gave the fence a sideways glance. That offered enough of an opening for Xttra. He fired a bolt from his eliminator. A spear head sailed past him at the same time.

Both struck Cliff.

He stumbled and fell forward, knocking Sam to the ground in the same motion. Sam peeled away Cliff's arm and rolled out from under the infected Earthian. Xttra turned and saw Kyra standing a few steps behind him. Her left arm hung limp and she grimaced as new pain burst through her wounded limb.

Norah sprang from the water. She laid eyes on Cliff's body sprawled out on the ground and let out an immediate anguished scream. The hybrid charged toward Xttra, intending to impale him with her stinger. He fired more bolts. One shattered the extended stinger. Others pierced her through the chest and belly.

Norah staggered a few steps and finally tumbled to the ground. She crawled over to Cliff's lifeless body, leaving a blood trail behind her. Tears raced down her cheeks as she lifted her fellow colonist up into a sitting position and hugged him.

Kyra raised her speargun to finish off the dying hybrid. Xttra shook his head and waved her off.

"I just want this nightmare to end." Norah's whispered voice broke while she talked to Cliff as though he still heard her. "I want to be me again. I want to be Norah. I want us to enjoy a happy life together again."

A lump formed in Xttra's throat when those words reached his ears. He lowered his eliminator and watched in silence as Norah rested her own forehead against Cliff's forehead. She closed her eyes, clenched her jaw, and mumbled other words Xttra could not discern. The Earthian let out a final pained gasp a second later. Both Norah and Cliff slumped over on the ground, her arms still encircling him.

Each one a victim, in their own way, of Delcor's past atrocities resurfacing.

"I owe you my life. Thank you."

Sam pressed his hand against his forehead and drew a sharp breath as he stood on his feet again. Xttra gave him a sharp glance.

His eyes trailed down the Earthian's body. Aside from sopping wet clothing, he spotted nothing out of the ordinary.

"Did the hybrid impale you with her stinger? Concealing any open wounds?"

Sam held out his arms away from his body.

"See for yourself. The only damage I suffered is a few new bumps and bruises. I got off lucky."

Kyra put away her speargun and shuffled over to him. She glanced up and down, searching for signs of puncture wounds or other similar injuries the dead hybrids may have caused. After a minute, the Confederation pilot stepped back and nodded.

"He's clean."

A wave of relief smacked Xttra. He returned his eliminator to its holster.

At once, a loud voice called out to Sam. All three turned to see Agent Wells and his fellow bureau agents approaching with pistols drawn.

"Impeccable timing." Sam made no effort to conceal his sarcasm. "You're right on time to clean up this mess."

Agent Wells frowned.

"The hybrids?"

"Both dead. The threat has been eliminated."

Agent Wells cracked a smile and shook his head.

"You seriously locked a cop up inside his own cruiser? The Sulphur PD wants your head on a platter."

Sam shrugged and hinted at a smile of his own.

"Too bad this is all a matter of planetary security. They can't do anything about it."

Agent Wells laughed and directed the other agents to go secure the dead bodies. Sam, Xttra, and Kyra started walking back toward the main gates.

"So, I guess you'll be heading back to Lathos now?" Sam asked, glancing over at Xttra.

"I can't afford to stay," he replied. "Every day spent on Earth is a day Calandra is put at further risk."

Kyra scowled. This time, her wounded arm was not the sole cause for her displeasure.

"We just barely landed on this planet. I'm under strict orders to forge an alliance with Earthian leadership. My hands are bound."

Xttra returned her scowl and jabbed his finger at her.

"Even traveling at the fastest possible speed, a year will have passed when I lay eyes on Calandra again. How can you deny me a speedy reunion? I helped you. I helped the Earthians. Now it's time to return the favor."

Sam extended his hand toward Kyra. She glanced down and back up at him with a confused look.

"We have forged an alliance," he said. "Your people are welcome to return to Earth in the future. We could use your help in moving forward with our planned extrasolar colony near Alpha Centauri. This isn't a goodbye. It's a hello."

Kyra hesitated. Her eyes flashed over to the pool where bureau agents fished out Xander's body and then refocused on Xttra.

"What guarantee do I have you won't imprison me and Cavac on the return journey to Lathos?"

Xttra licked his lips and bowed his head for a moment. He had not easily shaken off Kyra's earlier cruelty and willingness to threaten and torture him to suit her purposes. She deserved to face justice for her actions. Hearing Sam confirm his worst fears that the Earthians intended to settle planets beyond the Aramus system also did not sit well with him. Odds of other Earthian leaders experiencing a change of heart mirroring the change Sam made were slim at best.

Still, Xttra had to overlook these issues in favor of more pressing concerns. Delcor emerged as his true enemy and the chief sovereign had Calandra in his sights. Xttra needed to do everything in his power to save her.

"You don't need to worry about me," he said, lifting his chin again. "Your enemy is now my enemy."

# 31

Calandra studied the injector long after the blue light clicked on, and she had withdrawn the twin needles from her forearm. Even as an inanimate object resting in her hand, it mocked her. Taking bone strengtheners stood as an enduring symbol of the cruel role fate played in her life. Each turn fate took proved more vicious than the one that came before, sending her into a bottomless spiral.

She let out an anguished scream and threw the injector against the bathroom wall. The molded outer shell cracked open and scattered in pieces across the floor. Calandra sank to her knees and buried her face in her hands. Tears leaked out from under her palms as her sobs filled the room.

"I can't handle this burden." Her words came out in a strained whisper. "I feel so alone."

Xttra was stolen from her. Alayna was murdered. Calandra despaired at the thought of what other awful things lurked unseen behind the door. Her life was unraveling at the seams. All because their chief sovereign sought to conceal his awful crimes.

She despised him for what he had done and continued to do. Delcor was no exemplar of heroic virtue. All those stories detailing his courageous and wise leadership during the Separatist War, and since that time, rang false now. Each one no more than a twisted fable, dreamt up to obscure Ra'ahm's real history.

Noisy persistent beeps echoed from her bedroom. Calandra turned and stared at the open doorway. Her arca vox was the source. Multiple people tried to contact her over the last two days. Calandra never bothered to return contact or give her arca vox a second glance. Why involve them in her life at this point? They would only end up dead or missing in the end, like everyone else who mattered to her.

*You can't shut the rest of the world out forever. Stand and fight. Hope has not fled.*

Those words surged into her mind and burned inside her heart. Calandra drew in a sharp breath and rose to her feet. She steadied herself against the washbasin and brushed back her auburn hair.

"I need to stand against him. I can't let him threaten me into permanent silence."

Calandra whispered her vow as she wiped away tears. It fell on her shoulders to become an agent of change. For Xttra's sake. For Alayna's sake. Her grandfather lacked the courage to do the right thing. Calandra refused to let herself travel down a similar path.

Kevin was right. Her life had changed forever.

This fight belonged to her now.

The beeps ceased. Calandra smoothed out her long-sleeved shirt and walked straight into the bedroom to retrieve her arca vox. An urgent message flashed across the holoscreen when she activated the device.

It came from Bo'un.

"Where are you? What happened to you?" Fear and urgency spread through his voice. "I've been trying to reach you for two days.

I don't know if you're dead or alive. If you can hear this, Calandra, please contact me."

She bowed her head after the message finished. Calandra's decision to shut herself off from the rest of the world for two whole days created some unintended repercussions. Bo'un had no way of knowing if she was still alive. The last time they spoke, she was fleeing a would-be assassin. She said nothing to him since that time. Nothing to her parents or siblings either.

Guilt splashed over Calandra like a spray from a waterfall. How many people who cared about her were worried sick right now?

Calandra did not waste another second. She punched in the code for Bo'un's arca vox. Relief spread through her like a web when his image popped up on the holoscreen only a few seconds later.

"Calandra?"

Shock tinged his voice. Bo'un sank down into a chair behind him. He pressed his hand over his mouth.

"Apologies. I should have tried to contact you sooner." She cast her eyes at the ground for a moment and back up at him. "I've endured a few rough days."

Bo'un dropped his hand again and flashed a relieved smile at her.

"Praise Ahm—you're alive. I feared the worst when I didn't hear from you."

His smile disappeared as his eyes settled on her tear-stained cheeks and stoic frown.

"What happened?"

"Alayna is dead."

"Your friend?"

Calandra nodded.

"Someone murdered her. I found her dead body. They tried to … frame me … for ..."

Her lips quivered and tears flowed freely again. Bo'un rubbed the jagged scars on his jaw and neck. Concern filled his gray eyes as he pressed his lips together. He was at a loss for words.

She brushed away fresh tears with her right hand. Calandra swallowed away the lump forming in her throat and drew in a heavy breath.

"Why do these terrible things keep happening to us?" she asked. "What did we do to deserve it?"

A resolute frown deepened on his face.

"Nothing," Bo'un said. "We did nothing to deserve these things. Sometimes, people do evil things and innocents suffer the consequences. That's what makes them evil."

Calandra cast her eyes down at the floor. She knew what she needed to say. Dread clawed at her and ordered her to stay quiet for her own good. But she had to quash that feeling. Fear could not rule her any longer.

Someone else needed to know. Bo'un could help her expose the chief sovereign's deeds and shine a light on his true nature.

"He threatened my life, Bo'un."

"Who? Talan?"

"The chief sovereign."

Silence greeted her revelation. Calandra returned her gaze to the holoscreen. Bo'un's mouth hung partially open, and he stared unblinking at her. A numb shock threaded itself through his face.

"His hand guided everything that's unfolded," she said. "He gave my grandfather a choice of exile or death when he uncovered the sovereign's past crimes. Alayna and I uncovered the same crimes. He pressured me to stay silent in exchange for my life."

Bo'un stroked his chin, sinking into deep thought as Calandra recounted her encounter with Delcor in the holding cell. Her words rattled him. His worried eyes and intensifying frown told Calandra as much.

"Ominade was right," she said. "He intends to destroy everyone who survived our expedition to Earth. We can't let his plan succeed."

Bo'un answered her with a slow nod.

"That explains a few things on my end."

Calandra shot him a questioning look.

"What things?"

"Stellar Guard leadership pushed me to end my search for Xttra."

"What? They can't do that."

"One year has passed since his abduction. They want to declare him dead and close the case."

Anger surged inside Calandra and a fire filled her eyes. Stellar Guard leaders wanted to bury their collective heads under the sand and ignore what stared them in the face. Calling off the search for Xttra and pretending he was dead meant no one had to face uncomfortable realities about their chief sovereign.

"We can't let them get away with this."

Bo'un glanced off-screen and closed his eyes. He grimaced. Calandra realized he held back from fully sharing what occupied his mind.

"What are you not telling me? Did something else happen, Bo'un?"

He faced her again and opened his eyes.

"This is the end. I resigned from the Stellar Guard. I could not accept their decision. I can't abandon Xttra like that. Not after everything we all endured together."

Calandra sank down on her bed. She stared into space, at a total loss for words. The Stellar Guard had abandoned Xttra to his fate. They were on their own in finding him and bringing him home.

If he was still alive.

"Any word from Ominade?"

Bo'un's question triggered renewed anger. The Stellar Guard was not alone in abandoning them in this dark hour. Several days passed without a single word from Ominade or Kevin. He promised to put Calandra in contact with an underground refugee network that would help her flee Ra'ahm. His promise had gone unfulfilled. She pressed the Aracian letter on her contact block at random times since their meeting. Still, Kevin never appeared later. Neither did Ominade or another agent working for her.

The worst part is she did not know why. Did their silence mean something sinister also happened to them? Did they share Alayna's fate?

"I reached out to her many times." A fierce anger boiling inside Calandra swam among her words. "No luck. She has vanished as quickly as she appeared."

"Maybe it's time we paid the fake diviner another visit," Bo'un said. "Ominade led us down this path. The least she can do is travel the same path with us."

Calandra agreed wholeheartedly with that sentiment. They faced real jeopardy, in part, because of Ominade. If she and her agents were unwilling to act, they needed to find a way to shake them out of their complacency.

***

Raindrops pelted the aerorover's outer shell as Bo'un guided it toward a landing spot along a street around the corner from Ominade's shop. A fierce storm sent patrons and merchants scrambling from street markets as they sought shelter from the downpour. Calandra's eyes darted from one end of the street to the other as the aerorover descended. She wondered if Zatoriah or Talan tracked them from an unseen spot, waiting for the right moment to strike. Hidden eyes and ears could be lurking anywhere. Watching and listening.

Bo'un cast his eyes skyward once magnetic wheels touched stone pavement covering the street.

"I wish rainstorms turned on and off as easy as a holocaster," he said. "These are awful flying conditions."

"I know what you mean," Calandra said. "But we can't afford to wait around and do nothing."

Bo'un shut down the aerorover engine. They flung open their respective doors, shut both again quickly, and dashed down the street. Calandra shielded her eyes with her artificial arm as they rounded the corner. Water ran down her forearm and drizzled off her elbow. Raindrops also soaked Calandra's auburn hair and trailed down her forehead and cheeks. Her feet splashed through one growing puddle after another, shooting out splashes of water from each puddle.

Calandra glanced up at the square sign displaying the diviner's symbol and rushed toward the main door. It slid open with a metallic whoosh. Chimes rang out when she entered the shop, and again when Bo'un followed on her heels a second later. Calandra blinked away remnants of raindrops and brushed back wet strands of hair.

She cast her eyes around the shop. Her limbs tensed up and her spine tightened.

Empty space greeted her eyes.

Pendants. Trinkets. Rings. All vanished. A few empty shelves, a counter, and rotating poles which held the aforementioned items only inhabited the shop now. No other visible evidence remained to show Ominade ever occupied this place.

"Where did she go?"

Fear filled Bo'un's eyes and crept into his voice. Calandra sensed an identical fear sprouting inside her chest and extending roots through her limbs. Did the chief sovereign's agents finally track down Ominade? Did she and Bo'un inadvertently lead them here on their earlier trip to meet with her?

"This feels like a trap."

Calandra's quiet words were not quiet enough for her comfort. Even a whisper made a pointed echo in this empty shell of a room. She cast her eyes toward the stairs leading to Ominade's underground chamber. The metal chamber door had been sealed.

"I wonder if she concealed herself in her chamber." Calandra glanced over her shoulder at Bo'un. "Remember how Ominade told us magnetic door locks made it tough for unwanted visitors to go down there?"

Bo'un frowned.

"If those locks are active, we're not getting inside that chamber either."

She turned back and stared at the sealed door. Calandra tiptoed forward and waved her hand before the door, hoping to trigger a hidden sensor that would release the magnetic locks. The door did not budge, and she heard no noises to suggest a sensor activated.

"What do you think we should do?"

Calandra wheeled around and faced Bo'un again. An obvious answer to his question did not pop into her mind. If only they could break through the door, it might illuminate what transpired here.

"I don't suppose you have a cutter strong enough to punch a hole through this metal?" she asked. "It might be our only option at this point."

Bo'un stiffened. His hand dropped to a holster on his right hip. He drew out his eliminator. Calandra's eyes widened when she laid eyes on the weapon.

"What are you—"

Bo'un pressed his left index finger to his lips. Then he pointed at the ceiling. She nodded and swallowed hard. Her heart pounded against her ribs. Calandra dared not gaze up into the rafters to search out what he had seen. It already dawned on her what she would find. Someone else had hidden themselves inside the shop, spying on them from above.

She closed her eyes and tried to slow her intensifying breathing to a normal rate. When Calandra opened her eyes again, Bo'un had drawn out a thermal tracker from a pouch on his belt. The screen lit up. Several heat patterns materialized on the screen inside and outside the shop. He touched the screen and reduced the tracker range to only the shop itself. One red blob after another faded away until only four heat patterns showed on the screen.

Two were in the rafters directly above their heads.

Both resembled humanoid lifeforms.

Terror crawled up Calandra's spine. She dared not move a single step in any direction. What they found on the tracker screen only confirmed a lingering fear.

She and Bo'un were not alone inside the empty shop.

# 32

Bo'un refused to take his eyes off the ceiling. He extended his arm and handed the tracker off to Calandra. She tucked it in the palm of her metal hand. He raised his eliminator to eye level. Calandra finally forced herself to cast her eyes skyward. She needed to see who hid above the shop floor for herself, no matter how much that knowledge frightened her.

Her eyes traced a maze of long wooden rafters and hanging lights running along the ceiling. Mirror shades covered each light to boost illumination along the floor, leaving shadowy places in the rafters. It offered a perfect spot to spy on someone below while staying hidden to the naked eye. Calandra had excellent vision, but even her eyes played tricks on her in the shadows. No clues tipped her off to the lurkers' locations.

A laser bolt discharged from a spot above her head.

Calandra threw up an arm to shield herself and ducked down. Bo'un exhaled loudly. She snapped her head in his direction. He stumbled back a couple of steps. The bolt punched a hole through the right shoulder of his uniform, leaving singed and torn fabric in its wake.

His flex armor remained intact underneath.

Bo'un fired a bolt from his eliminator into the rafters. Splinters shot out from the blast point.

Calandra sprinted toward the counter. More bolts rained down from the ceiling. Splinters and wood chunks flew upward from impact points around her. Smoldering holes peppered the floor now. She dove behind the counter and pressed her back tight against it.

At once, a brilliant bluish white flash lit up the room behind her. Calandra saw the stun pebble's light bursting forth in her peripheral vision and quickly pinched her eyelids shut to avoid suffering accidental blindness. Screams from the rafters greeted her ears. A thud on the floor followed.

"I got one," Bo'un whispered.

Calandra's eyes popped open again. She peeked around the corner of the counter. Bo'un crouched under a pock-marked table. A dark-haired man lay motionless on the floor, his mouth partially agape.

"Is he—"

"Dead? Without a doubt. Broken neck."

She grimaced and averted her eyes from the body. It was not Talan. Calandra did not recognize the dead man. Kevin once informed her the chief sovereign used an extensive network of agents for carrying out his secret orders throughout Ra'ahm and the rest of Lathos. It meant a random attack on her could occur at any time or in any place.

That thought terrified her to the core. How could she ever sleep again?

"We need to get back to your aerorover," Calandra said. "I don't like our odds of survival staying in here."

"That's only one," Bo'un replied. "Where's the other one we detected on the tracker?"

She poked her head around the counter again. Bo'un's eyes still followed rafter beams and hanging lights. A fresh hole over his ribs adorned his shirt. His flex armor remained intact and kept the eliminator bolt from piercing flesh and bone. Still, their good fortune would fade away if they did not conceal themselves. Calandra did not have the security of wearing her own flex armor. The protective fabric was reserved alone for use by Stellar Guard officers and city guards. Taking a direct hit from an eliminator, like Bo'un had suffered twice now, would end her life.

He shot a questioning glance at her. Calandra remembered the thermal tracker was still in her metal hand. Her eyes dropped to the screen. One other heat pattern still lingered. The unseen person moved silently toward her until they were almost on top of Calandra.

She gulped and pointed directly above her head. Bo'un nodded and swung his eliminator upward. He angled the barrel at a narrow rafter beam running above her head and discharged two bolts from the eliminator. A pained groan followed.

Their would-be assassin, a woman wearing traditional silver Orontallan half-braids, staggered into the light and fell forward off the beam. She landed face-first on the counter with a crunch. Her left arm flopped down against the counter in front of Calandra. Blood dripped off the woman's fingertips and splashed on the floor. Her lifeless face possessed an eerie calm, her eyes unblinking. Calandra gasped and pressed a hand against her mouth to stifle a scream.

"That takes care of the immediate threat," Bo'un said. "Now we only need to worry about escaping from Luma unharmed."

Calandra stiffened and answered him with an unblinking stare. "How are we going to do that?"

Bo'un gazed at his eliminator and shrugged.

"We'll scale that cliff when we reach the mountain."

He did not inspire confidence. They dispatched two assassins who let their guard down while not expecting detection or resistance. Calandra held no illusions of a similar favorable scenario repeating itself if they crossed paths with more agents loyal to the chief sovereign along their escape route.

"Where are we going to go?"

"First stop is your apartment. Grab what we need to survive. From there, we'll take my aerorover into the Aurora Mountains and escape across the border into Daraconiah. We should be safe there. For the moment."

Bo'un's thermal tracker dropped from Calandra's hand and clattered against the floor. She buried her face in her hands and rubbed them down her cheeks.

"This is happening so fast," she said. "I don't know if I'm ready to leave my home and never come back."

Bo'un cast a worried stare at both dead bodies and then glanced back at the main shop door. No one else had tried to come inside, but his expression told Calandra he suspected their immediate peace would meet an abrupt end if they waited any longer.

"Neither of us wants this," Bo'un said. The tone in his voice grew more forceful. "I get it. I really do. I have a family too. But our choices are growing limited. These people waited here specifically to ambush us."

Calandra harbored the same suspicions. Evidence supporting his conclusion added up in her mind. She wondered if Delcor used them as bait all along to lure out Ominade and other rebels from the shadows. If his agents indeed found and executed the band of rebels, it meant both she and Bo'un had outlived their usefulness to the chief sovereign.

They needed to flee from Ra'ahm before the door closed on their freedom and their lives forever.

"I think we better find another way out of here." Calandra glanced at the main door. "My guess is more of the chief sovereign's agents are watching for us, waiting to shoot us down once we walk outside the door."

"You make a good point," Bo'un replied. "Look around. There must be an escape tunnel or a hidden exit somewhere in here."

Calandra rose to her feet. She joined him in scouring the empty room. They trailed their fingers along the walls and over shelves, searching for hidden buttons or sensors connected to a secret passage or door enabling a quick unseen escape.

She stooped down and ran her hand underneath the counter. At once, a sharp creaking noise greeted her ears. Calandra straightened up, wheeled around, and spotted a perfectly square hole on the floor between the counter and the wall. A section of wooden flooring slid inside a hidden slot, creating an opening large enough to admit an adult human.

"I think I found an alternate way out." She cast her eyes over at Bo'un. "I triggered a sensor that opened a trap door to a tunnel or cellar."

"Let's hope you're right for both our sakes," he said.

Narrow stairs led down into thick darkness. Calandra cursed her luck. She did not have a portable light on her. None were on hand inside the shop either. Climbing down below the floor without a light source was not an option. Experience taught her one false step could lead to a shattered foot. Or worse.

"We need a light, Bo'un." Calandra flashed a concerned frown back at him. "I can't risk stumbling around in darkness with my brittle bones."

He nodded and drew out a finger-length tube filled with translucent liquid from a pouch on his belt. Bo'un bent the tube toward him and let it snap back into place. The fluid swimming inside lit the tube up like a handheld ray of sunlight. He tossed it down the square hole ahead of them. The glowing tube exposed a narrow, arched tunnel leading away from thc stairs.

Calandra climbed down the stairs. She grasped rounded vertical handrails flanking each side of the stairs to support her balance and footing. Bo'un waited until Calandra reached the bottom stair and then climbed down behind her. She walked a few steps forward. At once, the section of flooring slid out again and sealed the opening above their heads.

Calandra flinched. Her heart pounded while she gazed up at the top of the stairs. If this did not lead to an actual exit, they would die trapped down here.

"Stick close to me," Bo'un said. "We'll see where this tunnel goes."

He snatched the glowing tube off the ground and started forward. A series of pops echoed down the tunnel. Short horizontal lights running across both walls sprang to life. Each embedded light resembled the tube Bo'un used to illuminate their path down the stairs. Abundant light now swallowed up what darkness lingered ahead.

The tunnel opened into a cramped room after they walked only a short distance. Calandra's eyes darted from wall to wall when she stepped inside the room. A series of chest-high shelves occupied much of the floor space. Most were empty or held items one would expect to find in a random storage room. Her eyes settled on a longer shelf mounted against the back wall.

She gasped.

This was no ordinary storage room.

Metallic plates and books, mirroring the records she studied inside the Central Archives, lay stacked on each row of the shelf. Calandra's eyes trailed across each one.

"There must be dozens of records stored inside this room," she said. "I wonder who made these records."

"Your guess is as good as mine," Bo'un said. "I do know one thing—if we stay here too long, we're begging for more trouble."

Calandra agreed with Bo'un in principle. Survival took priority over curiosity. Then again, they would not get another chance to examine these records. If Ominade went to such great lengths to hide them away from prying eyes, the records must hold valuable information.

"Guard the doorway." She glanced back at Bo'un. "I'm going to take a closer look."

Calandra approached the long shelf and picked up a book. She thumbed through metallic pages. It held meticulous records. Letters. Reports. Memos. Dates, events, and places linking the chief sovereign to unspeakable crimes. A distinct feeling struck her that the evidence from her trip to the Central Archives with Alayna was also here in these documents.

If that were true, though, why did Ominade withhold these records from her eyes? She reached out to Calandra in the beginning. Surely the rebel knew she would not have betrayed her confidence. Not with evidence of this magnitude. Of course, Calandra also realized she would have dismissed it all as a fabrication not too long ago.

"How many of these can you fit in your chest pouch?"

Bo'un furrowed his brow and glanced over at the tunnel. He fixed his eyes on her again and shook his head.

"Is that wise? Someone will notice if these records suddenly go missing."

"If someone other than Ominade and her rebel contacts was aware these records existed, they would have vanished. This is evidence implicating the chief sovereign."

Calandra started piling metallic books into her arms. She did not have enough time or strength to carry them all with her. Working quickly, she tried to pick out ones which—from a cursory glance—held enough valuable information to justify their rescue from this hidden room. Bo'un unstrapped his chest pouch and emptied the contents into his hand. He stuffed his arca vox inside a pants pocket and shoved a pair of books inside the pouch. Bo'un stretched the ebutoka leather tight over the metallic edges until it threatened to rip apart at the seams.

"Now let's get out of here," Calandra said.

They sprinted back into the tunnel. It branched off in another direction beyond the room. They followed this new path until reaching a sealed gray metal door. Bo'un slung the chest pouch across his chest again and raised his left armored sleeve. He moved his right hand over the door and the sides of the door. His motion triggered a hidden sensor. The door slid open with a whoosh and disappeared into a nearby slot.

Another darkened room stood before them.

"Do we dare go inside?" Calandra asked.

Her heart raced until it hammered her ribs. How far away were they from reaching Bo'un's aerorover? They would need to cover ground to his vehicle in a pouring rainstorm while carrying tons of records. Was it possible to go that far without drawing unwanted attention?

"We can't retrace the path we followed in here," Bo'un replied. "This is our only path forward—like it or not."

Calandra took a deep breath and uttered an unspoken prayer. If this offered their only way forward, they needed Ahm to shield her and Bo'un from potential dangers lurking outside the tunnel.

# 33

Windows revealed ashen storm clouds silhouetted by a scant amount of pale light. Calandra's eyes instinctively drifted to shadow cloaked corners. Large portable shelves covered much of the floor space. Each shelf held assorted goods ranging from handwoven baskets to polished stones. They had passed into another storage room.

Only this one held a door leading outside.

"We found our exit," Bo'un said.

Calandra wondered if other unseen adversaries tracked them along this new route. Tracing their steps as they crossed through the room. Waiting for the right moment to cut them both down.

A sensor activated when they reached the exit door. It slid open with a whoosh. Bo'un drew out his eliminator again and poked his head outside. His eyes darted one way, then the other. He glanced back at Calandra and nodded. Bo'un saw no danger.

They had to flee to the aerorover.

"Let's hope we don't have more company," he said.

The rainstorm had slowed to a drizzle when she stepped outside again. Calandra cradled metallic books and loose plates she gathered up from Ominade's hidden room, tucked between her artificial arm and her chest. Going through the tunnel led them out to a narrow street on the opposite side from where they started.

"How are we going to make it back to your aerorover unseen?" she asked.

"We'll get there," he said. "Have faith."

Bo'un set out on a brisk pace down the stone sidewalk. Calandra followed him with long-legged strides. They wanted to move fast while avoiding a full-on sprint that would draw unwanted attention. Once they rounded the corner, and she laid eyes on the aerorover again, Calandra let out a relieved sigh.

No visible sign of anyone watching or following.

Bo'un unsealed the magnetic locks and they both climbed inside. He extended the wings and retracted all four magnetic wheels. Then, Bo'un threw the main engine control knob forward. The aerorover shot upward until it hovered above scarlet treetops. It then shot forward and Bo'un charted a return course to Calandra's apartment.

No other vehicles gave chase as they followed the sky lane leading back to her apartment. They got away easier than she expected. Such a development did not put Calandra at ease. Fears of hidden agents following them at a safe distance only grew stronger inside her.

"I can't shake the feeling we're being watched," she said. "It's like we're back on Earth fleeing from hostile Earthians again."

Bo'un answered her with an uneasy frown.

"This feels so much worse than dealing with the Earthians for me," he said. "Apart from you, I don't know who I can trust any longer."

Calandra cast her eyes down at the plates and books resting on her lap. She started leafing through pages of a metallic book. She froze and doubled back to the first few pages. Somehow, Ominade obtained a travel log one of the chief sovereign's agents created.

The log noted several trips to the Aramus system.

The same system the chief sovereign and the Stellar Guard insisted carried a travel ban when she first discovered the probe from Earth.

"This is a travel log from one of the chief sovereign's agents." Shock gripped Calandra's voice. "It details multiple trips they made to the Aramus system."

"Aramus?" Bo'un cast a quick sideways glance at her. "You mean to tell me he sent agents to Earth before we went to that planet?"

She shook her head.

"Their log entries don't list a planet's name. Only a description of their destination as a small red planet."

"Didn't we pass a red planet on the way to Earth?"

"We did. And Doni didn't want us to visit that planet during our expedition even though it appeared desolate."

Bo'un's eyes locked into a straight-ahead unblinking stare as the aerorover approached Calandra's apartment. He began descent maneuvers and the vehicle plunged from the sky lane down to the street below.

"Why would they go to a barren planet?" he finally said. "What are they hiding there?"

Calandra glanced up from the page she studied. She knew enough Separatist War history to recognize the implications of one repeated word in the document.

Hybrid.

Travel logs detailed regular visits to supply nutritional and medical support to a hybrid lying in stasis inside a hibernation pod on the red planet.

"Evidence," she told Bo'un. "They're hiding evidence of the Chief Sovereign's war crimes."

"War crimes?"

"He's keeping hybrids in stasis. Keeping them ready to be used again."

Bo'un's face filled with fear.

"Hybrids? As in Rubrum-created hybrids?"

A lump formed in Calandra's throat. It pained her to give an affirmative answer to his question. So many things taught to them about the Separatist War, starting from childhood, were nothing more than carefully crafted lies originating from Ra'ahm's highest leaders.

"He did it," she said with a morose inflection in her voice. "The chief sovereign unleashed a legion of hybrids on Confederation cities. Just like Confederation leaders claimed all along. He really committed those atrocities."

Bo'un met her revelation with stunned silence. Calandra understood his wordless reaction. Learning the truth about Delcor and his evil nature shook her to the depths of her soul. She did not want these things to be real. She wanted to reclaim a long-lost naïveté where life's biggest worry lay in choosing a trail to explore deep within the Aurora Mountains.

They dashed from the aerorover as soon as Bo'un parked the vehicle. Calandra kept the travel log with her. If spies were indeed watching and waiting, she did not want to let this record leave her sight.

Each second that passed while the elevator climbed toward her apartment crawled along at an excruciating pace. She wanted to scream at the wretched machine to move faster. Calandra knew she would never again lay eyes on the place she called home once she packed and walked out the door. Collecting Bella mattered most now. No time to mourn what she was leaving behind. A new future lay ahead for her—one which, through Ahm's mercy, included a reunion with Xttra.

She only needed to survive long enough to get there.

Calandra and Bo'un attacked the hall at a brisk pace after the elevator doors slid open. When she reached her apartment door, Calandra froze. She cocked an ear toward the door.

Footsteps.

Inside her apartment.

Her green eyes grew as wide as plates. She wheeled around and stared like a frightened maniogo at Bo'un.

"Someone is inside." Her voice descended to a whisper. "I heard them."

Bo'un drew out his eliminator and aimed the barrel at the door. Calandra gulped and disengaged the magnetic lock. Her apartment door slid open with a whoosh. He stepped inside. She followed, hanging back a few steps.

They entered the living room at a measured pace. Bella poked her head out from under a couch cushion upon hearing Calandra and catching her scent. She refused to scurry out and greet her like normal. Unrestrained fear swam in the little cala's yellow eyes.

An identical sensation washed over Calandra. Her heart throbbed like a hammer repeatedly struck it. Her breaths devolved into shortened bursts. She clenched her natural hand tight to quash forming tremors threatening to break free.

Hidden eyes watched her and Bo'un. Calandra did not see those eyes with her own, but she felt their presence all the same.

"Where are you?" she whispered. "Show yourself."

The door to her studio opened.

Talan stepped out.

Bo'un swung his eliminator toward the treacherous navigator. His speed did not match Talan's quickness. A laser bolt struck him directly below his chest pouch. Bo'un gasped. The bolt's impact knocked him to the floor.

"Here I am." Talan flashed a vicious smirk. "Now what do you plan to do?"

Calandra's eyes fell on Bo'un. He groaned and raised his left armored sleeve holding razor discs. Talan shook his head and shot down the arm. He approached Xttra's fallen weapons officer with an arrogant calmness and delivered a brutal kick to his forehead. Bo'un's eyelids snapped shut and he slumped to the floor.

"Stay down!" Talan growled.

Calandra backed away from him. Her eyes darted from wall to wall, searching for anything she could turn into a weapon to defend herself. Terror seized every part of her body and squeezed with an iron grip. Her only weapon was to keep him talking. Distract him.

"Why are you doing this?" Her voice trembled as Calandra forced out the question. "I've done nothing to threaten you."

"You're a disgusting traitor." Talan spit his accusation at her with added venom. "You conspire with rebels to unseat our sovereign from his place as our true leader."

Calandra glanced down at the travel log still in her hands. She visualized throwing the metallic book at his head and retreating to a hiding place. Calandra dismissed that notion at once. He was too skilled with an eliminator. Talan would shoot her down without a second thought, exactly like he did with Bo'un.

"Why did you not leave well enough alone? Your obsessive search for Xttra led you down the wrong path."

Calandra backed away from Talan, keeping her eyes fixed on his weapon. She now stood inside her kitchen.

"What did you do to Xttra?"

Talan smirked again.

"Not what I wanted to do. We set it up beautifully to assassinate him on Fengar and blame the deed on a dissident faction. Some Thetians disrupted our plans and abducted him."

Calandra's eyes filled with horror as he unfolded the fate intended for her husband.

"It doesn't matter in the end," Talan continued. "He's out of the way. You and Bo'un were useful fools in leading us to a hidden network of rebels. They will pay a steep price for standing against our sovereign. As will you."

He walked between the couch where Bella concealed herself and a table. A faint growl emanated from under a cushion. Bella lunged forward.

She sank her sharp front teeth into his calf.

Talan screamed.

"Get off me you worthless cala!"

He stooped down and swatted Bella with the backside of his armored sleeve. She crashed on the floor and crawled away, whimpering. Anger swallowed the terror gripping Calandra. With Talan distracted, she charged toward him and swung the metallic book. It connected with his nose and left eye. The eliminator flew free as he brought his hand to his face. Talan stumbled sideways and crashed down on the table. The impact broke all three legs and cracked the tabletop down the middle.

"Don't touch my little Bella," she shouted.

He gazed up at Calandra and cradled his injured eye. Talan finally pulled his hand away, giving her a clear view of the damage. His nose now bent at an odd angle. A puffy purplish bruise overtook his eye and blood trickled from the corner down his cheek.

"I'll enjoy executing you," he seethed.

Talan's eyes darted over to his eliminator. Calandra cast a quick glance over at the same spot on the floor. They dove for the weapon at the same time. The metallic book fell from her hands to the carpet. She crawled forward and wrapped her fingers around the handle before he reached it. He elbowed Calandra in the jaw and strained at the eliminator with his other hand. Pain surged through her jawbone, but her grip held firm.

She elbowed him in the torso with her other arm. Talan gasped and Calandra rolled out from under him. She swung the eliminator around at him at the same time he scrambled to his knees and raised an armored sleeve to fire razor discs at her. A bolt haphazardly struck Talan in the left shoulder. He grunted in pain.

Talan pressed a button on his other armored sleeve. An arm saber popped out. He lunged toward her. Calandra fired another laser bolt. This one missed its intended target, sailing under his armpit, and left a smoking hole in the wall behind Talan. He slashed at her right arm and cut through both fabric and flesh.

Calandra cried out and dropped the eliminator. Blood seeped from the fresh wound on her arm as she backed away from him. Talan cracked a satisfied grin.

"You think you can stand against a Stellar Guard officer?" He edged closer until backing her against a wall. "I'm trained for combat. You are nothing more than a small thorn jabbing my skin."

He grabbed Calandra by her fresh wound. She cried out in pain again.

"Stand on your feet, you setaworm."

Talan rose to his feet and forced her to do the same. He marched Calandra toward the balcony door. She fought to free herself, but he only tightened his grip. More blood seeped out under his fingers.

"You are going to plunge from your balcony," he said. "Your 'tragic suicide' will help me finish this mission the right way."

"It's a little late in the game for that."

Calandra's eyes widened.

She knew that voice.

Talan wheeled around, trying to bring her around in front of him at the same time. Kevin stood before them. The Earthian had drawn a melter and pointed the barrel straight at the navigator.

He fired an acid pellet before Talan had a chance to use Calandra as a shield. The pellet hit him square in the torso. He gasped and then screamed as acid burned through his uniform and flesh. Calandra wrenched free from his grasp and Talan lurched forward. He raised his other arm to fire razor discs. Kevin fired a second acid pellet, hitting him in the upper chest.

Talan's eyes glassed over, and his lifeless body fell to the floor with a thud.

Calandra cast an unblinking stare at Kevin while she cradled her wounded arm. Her eyes drifted from his weapon to the contact block Ominade gave her earlier.

It did not glow this time.

"Kevin?" shock tinged her voice.

"I came as soon as possible." He flashed a warm smile at her. "I'm really here. In the flesh."

Calandra's face contorted as tears rushed unbidden from her eyes. She sprinted forward and he embraced her. Kevin saved her life.

For a second time.

"How did you know?" Her lips trembled as she forced out the question. "When I didn't hear from you—"

"Ominade's shop was raided hours after we spoke," Kevin said. He pulled back from the embrace and fixed his eyes on hers. "When I received word, I realized you were in danger. I sneaked back into Luma in the safest, speediest way possible."

"They were searching for you. How did you make it here undetected?"

"You know I used to be an army ranger on Earth. I have a few tricks hidden up my sleeve old Delcor's agents don't know about."

Calandra never realized Earthians also used items hidden in their sleeves. She glanced over at Bo'un. He lay motionless on the ground, fixed in the same spot where Talan shot him earlier. Her eyes darted over to the couch. Bella lay hidden underneath, still whimpering.

"Take care of Bella," Kevin said. "I'll check on Bo'un."

She tiptoed over to the couch and called out to the cala in soothing tones. Bella poked her head out from under the couch and looked at Calandra with a worried face. Her little nose and whiskers twitched.

Calandra knelt in front of the couch. She extended her natural hand, gritting her teeth as a new burst of pain shot through the laceration on her arm, and petted Bella gently on the head. She closed her eyes and bumped her snout against Calandra's wrist.

"You're a brave little cala. I love you."

Calandra rose to her feet again. She turned and looked over at Kevin. He bent over Bo'un and pressed his fingers against his throat.

"He still has a pulse," Kevin said. "If we get him some help, I think he'll recover."

Calandra studied Bo'un with a worried stare. Kevin pushed the chest pouch aside to check the extent of his eliminator bolt wound. She wondered how in the world he survived a blast in his lower chest at such close range.

"Bo'un is one lucky sucker," Kevin said as though he sensed her unspoken question. "His flex armor absorbed enough energy to keep this from being a fatal wound."

Still teary-eyed, Calandra flashed a grateful smile at her Earthian friend.

"I'm so thankful you didn't abandon me," she said. "You saved my life once again."

Kevin answered her with a renewed smile.

"I won't abandon you. Or Xttra. That's a promise."

# 34

Calandra paused after entering the assembly floor. Unsettled nerves tied her belly in knots. She mulled over what she wanted to say so many times in her head. Fear of the chief sovereign no longer controlled her actions. He had limited ability to harm Calandra now. Still, her words promised to make her clan a public target. Xttra's clan and Bo'un's clan also faced similar repercussions. Calandra understood the stakes. She also had no other choice except to travel this path.

The people of Ra'ahm deserved to know the truth he worked so hard to conceal.

She fixed her eyes straight ahead and marched toward the central platform. Calandra sensed eyes falling on her from both sides. A murmur swept through the chamber. Delcor stared at her wide-eyed, watching her approach the speaking platform with surprise and suspicion etched on his face. She halted atop the lowest stone step and gazed up at the chief sovereign's platform.

"I request permission to address this gathered assembly on an urgent matter."

Delcor narrowed his eyes and leaned forward in his chair. A half-frown graced his lips.

"Ra'ahm citizens are not allowed to address the assembly without an official invitation," he said in a stern voice. "Who extended such an invitation to you, Calandra Menankar?"

Calandra crossed her arms and answered him with an apologetic smile.

"I plead for you to let my voice be heard. Please do not bury my message under assembly protocols."

Guards flanking both sides of the chief sovereign's chair started forward, intending to subdue Calandra and arrest her. Delcor raised his hand and cast a glance at each guard. He waved both guards off and refocused his attention on Calandra.

"Those protocols exist for a wise reason. We value our citizens' voices. But order governs this place, not chaos."

Her eyes fell upon a few seated assembly members on her left side. Disdain for Calandra threaded through their faces. They placed themselves above her because of their exclusive access to the chief sovereign. Their arrogance sickened Calandra. They were all a collection of spineless traitors groveling for approval from a ruthless murderer rather than true representatives of Ra'ahm's people.

"I admit I'm not well versed in political matters," Calandra adopted an apologetic tone to buy herself time. She fixed her eyes on the chief sovereign again. "Is it not just and fair to allow a Ra'ahm citizen to present their message before deciding whether or not their voice should be silenced?"

"Not all messages are created equal," he said. "Trivial concerns have no place in this assembly."

Her eyes hardened. His haughty lecturing words would not deter Calandra from doing what she had to do.

"I assure you my words are not trivial," she said. "I only seek an audience to publicly reaffirm my loyalty to you and Ra'ahm."

Delcor allowed an amused smirk to cross his lips. The chief sovereign said nothing. If he felt threatened by Calandra, he hid visible signs of harboring such feelings. His arrogance would be his undoing.

Calandra climbed the steps and stood atop the round stone platform. She turned and faced the assembly.

"I imagine my presence is an unwelcome surprise. No doubt a few here hoped my voice would be silenced before I thought to raise it. No one will silence me."

Fresh murmurs swept through the chamber. Several assembly members leaned forward in their chairs. Her opening statement caught their attention.

Exactly as she hoped.

"The chief sovereign has taught us all that he is a benevolent ruler," Calandra said once the murmurs subsided again. "Filled with wisdom. Sanctioned by Ahm to lead our people. It is all a lie."

Angry shouts greeted her words. One bristling voice cut through the clamor.

"That's enough. Guards, remove Calandra Menankar from the assembly chamber at once."

She glanced over her shoulder at Delcor as he growled out his order. Both of his hands clasped the ends of the armrests on his chair. His arrogant smile had devolved into an angry frown.

Both of his guards drew out their eliminators and each one marched down a separate aisle toward the speaking platform. Calandra stood as firm as a statue, refusing to yield her spot.

"Valadius, our former prime oracle, uncovered his crimes. The chief sovereign tried to murder him. He failed. The prime oracle lives, hidden on a distant world."

Gasps splashed through the chamber right as the guards reached the platform. One guard reached out to seize her by her right arm.

His hand passed straight through flesh and bone.

Flickers marked the spot where the guard tried to make contact. Within seconds, Calandra regained a solid state again. She appeared as vivid and real as though she physically stood inside the chamber.

Fear flickered within Delcor's eyes. His guards stood frozen on the platform, staring at her as their mouths fell open. Several assembly members sprang to their feet. Pure silence replaced their earlier shouts and accusations.

"Where are you?" the chief sovereign said, looking around wildly. "How did you breach this chamber?"

Calandra flashed a knowing smile. Confusion washed over one face after another throughout the chamber. Their unfamiliarity with Peleusian technology gave her an unmistakable advantage over the assembly.

While the contact block remained concealed, they had no means of silencing her.

She pulled a metallic book from her chest pouch. The same book holding the travel log she discovered. Calandra hoisted the once-hidden record skyward.

"Now I know what he knew," she said. "Here is evidence showing crimes Delcor committed during the Separatist War. A travel log detailing where his agents hid remnant hybrids that he used to massacre Confederation civilians. Valadius paid a steep price for his knowledge. My own grandfather learned the same things and was given a choice of silent and permanent exile or death."

Delcor's face hardened like stone as he soaked in her words. A deepening scowl crossed his lips.

"Silence!" he thundered. "How dare you enter this chamber and bombard me with such vile accusations? I am your sovereign."

Calandra jammed the book back inside her pouch. She turned and faced the chief sovereign's seat, folded her arms, and answered him with an icy stare.

"You are not my sovereign."

Scattered voices instantly labeled her a traitor or a Confederation agent. Calandra shrugged off their accusations. Many assembly members were willfully blind. The same condition once afflicted her. Now her eyes beheld Delcor's real nature. His true ugliness and vileness were on display, hanging in the chamber like a vivid banner.

"You do not deserve to rule this people." Calandra paced back and forth on the speaking platform, never taking her eyes off Delcor. "You are a plague which has destroyed countless lives. The truth I bring is the cure."

Delcor slammed his fist down and rose to his feet.

"Such insolence! How dare you threaten me?"

He cast his eyes over at his guards on the platform.

"Search the entire chamber for the source of her transmission. We must silence these seditious lies."

"You see how he reacts to one who speaks the truth?" Calandra stopped, wheeled around, and jabbed her finger at the assembly members. "Is this the hallmark of a virtuous man? A benevolent ruler? Not as long as the sun crosses the sky. He is only a bloodthirsty tyrant!"

Murmurs swept through the gathered assembly members anew. Indignation permeated their faces. A few called her a liar.

"Many of you do not believe. But the truth is right here in these records and the people outside this chamber will believe." Calandra turned and faced Delcor a second time. She narrowed her eyes and knit her brows together. "When I open their eyes, all of Ra'ahm will see you for what you are. And then you will have no place among this people or hold power over us any longer."

Pure rage filled Delcor's eyes. She knew if he could crush her with his foot like an ictus bug, he would not hesitate to stomp.

"You are one person speaking unjustly against our sovereign." An aged assembly member rose from his chair and shook a finger at her like a club. "Why should we believe you? How do we know you did not fabricate these records yourself?"

Satisfied murmurs reverberated through the entire chamber. Delcor responded to the accusing questions with an approving nod.

"Calandra's voice is not the only one raised against this tyrant."

Her heart swelled within her when those words reached Calandra's ears. She could not believe it. She knew that voice. Tears brimmed in her eyes.

Praise Ahm.

She knew that voice.

Calandra turned toward the assembly chamber doors. Xttra approached the speaking platform. A joyful smile sprang up on her lips. Her year of heartache, loneliness, and crushing pain swept away in a moment.

He was alive.

Her husband was truly alive.

"Delcor arranged for my assassination on Fengar." Xttra stabbed a finger at the chief sovereign. "But his plan failed, and I uncovered evidence he helped create hybrids and subsequently ordered multiple hybrid attacks on Confederation cities."

"Your treasonous accusations will not go unpunished for long." Delcor's eyes revealed a hidden fear his words tried to mask. "You will be found and brought to justice."

His guards fired multiple eliminator bolts as Xttra reached the steps leading to the speaking platform. Each bolt passed through his body and struck the platform floor itself. Flickers marked the spots where the bolts struck his image. Xttra had also entered the assembly chamber with the aid of Peleusian technology.

"We are in a safe place far from your reach," he replied. Xttra removed a holocaster from his chest pouch. "A place where you cannot silence our voices."

A holoscreen materialized above the holocaster and a single enormous image appeared on the screen. It showed a hibernation pod with a Ra'ahm seal on the exterior.

"Confederation agents abducted me and took me to the Aramus system," Xttra explained. "There, we recovered this hibernation pod from a planet called Mars. The pod held a living hybrid who massacred a small Earthian colony on the planet. It unleashed a Ra'ahm Separatist War battle cry and attacked me before I executed the monstrosity."

Calandra's smile turned into a worried frown. Xttra faced greater danger during his absence than she ever imagined in her darkest moments. She was not alone in enduring life-altering ordeals while they were apart.

"We turned this evidence over to leaders from the Confederation and Daraconiah," Xttra said. "Your crimes will be exposed to all of Lathos."

Delcor sank back into his chair in stunned silence. Multiple assembly members joined his guards in searching high and low through the chamber, trying to find a way to end the transmission.

"Remember this day." Calandra picked up where her husband left off. "It is the beginning of your end."

A clamor erupted near the back end of the chamber.

"We found this device wedged in an alcove near the main doors," a breathless voice said. "It's the source of their transmission."

Calandra wheeled around and spotted an assembly member carrying a contact block resembling the one Ominade gave her earlier. A glow emanated around the Aracian letter etched on the block.

"Are they using a Peleusian imaging chamber?" a second voice called out.

Delcor's newly glum expression revealed how well he understood the implications of that revelation. Calandra's internal satisfaction seeped out on her face in the form of a triumphant smile. The chief sovereign would not uncover their location through the contact block. The virtual imaging chamber enabled a signal to travel from one side of the planet to the other.

"This is not the last time our faces will be seen and our voices will be heard in Ra'ahm," Xttra said.

Delcor seized the glowing block as soon as the assembly member approached his chair. He hurled the device to the floor, smashing it into several pieces. That became the final image Calandra saw before the assembly chamber faded away. Rows of narrow vertical lights rematerialized before her eyes.

"You took a major step forward today."

Calandra wheeled around on the circular platform and faced Kevin. Her Earthian friend cracked a smile. She stepped down from the platform. The vertical lights automatically switched off once she exited the virtual imaging chamber.

"Where is he?" Calandra's eyes darted around the room. "Where's Xttra?"

At once, a door slid open to a neighboring room. Xttra stepped through. They ran to each other, and he caught her in a tight embrace. Their lips locked together in the deepest, most passionate kiss Calandra ever experienced. She did not want to let him go. She wanted time to stand still and soak in his lips and his touch for a lifetime.

"I thought I lost you. I missed you so much," she said.

Tears rushed forth unbidden and choked her voice when Calandra pulled back and spoke to him for the first time in a year. Xttra's eyes also brimmed with tears, and he embraced her again.

"You're all I thought about over the past year," he said. "I missed you too. I love you."

"I love you too," she whispered.

They shared a tender, shorter kiss this time. Calandra tilted her head at Kevin after the second kiss. So many questions flooded her mind. She let go of Xttra and approached their Earthian friend.

"How did you find him? Where did you find him?"

"We tracked him down through a Confederation contact who aids our underground refugee network," he said. Kevin cast his eyes at the ceiling and back at her. "I won't bore you with the details. The important thing is we brought Xttra home."

"So, is this home now?" Xttra asked. "We obviously can't go back to Ra'ahm as long as Delcor remains the chief sovereign."

Kevin walked over to a nearby window and opened metal slats covering the glass. Sunlight filtered into the room holding the virtual imaging chamber. Calandra and Xttra clasped one another's hands and approached the window. Her eyes fell on the skyline of Daracos—an expansive Lathoan city. Many rectangular towers climbed skyward around her. Each tower featured a partially embedded spiraled column on every side. Numerous windows covered the columns.

"I'm told you're welcome to stay in Daracos," Kevin said. "Daraconiah will grant you asylum. You'll love it here. A free nation populated by good people."

"Will Bo'un also be resettled here?" Calandra asked.

"You bet. Once he's fully healed from his injuries, they've got a place waiting for him. Your families and his family will also be granted asylum in this land. The underground refugee network is gathering them from their homes as we speak."

Xttra looked over at him and nodded. He returned his gaze to the Daracos skyline.

"So, this is our new home."

Calandra stared out the window, letting those words soak into her mind. It did not matter what place they called home now.

She and Xttra were together again. His presence was more than enough to turn any place into her home. And, for the first time in their lives, they had a chance to experience true freedom.

THE END

# ALIEN WORDS PRONUNCIATION GUIDE

**Names:**

Calandra (Kaw-lan-druh)
Xttra (Ex-tra)
Ominade (Aw-min-aid)
Delcor (Dell-core)
Janthore (Jahn-thor)
Sarianna (Sar-e-ahn-na)
Oogan (Ooh-gun)
Menankar (Men-ann-kar)
Bathal (Baw-th-all)
Valadius (vah-lay-de-us)
Bo'un (Bow-un)
Kyra (Kai-rah)
Doni (Doh-knee)
Talan (Tay-lun)
Zatoriah (Zay-tor-eye-ah)
Cavac (Kay-vak)
Mikkah (Mee-caw)
Ohnro (on-row)
Ryollo (Rye-all-oh)
Alayna (Ah-lay-na)

**Locations:**

Lathos (Lay-thos)
Ra'ahm (Ray-ah-m)
Thetia (Thet-she-ah)
Peleus (Pell-e-oose)
Luma (Lou-mah)
Fengar (Fenn-gar)
Rubrum (Rube-rum)
Aramus (Air-am-us)
Sendala (sen-doll-ah)
Aracian (ar-ay-she-un)
Animo (ann-e-moe)
Serranta (Ser-ran-tah)

Nectura (Neck-tur-ah)
Daraconiah (dar-ah-co-ne-ah)
Daracos (dar-ah-cos)

**Plants, Animals, & Technology:**

Ebutoka (E-boo-tow-kaw)
Cala (Kaw-lah)
Sapinoa (Sap-eh-noah)
Senosa (See-nose-ah)
Fraxa (Frax-ah)
Arca vox (arc-ah-vox)
Syri'nai (sear-e-nye)
Russakin (Roose-ah-kin)
Ictus (Ick-tuss)
Setaworm (see-tah-worm)
Lupine (lou-peen)
Trique (Try-cue)
Mokai (Moe-kye)
Maidron (May-drawn)

# ABOUT THE AUTHOR

Being a storyteller is second nature to John Coon. Ever since John typed up his first stories on his parents' typewriter at age 12, he has had a thirst for creating stories and sharing them with others. John graduated from the University of Utah in 2004 and has carved out a successful career as an author and journalist since that time. His byline has appeared in dozens of major publications across the world.

John has published several popular novels. His debut novel, Pandora Reborn, became an international bestseller on Amazon and ranked as the no. 1 horror novel in Japan for a brief time. His novel Alien People earned distinction as a Top 100 new release and Top 100 bestseller in numerous science fiction categories on Amazon.

John lives in Sandy, Utah. Bookmark his official author page, johncoon.net, to get news and updates on his fiction. You can also connect with John on Twitter (@johncoonsports), Instagram (@jcoon312), and on Facebook (@jcoon).

CPSIA information can be obtained
at www.ICGtesting.com
Printed in the USA
LVHW031340200721
693179LV00011B/736